WITHDRAWN

The American Diary of a Japanese Girl

With Original Illustrations by

Genjiro Yeto

The American Diary of a Japanese Girl

AN ANNOTATED EDITION

Edited by

Edward Marx and

Laura E. Franey

TEMPLE UNIVERSITY PRESS PHILADELPHIA

TEMPLE UNIVERSITY PRESS
1601 North Broad Street
Philadelphia PA 19122
www.temple.edu/tempress

Copyright © 2007 by Temple University Press
All rights reserved
Published 2007
Printed in the United States of America

∞ The paper used in this publication meets the requirements of
the American National Standard for Information Sciences—Permanence of Paper
for Printed Library
Materials, ANSI Z39.48-1992

Library of Congress Cataloging-in-Publication Data
Noguchi, Yone, 1875-1947.
The American Diary of a Japanese Girl / written by Yone Noguchi; edited by Edward Marx and
Laura E. Franey. -- Annotated ed. p. cm.
Includes bibliographical references.
ISBN-13: 978-1-59213-554-7 ISBN 10: 1-59213-554-4 (cloth: alk. paper)
ISBN-13: 978-1-59213-555-4 ISBN 10: 1-59213-555-2 (pbk.: alk. paper)
I. Marx, Edward. II. Franey, Laura E., 1971- III. Title.
PR6027.O3A835 2006
895.6'442--dc22
2006020366

Quotations from the letters of Yone Noguchi are published with permission
from the Bancroft Library at the University of California, Berkeley

The illustrations are the work of Genjiro Yeto. All except two were published in
The American Diary of a Japanese Girl, New York: Frederick A. Stokes, 1902.
"One stupid wrinkle would be enough to stun me" and "A tea party in my honor" appeared
in the November 1901 excerpt printed in *Frank Leslie's Popular Monthly.*

2 4 6 8 9 7 5 3 1

Contents

Introduction

THE AMERICAN DIARY OF A JAPANESE GIRL* is both an entertaining book and one that deserves a special place in the history of American literature. The first long work of prose fiction by a person of Japanese descent in the United States, it counters the romanticized images of Japan and the infantilization of the Japanese, promulgated in some of the contemporaneous Orientalist fiction, and offsets the even more pernicious depiction of the Japanese as a "yellow peril" in some of the political discourse and media coverage at the turn of the twentieth century. To be sure, the book's peculiar syntax, the sometimes jarring shifts between episodes, and oddities such as a squirrel's first-person narrative about his dead wife might confuse the first-time reader at times, but the complex and wide-ranging *Diary* holds rich rewards for the reader willing to delve deeper into its content and history.[1]

When selections from *The American Diary of a Japanese Girl* first appeared in *Frank Leslie's Popular Monthly* in late 1901, and when the entire narrative was published in book form in 1902, the name "Miss Morning Glory" accompanied the title. This linking of title and name encouraged readers to assume that the first-person diarist, Miss Morning Glory, was the author of the text. Furthermore, most readers inferred that the book's daily entries concerning a young Japanese woman's visit to the United States with her uncle, an 1884 graduate of Yale and present "chief secretary of the Nippon Mining Company" (9), represented an authentic record. (In the book version, a prefatory letter to the empress of Japan purportedly written by Miss Morning Glory on her return to her native land is a device intended further to authenticate the *Diary*.)

Some early readers questioned the genuineness of the journal, while others claimed that the narrative must be authentic because, as a *Chicago Journal* reviewer declared, the "words [were] chosen as only a Japanese girl could choose them."[2]

The author behind the "Morning Glory" persona was not a Japanese girl but a young Japanese man, Yone Noguchi, who had been living in the United States since the mid-1890s. Born Yonejirō Noguchi in 1875 near Nagoya, Japan, he had been educated in schools in Nagoya and at Keiō University. Significantly for Noguchi's future, this Tokyo institution of higher education, established in 1858, was a private Western-oriented school whose founder, Yukichi Fukuzawa, was a keen proponent of Japanese modernization.[3]

After hearing positive accounts from young Japanese men who had visited the United States, Noguchi decided to emigrate to this country and arrived in San Francisco in December 1893 aboard the *Belgic* (the name he gave to Morning Glory's steamship in the *American Diary*). The young emigrant encountered many difficulties during his first few years in Northern California, working first for struggling Japanese-language newspapers in San Francisco and then as a house servant (or "schoolboy," as young Japanese men who worked in private domestic service were often called at that time). But after a brief stint in Palo Alto and a more permanent move in 1895 to a cottage on the Oakland Hills homestead of legendary California writer Joaquin Miller, Noguchi began to make a name for himself as a poet.[4] His years on Miller's seventy-one-acre spread greatly increased both his self-confidence as a writer and his familiarity with English and American literature. Though Miller did not keep books (other than his own writings) on the shelves of his cottages, he introduced Noguchi not only to the rich poems of Edward FitzGerald's *Rubáiyát of Omar Khayyám* but also to his circle of writer friends. Noguchi did some menial work at the Miller household in exchange for his room and board, but he never seems to have felt exploited, as he did in his "schoolboy" jobs. Miller always called him "Mr. Noguchi," a small but significant gesture of respect and a welcome change from the demeaning "Charley," "Frank," or "John." These were generic names many white Americans used for the Japanese they employed as servants. They were also names that some of Noguchi's own employers had used when addressing him. The stay on the Hights (as Miller spelled the name of his homestead) also afforded Noguchi an opportunity to participate in the natural world in ways not available to him in the city. The latter half of the *American Diary* consists largely of Noguchi's imaginative retelling of his experiences with the eccentric Miller and Miller's mother, Margaret. Miller appears in the novel as the writer Heine, who provides lodging, literary advice, and friendship for the young Japanese heroine, Miss Morning Glory.[5]

Writing and Collaboration:

The Creation of *The American Diary of a Japanese Girl*

In July 1896, a small but influential San Francisco magazine, *The Lark*, published a few of Noguchi's poems; the next year, with the support of his friends Gelett Burgess and Porter Garnett, Noguchi published two small volumes of poetry, *Seen and Unseen: Or, Monologues of a Homeless Snail* and *The Voice of the Valley*. The verse was mostly serious, concerned with nature, beauty, and philosophical reflection, but in late 1898, Noguchi began a writing project of a more playful, more immediate, and more satirical nature. Letters between Noguchi and Blanche Partington, a writer for the *San Francisco Call* and an enthusiast of Eastern religions, reveal that from December 1898 to May 1900 Noguchi worked on a series of vignettes and cultural critiques. Temporarily titled "O'cho San's diary," or Miss Butterfly's diary, his new project was no doubt partly inspired by Philadelphia writer John Luther Long's success in early 1898 with his story *Madame Butterfly*.

Worried that his knowledge of English was insufficient for the task he had set himself, Noguchi gave the entries to Partington for editing as he finished them. Yet Partington's influence extended well beyond changes to Noguchi's spelling and idiom. By mid-July 1899, Noguchi was complaining vehemently in his letters that she was introducing too much romance and too much novelistic plotting into his work.[6] He thus seems to have originally envisioned a series of social observations and believable daily occurrences in the life of a Japanese newcomer to America, and he wanted the diary entries to remain close to events he had witnessed. When Partington urged him to write on topics unfamiliar to him through personal experience, he told her: "You suggested to me to write on three more things, but now I have nothing to say about [them]. Yes, I have something to say about servants. By and by I will do it. I never saw any American wedding ceremony, therefore the difficulty is in my ignorance."[7] Besides clashing on these matters, Noguchi and Partington disagreed about the best venue for the *Diary*'s publication. Whereas Noguchi envisioned the series of diary entries by his protagonist—whom he was then calling "Miss Cherryflower"—serialized in a daily newspaper, Partington thought the manuscript should be published in a literary magazine. "'Miss Cherryflower,'" he wrote to Partington, "is the stuff more suitable to newspaper than magazine and it [the newspaper] pays more."[8]

When Noguchi left California in late May 1900, hoping to find success as a poet in the Eastern states, the *Diary* had not been published, though he was eager to see it in print. Taking about half the manuscript with him (Partington either could not find the remainder of the entries or did not wish to return them), he went first to Chicago and then to Washington, D.C., where he stayed with the writer Charles Warren Stoddard. After the visit to Stoddard, he settled in New York City. There, he later explained to Stoddard, he burned the original manuscript, started fresh on a new version, and hired a new editor, Léonie Gilmour, to "correct [his] English composition."[9] A gifted and creative woman who had majored in history and philosophy at Bryn Mawr and studied for a year at the Sorbonne, Gilmour was teaching Latin and French at a Catholic girls' school and hoping to find work in publishing.[10] Over the course of Noguchi's and Gilmour's work together, he asked her to excise unnecessary words, shorten his "horribly long paragraphs," and maintain the flavor of his "broken English" while ensuring that the *Diary* would still appear "good and artistic."[11]

By May 1901 Noguchi had completed the new version and sent it to *Frank Leslie's Popular Monthly* at the invitation of the magazine's editor, Ellery Sedgwick. Selections from *The American Diary of a Japanese Girl* appeared in the November and December 1901 issues. In September 1902 the full narrative appeared as a one-volume book, published by the Frederick A. Stokes Company, with illustrations by Genjirō Yeto, another young Japanese immigrant who was enjoying moderate artistic success in the United States.[12] Packaged in a protective box, the oversized book had a striking gold-printed cover with an inset color print; the spine and corners were bound "perishably and daintily," as one review noted, with exotic woven-bamboo fabric; and an ornamental border printed in yellow ink adorned each page. The book was priced for the Christmas market at $1.60. A chronicle of the daily adventures of Morning Glory, a well-to-do young Japanese woman, the diary extended from her early preparations for travel to the United States through her visits to four cities: San Francisco, Los Angeles, Chicago, and New York. The entries, from 23 September 1900 to 19 March 1901, presented Morning Glory's nightly ruminations on her encounters in multiracial America, her experiences of both prejudice and favorable treatment, and her adventures with friendship and romance. *The American Diary of a Japanese Girl* retained the spirit of light-hearted sociopolitical critique and "duck-out-of-water" observation of cultural customs that seems to have been Noguchi's primary aim when he started on the manuscript in California, while also providing more strident political criticism. For example, Morning Glory strongly satirizes racist perceptions of Japanese immigrants as suited only to domestic labor. When she pays her uncle to wash some windows at a cigar store that she is temporarily managing, she comments acerbically: "'It's good fun to hire the chief secretary of the Nippon Mining Company to rub windows, isn't it?'" (76).

Critique of Japonisme

In addition to social commentary the *Diary* contains a "love story" consisting of flirtation and talk of marriage between Morning Glory and a young American painter, Oscar Ellis. This plot element gave Noguchi free rein to satirize the portrayals of Japanese women and love in the Japanese-themed prose fiction and theatrical performances popular since the mid-1880s, when Gilbert and Sullivan's light opera *The Mikado* had initiated the "Japan" craze on stage. A biting satire of British politics and culture, the play was set in Japan, and its characters bore childish pseudo-Japanese names like Nanki-Poo and Pooh-bah. From 1896 onward, another musical production rivaled *The Mikado* on stages in both Britain and the United States—*The Geisha: A Story of a Tea House.* Its intertwined plots each featured the liberation of a woman from the machinations of unscrupulous men (both Asian and English) at the Tea House of Ten Thousand Joys, an establishment run by a money-hungry Chinese proprietor.[13]

The prose-fiction scene in the 1890s witnessed the growth of two types of representation of Japan and the Japanese—Westernized renditions of Japanese folktales, such as Lafcadio Hearn's *In Ghostly Japan* (1899), and contemporary romance narratives that featured interracial relationships. Three authors loomed large in the latter category: Pierre Loti (Julien Viaud), author of *Madame Chrysanthème* (1887); John Luther Long, whose *Miss Cherry Blossom of Tokyo* (1895) and even more famous *Madame Butterfly* (1898) shaped the parameters of much subsequent Asian-themed fiction; and Onoto Watanna (Winnifred Eaton), an Anglo–Chinese American writer whose fiction included *Miss Numè of Japan* (1899), *A Japanese Nightingale* (1901), and *The Heart of Hyacinth* (1903). Watanna's fiction added twists to the Chrysanthème and Butterfly storylines by portraying not only Japanese women in relationships with European or Euro-American men but also American-educated Japanese men enamored of Euro-American women.[14] Whereas Japanese women in some nonfiction accounts, as well as in Loti's foundational story, appeared flighty, fickle, and shallow, many fictionalized Japanese women, including Long's Butterfly and Watanna's Yuki (in *A Japanese Nightingale*), were devoted, faithful, and caring. Noguchi's *American Diary* injects a more realistic balance of traits into these starkly differentiated portrayals of Japanese women. Alhough often playful and even impish, Noguchi's Morning Glory also displays fond devotion to some of her new American friends and possesses critical acumen. Furthermore, her relationship with Oscar, mainly depicted through her love letters to him, does not follow the tragic pattern of turn-of-the-century Orientalist novels. Instead, through this relationship

Noguchi explores Japanese and American views of love and marriage, and critiques Orientalist fiction.

Some of Morning Glory's wittiest salvos skewer plays like *The Mikado, The Geisha,* and *Madame Butterfly* (impresario David Belasco had created a stage version of Long's story in 1900) for featuring white American actresses playing Japanese girls or women. A delicious send-up of theatrical Japonisme, for example, enlivens her diary entries for 1 and 17 November 1900. When Morning Glory's American friend Ada dresses up in a kimono and tries to walk like a Japanese woman, Morning Glory comments: "How ridiculously she stepped! / It was the way Miss What's-her-name acted in 'The Geisha,' [Ada] said" (31). And when Morning Glory herself poses for professional photographs, she objects to the photographer's attempts to make her—a real Japanese woman—look like an American actress's interpretation of a Japanese woman: "The photographer spread before me many pictures of the actress in the part of 'Geisha.' / She was absurd. / . . . What an untidy presence! / She didn't even fasten the front of her kimono" (40). When Ada and Morning Glory dress up together and begin creating characters for a private theatrical that Morning Glory calls "Two Cherry Blossom Musumes [young maidens]," the scene reveals the entwined layers of imitation involved when Euro-American women performed "Japaneseness." Contemporary imitative performance of this sort included both professional stage productions and private exhibitions like the "tableaux vivants, Japanese-style bazaars, and costume parties" popular with middle- and upper-class white women.[15] The *Diary* scene points up the absurdity of Ada's imitating what is itself an imitation (a white American actress playing a "geisha") rather than turning for a model to the flesh-and-blood Japanese woman in front of her.

Yet Noguchi's critique moves beyond inauthentic performances of "Japaneseness" by white Americans to imply that Japanese visitors or immigrants in the United States sometimes willingly commodified their cultural and ethnic identity to the point of misrepresenting themselves and their homeland. For example, contradicting Morning Glory's resistance to self-commodification represented in such statements as "I'll not play any sensational rôle for any price" (9) is her glee at possibly making money by selling the studio photographs of herself.

> If my first-rate picture by Mr. Taber were printed, it would be a whole thing in such a business. I thought the picture beautiful enough to sell at any stationer's of U.S.A. How many thousand could I sell in a week?

> Could I make money out of it? Some decent fortune, I mean, of course. (46)

Interestingly, Morning Glory considers the moneymaking potential of a photograph that she earlier condemned for portraying her as a false American "Geisha" with Chinese-style accoutrements. This about-face indicates that she is not always a mouthpiece for Noguchi's sociopolitical satire; sometimes she is its object. We should note, too, that the question of whether Morning Glory would choose to exploit her status as an exotic foreigner had parallels in Noguchi's experience. An editor at Funk and Wagnalls, for example, once returned a photograph of Noguchi in Western-style clothing and asked for a photograph of him in Japanese dress instead: "If not asking too much, won't you be so good as to favor us with one of your new photographs, the one you mention in your esteemed favor as being taken in your Japanese kimono?"[16] Whether or not Noguchi complied with this request, a couple of years later he tried to forestall a financial crisis by temporarily opening "a booth—a Japanese bazar—on [the] Madison Square Roof Garden," where he sold Japanese goods.[17]

Morning Glory frequently ridicules what she perceives to be Americans' inability to distinguish between things that are truly Japanese and things that are not. For example, she derides the cheaply made imitation of a Japanese-style table in her room at Mrs. Willis's "'high-toned' boarding house" on San Francisco's California Street (37). "I cannot sound Meriken jin's [Americans'] curiosity in prizing such a cheap thing," she grumbles. "The bamboo was painted. The cross nails glared from everywhere. I never saw such a Jap work in Nippon" (86). Similarly, Morning Glory's uncle criticizes traveling Japanese troupes and the Western audiences who unquestioningly accepted their performances as authentic reenactments of Japanese stage productions. (This kind of acceptance was evident, for instance, in the ultimate success of Otojirō Kawakami's troupe, which toured the United States and Europe from mid-1899 through mid-1902. The troupe featured a former geisha—Kawakami's wife—who had little acting experience but became famous as "star" actress Saddayakko during the Western tour. It also presented hybrid Japanese and Western theatrical performances that were often treated as true Japanese dramatic specimens by U.S. critics.)[18] As the uncle comments in one of his journal entries (quoted in Morning Glory's journal): "A year or two ago, one Japanese theatrical troupe roamed. They are not catalogued at home as actors. They chose to skip on the stage, simply because a bit more money is in it than in the calling of 'lantern-carrying for politicians.' Any wild animal can skip. I am now confronted with the question whether American generosity is not without sense. They piled up their money for them" (114).

Performance, Authenticity, and Identity

The critique of the bamboo table, the uncle's condemnation of the touring players, and Noguchi's satiric portrayal of Ada's dress-up show, suggest that Noguchi's despair over contemporary portrayals of Japan and the Japanese was grounded in a concern for authenticity. But we need to keep in mind that, despite Morning Glory's promise that she will one day produce a "genuine" Japanese novel to correct American readers' misperceptions, *The American Diary of a Japanese Girl* itself presents a male writer's impersonation of a Japanese female voice. Beneath the book's surface concern with authenticity, its complicated layering of performance, imitation, mimicry, and parody suggests a suspicion of fixed ethnic or racial identity. If we would do justice to the intricacies of the narrative itself and to Noguchi's experiences in the United States, we must resist the temptation to interpret it as trumping all the Orientalist texts written by non-Japanese writers simply because it was created by an ethnically Japanese author.

Even before Morning Glory arrives in the United States, she uses mimicry as she experiments with new appearances and new identities. While still at her family's home in Tokyo, she tries to reshape her body and her mannerisms to fit the pictures of women in U.S. magazines. After donning a pain-inducing corset and Western-style clothes and shoes, she is pleased to discover that a neighborhood dog does not recognize her as a Japanese girl: "I was glad, it amused me to think the dog regarded me as a foreign girl. / Oh, how I wished to change me into a different style! Change is so pleasing. / My imitation was clever. It succeeded" (10). Besides scenes of ethnic cross-dressing, Noguchi presents several episodes of gender and class cross-dressing. On one occasion, Morning Glory dresses up in her uncle's clothes privately in her closet: "At last I had an opportunity to examine how I would look in a tapering coat" (43). On another, she dons clothing she associates with gardeners, saying, "It wouldn't be a bad idea to play amateur gardener" (42), and later she tries on the Irish maid's clothes because she believes that "[a] white apron on [her] black dress makes [her] so cute" (45). In scenes like these, Morning Glory exudes a protean identity that continually adopts new shapes and characteristics. Thus, although the satirical bent of the story suggests that Noguchi was grieved by inaccurate representations of Japan and the Japanese, the emphasis on indeterminate play and fantasies of performance hints that ethnic, gender, and class identity may be malleable, shaped by an individual's needs and the needs of the community in which the individual lives.[19]

Wendy Doniger, a scholar of world religions, has identified what she terms "self-impersonation" as a significant trope in folk stories and national literatures around the world. "Through a kind of triple-cross or switchback,"

Doniger claims, "a person pretends to be someone else pretending to be precisely what he or she is." In one compelling example, she cites the moment in Hindu religious lore in which the god Krishna, "pretending to be a human cow-herd, teases the naked cow-herd girls by making them pretend that he is a god."[20] Similar cases of self-impersonation are woven into the fabric of the *American Diary*. Scenes in which Morning Glory assumes a male appearance display what Doniger calls self-impersonation because they represent the male author, Noguchi, pretending to be a female (Morning Glory) who is in turn pretending to be male. Similarly, in the scenes in which the high-born Morning Glory takes on the identity of a gardener, maid, waitress, or "shop girl" (77), we witness Noguchi, whose own father was a merchant, masquerading as a leisure-class person who is in turn masquerading as a member of the bourgeoisie or the working class.[21] Noguchi's self-impersonation through Morning Glory's role-playing should remind us that immigrants to the United States often adopted—or were forced by their circumstances to adopt—roles and identities that greatly diverged from their social, economic, cultural, or religious identities in the country of their birth. This adoption of new roles and identities could offer positive benefits to the Asian newcomer to the United States; as Tina Chen suggests in *Double Agency: Acts of Impersonation in Asian American Literature and Culture:* "Impersonation usefully encompasses a range of performative possibilities, and, in the final analysis, offers Asian Americans . . . the opportunity to im-personate themselves, to perform themselves into being as persons recognized by their communities and their country."[22]

The "switchbacks" in the *American Diary* might be read not so much as a postmodern endorsement of the idea that stable identity is more fantasy than reality, but as Noguchi's attempt to transform the sense of disempowerment experienced by many Japanese immigrants in turn-of-the-century America. Noguchi was one of approximately 27,440 Japanese who entered the continental United States between 1891 and 1900, the vast majority of whom were male.[23] Many of these early immigrants were laborers who came to the West Coast to find jobs with better wages and to enjoy better opportunities than were available in rural Japan. Emigration companies recruited numerous workers for the railroad companies and agriculture.[24] Continuing a trend that had been even more evident in the 1880s, however, many Japanese men who entered the United States in the 1890s had scraped up the money to emigrate in hopes of acquiring a Western education. As the *Japan Weekly Mail* reported a few years before Noguchi arrived in California: "The rank and file [of Japanese immigrants in San Francisco] are of the poor student class, youths who have rashly left their native shores. . . . Hundreds of such are landed every year, with miserably scant funds in their pockets. . . . Their object is to earn, with the labour of their hands, a pittance sufficient to enable them to pursue their studies in language, sociology, and politics."[25] All too often, however, these young men, many of whom envisioned returning to Japan permanently after their sojourns in the United States, discovered that enrolling in and graduating from U.S. schools was more difficult than they had imagined.[26] Lacking money, family support, and facility with the English language, many of these immigrants took jobs as family servants or as waiters while attending classes. In fact, in 1900, an astonishing 40.5 percent of employed Japanese men and 78 percent of employed Japanese women in the continental United States had jobs that fit within the broad category of "domestic and personal services."[27] Domestic service was likely very humiliating for many male immigrants like Noguchi, since "in Japan only lower class women worked as domestic servants. . . . When described in deprecating terms, the job [of 'schoolboy'] was referred to as *gejo hōkō* or maid-servant's work, which made it analogous to the tasks female domestics performed in Japan."[28] In view of the obstacles Issei immigrants faced, it is not surprising that Noguchi voiced his criticism of Euro-American stereotyping of Asian immigrants as domestic laborers and the consequent feminization of those laborers through the acerbic comments of a narrator who represented his sentiments but not his gender or class identity.

One episode from Morning Glory's stay in San Francisco perfectly illustrates Noguchi's dissatisfaction with some of his experiences in the United States. As the temporary manager of a cigar store owned by a Japanese couple, Morning Glory encounters a "funny drunkard" who puts out his "hairy hand" in greeting and says, "Hel-lo, Japanese!" (79). She responds to this gesture not with a friendly extension of her own hand but with violence: "I lengthened my arm, and slapped his face. I withdrew directly within, and watched him from a hole" (79). Unfazed by the slap, the man proceeds to steal a cigar, light it, and walk away singing a nonsense verse—"Pon pili, yon, pon, pon!"—reminiscent of the pseudo-Japanese baby-talk lyrics of some of the songs from productions like *The Mikado* and *The Geisha.* Morning Glory's slap represents physical power that Japanese immigrants, male or female, may have wished to display in response to the rock-throwing, spitting, and name-calling Asians sometimes experienced on the West Coast. A similar scene—minus the aggressive response—appears in Noguchi's collection of autobiographical essays, *The Story of Yone Noguchi* (1914). Recalling his first few days in San Francisco, Noguchi describes an American man accosting him rudely: "I was suddenly struck by a hard hand from behind, and found a large, red-faced fellow, somewhat smiling in scorn, who, seeing my face, exclaimed, 'Hello, Jap!' I was terribly indignant to be addressed in such a fashion; my indignation increased when he ran away, after spitting on my face" (28). Through the medium of a fictional diary, Noguchi depicts a real-life moment of vulnerability as a moment of aggressive physical resistance by an Asian immigrant.[29]

The unsettled nature of personal identities and the consistent references to boundary crossing in the *Diary* extend to the realm of sexual desire, making the book an especially interesting text for a twenty-first-century audience keenly aware of public and private debates over homosexuality, bisexuality, and "queerness." Sometimes Morning Glory appears to desire women—

> Ada caught my neck by her arm.
> She squandered her kisses on me.
> (It was my first taste of the kiss.)
> We two young ladies in wanton garments rolled down happily on the floor. (31)

At other times she appears to desire men: "I was wavering about my action, when I felt Oscar's firm arms around my waist. My small body was lifted on to the donkey's [back] by his careless gallantry. / What a sensation ran through me!" (62). Whether the object of attraction is male or female, such scenes connect the *Diary* with a popular fin-de-siècle genre: the confessional female diary. (For further discussion of this genre, see the Afterword.) The intertwining of homoerotic with heteroerotic scenes also reflects the complexities that characterized the intimate relationships Noguchi himself formed during the decade he spent in the United States. His correspondence suggests intimate relationships with at least two men: a fellow Japanese immigrant named Kosen Takahashi and Charles Warren Stoddard, a poet and teacher with whom Noguchi lived in Washington, D.C. for several intervals between 1900 and 1904. In addition, Noguchi became engaged for a time to Southern socialite and newspaper reporter Ethel Armes, whom he had met through Stoddard, and he had a sexual relationship with his second editor, Léonie Gilmour, that in 1904 produced a son who would become the renowned sculptor Isamu Noguchi.[30]

The *American Diary's* portrayals of desire and discussions of courtship and marriage carry not only personal but also political freight, for legal and social obstacles hindered marriage between "Caucasians" and "Orientals" at the time of its publication. For example, Section 69 of the California Civil Code, promulgated in 1880, prohibited the issuing of marriage licenses to couples consisting of a white person and a person from one of the following groups: "Mongolians, Negroes, mulattoes, and persons of mixed blood." (Japanese were classified as Mongolians.)[31] Morning Glory's uncle hypothesizes that Japanese men in California often looked sad and tired because they lacked female companionship, the result of the unbalanced ratio of male and female Japanese immigrants. Morning Glory suggests two possible solutions. First, male Japanese immigrants might begin relationships with "Meriken musume[s],"

American girls, rather than pining after faraway Japanese women (77). Second, the Japanese government might encourage more Japanese women to emigrate. Either solution to the problem of Japanese male immigrants' loneliness likely would have shocked—if not profoundly disturbed—some of Noguchi's white readers, but he still chose to provide these political comments on the touchy subjects of miscegenation and Asian female immigration.

Besides the above-mentioned obstacles to their enjoyment of a comfortable life in the United States, lack of fluency in English caused problems for many of the new arrivals in the 1880s and 1890s, Noguchi among them. As he reported in *The Story of Yone Noguchi:* "My first despair [in San Francisco] was my linguistic incompetency, which made me mad even to curse over the Japanese teachers who had not given me the right pronunciation of even one word" (36). He complained too about frequently being "taken for a deaf mute" because he carried a pencil and paper with him at all times to write down English words that Americans could not understand when he spoke them.[32] Interestingly, Morning Glory expresses none of the anxiety and anger over miscommunication found in *The Story of Yone Noguchi.* Instead, she is almost always at her ease, at least in terms of her linguistic abilities (again possibly fulfilling a fantasy for the immigrant writer). Though much of her phraseology does not conform to common American English usage, Morning Glory's ruminations in English are perfectly comprehensible to a U.S. audience.

One important difference between Noguchi's narrative and contemporaneous Orientalist stories like *Madame Butterfly* and *Miss Numè of Japan* is the fact that the protagonist's identity as a nonnative speaker of English is indicated not through a childish and unrealistic pidgin English but through the diarist's intriguing mixture of standard Japanese, standard English, and nonstandard English syntax and diction. (A characteristic pidgin-English statement by Long's Madame Butterfly runs thus: "Nob'y cannot git himself divorce, *aex*cep' in a large courthouse an' jail" [42, original emphasis]; similarly, Watanna/Eaton's Miss Numè is fond of saying things like "Japanese boy go long way from home—see all the big world; bud liddle Japanese girl stay at home with fadder and mudder, an' vaery, vaery good, *bud* parents luf *always* the boy" [87, original emphasis]). Morning Glory's repeated use of Japanese phrases, untranslated and unexplained, probably distracted her early-twentieth-century readers, but Noguchi likely thought that such phrases added an authenticity absent from contemporary novels, in which the authors only sprinkled the occasional "sayonara" or "shoji" amidst a profusion of pidgin English. The incorporation of two languages in Morning Glory's everyday writing neither diminishes the value of either language nor exploits language difference, as other uses of multiple languages or dialects sometimes did in

American literature at the turn of the century. Rather, Noguchi's linguistic experiments fall in the category of literary productions by those modernists who chose to reflect in their writings the rich cultural and linguistic traditions of various ethnic and national groups.

In the character of Morning Glory, Noguchi created an alter ego whose bubbly personality and witty satire might temper—and perhaps even mask—the sharpness of his critiques of both U.S. and Japanese culture. In one key passage, Noguchi has Morning Glory first discard and then attempt to rescue and reassemble some notes she has taken concerning "Things Seen in the Street." Ultimately, however, she jettisons them, ruminating that "I didn't come to Amerikey to be critical, that is, to act mean, did I? . . . / I must remain an Oriental girl, like a cherry blossom smiling softly in the Spring moonlight" (36). Like the text as a whole, this passage can be interpreted on at least two levels, in this case as a serious comment about the pressures to playact as a particular kind of "Oriental" girl and as a more playful allusion to Morning Glory's never really being "an Oriental girl" at all. As a literary creation, she was one of many interesting experiments Yone Noguchi undertook over the course of a long and impressive career.

The breadth of Noguchi's contribution to literature in English—as a writer of poetry, autobiography, essays, translations, literary and cultural criticism, art history, and political commentary—would be remarkable for any writer, let alone one battling the pioneer challenges he faced. In 1904, after publishing three volumes of English-language poems (two in the United States and one in Great Britain) and two books of fiction, Noguchi returned to Japan and became a highly respected professor of English literature at Keiō University. He published in all more than a hundred books (a third of them in English), as well as many hundreds of articles. The significance of these works is only now becoming clear, as scholars rediscover and reassess them in the more receptive critical climate of our day. In offering this annotated edition of *The American Diary of a Japanese Girl* to a new generation of readers, we are pleased to contribute to that reassessment.

Laura E. Franey

Notes to This Edition

Our text of *The American Diary of a Japanese Girl* follows the first edition published by Frederick A. Stokes in 1902 with a few relatively minor corrections: We have capitalized the name "Kikugoro" (77), substituted the date "7th" for "17th" (100), replaced "enshin" with "Enshiu" (135), and added missing quotation marks in several instances. Otherwise, we follow the text of the first edition as closely as possible, including the now slightly archaic English spelling of Japanese words and the somewhat unusual practice of not italicizing them. In our commentary and notes, however, we do make concessions to the practice of italicization and render Japanese words in a more contemporary form, using accented characters for long vowels (i.e., "*toō*" rather than "*toow*"), excepting words in common English usage (i.e., "Tokyo" rather than "Tōkyō"). For the sake of uniformity, however, we have retained Noguchi's preference of reversing Japanese name order according to English usage throughout.

Our most significant departure from the original text is the addition of an extensive set of annotations, incorporating glosses of Japanese words and explications of cultural references that may be unfamiliar to many readers. These include not only Noguchi's references to relatively unfamiliar aspects of Japanese culture but also his allusions to a wide range of literary works and now-forgotten elements of American popular or material culture. These annotations are fairly numerous, and since we have wished to retain the original condition of the text free of note numbers, we simply advise readers to consult the notes periodically or when in doubt. For the convenience of readers interested in the Japanese language, we also provide the Japanese equivalents of words employed by Noguchi and related terms where appropriate.

The illustrations follow the format of the 1902 edition with a few changes. The illustration "The guest of honour," which appeared as the frontispiece in the 1902 edition, is reproduced here as our cover illustration. And we have included two illustrations that originally appeared only in the November 1901 *Leslie's Monthly* excerpt: "One stupid wrinkle on my face would be enough to stun me" and "A tea party in my honor."

The border design that appears in yellow throughout the first edition is reproduced on our title page.

To Her Majesty

HARUKO

Empress of Japan

January, 1902

EVER since my childhood, thy sovereign beauty has been all to me in benevolence and inspiration.

How often I watched thy august presence in happy amazement when thou didst pass along our Tokio streets! What a sad sensation I had all through me when thou wert just out of sight! If only thou knewest, I prayed, that I was one of thy daughters! I set it in my mind, a long time ago, that anything I did should be offered to our mother. How I wish I could say my own mother! Mother art thou, heavenly lady!

I am now going to publish my simple diary of my American journey.

And I humbly dedicate it unto thee, our beloved Empress, craving that thou wilt condescend to acknowledge that one of thy daughters had some charming hours even in a foreign land.

Morning Glory

Before I Sailed

TOKIO, Sept. 23rd

My new page of life is dawning.

A trip beyond the seas—Meriken Kenbutsu—it's not an ordinary event.

It is verily the first event in our family history that I could trace back for six centuries.

My to-day's dream of America—dream of a butterfly sipping on golden dews—was rudely broken by the artless chirrup of a hundred sparrows in my garden.

"Chui, chui! Chui, chui, chui!"

Bad sparrows!

My dream was silly but splendid.

Dream is no dream without silliness which is akin to poetry.

If my dream ever comes true!

24th—The song of gay children scattered over the street had subsided. The harvest moon shone like a yellow halo of "Nono Sama." All things in blessed Mitsuho No Kuni—the smallest ant also—bathed in sweet inspiring beams of beauty. The soft song that is not to be heard but to be felt, was in the air.

'Twas a crime, I judged, to squander lazily such a gracious graceful hour within doors.

I and my maid strolled to the Konpira shrine.

Her red stout fingers—like sweet potatoes—didn't appear so bad tonight, for the moon beautified every ugliness.

Our Emperor should proclaim forbidding woman to be out at any time except under the moonlight.

Without beauty woman is nothing. Face is the whole soul. I prefer death if I am not given a pair of dark velvety eyes.

What a shame even woman must grow old!

One stupid wrinkle on my face would be enough to stun me.

My pride is in my slim fingers of satin skin.

I'll carefully clean my roseate finger-nails before I'll land in America.

Our wooden clogs sounded melodious, like a rhythmic prayer unto the sky. Japs fit themselves to play music even with footgear. Every house with a lantern at its entrance looked a shrine cherishing a thousand idols within.

I kneeled to the Konpira god.

I didn't exactly see how to address him, being ignorant what sort of god he was.

I felt thirsty when I reached home. Before I pulled a bucket from the well, I peeped down into it. The moonbeams were beautifully stealing into the waters.

My tortoise-shell comb from my head dropped into the well.

The waters from far down smiled, heartily congratulating me on going to Amerikey.

25th—I thought all day long how I'll look in 'Merican dress.

26th—My shoes and six pairs of silk stockings arrived.

How I hoped they were Nippon silk!

One pair's value is 4 yens.

Extravagance! How dear!

I hardly see any bit of reason against bare feet.

Well, of course, it depends on how they are shaped.

A Japanese girl's feet are a sweet little piece. Their flatness and archlessness manifest their pathetic womanliness.

Feet tell as much as palms.

I have taken the same laborious care with my feet as with my hands. Now they have to retire into the heavy constrained shoes of America.

It's not so bad, however, to slip one's feet into gorgeous silk like that.

My shoes are of superior shape. They have a small high heel.

I'm glad they make me much taller.

A bamboo I set some three Summers ago cast its unusually melancholy shadow on the round paper window of my room, and whispered, "Sara! Sara! Sara!"

It sounded to me like a pallid voice of sayonara.

(By the way, the profuse tips of my bamboo are like the ostrich plumes of my new American hat.)

"Sayonara" never sounded before more sad, more thrilling.

"One stupid wrinkle on my face would be enough to stun me"

My good-bye to "home sweet home" amid the camellias and white chrysanthemums is within ten days. The steamer "Belgic" leaves Yokohama on the sixth of next month. My beloved uncle is chaperon during my American journey.

27th—I scissored out the pictures from the 'Merican magazines.

(The magazines were all tired-looking back numbers. New ones are serviceable in their own home. Forgotten old actors stray into the villages for an inglorious tour. So it is with the magazines. Only the useless numbers come to Japan, I presume.)

The pictures—Meriken is a country of woman; that's why, I fancy, the pictures are chiefly of woman—showed me how to pick up the long skirt. That one act is the whole "business" of looking charming on the street. I apprehend that the grace of American ladies is in the serpentine curves of the figure, in the narrow waist.

Woman is the slave of beauty.

I applied my new corset to my body. I pulled it so hard.

It pained me.

28th—My heart was a lark.

I sang, but not in a trembling voice like a lark, some slices of school song.

I skipped around my garden.

Because it occurred to me finally that I'll appear beautiful in my new costume.

I smiled happily to the sunlight whose autumnal yellow flakes—how yellow they were!—fell upon my arm stretched to pluck a chrysanthemum.

I admit that my arm is brown.

But it's shapely.

29th—English of America—sir, it is light, unreserved and accessible—grew dear again. My love of it returned like the glow in a brazier that I had watched passionately, then left all the Summer days, and to which I turned my apologetic face with Winter's approaching steps.

Oya, oya, my book of Longfellow under the heavy coat of dust!

I dusted the book with care and veneration as I did a wee image of the Lord a month ago.

The same old gentle face of 'Merican poet—a poet need not always to sing, I assure you, of tragic lamentation and of "far-beyond"—stared at me from its frontispiece. I wondered if he ever dreamed his volume would be opened on the tiny brown palms of a Japan girl. A sudden fancy came to me as if he—the spirit of his picture—flung his critical impressive eyes at my elaborate cue with coral-headed pin, or upon my face.

Am I not a lovely young lady?

I had thrown Longfellow, many months ago, on the top shelf where a grave spider was encamping, and given every liberty to that reticent, studious, silver-haired gentleman Mr. Moth to tramp around the "Arcadie."

Mr. Moth ran out without giving his own "honourable" impression of the popular poet, when I let the pages flutter.

Large fatherly poet he is, but not unique. Uniqueness, however, has become commonplace.

Poet of "plain" plainness is he—plainness in thought and colour. Even his elegance is plain enough.

I must read Mr. Longfellow again as I used a year ago reclining in the Spring breeze,—"A Psalm of Life," "The Village Blacksmith," and half a dozen snatches from "Evangeline" or "The Song of Hiawatha" at the least. That is not because I am his devotee—I confess the poet of my taste isn't he—but only because he is a great idol of American ladies, as I am often told, and I may suffer the accusation of idiocy in America, if I be not charming enough to quote lines from his work.

30th—Many a year I have prayed for something more decent than a marriage offer.

I wonder if the generous destiny that will convey me to the illustrious country of "woman first" isn't the "something."

I am pleased to sail for Amerikey, being a woman.

Shall I have to become "naturalized" in America?

The Jap "gentleman"—who desires the old barbarity—persists still in fancying that girls are trading wares.

When he shall come to understand what is Love!

Fie on him!

I never felt more insulted than when I was asked in marriage by one unknown to me.

No Oriental man is qualified for civilisation, I declare.

Educate man, but—beg your pardon—not the woman!

Modern gyurls born in the enlightened period of Meiji are endowed with quite a remarkable soul.

I act as I choose. I haven't to wait for my mamma's approval to laugh when I incline to.

Oct. 1st—I stole into the looking glass—woman loses almost her delight in life if without it—for the last glimpse of my hair in Japan style.

Butterfly mode!

I'll miss it adorning my small head, while I'm away from home.

I have often thought that Japanese display Oriental rhetoric—only oppressive rhetoric that palsies the spirit—in hair dressing. Its beauty isn't animation.

I longed for another new attraction on my head.

I felt sad, however, when I cut off all the paper cords from my hair.

I dreaded that the American method of dressing the hair might change my head into an absurd little thing.

My lengthy hair languished over my shoulders.

I laid me down on the bamboo porch in the pensive shape of a mermaid fresh from the sea.

The sportive breezes frolicked with my hair. They must be mischievous boys of the air.

I thought the reason why Meriken coiffure seemed savage and without art was mainly because it prized more of natural beauty.

Naturalness is the highest of all beauties.

Sayo shikaraba!

Let me learn the beauty of American freedom, starting with my hair!

Are you sure it's not slovenliness?

Woman's slovenliness is only forgiven where no gentleman is born.

2nd—Occasional forgetfulness, I venture to say, is one of woman's charms.

But I fear too many lapses in my case fill the background.

I amuse myself sometimes fancying whether I shall forget my husband's name (if I ever have one).

How shall I manage "shall" and "will"? My memory of it is faded.

I searched for a printed slip, "How to use Shall and Will." I pressed to explore even the pantry after it.

Afterward I recalled that Professor asserted that Americans were not precise in grammar. The affirmation of any professor isn't weighty enough. But my restlessness was cured somehow.

"This must be the age of Jap girls!" I ejaculated.

I was reading a paper on our bamboo land, penned by Mr. Somebody.

The style was inferior to Irving's.

I have read his gratifying "Sketch Book." I used to sleep holding it under my wooden pillow.

Woman feels happy to stretch her hand even in dream, and touch something that belongs to herself. "Sketch Book" was my child for many, many months.

Mr. Somebody has lavished adoring words over my sisters.

Arigato! Thank heavens!

If he didn't declare, however, that "no sensible musume will prefer a foreign raiment to her kimono!"

He failed to make of me a completely happy nightingale.

Shall I meet the Americans in our flapping gown?

I imagined myself hitting off a tune of "Karan Coron" with clogs, in circumspect steps, along Fifth Avenue of somewhere. The throng swarmed around me. They tugged my silken sleeves, which almost swept the ground, and inquired, "How much a yard?" Then they implored me to sing some Japanese ditty.

I'll not play any sensational rôle for any price.

Let me remain a homely lass, though I express no craft in Meriken dress.

Do I look shocking in a corset?

"In Pekin you have to speak Makey Hey Rah" is my belief.

3rd—My hand has seldom lifted anything weightier than a comb to adjust my hair flowing down my neck.

The "silver" knife (large and sharp enough to fight the Russians) dropped and cracked a bit of the rim of the big plate.

My hand tired.

My uncle and I were seated at a round table in a celebrated American restaurant, the "Western Sea House."

It was my first occasion to face an orderly heavy Meriken table d'hote.

Its fertile taste was oily, the oppressive smell emetic.

Must I make friends with it?

I am afraid my small stomach is only fitted for a bowl of rice and a few cuts of raw fish.

There is nothing more light, more inviting, than Japanese fare. It is like a sweet Summer villa with many a sliding shoji from which you smile into the breeze and sing to the stars.

Lightness is my choice.

When, I wondered, could I feel at home with American food!

My uncle is a Meriken "toow." He promised to show me a heap of things in America.

He is an 1884 Yale graduate. He occupies the marked seat of the chief secretary of the "Nippon Mining Company." He has procured leave for one year.

What were the questionable-looking fragments on the plate?

Pieces with pock-marks!

Cheese was their honourable name.

My uncle scared me by saying that some "charming" worms resided in them.

Pooh, pooh!

They emitted an annoying smell. You have to empty the choicest box of tooth powder after even the slightest intercourse with them.

I dare not make their acquaintance—no, not for a thousand yens.

I took a few of them in my pocket papers merely as a curiosity.

Shall I hang them on the door, so that the pest may not come near to our house?

(Even the pest-devils stay away from it, you see.)

4th—The "Belgic" makes one day's delay. She will leave on the seventh.

"Why not one week?" I cried.

I pray that I may sleep a few nights longer in my home. I grow sadder, thinking of my departure.

My mother shouldn't come to the Meriken wharf. Her tears may easily stop my American adventure.

I and my maid went to our Buddhist monastery.

I offered my good-bye to the graves of my grandparents. I decked them with elegant bunches of chrysanthemums.

When we turned our steps homeward the snowy-eyebrowed monk—how unearthly he appeared!—begged me not to forget my family's church while I am in America.

"Christians are barbarians. They eat beef at funerals," he said.

His voice was like a chant.

The winds brought a gush of melancholy evening prayer from the temple.

The tolling of the monastery bell was tragic.

"Goun! Goun! Goun!"

5th—A "chin koro" barked after me.

The Japanese little doggie doesn't know better. He has to encounter many a strange thing.

The tap of my shoes was a thrill to him. The rustling of my silk skirt—such a volatile sound—sounded an alarm to him.

I was hurrying along the road home from uncle's in Meriken dress.

What a new delight I felt to catch the peeping tips of my shoes from under my trailing koshi goromo.

I forced my skirt to wave, coveting a more satisfactory glance.

Did I look a suspicious character?

I was glad, it amused me to think the dog regarded me as a foreign girl.

Oh, how I wished to change me into a different style! Change is so pleasing.

My imitation was clever. It succeeded.

When I entered my house my maid was dismayed and said:

"A new delight to catch the peeping tips of my shoes."

"Bikkuri shita! You terrified me. I took you for an ijin from Meriken country."

"Ho, ho! O ho, ho, ho!"

I passed gracefully (like a princess making her triumphant exit in the fifth act) into my chamber, leaving behind my happiest laughter and shut myself up.

I confess that I earned the most delicious moment I have had for a long time.

I cannot surrender under the accusation that Japs are *only* imitators, but I admit that we Nippon daughters are suited to be mimics.

Am I not gifted in the adroit art?

Where's Mr. Somebody who made himself useful to warn the musumes?

Then I began to rehearse the scene of my first interview with a white lady at San Francisco.

I opened Bartlett's English Conversation Book, and examined it to see if what I spoke was correct.

I sat on the writing table. Japanese houses set no chairs.

(Goodness, mottainai! I sat on the great book of Confucius.)

The mirror opposite me showed that I was a "little dear."

6th—It rained.

Soft, woolen Autumn rain like a gossamer!

Its suggestive sound is a far-away song which is half sob, half odor. The October rain is sweet sad poetry.

I slid open a paper door.

My house sits on the hill commanding a view over Tokio and the Bay of Yedo.

My darling city—with an eternal tea and cake, with lanterns of festival—looked up to me through the gray veil of rain.

I felt as if Tokio were bidding me farewell.

Sayonara! My dear city!

GOOD NIGHT—NATIVE LAND

On the Ocean

"Belgic," 7th

Good-night—native land!
Farewell, beloved Empress of Dai Nippon!

12th—The tossing spectacle of the waters (also the hostile smell of the ship) put my head in a whirl before the "Belgic" left the wharf.

The last five days have been a continuous nightmare. How many a time would I have preferred death!

My little self wholly exhausted by sea-sickness. Have I to drift to America in skin and bone?

I felt like a paper flag thrown in a tempest.

The human being is a ridiculously small piece. Nature plays with it and kills it when she pleases.

I cannot blame Balboa for his fancy, because he caught his first view from the peak in Darien.

It's not the "Pacific Ocean." The breaker of the world!

"Do you feel any better?" inquired my fellow passenger.

He is the new minister to the City of Mexico on his way to his post. My uncle is one of his closest friends.

What if Meriken ladies should mistake me for the "sweet" wife of such a shabby pock-marked gentleman?

It will be all right, I thought, for we shall part at San Francisco.

(The pock-mark is rare in America, Uncle said. No country has a special demand for it, I suppose.)

His boyish carelessness and samurai-fashioned courtesy are characteristic. His great laugh, "Ha, ha, ha!" echoes on half a mile.

He never leaves his wine glass alone. My uncle complains of his empty stomach.

The more the minister repeats his cup the more his eloquence rises on the Chinese question. He does not forget to keep up his honourable standard of diplomatist even in drinking, I fancy.

I see charm in the eloquence of a drunkard.

I exposed myself on deck for the first time.

I wasn't strong enough, alas! to face the threatening grandeur of the ocean. Its divineness struck and wounded me.

O such an expanse of oily-looking waters! O such a menacing largeness!

One star, just one sad star, shone above.

I thought that the little star was trembling alone on a deck of some ship in the sky.

Star and I cried.

13th—My first laughter on the ocean burst out while I was peeping at a label, "7 yens," inside the chimney-pot hat of our respected minister, when he was brushing it.

He must have bought that great headgear just on the eve of his appointment.

How stupid to leave such a bit of paper!

I laughed.

He asked what was so irresistibly funny.

I laughed more. I hardly repressed "My dear old man."

The "helpless me" clinging on the bed for many a day feels splendid to-day.

The ocean grew placid.

On the land my eyes meet with a thousand temptations. They are here opened for nothing but the waters or the sun-rays.

I don't gain any lesson, but I have learned to appreciate the demonstrations of light.

They were white. O what a heavenly whiteness!

The billows sang a grand slow song in blessing of the sun, sparkling their ivory teeth.

The voyage isn't bad, is it?

I planted myself on the open deck, facing Japan.

I am a mountain-worshipper.

Alas! I could not see that imperial dome of snow, Mount Fuji.

One dozen fairies—two dozen—roved down from the sky to the ocean.

I dreamed.

I was so very happy.

14th—What a confusion my hair has suffered! I haven't put it in order since I left the Orient. Such negligence of toilet would be fined by the police in Japan.

I was busy with my hair all the morning.

15th—The Sunday service was held.

There's nothing more natural on a voyage than to pray.

We have abandoned the land. The ocean has no bottom.

We die any moment "with bubbling groan, without a grave, unknelled, uncoffined, and unknown."

Only prayer makes us firm.

I addressed myself to the Great Invisible whose shadow lies across my heart.

He may not be the God of Christianity. He is not the Hotoke Sama of Buddhism.

Why don't those red-faced sailors hum heavenly-voiced hymns instead of—"swear?"

16th—Amerikey is away beyond.

Not even a speck of San Francisco in sight yet!

I amused myself thinking what would happen if I never returned home.

Marriage with a 'Merican, wealthy and comely?

I had wellnigh decided that I would not cross such an ocean again by ship. I would wait patiently until a trans-Pacific railroad is erected.

I was basking in the sun.

I fancied the "Belgic" navigating a wrong track.

What then?

Was I approaching lantern-eyed demons or howling cannibals?

"Iya, iya, no! I will proudly land on the historical island of Lotos Eaters," I said.

Why didn't I take Homer with me? The ocean is just the place for his majestic simplicity and lofty swing.

I recalled a few passages of "The Lotos Eaters" by Lord Tennyson—it sounds better than "the poet Tennyson." I love titles, but they are thought as common as millionaires nowadays.

A Jap poet has a different mode of speech.

Shall I pose as poet?

'Tis no great crime to do so.

I began my "Lotos Eaters" with the following mighty lines:

> "O dreamy land of stealing shadows!
> O peace-breathing land of calm afternoon!
> O languid land of smile and lullaby!

O land of fragrant bliss and flower!
O eternal land of whispering Lotos Eaters!"

Then I feared that some impertinent poet might have said the same thing many a year before.

Poem manufacture is a slow job.

Modern people slight it, calling it an old fashion. Shall I give it up for some more brilliant up-to-date pose?

17th—I began to knit a gentleman's stockings in wool.

They will be a souvenir of this voyage.

(I cannot keep a secret.)

I tell you frankly that I designed them to be given to the gentleman who will be my future "beloved."

The wool is red, a symbol of my sanguine attachment.

The stockings cannot be much larger than my own feet. I dislike large-footed gentlemen.

18th—My uncle asked if my great work of poetical inspiration was completed.

"Uncle, I haven't written a dozen lines yet. My 'Lotos Eaters' is to be equal in length to 'The Lady of the Lake.' Now, see, Oji San, mine has to be far superior to the laureate's, not merely in quality, but in quantity as well. But I thought it was not the way of a sweet Japanese girl to plunder a garland from the old poet by writing in rivalry. Such a nice man Tennyson was!" I said.

I smiled and gazed on him slyly.

"So! You are very kind!" he jerked.

19th—I don't think San Francisco is very far off now. Shall I step out of the ship and walk?

Has the "Belgic" coal enough? I wonder how the sensible steamer can be so slow.

Let the blank pages pass quickly! Let me come face to face with the new chapter—"America!"

The gray monotone of life makes me insane. Such an eternal absence of variety on the ocean!

20th—The moon—how large is the ocean moon!—sat above my head.

When I thought that that moon must have been visiting in my dearest home of Tokio, the tragic scene of my "Sayonara, mother!" instantly returned.

Tears on my cheeks!

Morning, 21st—Three P. M. of to-day!

At last!

Beautiful Miss Morning Glory shall land on her dream-land, Amerikey.

That's my humble name, sir.

18 years old.

(Why does the 'Merican lady regard it as an insult to be asked her own age?)

My knitting work wasn't half done. I look upon it as an omen that I shall have no luck in meeting with my husband.

Tsumaranai! What a barren life!

Our great minister was placing a button on his shirt. His trembling fingers were uncertain.

I snatched the shirt from his hand and exhibited my craft with the needle.

"I fancied that you modern girls were perfect strangers to the needle," he said.

He is not blockish, I thought, since he permits himself to employ irony.

My uncle was lamenting that he had not even one cigar left.

Both those gentlemen offered to help me in my dressing at the landing.

I declined gracefully.

Where is my looking-glass?

I must present myself very—very pretty.

IN AMERIKEY

In Amerikey

San Francisco, night, 21st

"Good-Bye, Mr. Belgic!"

I delight in personifying everything as a gentleman.

What does it mean under the sun! Kitsune ni tsukamareta wa! Evil fox, I suppose, got hold of me. "Gentlemen, is this real Amerikey?" I exclaimed.

Oya, ma, my Meriken dream was a complete failure.

Did I ever fancy any sky-invading dragon of smoke in my own America?

The smoke stifled me.

Why did I lock up my perfume bottle in my trunk?

I hardly endured the smell from the wagons at the wharf. Their rattling noise thrust itself into my head. A squad of Chinamen there puffed incessantly the menacing smell of cigars.

Were I the mayor of San Francisco—how romantic "the Mayor, Miss Morning Glory" sounds!—I would not pause a moment before erecting free bath-houses around the wharf.

I never dreamed that human beings could cast such an insulting smell.

The smell of honourable wagon drivers is the smell of a M-O-N-K-E-Y.

Their wild faces also prove their likeness to it.

They must have furnished all the evidence to Mr. Darwin. "The better part lies some distance from here," said my uncle.

I exclaimed how inhospitable the Americans were to receive visitors from the back door of the city.

We are not empty-stomached tramps rapping the kitchen door for a crust of bread.

We refused hotel carriage.

We walked from the Oriental wharf for the sake of the street sight-seeing.

Tamageta wa! A house was whirling along the street. Look at the horseless car! How could it be possible to pull it with a rope under ground!

Everything reveals a huge scale of measurement.

The continental spectacle is different from that of our islands.

We 40,000,000 Japs must raise our heads from wee bits of land. There's no room to stretch elbows. We have to stay like dwarf trees.

I shouldn't be surprised if the Americans exclaim in Japan, "What a petty show!"

Such a riotous rush! What a deafening uproar!

The lazy halt of a moment on the street must have been regarded, I fancied, as a violation of the law.

I wondered whether one dozen were not slain each hour on Market Street by the cars.

Cars! Cars! And cars!

It was no use to look beautiful in such a cyclone city. Not even one gentleman moved his admiring eyes to my face.

How sad!

I thought it must be some festival.

"No, the usual Saturday throng!" my uncle said.

Then I asked myself whether Tokio streets were only like a midnight of this city.

My beloved minister kept his mouth open—what heavy lips he had!—amazed at the high edifices.

"O ho, that's astonishing!" he cried, throwing his sottish eyes on the clock of the *Chronicle* building.

"Boys are commenting on you," I whispered.

I beseeched him not to act so droll.

He tossed out in his careless fashion his everlasting heroic laughter, "Ha, ha, ha—"

A hawkish lad—I have not seen one sleepy fellow yet—drew near the minister shortly after we left the wharf, and begged to carry his bag.

He was only too glad to be assisted. The brown diplomatist thought it a loving deed toward a foreigner.

He bowed after some blocks, thanking the boy with a hearty "arigato."

"Sir, you have to pay me two bits!"

His hand went to his pocket, when my uncle tapped his stooping back, speaking: "This is the country of eternal 'pay, pay, pay,' old man!"

"What does a genuine American beggar look like?" was my old question.

The Meriken beggar my friend saw at Yokohama park was dressed up in a swallow-tail coat. Emerson's essays were in his hand. He was such a genteel Mr. Beggar, she said.

I often heard that everybody is a millionaire in America. I thought it likely that I should see a swell Mr. Beggar among the Americans.

How many a time had I planned to make a special trip to Yokohama for acquaintance with the honourable Emerson scholar!

Alas, it was merely a fancy!

I have seen Mr. Beggar on the street.

He didn't appear in the formal dignity of a dress coat.

Where was his Emerson?

He was not unlike his Oriental brothers, after all.

He stood, because he wasn't used to kneeling like the Japs.

The only difference was that he carried pencils instead of a musical instrument.

He is a merchant,—this is a business country,—while the Japanese Mr. Beggar is an artist, I suppose.

My little gold watch pointed eleven.

I have been writing for some hours about my first impression of the city from the wharf, and my journey from there to this Palace Hotel.

The number of my room is 489.

I fear I may not return if I once go out. It's so hard to remember the number.

The large mirror reflected me as being so very small in the big room.

Such a great room with high ceiling!

I don't feel at home at all.

Not a petal of flower. No inviting picture on the wall!

I was tired of hearing the artificial greeting, "Irasshai mashi," or "Honourable welcome," of the eternally bowing Japanese hotel attendants.

But the too simple treatment of 'Merican hotel is hardly to my taste.

Not even one girl to wait on me here!

No "honourable tea and cake."

22nd—I need repose. The last few weeks have stirred me dreadfully. I will slumber just comfortably day after day, I decided.

But the same feeling as on the ocean returned.

My American bed acted like water, waving at even my slightest motion.

I fancied I was exercising even in sleep.

It is too soft.

Nothing can put me at complete ease like my hereditary lying on the floor.

I was restless all the night long.

I got up, since the bed was no joy.

Oh, the blue sky!

I thought I should never again see a sapphire sky while I am here. I was wrong.

This is church day.

The bells of the street-cars sounded musical.

The sky appeared in best Sunday dress.

I felt happy thinking that I should see the stars from my hotel window to-night.

I made many useless trips up and down the elevator for fun.

What a tickling dizziness I tasted!

I close my eyes when it goes.

It's an awfully new thing, I reckon.

Something on the same plan, I imagine, as a "seriage" of the Japanese stage for a footless ghost rising to vanish.

It is astonishing to notice what a condescending manner the white gentlemen display toward ladies.

They take off their hats in the elevator—some showing such a great bald head, like a funny O Binzuru, that is as common as spectacled children—if any woman is present. They stand humbly as Japs to the august "Son of Heaven." They crawl out like lambs after the woman steps away.

It puzzles me to solve how women can be deserving of such honour.

What a goody-goody act!

But I wonder how they behave themselves before God!

23rd—It is delightful to sit opposite the whitest of linen and—to portray on it the face of an imaginary Mr. Sweetheart while eating.

Whiteness is appetising.

And the boldly-marked creases of the linen are so dear. Without them the linen is not half so inviting.

I was taught the beauty of single line in drawing class some years ago.

But now for the first time I fully comprehended it from the Meriken tablecloth.

I wished I could ever stay gazing at it.

If I start my housekeeping in this country—do I ever dream of it?—I shall not hesitate to invest all my money in linen.

I laughed when I fancied that I sat with my husband—where's he in the world?—spreading a skilfully ironed linen cloth on the Spring grasses (what a gratifying white and green!), and I upset a teapot over the linen, while he ran after water;—then I picked all the butter-cups and covered the dark red stain.

The minister makes a ridiculous show of himself in the dining room.

His laughter draws the attention of every lady.

This morning he exclaimed: "Americans have no courtesy for strangers, except meaning money."

And he finished his speech with his boisterous "Ha, ha, ha!"

A pale impatient lady, like a trembling winter leaf, sitting at the table next to us, shrugged her shoulders and muttered, "Oh, my!"

I hoped I could invent any scheme to make him hasten to his post—Kara or Tenjiku, whatever place it be.

He is good-natured like a rubber stamp.

But I am sorry to say that he does not fit Amerikey.

I was relieved when he announced that his departure would occur to-morrow.

My dignity was saved.

I cut a square piece of paper. I pencilled on it as follows:

To the Japanese Legation The City of Mexico Handle Carefully, Easily Broken.

I put it on the large palm of the minister. I warned him that he should never forget to pin it on his breast.

"Mean little thing you are!" he said.

And his great happy "Ha, ha, ha!" followed as usual.

Bye-bye!

The negroes are horrid. I scanned them on the first chance of my life.

What is the standard of beauty of their tribe, I am eager to be informed!

I searched for "coon" in my dictionary. The explanation was unsatisfactory.

The ever-so-kind Americans don't consider them, I am certain, as "animals allied to the bear."

Tell me what it means.

24th—Spittoon!

The American spittoon is famous, Uncle says.

From every corner in this nine-story hotel—think of its eight hundred and fifty-one rooms!—you are met by the greeting of the spittoon.

How many thousand are there?

It must be a tremendous task to keep them clean as they are.

I wonder why the proprietor doesn't give the city the benefit of some of them.

San Francisco ought to place spittoons along the sidewalk.

The ladies wear such a long gaudy skirt.

And it is quite a fashion of modern gents, it appears, to spit on the pavements.

This Palace Hotel is a palace.

You drop into the toilet room, for instance.

You cannot help exclaiming: "Iya, haya, Japan is three centuries behind!"

Everything presents to you a silent lecture of scientific modernism.

Whenever I am bothered too much by my uncle I lock myself up in the toilet room. There I feel the whole world is mine.

I can take off my shoes. I can play acrobat if I prefer.

Nobody can spy me.

It is the place where you can pray or cry all you desire without one interruption.

My room is great, equipped with every new invention. Numbers of electric globes dazzle with kingly light above my head.

If I enter my room at dusk, I push a button of electricity.

What a satisfaction I earn seeing every light appear to my honourable service!

I look upon my finger wondering how such an Oriental little thing can make itself potent like the mighty thumb of Mr. Edison.

25th—What a novel sensation I felt in writing "San Francisco, U. S. A.," at the head of my tablet!

(What agitation I shall feel when I write my first "Mrs." before my name! Woman must grow tired of being addressed "Miss," sooner or later.)

I have often said that I hardly saw any necessity for corresponding when one lives on such a small island as Japan.

I could see my friends in a day or two, at whatever place I was.

I have now the ocean between me and my home.

Letter writing is worth while.

I did not know it was such a sweet piece of work.

I should declare it to be as legitimate and inexpensive a game as ever woman could indulge in.

I was stepping along the courtyard of this hotel.

I have seen a gentleman kissing a woman.

I felt my face catching fire.

Is it not a shame in a public place?

I returned to my apartment. The mirror showed my cheeks still blushing.

The Japanese consul and his Meriken wife—she is some inches higher than her darling—paid us a call.

I said to myself that they did not match well. It was like a hired haori with a different coat of arms.

The Consul looked proud, as if he carried a crocodile.

Mrs. Consul invited us for luncheon next Sunday.

"Quite a family party—O ho, ho!"

Her voice was unceremonious.

I noticed that one of her hair-pins was about to drop. I thought that Meriken woman was as careless as I.

How many hairpins do you suppose I lost yesterday?

Four! Isn't that awful?

My uncle innocently stated to her I was a great belle of Tokio.

I secretly pinched his arm through his coat-sleeve. My little signal did not influence him at all. He kept on his hyperbolical advertisement of me.

She promised a beautiful girl to meet me on Sunday.

I fancied how she looked.

I thought my performance of the first interview with Meriken woman was excellent.

But my rehearsal at home was useless.

26th—I lost my little charm.

It worried me awfully.

It was given me by my old-fashioned mother. She got it after a holy journey of one month to the shrine of Tenno Sama.

I should be safe, Mother said, from water, fire and highwayman (what else, God only knows) as long as I should carry it.

I sought after it everywhere. I begged my uncle to let me examine his trunk.

"Cast off an ancient superstition!" Uncle scorned.

I sat languidly on the large armchair which almost swallowed my small body.

I imagined many a punishment already inflicted on me.

The tick-tack of my watch from my waist encouraged my nervousness.

There is nothing more irritating than a tick-tack.

I locked up my watch in the drawer of the dresser.

I still felt its tick-tack pursuing my ears.

Then I put it under the pillow.

27th—How I wished I could exchange a ten-dollar gold-piece for a tassel of curly hair!

American woman is nothing without it.

Its infirm gesticulation is a temptation.

In Japan I regarded it as bad luck to own waving hair.

But my tastes cannot remain unaltered in Amerikey.

I don't mind being covered with even red hair.

Red hair is vivacity, fit for Summer's shiny air.

I remember that I trembled at sight of the red hair of an American woman at Tokio. Japanese regard it as the hair of the red demon in Jigoku.

I sat before the looking-glass, with a pair of curling-tongs.

I tried to manage them with surprising patience. I assure you God doesn't vouchsafe me much patience.

Such disobedient tools!

They didn't work at all. I threw them on the floor in indignation.

My wrists pained.

I sat on the floor, stretching out my legs. My shoe-strings were loosed, but my hand did not hasten to them.

I was exhausted with making my hair curl.

I sent my uncle to fetch a hair-dresser.

28th—How old is she?

I could never suggest the age of a Meriken woman.

That Miss Ada was a beauty.

It's becoming clearer to me now why California puts so much pride in her own girls.

Ada was a San Franciscan whom Mrs. Consul presented to me.

What was her family name?

Never mind! It is an extra to remember it for girl. We don't use it.

How envious I was of her long eyelashes lacing around the large eyes of brown hue!

Brown was my preference for the velvet hanao of my wooden clogs.

Long eyelashes are a grace, like the long skirt.

"SUCH DISOBEDIENT TOOLS!"

I know that she is a clever young thing.

She was learned in the art of raising and dropping her curtain of eyelashes. That is the art of being enchanting. I had said that nothing could beat the beauty of my black eyes. But I see there are other pretty eyes in this world.

Everything doesn't grow in Japan. Noses particularly.

My sweet Ada's nose was an inspiration, like the snowcapped peak of O Fuji San. It rose calmly—how symmetrically!—from between her eyebrows.

I had thought that 'Merican nose was rugged, big of bone.

I see an exception in Ada.

She must be the pattern of Meriken beauty.

I felt that I was so very homely.

I stole a sly glance into the looking-glass, and convinced myself that I was a beauty also, but Oriental.

We had different attractions.

She may be Spring white sunshine, while I am yellow Autumn moonbeams. One is animation, and the other sweetness.

I smiled.

She smiled back promptly.

We promised love in our little smile.

She placed her hand on my shoulder. How her diamond ring flashed! She praised the satin skin of my face.

She was very white, with a few sprinkles of freckles. Their scattering added briskness to the face in her case. (But doesn't San Francisco produce too many freckles in woman?) The texture of Ada's skin wasn't fine. Her face was like a ripe peach with powdery hair.

Is it true that dark skin is gaining popularity in American society?

The Japanese type of beauty is coming to the front then, I am happy.

I repaid her compliment, praising her elegant set of teeth.

Ada is the free-born girl of modern Amerikey.

She need never fear to open her mouth wide.

She must have been using special tooth-powder three times a day.

"We are great friends already, aren't we?" I said.

And I extended my finger-tips behind her, and pulled some wisps of her chestnut hair.

"Please, don't!" she said, and raised her sweetly accusing eyes. Then our friendship was confirmed.

Girls don't take much time to exchange their faith.

I was uneasy at first, thinking that Ada might settle herself in a *tête-à-tête* with me, in the chit-chat of poetry. I tried to recollect how the first line of the "Psalm of Life" went, for Longfellow would of course be the first one to encounter.

Alas, I had forgotten it all.

I was glad that her query did not roam from the remote corner of poesy.

"Do you play golf?" she asked.

She thinks the same things are going on in Japan.

Ada! Poor Ada!

The honourable consul and my uncle looked stupid at the lunch table.

I thought they were afraid of being given some difficult question by the Meriken ladies.

Mrs. Consul and Ada ate like hungry pigs. (I beg their pardon!)

"You eat like a pussy!" is no adequate compliment to pay to a Meriken woman.

I found out that their English was neither Macaulay's nor Irving's.

29th—I ate a tongue and some ox-tail soup.

Think of a suspicious spumy tongue and that dirty bamboo tail!

Isn't it shocking to even incline to taste them?

My mother would not permit me to step into the holy ground of any shrine in Japan. She would declare me perfectly defiled by such food.

I shall turn into a beast in the jungle by and by, I should say.

My uncle committed a greater indecency. He ate a tripe.

It was cooked in the "western sea eggplant," to taste of which brings on the smallpox, as I have been told.

He said that he took a delight in pig's feet.

Shame on the Nippon gentleman!

Harai tamae! Kiyome tamae!

30th—"Chui, chui, chui!"

A little sparrow was twittering at my hotel window.

I could not believe that the sparrow of large America could be as small as the Nippon-born.

Horses are large here. Woman's mouth is large, something like that of an alligator. Policeman is too large.

I fancied that little birdie might be one strayed from the bamboo bush of my family's monastery.

"Sweet vagabond, did you cross the ocean for Meriken Kenbutzu?" I said.

"Chui, chui! Chui, chui, chui!" he chirped.

Is "chui, chui" English, I wonder?

I pushed the window up to receive him.

Oya, ma, he has gone!

I felt so sorry.

I was yearning after my beloved home.

This is the great chrysanthemum season at home. I missed the show at Dangozaka.

How gracefully the time used to pass in Dai Nippon, while I sat looking at the flowers on a tokonoma.

Every place is a strange gray waste to me without the intimate faces of flowers.

Flowers have no price in Japan, just as a poet is nothing, for everybody there is poet. But they have a big value in this city—although I am not positive that an American poet creates wealth.

I purchased a select bouquet of violets.

I passed by several young gentlemen. Were their eyes set on my flowers or my hands?

I don't wear gloves. I don't wish my hands to be touched harshly by them. Truly I am vain of showing my small hands.

I love the violet, because it was the favourite of dear John—Keats, of course.

It may not be a flower. It is decidedly a perfume, anyhow.

31st—I have heard a sad piece of news from Mrs. Consul about Mr. Longfellow.

She says that he has ceased to be an idol of American ladies.

He has retired to a comfortable fireside to take care of school children.

Poor old poet!

Nov. 1st—American chair is too high.

Are my legs too short?

It was uncomfortable to sit erect on a chair all the time as if one were being presented before the judge.

And those corsets and shoes!

They seized me mercilessly.

I said that I would spend a few hours in Japan style, reclining on the floor like an eloped angel.

I brought out a crape kimono and my girdle with the phoenix embroidery, after having locked the entrance of my room.

"Kotsu, kotsu, kotsu!"

Somebody was fisting on my door.

Oya, she was Ada, my "Rose of Frisco" or "Butterfly of Van Ness."

(She was quartered in Van Ness Avenue, the most elegant street of a whole bunch.)

She was sprightly as a runaway princess. She blew her sunlight and fragrance into my face.

I was grateful that I chanced to be acquainted with such a delightful Meriken lady.

"O ho, Japanese *kimono*! If I might only try it on!" she said.

I told her she could.

"How lovely!" she ejaculated.

We promised to spend a gala day together.

"We will rehearse," I said, "a one-act Japanese play entitled 'Two Cherry Blossom Musumes.'"

I assisted her to dress nip. She was utterly ignorant of Oriental attire.

What a superb development she had in body! Her chest was abundant, her shoulders gracefully commanding. Her rather large rump, however, did not show to advantage in waving dress. Japs prefer a small one.

My physical state is in poverty.

I was wrong to believe that the beauty of woman is in her face.

It is so, of course, in Japan. The brown woman eternally sits. The face is her complete exhibition.

The beauty of Meriken woman is in her shape.

I pray that my body may grow.

The Japanese theatre never begins without three rappings of time-honoured wooden blocks.

I knocked on the pitcher.

Miss Ada appeared from the dressing room, fluttering an open fan.

How ridiculously she stepped!

It was the way Miss What's-her-name acted in "The Geisha," she said.

She was much taller than little me. The kimono scarcely reached to her shoes. I have never seen such an absurd show in my life.

I was tittering.

The charming Ada fanned and giggled incessantly in supposed-to-be Japanese *chic*.

"What have I to say, Morning Glory?" she said, looking up.

"I don't know, dear girl!" I jerked.

Then we both laughed.

Ada caught my neck by her arm. She squandered her kisses on me.

(It was my first taste of the kiss.)

We two young ladies in wanton garments rolled down happily on the floor.

2nd—If I could be a gentleman for just one day!

I would rest myself on the hospitable chair of a barber shop—barber shop, drug store and candy store are three beauties on the street—like a prince of leisure, and dream something great, while the man is busy with a razor.

"O ho, Japanese kimono!"

I am envious of the gentleman who may bathe in such a purple hour.

I never rest.

American ladies neither!

Each one of them looks worried as if she expected the door-bell any moment.

I suppose it is the penalty of being a woman.

3rd—My little heart was flooded with patriotism.

It is our Mikado's birthday.

I sang "The Age of Our Sovereign." I shouted "Ten thousand years! Banzai! Ban banzai!"

My uncle and I hurried to the Japanese Consulate to celebrate this grand day.

4th—The gentlemen of San Francisco are gallant.

They never permit the ladies—even a black servant is in the honourable list of "ladies"—to stand in the car.

If Oriental gentlemen could demean themselves like that for just one day!

I should not mind a bit if one proposed to me even.

I love a handsome face.

They part their hair in the middle. They have inherited no bad habit of biting their finger-nails. I suppose they offer a grace before each meal. Their smile isn't sardonic, and their laughter is open.

I have no dispute with their mustaches and their blue eyes. But I am far from being an admirer of their red faces.

Japs are pygmies. I fear that the Americans are too tall. My future husband is not allowed to be over five feet five inches. His nose should be of the cast of Robert Stevenson's.

Each one of them carries a high look. He may be the President at the next election, he seems to say. How mean that only one head is in demand!

A directory and a dictionary are kind. The 'Merican husband is like them, I imagine.

I have no gentleman friend yet.

To pace alone on the street is a melancholy discarded sight.

What do you do if your shoe-string comes untied?

I have seen a gentleman fingering the shoe-strings of a lady. How glad he was to serve again, when she said, "That's too tight!"

Shall my uncle fill such a part?

Poor uncle!

Old company, however, isn't style.

He is forty-five.

Why can I not choose one to hire from among the "bully" young men loitering around a cigar stand?

5th—My uncle was going out in a black frock-coat and tea-coloured trousers. I insisted that his coat and trousers didn't match.

How can a man be so ridiculous?

I declared that it was as poor taste as for a darkey to wear a red ribbon in her smoky hair.

Uncle surrendered.

He said, "Hei, hei, hei!"

Goo' boy!

He dismissed the great tea-colour.

6th—We had a shower.

The city dipped in a bath.

The pedestrians threw their vaguely delicate shadows on the pavements. The ladies voluntarily permitted the gentlemen to review their legs. If I were in command, I would not permit the ladies to raise an umbrella under the "para para" of a shower. Their hastening figures are so fascinating.

The shower stopped. The pavements were glossed like a looking-glass. The windows facing the sun scattered their sparkling laughter.

How beautiful!

I am perfectly delighted by this city.

One thing that disappoints me, however, is that Frisco is eternally snowless.

Without snow the year is incomplete, like a departure without sayonara.

Dear snow! O Yuki San!

Many Winters ago I modelled a doll of snow, which was supposed to be a gentleman.

How proud I used to be when I stamped the first mark with my high ashida on the white ground before anyone else!

I wonder how Santa Claus will array himself to call on this town.

His fur coat is not appropriate at all.

7th—Why didn't I come to Amerikey earlier—in the Summer season?

I was staring sadly at my purple parasol against the wall by my dresser.

I have no chance to show it.

I have often been told that I look so beautiful under it.

8th—My darling O Ada came in a carriage. Her two-horsed carriage was like that of our Japanese premier.

She is the daughter of a banker.

The sun shone in yellow.

Ada's complexion added a brilliancy. I was shocked, fearing that I looked awfully brown.

Ada said that I was "perfectly lovely." Can I trust a woman's eulogy?

I myself often use flattery.

A jewel and face-powder were not the only things, I said, essential to woman.

We drove to the Golden Gate Park and then to the Cliff House.

What a triumphant sound the hoofs of the bay horses struck! I fancied the horses were a poet, they were rhyming.

I don't like the automobile.

Ada was sweet as could be.

"Tell me your honourable love story!" she chattered.

I did only blush.

I hadn't the courage to burst my secrecy.

I loved once truly.

It was an innocent love as from a fairy book.

If true love could be realised!

In the park I noticed a lady who scissored the "don't touch" flowers and stepped away with a saintly air. The comical fancy came to me that she was the mother of a policeman guarding against intruders.

We found ourselves in the Japanese tea garden.

A tiny musume in wooden clogs brought us an honourable tea and o'senbe.

The grounds were an imitation of Japanese landscape gardening.

Homesickness ran through my fibre.

The decorative bridge, a stork by the brook, and the dwarf plants hinted to me of my home garden.

A sudden vibration of shamisen was flung from the Japanese cottage close by.

"Tenu, tenu! Tenu, tsunn shann!"

Who was the player?

When I sat myself by the ocean on the beach I found some packages of peanuts right before me.

The beautiful Ada began to snap them.

She hummed a jaunty ditty. Her head inclined pathetically against my shoulder. My hair, stirred by the sea zephyrs, patted her cheek.

She said the song was "My Gal's a High-Born Lady."

Who was its author? Emerson did not write it surely.

When I returned to the hotel, I undertook to place on the wall the weather-torn fragment of cotton which I had picked up at the park.

These words were printed on it

"KEEP OFF
THE GRASS."

I decided to mail it to my Japan, requesting my daddy to post it upon my garden grasses—somewhere by the old cherry tree.

9th—To-day is the third anniversary of my grandmother's death.

I will keep myself in devotion.

I burned the incense I had bought from a Chinaman. I watched the beautiful gesticulation of its smoke.

Good Grandma!

She wished she could live long enough to be present at my wedding ceremony. She prayed that she might select the marriage equipage for me.

I am alone yet.

I wonder if she knows—does her ghost peep from the grasses?—that I am drifting among the ijins she ever loathed.

I don't see how to manage myself sometimes—like an unskilful fictionist with his heroine.

When shall I get married?

10th—I yawned.

Nothing is more unbecoming to a woman than yawning.

I think it no offence to swear once in a while in one's closet.

I was alone.

I tore to pieces my "Things Seen in the Street," and fed the waste-paper basket with them.

The basket looked so hungry without any rubbish. An unkept basket is more pleasing, like a soiled autograph-book.

"I didn't come to Amerikey to be critical, that is, to act mean, did I?" I said.

I must remain an Oriental girl, like a cherry blossom smiling softly in the Spring moonlight.

But afterwards I felt sorry for my destruction.

I thrust my hand into the basket. I plucked them up. They were illegible as follows:

"   women coursing like a 'rikisha of 'Hama   their children crying at home   left somewhere their womanliness gentleman with stove-pipe hat blowing nose with his fingers young lady kept busy chewing gum while walking. If you once show such a grace at Tokio, you shall wait fruitlessly for the marriage offer.

" old grandma in gay red skirt aged man arm-in-arm with wife so young What a martyrdom to marry for G-O-L-D! policeman has no

"San Francisco is a beautiful city, but 'vertisements of 'The Girl from Paris'

W————d's Beer

with the watches hanging on their breasts God bless you, red necktie gentleman woman at the corner chattering like a street politician."

And I missed some other hundred lines.

11th—A letter from the minister arrived.

(I'd be a postman, by the way, if I were a man. A noble work that is to deliver around the love and "gokigen ukagai.")

I clipped off the Mexican stamp.

I will make a stamp book for my boy who may be born when I become a wife.

Before opening the letter I pressed it to my ear. My imaginative ear heard his illustrious "Ha, ha, ha——" rolling out.

How I missed his happy laughter!

Can he now pronounce a "How do?" in Mexican?

12th—It surprises me to learn that many an American is born and dies in a hotel.

Such a life—however large rooms you may possess—is not distinguishable, in my opinion, from that of a bird in a cage.

Is hotel-living a recent fashion?

Don't say so!

The business locality—like the place where this Palace Hotel takes its seat—does not afford a stomachful of respectable air.

I preferred some hospitable boarding house in a quiet street, where I might even step up and down in nude feet. I wished to occupy a chamber where the morning sun could steal in and shake my sleepy little head with golden fingers as my beloved mama might do.

We will move to the "high-toned" boarding house of Mrs. Willis this afternoon.

Her house is placed on the high hill of California Street.

I am grateful there is no car quaking along there.

My uncle says I shall have a whole lot of millionaires for neighbours.

California must be one dignified street.

The Chinese colony is close at hand from Mrs. Willis', —the exotic exposition brilliant with green and yellow colour. The incense surges. So cute is the sparrow-eyed Asiatic girl—such a "karako"—with a small cue on only one side of the head. Dear Oriental town!

Good luck, I pray, my Palace Hotel!

Sayonara, my graceful butlers!

I shall hear no more of their sweet "Yes, Madam!" They talk gently as a lottery-seller.

The more they bow and smile the more you will press the button of tips.

They are so funny.

So long, everybody!

13th—The savour of the air is rich without being heavy.

The Tokio atmosphere emits a lassitude.

It's natural that the Japs are prone to languor.

A good while ago I pushed down my window facing the Bay of San Francisco. I leaned on the sill, my face propped up by both my hands.

The grand scenery absorbed my whole soul.

"Ideal place, isn't it?" I emphasised.

The bay was dyed in profound blue.

The Oakland boat joggled on happily as from a fairy isle. My visionary eyes caught the heavenly flock of seagulls around it.

If I could fly in their company!

The low mountains over the bay looked inexpressively comfortable, like one sleeping under a warm blanket.

The moon-night view from here must be wonderful.

I felt a new stream of blood beginning to swell within my body.

I buzzed a silly song.

I crept into my uncle's room.

I stole one stalk of his cigarettes.

I bit it, aping Mr. Uncle, when my door banged.

14th—I bustled back to my room.

My breast throbbed.

A naked woman in an oil painting stood before me in the hall.

Is Mrs. Willis a lady worthy of respect?

It is nothing but an insulting stroke to an Oriental lady—yes sir, I'm a lady—to expose such an obscenity.

I brought down one of my crape haoris, raven-black in hue, with blushing maple leaves dispersed on the sleeves, and cloaked the honourable picture.

My haori wasn't long enough.

The feet of the nude woman were all seen.

I have not the least objection to the undraped feet. They were faultless in shape.

I myself am free to bestow a glimpse of my beautiful feet.

I turned the key of my door.

I stripped off my shoes and my stockings also.

Dear red silken stockings!

I scrutinised my feet for a while. Then I asked myself:

"Which is lovelier, my feet or those in the painting?"

15th—I couldn't rest last night.

The long wail of a horn somewhere in the distance—at the gate of the ocean perhaps—haunted me. The night was foggy.

I had a wild dream.

The fogs were not withdrawn this morning.

I was discouraged, I had to go out in my best gown.

Wasn't it a shame that two buttons jumped out when I hurried to dress up?

"Are the buttons secure?" is my first worry and the last.

Why don't Meriken inventors take up the subject of buttonless clothes?

Woman cannot be easy while her dress is fastened by only buttons.

16th—I wish I could pay my bill with a bank check.

Have I money in the bank with my name?

I fancied it a great idea to sleep with a big bank book under the pillow.

I decided to save my money hereafter.

How often have I expressed my hatred of an economical woman!

I detested the clinking "charin charan" of small coins in my purse. Very hard I tried to get from them.

Extravagance is a folly. Folly is only a mild expression for crime.

I deducted ten dollars from the fifty that I had settled for my new street gown. I dropped a card notifying my ladies' tailor that I had altered my mind for the second price.

"Ten already for the bank!" I said.

I took it to the "Yokohama Shokin Ginko" of this city.

I was given a little book for the first time in my life.

I thought myself quite a wealthy woman preserving my money in the bank.

I pressed the book to my face. I held it close to my bosom as a tiny girl with a new doll.

And I smiled into a looking-glass.

17th—I went to the gallery of the photographer Taber, and posed in Nippon "pera pera."

The photographer spread before me many pictures of the actress in the part of "Geisha."

She was absurd.

I cannot comprehend where 'Mericans get the conception that Jap girls are eternally smiling puppets.

Are we crazy to smile without motive?

What an untidy presence!

She didn't even fasten the front of her kimono.

Charm doesn't walk together with disorder under the same Japanese parasol.

And I had the honour to be presented to an extraordinary mode in her hair.

It might be entitled "ghost style." It suggested an apparition in the "Botan Toro" played by Kikugoro.

The photographer handed me a fan.

Alas! It was a Chinese fan in a crude mixture of colour.

He urged me to carry it.

I declined, saying:

"Nobody fans in cool November!"

18th—We had a laugh.

Ada, my sweet singer of "My Gal's a High-Born Lady," accompanied me to a matinée of one vaudeville.

This is the age of quick turn, sudden flashes.

The long show has ceased to be the fashion. Modern people are tired of the slowness of old times which was once supposed to be seriousness.

Could anything be prouder than the face of the acrobat retiring after a perilous performance?

Woman tumbler!

I wondered how Meriken ladies could enjoy looking at such a degeneration of woman.

I was glad, however, that I did not see any snake-charmer.

What a delightful voice that negro had! Who could imagine that such a silvery sound could come from such a midnight face? It was like clear water out of the ground.

I was struck by a fancy.

I sprang up.

I attempted to imitate the high-kick dance.

I fell down abruptly.

"Jap's short leg is no use in Amerikey—can't achieve one thing. I am frankly tired of mine," I grumbled.

19th—The Sunday chime was the voice of an angel. The city turned religious.

Mrs. Willis—I had no curiosity about her first name; it is meaningless for the "Mrs." of middle age—indulged in chat with me.

If I say she was "sociable"?—it sounds so graceful.

She announced herself a bigot of poetry. She was bending to make a full poetical demonstration.

Of course it was more pleasing than a mourning-gowned narrative of her lamented husband. (I suppose he is dead, as divorce is too commonplace.)

But it were treachery, if I were put under her long recital of the insignificant works of local poets.

Tasukatta wa!

A little girl came as a relief.

Dorothy! She is a boarder of Mrs. Willis', the golden-haired daughter of Mrs. Browning.

(Mrs. Browning was a disappointment, however. I fancied she might be a relative of the poet Browning. I asked about it. Her response was an unsympathetic "No!")

"O' hayo! " Dorothy said, spattering over me her familiarity.

It takes only an hour to be friends with the Meriken girl, while it is the work of a year with a Japanese musume.

"Great girl! Your Nippon language is perfect? Would you like to learn more?" I said.

"I'd like it," was her retort.

Then we slipped to my room.

I wonder how Mrs. Willis fared without an audience!

I was sorry, thinking that she might regard me as an uncivil Jap.

"Chon kina! Chon kina!"

Thus Dorothy repeated. It was a Japanese song, she said, which the geisha girls sung in "The Geisha."

Tat, tat, tat, stop, Dorothy!

Truly it was the opening sound—not the words—of a nonsensical song.

I presume that "The Geisha" is practising a plenteous injustice to Dai Nippon.

I recalled one Meriken consul who jolted out that same song once at a party.

He became no more a gentleman to me after that.

20th—I pasted my little card on my door.

I wrote on it "Japanese Lessons Given."

I gazed at it.

I was exceedingly happy.

21st—A gardener came to fix our lawn.

There is nothing lovelier than verdant grasses trimmed neatly. They are like the short skirt of the Meriken little girl.

We women could be angels, I thought, if our speech lapped justly. Women talk superfluously. I do often.

What language did that gardener use?

It must be the English of Carlyle, I said, for its meaning was intangible.

I discovered, by and by, that German English was his honourable choice.

My eyes could express more than my English uttered in Nippon voice. My gestures helped to make my meaning plain.

He became my friend.

He carried a red square of cotton to wipe his mouth, like the furoshiki in which a Japanese country "O' ba san" wraps her New Year's present.

And again as he was leaving I saw a red thing around his neck.

Was it not the same furoshiki which served for his nose?

It wouldn't be a bad idea to play amateur gardener.

The season wasn't fitting for such a performance, however.

A large summer hat! That was the customary attire.

But my light-hearted straw one with its laughing bouquet was not adapted to November, however gorgeously the sun might shine.

And it's sheer stupidity to track after a tradition.

I wound a large flapping piece of black crape about my head. (How awfully becoming the garb of a Catholic nun would be! I do not know what is dear, if it is not the rosary. A writhing rope around the waist is celestial carelessness.)

I appeared on the lawn, but without a sprinkler and rake. It would have been too theatrical to carry them.

I gathered the small stones from amid the grasses into a wheelbarrow near by.

Just as my new enterprise was beginning to seem so delightful, the luncheon gong gonged.

My uncle goggled from the hall, and said:

"Where have you been? I was afraid you had eloped."

"I've no chance yet to meet a boy," I spoke in an undertone.

Afterward I was ashamed that I had been so awkwardly sincere.

22nd—There was one thing that I wanted to test.

My uncle went out. I understood that he would not be back for some hours.

I found myself in his room, pulling out his drawer.

"Isn't it elegant?" I exclaimed, picking up his dress-suit.

At last I had an opportunity to examine how I would look in a tapering coat.

Gentleman's suit is fascinating.

"Where is his silk hat?" I said.

I reached up my arms to the top shelf of a closet, standing on the chair.

The door swung open.

Tamageta! My liver was crushed by the alarm.

A chambermaid threw her suspicious smile at me.

Alas!

My adventure failed.

23rd—I mean no one else but O Ada San, when I say "my sweet girl."

She was tremendously nice, giving a tea-party in my honour.

The star actress doesn't appear on the stage from the first of the first act. I thought I would present myself a bit later at the party, when they were tattling about my delay.

I delight in employing such little dramatic arts.

I dressed all in silk. It's proper of course, for a Japanese girl.

I chose cherry blossoms in preference to roses for my hat. Roses are acceptable, however, I said in my second thought, for they are given a thorn against affronters.

I went to Miss Ada's looking my best.

They—six young ladies in a bunch—stretched out their hands. I was coaxed by their hailing smile.

Ada kissed me.

I had no charming manner in receiving a kiss before the people no more than in giving one. I blushed miserably. I knew I was bungling.

O Morning Glory, you are one century late!

They besieged me.

None of them was so pretty as Ada. Beauty is rare, I perceive, like good tweezers or ideal men.

I distributed my Japanese cards.

All of my new friends held them upside down.

Is it a modern vogue to be ignorant?

Ada played skilfully her role of hostess, which was a middle-aged part. She didn't even spill the tea in serving. Her "Sugar? Two lumps?" sounded fit. She divided her entertaining eye-flashes among us.

Tea is the thing for afternoon, when woman is excused if she be silly.

We all undressed our too-tight coat of rhetoric in the sipping of tea.

We laughed, and laughed harder, not seeing what we were laughing at.

I couldn't catch all of their names.

Such a delicious name as "Lily" was absurdly given to a girl with red blotches on her face.

(A few blemishes are a fascination, however, like slang thrown in the right place.)

Her flippancy was like the "buku buku" of a stream.

Lightness didn't match with her heavy physique.

"How lovely an earthquake must be!" she chirruped. "Shall I go to Japan just on that account? A jolly moment I had last February. A baby earthquake visited here, as you know. I was drinking tea. The worst of it was that I let the cup tumble on to my pink dress. I prayed a whole week, nevertheless, to be called again."

Woman has nothing to do with a hideous make-up. Miss Lily should not select a pink hue.

"A tea-party in my honour."

"You are awful!" I said.

I told about the horror of a certain famous Japanese earthquake. They all breathed out "Good heavens!"

There was one second of silence.

Ada struck a gushing melody on the piano.

The lively Meriken ladies prompted themselves to frisk about.

I was ready to cry in my destitution.

One girl hauled me up violently by the hand.

"Come and dance!"

Her arm crawled around my waist, while she directed:

"Right foot—now, left!"

I returned to Mrs. Willis', my thoughts absorbed in a dancing academy.

"I must learn how to skip," I said.

24th—I hate the alarm clock, simply because it is always so punctual.

"I was too late" is a delightful expression.

Mrs. Willis' breakfast is at quarter-past eight!

Isn't that "quarter-past" interesting?

And I can never be ready before nine.

25th—I dragged my uncle off to the Chute to enrich my store of zoology.

"One gape more, Uncle, to count up one dozen!" I said, and pulled his mustache in the car.

It was lucky that no one saw my act.

Poor Oji San! Playing chaperon is not a very promising occupation, is it?

I stood by the "happy family" of monkeys. I tried to descry their point of view in orations.

I gave it up.

The vain Miss Polly worked hard to bring everybody to an understanding with one eternal "Hello, dear!"

I found such grace in the elephant when he waved his honourable trunk.

The stupid Mr. Elephant wasn't stupid a bit in accepting my present.

How philosophically he gazed at me! Very likely I was the first Jap girl to his audience.

What respectable eyes!

"You'll bankrupt yourself in peanuts," my uncle warned.

26th—A white apron on my black dress makes me so cute.

I am just suited to be a chambermaid. Shall I volunteer as a servant?

I bought an apron.

To-day is house-cleaning day.

I kept busy a good while arranging my theatrical costume as a maid.

Wasn't it fun?

I was ready to scrub the floor, when I heard "kotsu kotsu," on my door.

It was Annie with a broom.

"I'm your help. Just a moment! I have forgotten the finishing glance in my mirror."

27th—I have been studying the catechism.

I am afraid to go to church, for the minister may put many a question to me.

Is Miss Ada a dutiful church-goer?

I don't think so.

She would rather mumble a nigger song than a chapter from the Bible.

I will ask her a few things from the catechism at my first opportunity.

28th—"Hand me your cup after you are done with your tea!" Mrs. Browning requested. "I will ponder on your fortune."

"How delightful!" I said.

My fortune?

I remembered how I used to scatter my pocket money among the fortune-tellers, pleased to be informed of a lot of nice things.

What meaning she could find in a cup!

I felt like a mother with her children already in bed, when I dropped my spoon into my tea.

I felt mistress of the situation.

Was there ever anything more welcome than to learn your fortune?

"A young American (rich, very rich—indeed) will win your affection. The marriage will be a happy one," she prophesied.

Is that so?

Life is becoming very interesting.

I wonder where my would-be husband is seeking me.

Shall I advertise in a paper?

How?

If my first-rate picture by Mr. Taber were printed, it would be a whole thing in such a business.

I thought the picture beautiful enough to sell at any stationer's of U. S. A.

How many thousand could I sell in a week?

Could I make money out of it? Some decent fortune, I mean, of course.

29th—Ho, ho, such a day!

I was aroused by the roar of a milk-wagon early in the morning.

I sought a pin in vain.

I tore my skirt on a sneering nail at the door.

I upset my flower-vase.

I sat by my window. A vegetable pedlar howled to me, "Potatoes? Potatoes?"

I couldn't recall a sweet dream I had last night.

The clamour of a Chinese funeral passed under my room. The carriages were packed with hired "crying women." Isn't it a farce?

I went out. My street-car ran off the track.

A fire-engine deafened me.

I passed by an undertaker's. It was cold like a grave.

The sight stunned me.

30th—Is my nose high enough?

I bought a pair of "nose spectacles."

Those with wires to circle the ears, which are Oriental (that is to say old-fashioned), would suit even a noseless Formosa Chinee.

But how many Japs could show themselves ready for nose spectacles?

The optician asked if they were for myself.

He was a trifle uncertain about my nose, I suppose.

"No! For my friend," I said.

It was a white lie.

I blushed as if I had committed a heavy crime.

I hoped I had not.

I put my new spectacles on my nose, as soon as I returned to my room. Very well they stayed. Mother Nature was specially kind to me.

But what a depression—also what torture—I felt from their clutch!

I was pleased, however, seeing myself somewhat scholarly.

Aren't spectacles an emblem of wisdom?

The first requirement to be a critic should be spectacles. The second is a pessimistic smile, of course.

My mirror told me that I looked quite modern.

"Book!" I exclaimed.

I must see what effect I could produce with a book on my lap.

I leaped from the chair to fetch one.

My spectacles dropped from my honourable nose on to the hearthstone. My nose was exceedingly stupid.

Alas, and alas!

The spectacles were crushed to pieces.

I was broken also.

I buried my face in the pillow for some time.

Then I said: "I'm not short in my sight. I have no use for them except for fun."

I wiped my disturbed eyes with a handkerchief. My finger felt the rude marks printed on both sides of my nose.

Dec. 1st—I bought a Louisiana lottery ticket through Annie.

Like any other domestic girl, she has no key to her mouth. She is like a sentence that has forgotten to add the period.

I begged all sorts of gods to drop the capital prize on me.

Thirty thousand dollars! Think!

How shall I manage with them when I have won?

2nd—If I were a painter!

My eyes were fixed upon the dying sun. Its solemnity was like the passing of a mighty king.

Some time glided by.

My thought was pursuing the sun.

The twilight!

Oh, twilight pacifying me as with the odour from a magical palace!

Hush!

The melody of a piano effused from my neighbour.

The best thing in the world is to play music. The very best is to listen to the profuse melody evoked by a master.

Was it a superb execution?

My soul was dissolved, anyhow, in the rapture.

I left my uncle's room where I saw the grand sun pass away.

I put me in my bed, because my visionary mood was not to be stirred for the world, and because I wished to dream a romance without the delay of a moment.

But I could not slumber.

And I missed my dinner.

I petitioned my uncle to step out into the street for my beloved chestnuts.

Dear Italian chestnut vendor!

I never pass by without buying.

3rd—We start tomorrow for Los Angeles of Southern California.

Mr. and Mrs. Schuyler have invited us to spend some weeks with them.

The gentleman was the former consul at Yokohama. My uncle is his intimate friend.

My new trunk was brought in from the store.

It bears my name in Roman of commanding type.

I stared at the characters as upon an ancient writing whose meaning could only be imagined.

"Doesn't 'Miss Morning Glory' suggest that the owner is a charming young lady?"

My little smile smiled, as I thought that it would, of course.

A new trunk, I am sorry to say, lacks a historical look. An old one is more gratifying, like old brocade or an old ring.

Au revoir, my Ada!

South-bound train, 4th—I was lavish of my art of "bothering."

My poor uncle—my eternally "poor uncle" was the victim. I wanted some diversion at any price.

His face scowled as I bored him with my successive questions.

I thought his irritated face fascinating.

When I presented another question, he was droning a genteel snore.

I twisted an edge of a newspaper into a roll. I thrust it into his nose.

There was no doubt about his starting.

"Bikkurishita!" he exclaimed.

Then he begged to be allowed some chance to rest.

This is a "bad year for cucumbers" for him. He made a mistake in accompanying me on Meriken Kenbutsu.

Honestly I have to behave nicely.

My opening question to Uncle was: "What's the derivation of 'damn'?"

"Imperialism" was my last.

I have a high regard for the people dignified by using the capital "I" for the personal pronoun.

But if I were the President I should not wish to be addressed with that hackneyed, unromantic "Mr."

The cartoonists making sport of the President shock me.

How big-hearted the President is!

Those "devils" would be beheaded in the Orient.

Los Angeles, 5th—No one bangs the door at Schuyler's.

The servants drop their eyes meekly before they speak.

A well-bred atmosphere circulates.

A woman over forty-five is nothing if she isn't motherly enough to let one feel at home. Mrs. Schuyler's silence is a smile. I loved her from my first glance. I thought I could ask her to wash my hair some sunny day. I could fancy how pleasant it would be to immerse myself in her chat—such sort of talk as an old-bonneted "how to keep house"—while I was drying my hair in the indolence of a sea-nymph. Modern topic is like black coffee, it is too stimulating. There is nothing dearer than a domestic subject.

I have no hesitation in accepting her as my Meriken mother.

I am positive I would feel more comfortable if I had one in this country.

How good-naturedly she was fattened!

A somewhat stout woman looks so proper for a mother.

I wished I could lean on her plump shoulder from the back in Japanese girl's way, and play with her hair, and ask a few innocent questions like "What have I to eat for dinner?"

She talked about the Japanese woman, principally praising her shapely mouth.

I felt conceitedly, because I was given one classical little mouth, if I had nothing else to be noticed.

Mr. Schuyler grasped my hand ever so hard. My hand was buried in his palm. His manner was courteously boyish.

His body is erect like a redwood.

Such an old gentleman gives me the impression of another race from the divine realm of everlasting youth. A Jap after fifty is capped with "retired."

But the work of the American gentleman is only finished when he dies.

Great Meriken Jin!

Mr. Schuyler shows more civility to his servants than to his wife.

Here I can study the typical household of America's best caste.

6th—"Anata donata?"

I rubbed my dreamy eyes, scanning my room.

Who was the Japanese speaker?

I crept to the door, and opened it slightly. Not a soul was there.

I heard the trivial clatter of the kitchen stepping up.

I dipped into my bed again. I smiled sceptically, thinking that I must have been dreaming.

"Gokigen ikaga?"

I was addressed again by the same voice.

I said that there was positively some mischief in my room.

I leaped down from the bed.

I inspected my slippers. I made sure there was nothing strange under the pictures on the wall. I tugged at the drawers. I tumbled every blanket. I pried in the pitcher.

I sat on the bed wrapped in fog.

The blind rustled.

The sunbeams crawled in marvellously.

Then I was frightened by another speech, "Nihonjin desu."

I declared that it flew in from the outside.

I rolled up the blind.

Oya, oya! There was a parrot perching in a cage by my window!

He adjusted his showy coat first, and then sent me his inquisitive eyes.

"Anata donata?" he repeated.

"Morning Glory is my insignificant name, sir," I replied.

A trifling toss of his head showed his satisfaction in my name. I thought he was trying to set me at ease with his smile.

"Gokigen ikaga?"

"I feel splendidly, thank you, Mr. Parrot!" I said.

Then pressing his head backward he looked haughtily at me with fixed eyes, and announced:

"Nihonjin desu."

"I'm also a Jap," I muttered.

He was the most profound Japanese scholar, Mrs. Schuyler said, in all Los Angeles. Mr. Schuyler Jr. brought him from Kobe last spring.

I told her the incident of this morning.

She laughed, she said she expected it.

Bad Mother Schuyler!

7th—Dear Baby! Kawaii koto!

I hugged the baby of Mrs. Schuyler Jr. and kissed it.

Her husband is away in Japan for the tea business.

It was the darling baby, I thank the gods, who received my first kiss.

It's heavenly to stamp love with a kiss. Lips are the portal of the human heart.

Kiss is sweet.

I say that it marks an epoch in the spiritual evolution of the Japanese when they learn what a kiss is—but not how to kiss.

The baby crawled like a sportive crab. It orationed. It! I felt sorry that "It" would soon be changed to "He" or "She." It caught sight of a piece of burnt match in the course of its expedition. It turned its way and clinched it with its fingers. It hastened to the mother to exhibit it, and waited patiently with its great game for Mamma's praise.

I nearly cried in my excitement at such a pathetic revelation.

Lovely thing!

The baby had blue eyes.

My preference wasn't for blue eyes. I often snapped at them, saying that they were like a dead fish's eyes.

But how long can I keep up my ill-will, when I look with delight upon the blueness in water, sky and mountain?

Isn't it precious to see the blue pictures on china?

A blue pencil is just the thing to mark on the margin of a pleasing book.

Blue is a poetical hue.

Robert Burns was blue-eyed.

I recalled the first American I met in Tokio, who seriously questioned whether it was a fact that Japs butcher a blue-eyed baby.

Bakabakashii wa!

Japan has no blue eye.

And Japanese are worshippers of any sort of baby.

If American babies were like Chinese girls!

I would pile up all my coins to buy one.

Meriken baby understood how to smile before how to cry. It is a lady or gentleman already.

I will serve as baby's nurse if I must support myself.

It's a high task to be useful to the baby, and watch its growth as a silent astronomer watches the stars.

I wish I could roll the baby's carriage day after day.

How sweetly the world would be turning then!

Shall I hire Schuyler's baby for one day?

8th—Is there any more gratifying word than dinner?

I had a "hipp goo" dinner. (Permit a Chinese-English expression for once.)

Its inviting heaviness was like an honourable poem by Milton.

Schuyler's house has a Miltonic presence.

Electric light is too imposing.

Candelabra are like a moon whose beams are a lenitive song.

The nude shoulders of Mrs. Schuyler, Jr., crimsoned in the rays from the candelabra.

The exposure of some part of the skin is the highest order of art. How to show it is just as serious a study as how to clothe it.

If I had such supreme shoulders as hers, I would not pause before displaying them.

What falling shoulders are mine!

The slope of the shoulders is prized in Japan. Amerikey is another country, you know.

I appeared at the dinner in my native gown.

The things on the table had a high-toned excellence.

I will not forget to have my initials engraved if I happen to buy any silver.

Coffee was served. I felt that an old age had returned, when eating was only a dissipation.

I'm growing to love Meriken food.

I am glad that I don't see any musty pudding at Schuylers', a sight that makes me ten years older.

And another thing I hate is the smell of cabbage.

How pleased I was to see a "chabu chabu" of shallow water in my finger bowl! Just a glimpse of water is tasty.

Our taciturn butler retired from the dining-room with graceful dignity.

The butler has ceased to be a common servant. He has advanced, I suppose, to the rank of an ornament of the Meriken household.

The sister of Mother Schuyler and her husband dined with us.

The funniest thing about her was that she kept a few long hairs on her cheek. They grew from a mole.

It may be good luck to preserve them.

Her husband was surprised when he heard that we do not use knife and fork at home.

Bamboo chop-sticks! How dear!

9th—I have no belief in the earring.

It is a savage mode, like the deformed feet of the Chinese woman.

But why did the Meriken lady discard her veil?

Her face behind the veil would appear like a rose through the Spring mist. It is a charming thing as ever was fashioned for woman.

I have seen no lady with a veil in this town.

I suppose the Los Angeles women confide in their faces.

They strew more liberty in their grace than the San Franciscans.

Their beauty is informal.

The city is enchanting.

I am pleased that I am not shown here so many a "To Let" as in Frisco.

Even the barefooted Arabs, those street sparrows, are quite a picture.

10th—I promised Mrs. Schuyler, Jr., good care of her baby for half an hour.

I carried it firm on my arms.

I jogged out to the garden.

The baby faced toward me and said:

"Bu, bu! Bu, bu, bu!"

I felt grateful, thinking that it counted me among its friends.

I laid its head on my breast.

I sang a little Japanese lullaby:

> "Nenneko, Nenneko,
> Nennekoyo!
> Oraga akanbowa
> Itsudekita?
> Sangatsu sakurano
> Sakutokini!
> Doride okawoga
> Sakurairo."

(Sleep, sleep, sleep! When was our baby made? Third month, when the cherry blossoms. So the honourable face of our child is cherry-blossom coloured.)

The breezes billed and cooed upon the grasses. An imperial palm cast its rich shadow.

The affectionate sunlight made me think of a "little Spring" of the Japanese September. Everything inclined to a siesta in the yellow air.

A tropical touch is the touch of passion.

Can you fancy this is the month of December?

I cannot.

After I put the baby to its nurse, I paced around a bronze statue upon the lawn, losing myself in Greek beauty.

Then I snatched a rose.

I pressed it to my nose-tip.

12th—Where's my painstaking description of Echo Mountain?

I made a pleasant trip there yesterday with Schuyler's party.

I lost my writing penned last night.

Such a heedless tomboy!

I idled, watching a spider from my window. It was framing a net amid the garden trees. An awfully dignified tom cat glared from under a bush. I was sorry no game came upon the scene to his honour. My profound Japanese scholar was not discouraged by the lack of an audience. He was busy presenting his polite "Gokigen ikaga?"

Then I found what I did with my yesterday's diary.

Areda mono!

I wiped my oily hands with it and buried it in a trash basket.

I fixed my hair this morning.

Morning Glory San, you have to keep your Nikki in a safe!

Great Carlyle wrote his "French Revolution" twice.

I wish I had been given a slice of his persistency.

13th—A Bishop visited and lunched with us.

Bishop! How I desired to meet one!

It had been my fancy, ever since I read of the venerable Bishop who threw out candle-sticks to Jean Valjean in Hugo's book.

His name was Myriel.

What is my friend's name? After a man reaches the bishop's see, his own name should retire from actual service. People call him "Bishop! Bishop!" as if it were a nickname.

My bishop had a holy face.

"Who is this good man who is staring at me?" I said to myself at first sight, as Napoleon said when he saw Myriel.

A young churchman is unnatural.

The customarily pessimistic face of the Japanese priest causes aversion.

I got what I wanted in my new friend.

If I were his daughter, I would comb his silken hair before he goes to church on Sunday.

I was glad he was not thin.

Ho, ho, ho! He ate meat like anybody else.

He would seem holier if he merely bit a crust of bread, and sipped three spoonfuls of tea.

After luncheon we strolled through the garden arm in arm.

Not a bit I blushed. I was as completely at ease with him as with my papa.

He told me of the beauty of Christ. His soft, deep voice was as from a far-away forest.

I plucked a few stems of violets. I fitted them to his buttonhole.

Such a little thing pleased him immensely.

Dear, simple Bishop!

I digested what he spoke. I declared that Christianity was the sun, while Buddhism was the moon.

The sun is day and life, and the moon night and rest.

How can we live without the sun? The moon is poetry.

14th—The sky became low, its colour frowning gray.

The winds snarled.

December was suddenly calling us.

We sat by a snug fire at evening.

Its yellow flame suggested a preacher uplifting his hands in prayer. The fire flickered in jollity.

"Pachi, pachi, pachi!"

The parlour was not lighted.

The pictures on the wall were impressive in the firelight

Any woman looks charming at night and by the fireside. I felt happy imagining that I must appear lovely.

The fireplace is so dear, like mamma's lap.

Mr. Schuyler brought a chess-board and challenged.

I offered me for a fight.

I used to play American chess with a Meriken missionary who lived in my neighbourhood.

I thought it fun to beat an old man.

"Namu Tenshoko Daijingu!" I repeated.

The gentleman asked what I muttered.

"Never mind! Only a little spell!" I replied in the lightest fashion.

The chess-board was placed between us.

"Mr. Schuyler, can you sacrifice anything for the game?"

"Whatever you please, my little woman!"

"Well!"

"Well, then!"

"Suppose you make Mrs. Schuyler your stake! My uncle will be mine."

"Ha, ha! Very well!"

He was a tactician. I fought hard.

Alas, my game was lost!

My second stake was myself.

"It means that I may marry you, doesn't it?"

"As you please, sir!"

Iyani natta!

He was far superior.

Oya, oya, I was a loser again!

I looked sadly on my uncle, and said:

"Uncle, you cannot return home! We are the property of Mr. Schuyler. Isn't it really too bad?"

15th—Shall I make a little kimono for Schuyler's baby?

It would be a souvenir of my visit.

The crape kept in the Jap stores of this town isn't appropriate for a baby's "bebe." My flower-dyed under-kimono should be utilized.

I opened my trunk.

Mother Schuyler brought in a young lady. She was her niece, that is to say, the daughter of Mrs. Ellis. Mrs. Ellis is the one with the long hair on her cheek.

I told them of my new drift.

They were surprised at my determination.

Miss Olive applied to be my pupil in Japanese sewing.

What a southern name! Olive perfectly fits for a girl born in the passionate breeze.

Her "Is that so?" or "Don't you?" fluttered affectionately like golden sunshine.

Mrs. Schuyler bade her servant to move in the machine.

I objected.

Machine-clicking is not Oriental. The "bebe" has to be done in pure Japanese.

16th—I found a hammock on the veranda.

It is the thing for summer, of course.

I never laid me in it before in my life.

I thought that I would see how I would feel.

I hanged it.

I romped in it.

It was delightful. I fancied that we—I and who?—hammocked among the summer breezes. Then a star appeared. He said, "How beautiful the star is!"

What did I fancy next?

Oh, never mind!

I tossed my feet. The skirt fluttered. My new satin slippers—number one and a half—were all seen. I drew up my skirt a little, and made a whole show of my honourable legs.

I prayed that somebody would pass by to fling an adoring glance at them.

No one roamed along. I scorned my frivolity.

The Bible by me wasn't open at all.

I decided to read it to-day although religion isn't so becoming.

My Bishop sent it this morning. Dear old Bishop! He thought me quite a docile "nenne."

I stretched my body in the hammock.

Alas, ma!

My hana kanzashi with the butterflies was caught by the meshes. The wings of one butterfly were tortured. Yes, I had put a Japanese pin on my hair this morning.

I hoped I could pay a bit more attention to my head all the time.

I was sad for a while.

17th—Good Annie wrote me from Mrs. Willis'.

What a scrawl!

But woman's bad grammar and infirm penmanship are pathetic, don't you think so?

It might look better on a thin blue tablet.

But poor Annie chose such thick smooth paper.

Oya! What?

A five-dollar check?

My goodness, I had forgotten all about my lottery! Even the ticket I have lost. It drew out five dollars.

Why not thirty thousand dollars?

It was better than a blank, anyway, I said philosophically.

Now let me send a little present to my home!

A little thing is a deal sweeter.

I ordered fourteen packets of N. Y. Central Park lawn seed from a nursery.

New York Central Park!

Doesn't it sound grand?

And other flower seeds also.

The dwarf sweet pea is named "Cupid."

It will be no wonder if my father mistakes it for a kibisho.

Cupid is a handsome boy, not a bullfrog-looking teapot, funny papa!

He is garden crazy. I can imagine how conceited he will be showing around his western sea flowers when they are in bloom.

I asked my uncle to translate the directions.

Isn't it handy to keep a secretary?

I'll not miss signing my name on the translation.

My daddy may think it was done by myself.

Woman is a snob.

Now what for mamma?

18th—Mother Schuyler took me to her church.

Such a heathen me!

I felt that I was "sitting on needles," when I slipped into the Meriken church without glancing at even one page of the Bible. It was as risky a venture as to face an examination before fitting.

The service hadn't begun.

Many ladies were introduced to me by Mrs. Schuyler.

They talked about—what?—anything but religion.

I was fanned continually by an offensive odour. Some one had left her perfume at home.

Honourable arm-pit smell!

Amerikey cultivates many a disagreeable sort of thing, doubtless.

The ladies seemed to regard the church as another drawing parlor.

My mind was calmed within ten minutes.

Ureshiya!

The Meriken church is not a difficult place at all.

A Japanese church is ever so sad-faced. No woman under thirty is seen there. I laughed at the thought of an "incense-smelling" young girl.

Isn't it strange that Meriken girls love the church?

Is it because they cannot marry without it?

Sunday amusement doesn't begin before noon. What would girls do if there were no church where they could burst into song?

How classically the bald head of the minister shone!

There is nothing more pleasing than a sweeping sermon on a bright day.

But my mind strayed, wondering why all those ladies were so homely.

I snatched my hat off, wishing to be different from the rest.

I fancied the reason why their hats were eternally glued to their heads was because their hair was never in first-rate order for exhibition.

Many years ago I used to steal into a Buddha temple, being a little "otenba," and tap an idol's shoulder, saying: "How are you getting along, Hotoke Sama?"

Not one idol here!

No incense!

How uninteresting!

How silly I was inventing some clever thing for the occasion when I should be forced to confess! The church was not Catholic.

When we returned home, Mrs. Schuyler asked me what was the text.

"Let me see——"

I made as if I had been a listener to the sermon.

"Dear Mrs. Schuyler, what was it?" I exclaimed as if I had accidentally forgotten.

19th—Miss Olive offered to show me how to play golf.

I went to her home at Pasadena.

Pasadena is a luxurious Winter resort of cheerful aspect.

Its water is blessed.

Even the street cars run like a well-bred gentleman. The dog never growls around. It only wags its tail. No beggars.

America's outdoor diversion demands a great deal of strength

What an imbecile "anego!"

After fifteen minutes I found two bean-like blisters on each palm.

I gave up the game.

I bought a golf outfit, nevertheless, in a store on my way home. The sight of a lady carrying it once stamped itself on my mind as so charming.

What attire would be becoming to me?

I said that my waist should be of deep red wool. Skirt? It must also be of wool, of course, with a large checkerboard pattern. Silk isn't gamesome, is it? And the hat should be a mouse-coloured felt, which must be thrust carelessly by my big gold pin with a coral head.

I well-nigh decided to dye my hair red.

What will my uncle say?

20th—Schuyler's cook wasn't acquainted with the art of rice-cooking.

Mother Schuyler said explanatorily that she had never tasted properly cooked rice since the day at Yokohama.

The rice was pasty.

I thought I would boil the rice according to Japanese prescription for to-day's dinner.

I stepped down to the kitchen.

I put three cupfuls of rice in a saucepan, and dipped my hand in it, and supplied water as much as to my wrist

I placed it on the splendid fire till the agitated water pushed up the lid. Then I moved it on to a gentle fire. The cooking was done after twenty minutes.

I was honoured by everybody at the dinner. The rice was singularly fine. The grains kept their own perfect shapes.

After the dinner I approached Mrs. Schuyler with ink and paper.

"Will you write your recommendation of my rice-cooking?" I said.

She gazed at me questioningly.

"What a funny girl! What shall I say?"

Then I dictated solemnly thus:

"To whom it may concern:

I highly recommend Miss Morning Glory with her honourable art of rice-cooking. Her method is Japanese, that is to say, the best in the world.

MRS. SCHUYLER"

21st—Without a nephew Mother Schuyler wouldn't be a complete old dear.

She has one fortunately.

Olive San told me a whole lot about her great brother.

He is a promising artist.

Artist?

Doesn't an artist affect boorish hair? I was anxious to know how his hair was, because I hated anything long except a frock-coat.

Miss Olive declared him one handsome boy. (I thought how ridiculous is the American girl to praise her brother. It is Japanese etiquette to undervalue one's relatives in describing them.)

I finished my imaginary sketch of his face before we intruded in his studio.

Olive presented me to him.

He was a comely young man.

What gratified me most about him was his shapely shoes, well-polished.

He knew how to talk with girls.

I was instantly put on unceremonious terms.

How beautifully he once slipped "Miss" in addressing me! His gracefully sounding "Pardon me, I mean Miss Morning Glory!" pleased me enormously.

I told him that it was a regular humbug to be particular.

"I will call you Oscar, shall I?" I said, winking.

I felt some fervid water oozing down my cheeks. I was blushing.

I was glad that he was not Mr. Ellis, Jr. The word "Jr." appears to me like a ragged papa's old coat which is dreadfully out of fashion.

"Will you let me paint you?" he requested.

"Am I beautiful enough, do you think?" I said, dropping my eyelids.

"Only too charming!" he said bravely.

I always think every gentleman whom I meet falls in love with me.

I regarded Mr. Oscar Ellis already as an adorer.

O sentimental Morning Glory!

When I returned to Schuyler's my mind was completely occupied with an absurd fancy.

I was thinking what I shall do when he proposes to me. Shall I say yes?

For a girl to fall in love with one while she is staying at his aunt's isn't romantic a bit, is it?

I don't care, anyhow, for an artist lover.

It is a worn-out hero in old fiction.

Doesn't the word "artist" ring like a synonym for poverty?

22nd—Mrs. Ellis invited me to dinner.

I went to Pasadena with Mrs. Schuyler, Jr.

The evening was fragrant.

After the dinner we stepped out to the garden. It was dusky.

By and by, twenty Japanese lanterns were candled among the trees in my honor.

I was in a sprightly bent.

I was whispering a little Jap song, when Oscar led out two donkeys.

Olive sprang upon the back of one in gracious audacity.

"Jump, Morning Glory!" she exclaimed.

I was wavering about my action, when I felt Oscar's arms around my waist. My small body was lifted on to the donkey's by his careless gallantry.

What a sensation ran through me! It was the first occasion to put me into so close contact with a Meriken young man.

My skirt was caught by the saddle. I made a whole exhibition of my leg.

But I was glad the stocking was beautiful.

Oscar held my bridle, pacing by my side.

Alas!

My donkey acted awfully.

Did he take it as a degradation to be whipped by a Jap?

Suddenly it dropped its honourable rump. I should have been pitifully thrown out, if my arm had not seized Oscar's neck. I looked apologetically at him. He turned his delighted face.

I could not stay a minute longer.

When I got me off from the donkey, I observed the new moon over my right shoulder.

"Good luck!" Olive San said.

Why?

Mr. Oscar began to whistle somewhat as follows:

"Ho pop pop pop, ho pop pop pa!"

23rd—To-day is Mrs. Schuyler's reception day.

She set two Japanese screens in the drawing room, moving them from her chamber. She sprinkled a great lot of exotic bric-a-bric about.

She opened a regular Chinese bazar which expressed every poor taste. Such confusion!

I fancied she wanted the callers to recollect that she was Mrs. Ex-Consul of the Orient.

Japan teaches nothing but simplicity. Simplicity is the philosophy of art.

I wondered how she lived there without learning it.

Every inch of Schuyler's parlour means a heap of money.

But is there anything more displeasing than tasteless luxury? Sufficiency is grateful, but superfluity is nothing but offence.

I thought that Americans buy things because they love to buy, not because they have to buy.

Meriken jin has to study the high art of concealing.

The brown people look upon the scattering of things (however costly they be) as lower than barbarity. Japs believe in the sublimity of space.

Isn't it delightful to sit on the new matting of a Japanese guest-room? Its fresh whiteness used to cure my headache.

Isn't it taste to place just one seasonable picture on the tokonoma?

So many a Mrs. Brown and Mrs. Smith called.

They surrounded me.

I asked myself whether they paid a visit to Mother Schuyler or to me.

They incessantly threw the following questions at me:

"How do you like America?"

"How long do you expect to stay?"

Such an inquisitive Meriken woman!

I wished I had been bright enough to print a slip with my reply.

Each lady wore four rings at least.

Are they real things?

Diamond is hardly my choice. Haughtily cold, isn't it?

I declared that their shapeless fingers were not fit to show without embellishment.

If I had money for a ring I would use it for 365 pairs of silk stockings. Isn't it a joy to change everyday?

Schuyler's baby made a hit with its kimono.

All the ladies kissed and kissed.

The baby wondered at their act, rolling its eyes.

Mother Schuyler was quite fussy with a little speech about the history of its Japanese gown.

Funny old dear!

24th—Mr. Oscar Ellis came to paint me.

Dear Oscar!

I have never before left my face alone for such a close scrutiny.

I was restless at first, fancying that he was gathering all my flaws.

Then it happened in my thought that his absorption had something of religious devotion in it.

I grew easy.

I began to feel like a star with all the admirers in the earth.

A garden tree sent its shadow through the window. The time passed as gracefully as a fairy on tiptoe. The air was purple.

Oscar San chatted freely.

I never took the part of a listener before in my life. I found listening honourable.

"So you like the Oriental woman?" I said.

He said American beauty was rather external, like a street shop window. He would like to know, he said, if there was any word more pathetic than "sayonara."

"Isn't the Japanese woman like it?" he asked.

I thought he was correct.

He continued:

"I read in a modern poet the following lines:

> '. . . full of whispers and of shadows,
> Thou art what all the winds have uttered not,
> What the still night suggesteth to the heart.'

Such is the vague Japanese beauty in my idea."

"I am not so nobly sweet, am I?" I exclaimed.

He cast a strong look, as if he were trying to put his final judgment upon me.

He moved his brush slowly on the canvas.

I bowed a profound bow.

"Gomen kudasai!" I said.

And I laid me on the floor, stretching out my legs.

25th—I bought two dolls.

One for Schuyler's baby, as my Christmas gift.

I slept with the other last night. I squeezed my ear to the dolly, fancying I might hear a few scratches of human voice. I kissed it. I laughed, saying that the doll was the thing for my starting to learn how to kiss.

"Sleep till mamma comes back, darling!" I said in the morning when I stepped down for my breakfast.

I left the table before I had half-finished, on account of my anxiety lest the upstairs girl might tattle of my childishness, if she found the doll in my bed.

Thank Heavens!

The girl hadn't come around yet.

I locked it up in my trunk.

What name shall I give it?

Charley?

I was disgusted at the thought, because every Chinee—ten thousand Mongols in all—is named one Charley.

Merry Christmas, all of you!

26th—It rained.

I implored Mother Schuyler to select a book from her library.

All the literature was packed in there, beginning with Socrates, sane as a silver dollar.

Every book was without finger-marks. Book without finger-mark is like bread without brown crust. Dear finger-mark!

The fashion is to buy books and to glance at their covers, I suppose, but not to read them. Modern publications aren't meant to be read, are they? The authors have degenerated to the place of upholsterers. Isn't it a shame?

Mrs. Schuyler picked out for me "Rubaiyat of Omar Khayyam."

My uncle said: "American woman can't keep away from Omar and chicken-salad."

I began to peruse it.

The raindrops by my window tuned:

"Tap, tap, tip, tap, tap!"

I thumped the book on the floor, and exclaimed:

"Mr. Khayyam!"

Rubaiyat is a menace against civilisation.

Americanism is nothing but the delight in life and the world.

I wonder why the wise government of Washington does not oppose its pagan circulation.

It is leprosy.

But I thought how truly true was his "I came like Water, and like Wind I go."

I took up the book and opened it again.

Then I shut it.

I listened to the "Tap, tap, tip!"

Doesn't it sound like a wan voice of Omar?

Yes!

27th—A lady whom I met at Mrs. Schuyler's reception sent me a mass of distinguished roses.

Loving American!

I said I would arrange them in Japanese cult.

My style is the Enshiu.

Amerikey is destitute of flowers.

Nippon is known as a paradise of botanists. The "scientists" of flower decoration (if I may call them so) are given a great advantage in their craft of delineating beauty.

The rose is not much of a flower to the Jap mind.

"So you like the Oriental woman?"

They never employ it in their work. It has no grace of line. Its perfume cannot indemnify for its being thorny. Things not qualified to convey charm are declined from the tokonama.

I love roses awfully well myself.

I will make the best of them in my art.

Is there any proper vase in Schuyler's house?

Mother Schuyler fetched me two pieces.

One was a silver vase and the other a china one.

I couldn't use them, I was sorry. Silver was commercial-looking. The painting on the china a hodge-podge of a joss house.

Then I was seized with a thought.

I ran down to the kitchen.

I borrowed an old scrubbing bucket.

"Such a soft antique hue!" I exclaimed with delight.

I elected one imperial rose and one little one for a "retainer."

I fixed them in the bucket.

I thought it was verily the simplicity of the illustrious Mr. Rikiu.

I presented the rest of the roses to Mrs. Schuyler, Jr.

She stared at the bucket without a word. I knew that her silence was the most forcible irony. She didn't approve of setting such a bucket on the table.

"Meriken jins don't know any art!" I said, when she left.

My uncle begged me not to act so fantastically.

28th—"Here's a shamisen, Morning Glory!" Mother Schuyler cried from the hall.

I darted out of my room.

"Well!" I exclaimed.

Shamisen?

It is a three-stringed guitar of Japan.

Mr. Schuyler, Jr., had sent it from Yokohama, as she explained.

She wished me to tinkle a little gamboling music in the parlour before dinner.

It is a hard implement to handle. It has no notation. Attainment is through unending blind practice.

I was compelled to learn by mother, many a year ago, but I soon gave it up for an English spelling-book.

But I daresay I can play.

I regulated the key to begin with.

"Ting, ting! Chang, chang, ting!"

"What to hum, Uncle?" I asked, facing aside.

"Love ditty is desirable," Oji San considered.

"Don't fancy me a geisha!" I said in defending laughter.

Then I murmured an old hauta, "Haori kakushite," which was Englished by some one.

> "She hid his coat,
> She plucked his sleeve,
> 'To-day you cannot go!
> To-day, at least, you will not leave,
> The heart that loves you so!'
> The mado she undid
> And back the shoji slid:
> And clinging cried, 'Dear Lord, perceive
> The whole world is snow!'"

29th—We went to a theatre last evening.

Dear, classical "flower path"!

How I missed it in the Meriken stage!

Flower path?

It is a projection into the auditorium used to represent when one starts out of the house or returns.

So the American stage has no front gate scene! Everyone enters very likely from the kitchen door.

The stage never turns round like the Japanese stage.

Oh, dear, iyadawa!

American play has too much kissing. Each time I was electrified.

The pit was filled with a well-behaved throng. All the ladies took off their hats. Do they pay more respect than in church? The gentlemen never whiffed smoke.

Japan theatre is a hurly-burly.

The "boys" roar up "Honourable tea—O'cha wa yoroshi? Honourable cake?" The attendants of tea houses bow around to the beneficent habitues, like inclining puppets.

Women sob. They laugh, stuffing their sleeves into their mouths. They are ready to put themselves in the play. They are sentimental.

Meriken women place themselves above the play.

I doubted whether they were criticising or enjoying.

Some lady even used a spy-glass to examine the face of a player.

I thought it decidedly an impertinence.

What a pry!

I will not act to such an assembly, if I ever happen to be an actress.

What was the title of the play?

I could hardly understand half of it.

I tried hard to swallow my gape.

30th—Mr. Oscar Ellis came to put the finishing touch to my picture.

The execution was subtle sureness.

He said that he would offer it to his beloved aunty—Mother Schuyler, of course—begging to let it ornament the wall of my room.

My room?

It is "my room" for a few days yet.

I thought it exceedingly sweet.

The wall is duskily red. The effect would be superb.

When I announced to him that our leave would take place on the approaching fourth, he started as if he had received a stroke.

"So soon?" he said.

"Yes," I said, turning my uneasy face.

"We are only beginning to understand each other."

"I am a bird of passage, as you know. I have to fly on my road."

The air grew tragic.

Then Oscar said:

"What will you do when you tire of flying?"

"Sah!"

"Well?"

"I'll return to Los Angeles and induce you to marry me with my honourable Oriental oratory. Will that do?"

We interchanged our nimble look. We laughed afterward.

After he left Schuyler's, I said to myself that I would not mind positively if he would kiss me. The kiss must be on my brow, however. Lips are too personal.

I wrote a note, beseeching him not to forget to kiss me at my farewell.

Then I chewed the note.

I reviled my folly.

31st—Street walking is a delight.

I'll mirror my face in the glass of the shop windows ambling by.

I dropped a handkerchief to-day.

A gentle gentleman—man behind me should be young and good-looking always—picked it up. His respectful "Pardon me—" made me feel as if I were living in the silver-armoured age of chivalry.

Shall I drop something again?

I observed a variety of form in raising the skirt.

One lifted a bit of the left by her finger-tips. Another pulled up the right edge of her front. Another clinched out the centre of her back, showing a significant fist. A corpulent one stepped, holding up both sides of her front. The miserable underskirt revealed itself in red.

Which mode is becoming to me?

Jan. 1st, 1900—Is to-day the opening of another century?

Happy New Year!

I will send a lot of "Shinnen omedeto" to Tokio.

Isn't this a queer New Year?

No shimenawa along the façades with flitting gohei!

No "gate pine tree"!

No sambow for an oblation unto the gods in any room!

No rice-bread! No golden toso for the cup!

I mingled with a neighbour's girls for a "rope-jumping."

We played hide-and-seek. I offered ten cents reward to the one who detected me. I abandoned the unprofitable job after emptying out all my change.

Miss Olive called on a bicycle.

I persuaded her to let me try on her bloomers. She exchanged them for my walking skirt which was four inches shorter.

We hurried to the garden.

She helped me on the wheel.

Such a bad Meriken girl!

She slipped her hand from it. I fell on a bush. The touchy rose thorned in my hand.

2nd—I made a discovery.

Mother Schuyler's teeth are all false.

I have no chance to explore whether her hair is a wig.

She chains a big bunch of keys to her waist. Its rattle sounds housewifely.

She forgot it, laying it on the sitting-room table.

I knotted it to my waist-strap.

I jiggled it.

"Jaran, jaring, jaran, jaran!"

3rd—The sayonara dinner was given. Mrs. Ellis' folks joined us.

Mother Schuyler repeated every ten minutes her query, "when would I visit them again?"

Mr. Oscar set his depressive look on me. I wasn't brave enough to encounter it.

I slid away from confronting him.

I found him an elegant young man. He impressed me as an image of Apollo.

Only God knows when I will reprint my footsteps on the soil of Los Angeles!

I felt awfully sorry in leaving such an agreeable company.

"Fold your tent like the Arabs,
And silently steal away."

How sad!

4th—Good-bye, Mr. Parrot!

San Francisco, 5th

I am again at Mrs. Willis'.

San Francisco!

Such miraculous San Francisco water!

I will taste bliss again in drinking the midnight water, stretching out my arm from the bed.

6th—I tied Dorothy's hair in Nippon style.

She pleased me much by remembering the Japanese words I taught her.

She is a cute dear.

The mode had been the "O'tabaco bon."

I straightened her hair with my wet hand.

I added a tiny bit of crimson crape.

She looked a lovely fairy.

7th—Rainy day!

The heavily reserved weather confines me in the pose of genius.

My hair lounged down my shoulders. Disorder is the first step in being a genius, I fancy. My eyes should be rolled up to the sky in divine tragicalness.

I have had a greediness for the name of novelist.

To-day I found myself in the crisis where I must scribble or die.

I regret to say that mine is a love story also, as every beginner's book has been. I hope everybody will be contented with "The Destiny," a respectable title for my fiction. Who says it is the style of name employed one hundred years ago?

The book will be concluded with three hundred pages.

Now I wonder whether a long story is in demand.

Chapter I. is as follows:

WHEN THE MOON ROSE.

This story begins when the moon rose.

Its silvery rays—it was six P. M. of April—fell on the Shiba park in laughter.

My heroine jogged along into the park, singing a light song.

> "Miss Honourable Moon, how old are you?
> Thirteen and seven, you say?
> You are young enough to marry—"

Let me explain about her a bit!

Her name is O Hana San.

Thirteen years old. Thirteen? It is the age when the flower of girlhood starts to bloom.

Bewitching Hana!

Do you remember a well by the glorious cherry tree in the park? The 'rikisha men moisten their parched lips at the "Heaven-Sent." That is its name, sir.

Miss Hana looked down into the well.

She began to adjust her hair. The first worry of a girl after thirteen would naturally be about her hair.

She gazed up to the cherry blossoms and exclaimed:

"Utsukushii nah! Lovely!"

Then she found her face again in the well-mirror, thinking what a charming O Hana San it would make with the flowers on her hair.

My worthy readers, I suppose it is the time some one must enter.

He came.

He was a little boy.

I will not mention his name just yet.

He came close to her and pinched her little back. Both blushed, facing each other. They were quite strangers.

The evening zephyrs stirred the cherry blossoms. They planted themselves silently among the falling petals, as ethereal as snow.

"I delight to stand in the storm of petals, don't you?" Hana inclined her head a trifle in speaking.

The woman always speaks first.

"Let me see your school book!" again she said.

"Why?"

He put it in her tiny hand.
"Thanks! Arigato!"
She bowed low. When she put the book on her shoulder, she was running away, singing:

"Miss Honourable Moon, how old are you?"

The boy stood aghast.

* * * * * * *

The author of this story found O Hana San again by the same well on the next evening.
The boy's book in her hand, of course.
She paced around the well, muttering:
"He must come, because the moon rose."
But he was not seen.

My next chapter will be "The Second Meeting."

8th—My precious Ada again!
How could I live without her?
We hastened to a circus.
If I were a boy, I could earn a heap of money selling "Pea—nuts! Lemon—ade!"
How those clowns did tumble!
If I could share in such fun!
The ringmaster was the handsomest man in the world, in shiny boots and heavenly hat. How splendidly his whip cracked!
The clack dashed like a burst of bamboo.
"Wouldn't you be glad to be the lady on horseback? I would truly. Glance at her daring grace!" I whispered to Miss Ada.
Even the seal performed.
We laughed till tears dropped.
The circus had twenty elephants. Think!
Our Imperial Menagerie of Tokio has only one. How poor!

9th—Last night I went over to Mrs. Consul's to be given a lesson in card-playing.
"Cribbage would be the thing. Why? Because the Lambs took much pleasure in it," she said.

"How is poker?" I suggested.

"Gambling game!" she protested.

"I delight in gambling, Mrs. Consul," I proclaimed.

I had a wicked dream.

What do you imagine?

I ran away with a circus rider.

10th—I made the acquaintance of a Japanese woman.

She must have been passing her thirty springs. I could be accurate in my scale, being one of her sisterhood.

A cigar-stand keeper in Dupont Street.

Her name is O Fuji San.

Mrs. Wistaria brought a box of cigarettes that my uncle had ordered.

The morning is unoccupied in such a retail shop. Nobody puffs much before lunch. She set herself in a tête-à-tête.

The chastity of a wife may be measured by her solo on her husband. Woman's greatest joy often lies in lamenting the faults of her teishu.

Mrs. Wistaria spoke of her husband's being ill. I was to accept any chance for squandering my feelings. I sympathised, repeating, "Komaru nei! How sad!"

She said that she was going to leave the city for a week for the spring of San Jose, to take care of her infirm dear.

"I fear I may lose my customers," she flagged.

Her husband was afflicted with rheumatism.

I promised to call at her store.

Japs never visit an invalid without a present.

Champagne? It's too ostentatious a drink. It's like a highly rouged woman.

The loving-eyed claret should be chosen.

I sent half a dozen bottles to Mrs. Wistaria's.

A charity woman should be dressed in black and white. I went to Dupont street, however, in my grey dress.

Her husband struggled to entertain me. His clumsy smile appeared all the time at the wrong cue.

Poor Mr. What's-his-name!

Their business was an absurdly small affair.

The whole stock hardly valued above one hundred dollars.

I thought I could conduct it rightly.

I was carried away by a sudden fancy.

"Can't you leave your store in my hands, while you are away? Say yes! No?" I pressed myself upon them eagerly.

They were amazed.

"High-born lady like you? Oh, no! Doshite, doshite! Think! Do you know this is the toughest part of the town?" Mrs. Wistaria tried to make me retreat.

I couldn't listen to her, my whole soul being absorbed in my new caprice.

I thought it remarkably romantic.

I left the store to bring uncle to talk the matter over.

Mrs. Wistaria's store was neighboured by every saloon. The fuddling sounds overflowed in song:

"Hello ma baby, hello ma honey——"

11th—Now he is my beloved uncle.

He assured me of his help in carrying out my freak.

"You are fitting me for a slightly better rôle, I fancy," he said, venturing to add even one or two of his good-natured giggles. "The secretaryship of a cigar-stand is a rather more hopeful occupation than carrying your wraps through the street."

Everything was arranged.

Mrs. Wistaria and her husband set off for San Jose.

I am a merchant-lady.

The first thing I did was to put up a dignified sign with the following black letters:

MORNING GLORY CIGAR STORE

I borrowed a picture from Mrs. Willis' parlour, and placed it by the slot machine.

It is the picture of a dear Injun sitting against a woodland fire with a respectable pipe, whose smoke sails up to the yellow moon. What resignation! What dream! What joy! It did suit beautifully for the cigar-stand.

I love to see a man smoking. The elfish smoke acts like a merry-hearted May gossamer. When I observe a man's eye pursuing his smoke, I say to myself that his soul must be stepping nearer to his ideal. The road of smoke is the road of poesy.

A noble trade is tobacco.

Man's hermitage is situated only in smoking, I should say.

I divested my uncle of his coat. I begged him to hold a bucket and a piece of cloth for a moment.

"Are you ready to wash the windows, Uncle?" I said.

"Traitor, Morning Glory!" He flashed his accusing glare.

Docile old man!

He cleaned four windows of the kitchen, which was also the dining-room and the parlour.

I paid him five cents for each.

I said: "It's good fun to hire the chief secretary of the Nippon Mining Company to rub windows, isn't it?"

And I laughed.

Then I forced him to buy a cigar.

"You made some twenty cents out of me. Your turn is coming, my uncle!" I said.

I sold him a box of Lillian Russell cigars for three dollars. The real price was two.

Ha, ha, ha!

12th—I invited my precious Ada to my store to dine *à la Japonaise.*

One Jap restaurant catered to it.

"Irrashaimashi! Condescend to enter!" I showered my wooden-clogged greeting over Ada.

From "The Klondyke," my neighbouring saloon, a nigger song was flapping in.

"If you ain't got no money, you needn't come round."

Happy Ada San!

She was about to join in it, when I brought her into my great dining-room.

(Beg pardon, it was a paltry kitchen!)

Everything was seen on the table.

Japanese dinner has no strict order of courses. You are a frolicsome butterfly among the dishes set like flowers before you. You may flit straight to any one which catches your whim.

"Take your honourable chop-sticks!" I said.

Poor Miss Ada!

"How shall I manage with one stick?" she raised her eyelids in questioning meekness.

I bade her to split the stick in two. It was a brand new wooden one. I showed her how to finger it.

She nibbled a bit from each dish. Every time she tasted she looked upon me with a suspicious smile.

And how she slipped her sticks at the critical moment!

The sight amused me hugely.

"How dare I swallow raw fishes!" she said shrinking.

"What delight I taste in them!" I slammed back at her timidity.

Then I dipped a few cuts of the fishes into a porcelain soy pan for my mouth.

I even trampled into her fish-dish by and by.

She was literally terrified.

The feast was over. I said, "Go yukkuri! Honourable not-to-be-in-a-hurry!" I slid away.

I tied my white apron like a shop girl. I was glad that I did not forget to push a lead-pencil through my hair. I presented myself to Ada carrying a cigarette box.

"Will you buy tobacco for your lord?"

I spread the box before her.

"How much for one packet," she asked with the charming arrogance of a customer.

She was acting also.

"To-day is the memorial day of Lord Nono Sama. My sweet Oku San, allow me to make a reduction!"

Then we laughed.

13th—I created much noise in the Jap colony!

Why not?

Many brown men pause by my store and buy, simply because they can address a word or two to me.

They are silly, aren't they?

I announce that I am tired of their faces. I have never met one progressive-seeming Oriental since I landed. They are like a dry tree. Are their souls dying?

"Well, that's why, they have no girl," my uncle conclusioned.

He is so bright once in a while.

Why not make love with Meriken musume?

I said I would petition the Tokio government to transplant her women.

It may ruin the Japanese girl's name, was my afterthought, if they ship only the homely gang.

Lovely girl has no longing to sail over the ocean. She has plenty of chance to grow a flower bride at home.

I pity my native boys of this city.

"Jap! Jap!"

They are dashed with such exclamations from every corner.

"How dare I swallow raw fishes!"

As for me the sound of "Jap" is my taste, so I spray it in my writing.

I took up again my knitting work which I had commenced on the seas. Nothing could be more decent to fill up my leisure in the store.

My little neck fell, as I was intent on my stocking.

Some one spoke above my head: "How is business?"

"So, so!" I replied in businesslike reserve.

I lifted my face.

Oya, he was Mr. Consul.

"Will you sell me a cigar?"

"Things are becoming awfully high. Mine is a distinctly dear store. Do you know it, Mr. Consul?"

"I'm prepared to pay more at the beautiful girl's," he began to titter.

"General Arthur cigar has leaped one dollar higher since Monday, and——"

"You don't mean it!" He mimicked a sudden alarm.

14th—O funny drunkard!

To-day one fellow established himself before my store. He fixed his amazing eyes on my face, and extended his hairy hand.

"Hel-lo, Japanese!" he stuttered.

He wanted to shake hands with me.

I lengthened my arm, and slapped his face. I withdrew directly within, and watched him from a hole.

"Ha, ha! She got mad—ha, ha, ha!"

He was in a tip-top state of mind.

"Let me help myself!"

He pilfered one cigar from the shelf. He struck a match. He bit the cigar.

"Good!" he muttered.

He tossed himself away with ludicrous dignity, singing:

"Pon pili, yon, pon, pon!"

"This is undeniably a tough place!" I exclaimed.

15th—Night has just arrived.

Only ten minutes ago a white-capped "Jim" (I overheard people calling him so) lighted a paper lantern labelled "Tomales." He is an eating-stand keeper across the street. The loafers passed. There was some time to watch the lazy parade. It was a blank hour of Saturday when he could puff a whiff of smoke.

The prankish songs ceased.

Even in Dupont Street I am given a page of dream.

The barkeeper of "Remember the Maine" called at my store.

"Remember the Maine?"

It is a name cheap as the grimness of a toothless woman.

Mr. Barkeeper had something to say, I imagined.

I offered a stem of cigarette.

"Do you ever hear a bloody cry at night?" he began his chapter, gathering a medley of gravity on his brow.

"Scream? No!"

"Never mind!"

He turned aside. I thought he was playing a threadbare artifice of a story-teller to tantalise my fancy.

"Tell me why!"

I knew I became his victim.

"I fear I do scare you."

"No! I never——" I leaned forward.

"To begin with——"

He stopped, looking around.

"Your kitchen—don't be scared—is close by a haunted room of a house on Pine Street. It's no story. A chorus girl lived—well, some five years ago—in that house with her stepmother. Just think! The old hen of sixty-five fell in love with her daughter's lover. Do you understand? She saw one morning the young fellow kissing her daughter. She went crazy. She shot him. Isn't it awful? The murderess leaned against the wall by your kitchen, and cried, 'I killed him!' I swear to you that it is all true. So, people say, a wail is heard at night from your side."

"Mah! Mah!" I breathed.

"That is all."

He retired heavily.

Do I believe it?

"No! No!" I denied.

But I was thickly swarmed by sickening air. How could I trust me in the kitchen!

I closed the store.

I pasted up a piece of paper whereon was written: "NO BUSINESS TO-NIGHT."

16th—I had a stomach-ache this morning. I couldn't rise.

The maid fetched me some toast and a cup of coffee. I think it is very nice to eat in bed.

17th—Mrs. Wistaria and her husband returned from San Jose.

She lavished on me her thousand arigatos.

She said I sold sixty per cent more than on any previous week.

She wished me to condescend to accept a "meager" fifteen dollars as a share of the profits.

I refused it.

18th—My letter to Miss Pine Leaf (who wept with me reading Keats' love-letters one mournful night) is as follows:

"Matsuba San:

'Hitofude mairase soro.

"'I have the honour to present a brief writing.'

"Let me omit the shopworn form of Japanese letter-writing! Its redundant 'honourables' are more cheap than honourable.

"Satetoya!

"Shall I begin my letter with a deep bow?

"Bow?

"I use it occasionally before Meriken San for sport's sake. But it is degenerating, in my opinion, to comic opera, like the tortoise-shell-framed spectacles of a Chinese doctor.

"Now I address you with a thousand kisses.

"The kiss is the thing to begin with for up-to-date girls.

"It is useful, as a poem is useful in filling up space in magazine-making. Woman—even a loftily learned American woman—cannot be ready always with her rhetoric of expression. The kiss comes to her relief in the crisis whenever she fails in speech.

"The kiss is everything.

"The Jap girl is intimate with the art of crying.

"A kiss is as eloquent as a tear.

"I suppose the cleverness of American woman is graded by the way she handles it. It strikes me that every white girl is perfectly at home with it.

"She is awfully bright.

"You wonder why she is so?

"There is one reason that I can tell you. It is because she has a serious job to pick out her husband herself. I don't think it is fair to blame her growing insipid after marriage. Every one feels tired when a weighty work is done. What would be her doom if she were stupid? An old maid is such a sad sight, like a broken clock, or a cradle after baby's death. Isn't it dreadful to have nothing to rejoice in but a customary tea or books? Literary critic is one occupation left for her. Worse than death!

"I am pained to state that our brown sisters are extremely behind time.

("There are lots of exceptions, of course, like honourable you and Miss M. G.)

"I am talking of common Jap musumes.

"Naturally so.

"They are like those waiting at the station for the next train. They have only to doze and wait for the footsteps of a matchmaker with a young man.

"I am grateful to the Nippon government for stimulating education in women.

"But I advise her to imprison all the matchmakers. Then the girls will wake up at once, like one who has everything on her back after papa's passing.

"That is one process to brighten them, I think.

"Am I not logical?

"Your last tegami questioned me whether the American lady was charming.

"Are you attentive to western sea painting?

"How does it impress you when you are close by it? Only a jumble of paint, isn't it? So with Meriken woman!

"You should be off half a dozen steps to estimate her beautiful captivation. You would be horrified, otherwise, by her hairy skin.

"I love her.

"She has no headache like the Japs. (By the way, I will call Japan, hereafter, the country of headache.) She lives in a comedy.

"Nothing turns bad in Amerikey.

"'Tragedy To Be a Woman,' could only be seen on a fiction thrown in a moth-trodden second-hand store.

"Police never bother.

"Such a deliverance!

"I am delighted with my Meriken Kenbutsu.

"Sayonara!

Yours,
"Morning Glory"

19th—I forced Uncle to swear to me that he would overlook everything I did, in consideration of my great service in darning his socks.

I peeled off my shoes to begin with.

I sat like a Turk.

"Why do you frown like an Oni in hell?" I acidified my smile. I held my needle and thread suspended in the air, while I said: "What is a Trust?"

"Be quiet!" he exclaimed.

He didn't even glance at me, being engaged in writing in the other nook.

"Uncle, your hair ought to be curled. I will step in to-morrow morning, and turn it up before you awake. What do you think, Uncle? Oji San!"

"Morning Glory San!"

He emitted a growl of satanic despotism, and soon resumed his work gracefully.

I thought what a scandal if he were penning a love letter to Mrs. Schuyler junior.

I rose. I approached him with secret step. I fell on him from his massy back and cried:

"What are you scribbling?"

Erai, my honourable uncle!

He was translating Gibbon's "History of Rome."

I was stunned from the shame of taking him to be in such a wretched line even in fancy.

I vowed to myself—with three low bows—to take perfect care of my noble worker.

Then I gave him my sweet smile.

"Uncle, let me fix something more! Haven't you anything? Tear your shirt or pull off the buttons, then!"

20th—Already I could suck from the agile air the flavour of spring upon the lawn.

I was roving by the rose-bushes along the street with scissors.

A gentleman passed by me. How sluggish his shoes sounded! He stopped, waving his old-scented smile, and addressed me:

"Good morning, young lady!"

"Ohayo!"

"I perceive that you are Japanese."

"Yes, sir!"

He stepped nearer to me. I took a peep at the Bible under his arm.

"Are you a Christian?" he lowered his tone.

"Don't you read the Gospel?" his voice rose higher.

"Don't you attend church?" his sound grew higher still.

"I love to be shocked. I couldn't sustain myself against a bore. Church? It's too sleepy, don't you know? I have remarked that God is with me without any sort of prayer, if I trace the path of righteousness. A minister is only a meddling grandmamma to my mind. If I ever build my ideal city, two things shall not be tolerated. One is a lawyer's office and the other is a church. Church, sir! May I present you with one rose?"

I raised me to place it in his coat.

"Here's a letter for you, Morning Glory!"

I was rescued by my uncle. How angelic his voice rang!

"I'm sorry, I'm much occupied this very morning," I said, bowing slightly.

I pushed myself within the door.

Poor preacher!

21st—My answer to Oscar is as follows:

"Dear Honourable Mr. Ellis:

"Let me begin in respectable fashion.

"A Jap girl is awfully formal.

"Do you know, Mr. Ellis, whom you are addressing?

"I am an Oriental.

"Nippon daughters believe 'ev'rithin" a gentleman mentions.

"They have been fooled enough, I should declare, in American fiction. Oscar—no, Mr. Ellis—don't let me earn the anecdote that I drifted to Ameriky to be toyed with! My ancestor did a harakiri. I am pretty sure I have, then, to kill myself.

"Don't recite again your honourable confession of love!

"It made me cry.

"My dark face with drenched eyes will degrade me to a hired Chinese 'crying woman.'

"Your narration was dramatic.

"Your cleverness is the most lamentable thing about you. Woman used to love a bright fellow many years ago. Do you know that the modern girl woos a stupid man?

"Please, don't repeat again such an adjective as 'heavenly' for my face! No one utters the word 'heaven' except in swearing. Even ministers juggle with it for a jest in church, I suppose. My face isn't heavenly at all. You know it, don't you?

"You amused me, however, when you told how you had pillaged my picture from Mother Schuyler's room to put in your own, feigning that it needed to be retouched.

"Poor Mother Schuyler!

"If she knew your secret!

"Frankly, I fear that such a gentleman as you does commit forgery always. Have you no consanguinity with a convict?

"O such a wretched boy!

"The saddest thing about a woman is that she is glad to fall in love with the worthless.

"Do I love you?

"Give me time to reply to the question!

"Everything is tardy with a Japanese. I was educated by slowness; I bow one dozen times before I speak.

"O Oscar, you got to think of my side a little bit!

"Every girl claims that she has half a population as adorers in her pocket handkerchief.

"You are the only one young American I ever met.

"If I accept your love, I am afraid one may satirise my destitution.

"You'll write me soon, won't you?

"Yours, M.G.

"P.S.—I wish I could show you how charmingly I smoke. I learned the art recently. I tap the cigarette with my middle finger to knock the ashes off. It is delightful to heap a hill of ashes on the table edge. When I puff, finding no word after 'And—' the smoke seems to be speaking for me.

"But I assure you that I smoked only before my uncle.

"I was a pretty naughty girl at home, but I flatter myself that I can easily be classed among the best in this country.

"White women behave terribly, you know."

22nd—I passed the afternoon at Mrs. Consul's. She gave me her "favourite" discourse on Walt Whitman.

I delivered to my uncle what I had learned.

"No newness in it. It is what dear John Burroughs or Mr. Stedman said."

He overturned my castle with one blow, and lit his cigar with a victorious air.

I was enraged.

"Yes, yes, eraiwa! Oriental gentleman knows everything we poor women know," I said.

I sulkily drew away to my room with Mr. Whitman's fat book, that I borrowed from Mrs. Consul.

23rd—A letter from my father arrived.

"O Papa, please don't! I am tired of such a dirty conference". I scoffed.

I tore the paper into shreds.

"What a sullen lady! What did Otto San write? Marriage proposal, I reckon!" my uncle intruded.

"Papa threatened me with a list of suitors. He cried, 'Chance, chance!' like the gateman of an ennichi show. Pray grant me for once in my life, Uncle, to say: 'The marriage lottery go to the dogs!' How many Jap girls kill themselves from the burden of such a glued union, do you suppose?"

"Then, 'free marriage'?"

"Of course!"

"It's very beautiful, Miss Morning Glory."

"Why not?"

"You are Japanese, aren't you?"

"Did you ever think I was a Meriken jin?"

"Well, then, how did you come to know young men in a country where familiarity with one is regarded as a crime for a girl?"

"Things all wrong in Nippon, Uncle!"

"I am sorry you were born a Jap."

"I'll never go back to Japan, I think. The dictionary for Jap girls comprises no such word as 'No.' But you must remember, Uncle, I have the capital 'No' in my head. I am a revolutionist," I proclaimed.

Then I thought much of my dear Oscar.

24th—My worthy labourer upon Gibbon's work sat before the table for some hours.

I stood behind him and dropped the fluid from a bottle on his head.

"Cold! What are you doing, my little romp?" He looked up in a fright.

"No harm, Uncle! It is only a remedy. Your hair is growing so thin. Do you know it? I think it a shame to appear in Greater New York with a bald gentleman."

I bought the bottle this morning.

25th—A bamboo table in my room reminded me of a take bush in the neighbouring churchyard of my Tokio home.

(I cannot sound Meriken jin's curiosity in prizing such a cheap thing. The bamboo was painted. The cross nails glared from everywhere. I never saw such a Jap work in Nippon.)

Dear take, O bamboo bush!

How I used to laugh, breaking the dreams of sparrows by wriggling the bush!

I was so ungoverned.

If I could be a grammar school girl again!

I secured a reader at a bookstall. My mind was made up to present myself in the Lincoln night school and mingle with the girls in "SEE THE BOY AND THE DOG!"

What fun!

I went to see the stooping principal. His tarnished frock-coat—I fancied he was an old bachelor, as one button was off—was just the thing for such a *rôle*.

I seemed to him a regular nenne of thirteen.

He was heartily pleased with my greediness for learning English.

Poor soul!

He ushered me into the class for which I had brought the book.

It was the hour for composition. "Ocean," the subject.

When I was seated, the girl next me winked charmingly. She threw me a note within a minute, to which I promptly replied, "Morning Glory." My note was answered "Miss Madge, 340 Mission Street." I wrote her, "May I call on you to-morrow?" for which she wrote, "As you please."

I was placed on the dangerous verge of clapping Byron's poem into my "Ocean." I manufactured one dozen of spelling errors.

"You should belong to some higher class. Take this slip to the principal!" the teacher said. "You have an imagination." She wiped her spectacles slowly.

I left the room remarking, "Because I am a Japanese."

I slipped away from the school altogether.

"One experience is plenty," I declared.

26th—I went to Mission Street to call on Madge.

From both sides of the street peeped the famous Jewish noses. The second-hand clothing shops parade. How droll to see those noses shrivelling like a lobster!

Madge's father owns a despicable restaurant with only four eating tables. Mamma cooks, while she sits on the counter.

When I appeared, she shot out, greeting me: "Hello! Morning Glory!"

"Awfully glad to see you! I have come to help you, haven't I?"

I was ready to strip off my jacket and wind myself in her apron.

Her papa was dumbfounded by my sudden action.

The outside board with the bill of fare was scraped out by this morning's rain. It looked as miserable as an Italian vegetable wagon under the rain.

My first work was to rewrite it.

I saw a Jew at a neighbouring door striving with one about the value of pants. A shoe-maker's "pan, pan" hammered on my head from the opposite house.

Mission Street is the street of horse-dung.

When my job was over, an honourable Mr. Wagon Driver leaped in, bidding me serve some soup.

I ran into the kitchen to fetch it.

I spilled it on the table.

"That's all right, honey!" he said in patronising aloofness, and pierced my face with his gummy red eyes.

O Kowaya! Shocking!

I put one five dollar piece of gold on Madge's palm when I left her.

Because her shoes were heelless.

Pity the musume!

27th—I bought one book, being captivated by its title. Isn't "When Knighthood was in Flower" beautifully chivalrous?

I have remarked that every Imperial cruiser anchors at an isle close by Loo Choo, just on account of the enticement in the name "Come and See."

I found in my trunk an introduction to Miss Rose by my professor friend of Tokio 'versity.

Miss Rose?

My imagination started to move like a watch. I fancied she should be nineteen, since she was a Miss. No Rose girl can be homely.

I went to see her.

Alas!

She was a lady like a beer-barrel. Her finger-nails were black.

I left her like a miner stepping out of a gold mountain with empty hands.

I wonder why the mayor didn't object to letting an ugly woman be crowned with a pretty name.

Fifty-years-old Miss Rose!

Now I fear to read Mr. Major's book.

28th—The following is my letter to Mr. Oscar:

"OSCAR SAN! ELLIS SAN!

"I never liked your profession, simply because it is too beautiful.

"I don't see why you cannot transfer to some other business.

"I have been ever so much fascinated with odd sorts of manual work. If I were a gentleman, I would very likely pursue the calling of grave-digger or sea-diver.

"Yesterday I passed by some labourers breaking massive stones. They lifted their hammers (O Oscar, look at their muscles!) and knocked them down to the sound of 'Sara bagun!' They jerked the 'sara bagun,' Oscar. Does it mean 'ready?' Mrs. Willis' Century dictionary must be imperfect, since it does not contain such a word. Am I misspelling?

"Suppose I marry one of those!

"He will return home awfully tired. He will naturally doze after dinner. When his smoking pipe has slipped from his lips and burned my best tablecloth, isn't it possible that I will be mad? . . . . I startled him, pulling his hair ever so hard. Now you must think that he grew mad also. He seized my arm, and beat me. O Oscar, he beat me surely! . . . . Then he will repent his conduct, and kneel by my side, begging my forgiveness. He will say, 'My dear sweet wife—'

"Do you know how interesting it is to be beaten by a husband?

"I well-nigh fixed my mind never to affiance with a man too genteel to hit me.

"Woman is a revolting little bit of thing.

"If you say 'Yes,' I am quite ready to slam my 'No!'

"Oscar San!

"I am afraid that you are too amiable.

"What you have to do for your next missive is to collect every kind of dreadful adjectives from your dictionary, and throw them in.

"You know what to do when I get angry, don't you?

"Ellis San!

"You are too handsome.

"I am fond of a comely face as anybody else.

"But I fancy often how it would be if I fell in love with a deformity.

"People would laugh at me doubtless. But how dramatic it would be when I proclaimed, 'Because I love him!'

"What a romantic phrase that is!

"Can't you deform yourself?

"Sayonara,

"With a thousand bows,

"M.G.

"P. S—My letter never finishes without a P.S.

"Isn't that awful?

"My uncle asked me whom I was corresponding with. I mentioned 'Olive.'

"Old man is jealous always.

"So you got to counterfeit your sister's penmanship for your envelope."

29th—I drank the last drop of my coffee.

"Oji San, when shall we go to New York?" I said, pillowing my face on my hands on the breakfast table.

"As soon as spring begins to flicker in the East, my little woman! It's snow and snow there at present."

"I love snow, Uncle."

"Old gentleman can't bear tyrannical cold, Morning Glory."

"Don't you notice how tired I am of Frisco? Aren't you tired?"

"Yes—frankly!"

"Why don't you then contrive some novel diversion to pass a month?"

"I've a fancy, but——"

"What is it?"

"It may not strike you as romantic."

"Tell me!"

"I am known to one poet who dreams and erects a stone wall on the hill-side. He is unlike another. His garden and cottage are open to everybody. I ever incline to loaf in an irregular puff of odour from his acacia trees. If you lean towards a poetical life, I have no hesitation in seeing him to make an arrangement."

"Great Uncle, it's romantic! Is he married?"

"Why?"

"Because a poet is not one woman's property, but universal. My ideal poet is melancholy. Fat poet is ridiculous. Happy poet isn't of the highest order. Tennyson? I wish his life had been more hard up. I suppose your friend-poet won't mind if I sleep all day. Is he particular about the dinner time? Does he look up to the stars every night? Does he wash his shirt once in a while?"

"Stop!"

Then I asked respectably:

"Is the sight from there beautiful?"

"Wonderful! The only place where you can breathe the air of divinity!"

"Very well, Uncle. We will settle there, and hasten to become poets."

"It wouldn't be a bad idea, I say, to start again with your honourable 'Lotos Eaters!'"

"'Paradise Lost' shall be my next subject."

"If nobody publishes it?"

"I will present it solemnly to our Empress. She is a poetess, you know."

My uncle went to see Mr. Poet.

30th—Uncle said that the poet said: "You are welcome, sir. The cottage for your young lady lies by one willow tree. The waters, the air, the grand view, are God's. It costs a wee bit of money to provide the best coffee. I tell you that my claret is superb. You shall be my guest as long as you please. Present my love to Miss Morning Glory! Everything will be ready when you come."

"Isn't he adorable?" I ejaculated.

I stirred my trunk, and sifted out the things needful for my adventure.

31st—To-morrow!

"The Heights, Feb. 1st

Let me recline heart-to-heart on the breast of Mother Nature! Let me retreat to a hillside not far from the city, yet verily near to God! Let me go to my poet abode!

We abandoned the Fruitvale car at the hill-foot.

My uncle picked out our destination from the speckles in the distance.

The breeze (how heavenly is a country breeze!) enticed my soul—a Jap girl also is provided with some soul—into "Far-Beyond."

"I feel myself another girl, Uncle."

"How?"

"I'm a poet already. The poet without poem is greater, don't you know?"

We climbed the hill slowly. Every step enlarged the spectacle.

When we attained to one wildly well-kept garden, the whole bay of the Golden Gate stretched before us. A thousand villages knelt humbly like vassals.

I saw a tiny gate with the sign:

"Fruit Grower."

An old gentleman appeared from a cottage, singing:

"Ah, take the Cash, and let the Credit go,
Nor heed the rumble of a distant Drum!"

"Poet!" Uncle whispered.

Let me now examine him!

What lengthy hair he wore!

It didn't annoy me, however, because he stamped himself on my mind as if he were an ancient statue. I imagined him a type of mediaeval squire. I thought of him truly as one metamorphosed from the frontispiece of a wholly forgotten volume in a cobwebbed recess of a library.

His courteous voice was simply dignified.

"Nature never hurries. God commands you every happiness and all repose. Here's your little home, my gentle lady! I am at your service any time. I hope you will find it comfortable."

He set me at the "Willow Cottage."

He slipped gracefully away.

There was some time before I heard his "kotsu kotsu" on my door.

I opened it.

"Greeting from the host!" Mr. Heine offered me a tuft of brisk roses.

Heine was the poet's name.

How loving!

I buried myself in the thought of straying to a fairy isle, and being accepted romantically by the dwellers.

I suspected that I was dreaming.

"Arcadia!" I exclaimed, when the poet announced that supper would be prepared within half an hour.

I spied him through the window, gathering the loppings of trees and leaves. He made a camp-fire. Its soft smoke surged into the sky. Oh, smell it!

How fascinating is the Poet's life!

I ran out, crying:

"Pray, make me useful!"

2nd—Dream and reality are not marked here by different badges. They waltz round. Dear poet home!

Was it in my dream, that I heard the tinkle of bells?

I thought something was going on.

I parted from the bed. I pushed out my face from the window.

Look at the procession of cows!

I have read much of them, but I admit that it was my first occasion to admire them. I am a trivial Jap, only acquainted with cherry blossoms and lanterns. How I wished to knot the bells round my waist, and whisk down the path by the violets!

"Lover's lane!"

It should be the title for that path, I thought, if I were Mr. Poet.

I finished my toilet. I leaped out upon the grasses smiling up to the sunlight.

I congratulated myself on my new life.

Then I found my uncle sitting by the campfire.

"Ohayo!" I said, filling the seat on another side.

I remember one Japanese essay, "The Poetry of a Tea Kettle." Indeed! The kettle was a singer. Its melody was far-reaching. It was like a harp of pine leaves fingered by the zephyr.

I faced up, and saw my poet moving down from the lily pond. Two frogs in his hand.

"Frogs?" I cried.

"They will complete our table. How did you sleep, my lady?"

"Splendid!"

"Do you love the country?"

"I begin to taste a greater joy in Nature."

"I'm happy to hear it, my dear. My life is like the life of a bird. I awake when the sun rises. I lay me in the bed at the bird's dipping into its nest. God made the night for keeping quiet. That is better than prayer itself. I light neither lamp nor candle. I presume that every young lady has certain secret work at night. Let me offer you a few candles!"

We ate breakfast from the table by the fire.

Frogs supplied a special dish.

I couldn't touch it, thinking of the songs of frogs that I had heard all the night long.

Such a song! It was the muddy-booted song of the countryside. No valuable quality in it, of course. But I should say that they tried the best they could.

Poor Messrs. Frog!

I fancied the leg in my dish was that of one who volunteered to sing my lullaby.

I almost cried in grief.

The poet was ready to wash the dishes. I was quick to snatch his job. My uncle wiped them.

Stupid uncle!

He broke two dishes.

I collected the bones of the frogs, and buried them. On the stone above them I wrote with a pencil:

"Tomb of Unknown Singers."

What time was it when we were done with our breakfast?

I couldn't tell.

The first thing I did yesterday was to stop the tick-tack of my watch, and hide it in the lowest drawer.

The watch is a nuisance since I am thrown in THE GARDEN OF ETERNITY.

3rd—I searched for a pen and ink in my Willow Cottage.

Nothing like those.

Foxy Poet!

He hid them from view, I fancied, in the opinion that playing with them for a girl is more jeopardous than swallowing needles.

I say that letter-writing—particularly a decent love letter, if there is one—isn't half so grave a crime as rhyming.

I was spraying some water on a rose by the gate, when I caught sight of a white quill by my shoes.

"This will serve me perfectly," I said.

I had not one thing with any tooth except my comb. (Comb? Luckily I have not lost it. Ara, ma, my hairpins! Five of them vanished from my head while I was springing amid the rocks. By and by the stems of acacia leaves shall be used in their places. Don't you know this is quite a remote spot from civilisation?) A kitchen knife shaped my quill as a pen.

Now only ink!

I begged Uncle to run down three miles to fetch one bottle.

4th—We went to "breathe the song of the forest."

The forest laces the poet's canyon.

(By the way, poet's ground spreads over one hundred and fifty acres. Does he pay taxes?)

We climbed the "Road to the Milky Way." I beseech your forgiveness, it was merely the name I wished for the path to the poet's hilltop. I felt as if I were hurrying to the "Sermon on the Mount." You would hardly believe Morning Glory if she said that sublimity vibrated in her soul, because she was just a little Oriental. How grand! We faced toward the Gate of the Pacific Ocean. We were still. Why? Because we were thinking the same thing.

We traversed the poet's graveyard.

How romantic to put up a tombstone while living!

How romantic to lie in the ecstasy of a marvellous view! We could be nearer the stars here.

We stepped down to the canyon.

The poet said solemnly:

"Lady and gentleman, this is a holy place where you can pray heartily."

My uncle started to drone Bryant's hymn:

"The groves were God's first temples."

"Did you ever read Thanatopsis, my dear?" Mr. Heine asked.

"Yes, sir!"

"It's a noble piece. So many thousand Asiatics converted every year to the English alphabet. Wonderful!" he soliloquised.

We seated ourselves by a brook.

"Such a lesson in Nature! We endeavour to transcribe, but fail," he sighed, looking on the trees.

Then he turned to me questioning:

"Do you hear the silent song of the forest?"

I nodded.

"Silence! Silence!" he muttered.

We walked among the trees. We came back to the same hilltop, when the large red ball of the sun sank heavily from the Gate.

"Bye-bye!" I shook my handkerchief.

The playful breeze carried it away. It glimmered like a silvery inspiration. Who knows how far it sailed?

I thought a huge statue of the Muse bidding sayonara to the dying sun would be the fitting ornamentation for these Heights. Countless numbers of people would look upon it from the valley. It would be a salvation, if they could bind themselves with Poesy by its noble figure. There was no question it would be more effective than a thousand pages of poem.

"I have no coin to build it," the poet said, in dear openness.

"Let me present it by and by!"

"When?"

"When? It must be after I get married to a rich philanthropist."

We laughed.

We rolled down the hill in the purple fragrance of evening. The evening was sweet like a legend.

5th—I wrote a letter to the artist:

My Sweet Oscar:

"You will love no more your Morning Glory, I am certain, when you are informed how she looks nowadays.

"She inclines against a willow trunk by her cottage. Were you ever acquainted with the great repose of a poetess? Her eyes flash in divine sarcasm. She will shoot them down to the mortal domain (she lives on the mountain), while she murmurs in tragical accents: 'I pity you, ant-mortals!'

"Isn't she shocking?

"Oscar, I have withdrawn to the Heights, and am prying into the Incomprehensible of Nature with Mr. Heine.

"He is unique.

"I take it upon me to say that he is a great poet. Because, in the first place, he never asked me yet, 'Do poems pay in Japan?'

"It's such a trying work for an old man like him to pose as a poet all the time.

"Poet is a sensitive creation. He fancies, I think, the whole world is staring at him. Poor Poet! He keeps up, and tries to be picturesque as he can.

"I am grieved to state, however, that his picturesqueness frequently drops into silliness.

"The absurd thing is that even my uncle takes a part in his farce.

"We had no meat to bite yesterday.

"The poet had no shot left for his gun.

"What did he plan, do you imagine?

"He went up the hill, shouldering his pick. My uncle retainered him with a spade.

"'We will soon bring back a squirrel which we will dig out, Miss Morning Glory,' the poet said.

"Could you ever suppose, Oscar, that any animal except an invalid (an animal who has four feet at that, instead of two like my venerable gentlemen) could permit itself to be so slow like them?

"I laughed till my side ached.

"Funny old men!

"Every sort of sweat fell from their brows when they dragged their fatigued feet home not accompanied by even one inch of any animal tail.

"'I have never heard yet, Mr. Poet, of a squirrel turned to turnip,' I gibed.

"I dread old age, because it makes woman inquisitive, and man silly. Inquisitiveness is tasteless like wax, while silliness is helpless, like a fish on the sand.

"I fear you are silly already, when you say that you sat up late looking at my picture.

"Sat up late?

"What will you do if your mamma thinks you can't sleep from hard drink when you yawn continually at the table?

"Please, don't do it again!

"Step to your bed at half-past six as I do!

"Are you sure that my picture approved your act?

"I guess it shrugged its shoulders from contempt, the delicious moment of blushing being passed.

"If my picture is so precious, I advise you to alter it to ashes. You will take two spoonfuls of the ashes every morning. I am sure, then, your soul will be saved.

"O my darling, I love you!

"I am your

LITTLE JAP GIRL

"P. S.—This letter was written by my duckquill. My new invention, you know.

"My handwriting is clumsy enough, I suppose, to sell as high as any ancient author's autograph.

"Sayonara!"

6th—O poppy, beloved harbinger of California spring!

I "hung on the honourable eyes" of a poppy by my door. Its quaking cup burnt in love (for a meadow-lark perhaps).

"Let me feed you, my new friend!" I said, and brought out a cupful of water.

I moistened it.

A golden flake of the sun-ray came down to it. It smiled, daintily thanking me for my humble treat.

I stared at it, slowly fabricating a fable of its love affair, when the breeze sent me a dreamy song.

The song was old-fashioned, like the afternoon snore of a water-wheel.

I plunged into the song, not knowing who was the singer.

"Ara, ara, Grandmamma's song!" I exclaimed.

She is the aged mother of our poet. She is within the rim of ninety. I suspected her of having discovered the "Elixir for Preserving Eternal Girlhood." You cannot help esteeming her a philosopher when you are told that she has visited San Francisco only twice in ten years. I have no bit of doubt that she would die if you were to rob her of the sight of her flower garden and one stout scrap-book about her son's poems. They work a miracle. What a mystery is human life!

I say that I'm touched by superstition.

I have read of a villainous fox who masquerades in the shape of an old woman.

My wretched fantasy about Mrs. Heine passed, when I heard that no fox resided in the hill.

She is such a dear grandma.

She has no hostile grimace against age. She welcomes it. Her wrinkles are all her beauty. Natural ripening in age is but another form of girlhood.

She is happy as a sparrow.

(Sparrow never forgets, it is said in Nippon, to dance in its hundredth year.)

She hoes round her garden. Her vanity is to make her table rich with her own potatoes and roses.

She lives alone by herself in a cottage some hundred steps from mine.

Did you ever taste her cooking?

"Good morning, Mrs. Heine!" I said.

"Come in!"

She showed herself, extending her large hands. They were damp. I thought she was employing herself in washing.

Is there any sweeter occupation than service to an old lady?

"Let me help you!"

I carried out a bucket to a spring in the backyard.

I brimmed it with the waters. It was so weighty. A naughty stone bounced under my heel. I was thrown down like a toy.

Alas!

My bucket was upset over my skirt.

I had made myself a specimen of misery.

"O grandma, it's raining awfully outside!" I cried.

7th—To-day I was the *chef*, while my uncle was second cook.

I placed a heroic iron pot over the campfire. I dropped a lump of beef in, and afterward the mass of potatoes, carrots, and onions. Mr. Poet's directions were that they should boil for two hours.

Mr. Heine intruded, saying that he would like to season them himself.

"Longfellow, Lowell—they all loved high seasoning as I," he said, snatching a pepper-box from my hand.

He kept tapping the bottom of the box, when the cover fell into the pot.

Oya!

The red pepper garmented the whole thing.

"Go, Mr. Poet! Why don't you mind your own business? You are butler to-day." I spoke in rough sweetness, and drove him away.

He began to place a linen cloth on the table, while I dipped up all the pepper. He picked up one dozen pebbles to weight the tablecloth. The first thing he put on the table was his claret bottle. How could he lose it from sight! When he said that everything was in place, he had forgotten the knives and forks. Dear old poet!

We sat at the table under the wild rose bushes.

Mr. Heine read aloud the following menu:

"PERFUME OF OMAR'S ROSE
WATER OF JORDAN RIVER
MOTHER LOVE BROTH
MEAT OF WISDOM
POTATOES OF SIMPLICITY
PASSION CARROT
ONION OF WIT
DREAM COFFEE.

DESSERT

TYPICAL TOKIO SMILE OF MISS MORNING GLORY."

My grandmamma was our guest.

"Mother, you talk too much always. Remember, this is a sacred service. Silence helps your digestion. Eat slowly, think something higher, and be content!" Poet said.

We smelled the "Perfume of Omar's Rose," and wet our lips with the "Water of Jordan River."

The broth was served.

Everybody choked with its pungent fire.

Poor Mrs. Heine!

She was showering her tear-beans.

"This is perfectly seasoned. Send up your bowl again, ladies and gentlemen!"

Mr. Poet's performance was beautifully buffoonish.

We finished our meat and vegetables.

I smiled lightly, and said: "Are you ready for the Tokio smile?"

"Just ten minutes yet, my dear!" The poet smoothed such a lengthy gray beard.

I winked to Grandma. We looked upon him slyly.

8th—The poet was hoeing in his vegetable garden.

His attire was theatrical.

His red crape sash laxly surrounding his trousers lacked, I am sorry to say, a large Japanese tobacco bag. The cap with gay ribbons was like one of Li Hung Chang's. His back carried a bearskin, inside of which some slovenly yellow silk flapped down.

How tall he was!

"Please, don't dig over there, Mr. Heine, because I buried my poem there," I said.

"What poem, my lady?" he asked.

"The poem to be read at the unveiling of my statue of the Muse on your mountain top, which may occur possibly within five years. The opening lines sound thus:

'Victor of Life and Song,
O Muse of golden grace!'"

"That's great! Why did you bury it?"

"Don't you bury your poems? The best poems are those not published. The very best are those not written. Dante Gabriel Rossetti buried his 'House of Life,' because they were not for a gaping millionaire's wife, but only for his own little wife. But his greatness was ruined when he dug them up and sold them. Poor poet! What all the poets ought to do, I think, is to bury their poems in a potato garden. What a shame even the poets have to eat once in a while! They should wait till the potatoes grow, and then sell them in a vegetable stand, calling 'Poetical Potatoes!' Do you sell your poems, Mr. Heine?"

"Yes."

"Aren't you making your living with your fruits?"

"I never sell them, my dear."

"What do you do?"

"I give them to needy persons. But I was obliged, last year, to hang up a sign, 'No Fruit Lover is Wanted.' I told an Oakland minister to come up and eat *some* plums. He brought his wife and children, even his grandmother. They shouldered away every bit of fruit from half a dozen trees. Next day so many people trampled in with an introduction from the minister."

"Such a minister! I see no use to have the sign, 'Fruit Grower,' if you don't sell."

"Well, my dear lady, God will be merciful to let me use it in place of 'Poem Manufacturer!'"

My uncle announced that tea was boiled.

We left the garden.

9th—The fogs held possession of our world, like the darkness of night.

Where did they invade from?

Pacific Ocean?

Our hillside cottages looked like a tottering ship having no hope for any haven.

Tremendous sight!

I planted me on the hilltop. My mind merged in Japanese mythology. I felt as if I were the first goddess, Izanagi, standing on the "Floating Bridge of Heaven," before the creation.

The divine ghastliness bit my little soul.

I couldn't stand against it. I crept down like a mouse.

The poet said he was preparing a lecture. Its title was "Not in Books."

He in his bed—there he passes every forenoon—was reciting his song.

The words leapt like a leaping sword:

"Sail on! Sail! Sail on! And on!"

I threw a bunch of roses over to his bed as an admirer does to a star.

Then I clapped my hands.

"Pan, pan! Pan, pan!"

10th—I went up the hill to gather mushrooms and watercresses.

I filled a huge basket with them.

I carried it down on my shoulder in Chinese laundry style. I paused every twenty steps.

I slipped within the gate of Mrs. Heine's back garden.

"Mush — rooms! Water — cresses!" I called boisterously.

"My dear girl!" Grandma smiled out from her door.

"Keep your hands off, please! They are things for sale. To-day they are uncommonly cheap. Will you buy them?"

"How much do you charge?"

"Two thousand words of the story about your illustrious son's life."

"What a funny vender!"

"Tell me something about him! I'm ready to leave you the whole business."

"Shall I narrate to you how he started to write?"

"How interesting!" I ejaculated.

"Let me see your things first!" she said, tugging the basket nearer.

"My dear child, they aren't watercresses, but baby weeds. I don't consider they are legitimate mushrooms, either."

She turned upon me with compassionate objection.

"Oya, oya, you don't say so!" I exclaimed. "Then, no story, Grandma?" I looked up meekly.

11th—We had sipped our supper tea some time ago.

A band from the bay sent up irregularly the melody of the love and prowess of dear mariners.

The white moon rose.

I sat alone on my front step, and watched tenderly by the poppy.

My darling Miss Poppy shook herself prettily, as if she uttered a sweet word out of her heart. I imagined every sort of speech that may come from such a tiny bit of flower.

"Sodah, she said that she loved me!" I murmured.

I made a little letter.

"MISS POPPY:

"I love you too.

"Yours,

"MORNING GLORY."

I rolled it to a ball. I dropt it in her cup.

The moon turned gold. The evening odour filled the air.

Look!

She was folding her cup, pressing my missive to her breast. There was no question that she understood.

Dearest friend!

Was it silly that I cried?

12th—The poet left the Heights to exchange his MS. for a gallon of whiskey.

He carried a demijohn, which was as apt to him as a baby to a woman.

I volunteered to clean his holy grotto.

The little cottage brought me a thought of one Jap sage who lived by choice in a ten-foot square mountain hut. The venerable Mr. Chomei Kamo wrote his immortal "Ten-Foot Square Record." A bureau, a bed, and one easy chair—everything in the poet's abode inspires repose—occupy every bit of space in Mr. Heine's cottage. The wooden roof is sound enough against a storm. A fountain is close by his door. Whenever you desire, you may turn its screw and hear the soft melody of rain.

That's plenty. What else do you covet?

The closetlessness of his cottage is a symbol of his secretlessness. How enviable is an open-hearted gentleman! Woman can never tarry a day in a house without a closet.

He never closes his door through the year.

A piece of wire is added to his entrance at night. He would say that that will keep out the tread of a dog and a newspaper reporter.

Not even one book.

He would read the history written on the brow of a star, he will say if I ask him why.

Every side was patched by pictures and a medley of paper clippings. Is there anything sweeter to muse upon than personal knicknacks?

O such a dust!

I swept it.

But I thought philosophically afterward, why should people be so fussy with the dust, when things are but another form of dust. What a far-away smell the dust had! What an ancient colour!

I observed on the wall an odd coat and boots that dear old Santa Claus might have lost.

"Klondyke costume!" I exclaimed.

I undressed myself, and tried them on.

When I was ready to put on a fur cap, Mrs. Heine wandered down, calling me.

"Morning Glory! Morning Glory!"

I trembled in deadly fear.

I hid me promptly by the bureau, under the bed. I shut my eyes, praying:

"Namu Daijingu, don't let her find me!"

13th—Last midnight (O voicelessness of the hillside yonaka!) I woke up. The moon peeped into my sitting room. She laid a square looking-glass on the floor.

I abandoned my bed, and sat by the glass.

I spread on it the letter from my sweetheart.

I read it over and over, till I couldn't read any more, the moon being kidnapped by the cloud-highwayman.

"O Oscar!"

I cried in the darkness.

I could not slumber all the night, on account of my thought of him.

A letter was written to him to-day.

Nature and love! I am now living with them.

14th—I elaborated a nosegay.

The poet and uncle dignified themselves in frock-coats.

The coming of the coffin was slow.

Mr. Poet had proffered his own graveyard to let an unknown poet lodge there. "Is it because you want some one to greet you when you die?" I said in laughter.

I seated myself by a creek.

I entered involuntarily into the riddle of Life and Death.

The water under my feet rolled down, positively not knowing why nor whence. The wind passed, "willy-nilly blowing." I wondered whither it went. Mr. Omar is unquestionably a true poet. The petals of a rose before me fell.

I murmured:

> "Each Morn a thousand Roses brings, you say;
> Yes, but where leaves the Rose of Yesterday?"

I was crying in sadness when the coffin arrived.

Mr. Heine and my uncle lifted it by either edge. The neighbouring farmers and two sardonically cool gentlemen from the undertaker's aided them. The jaw-fallen papa of the dead carried all the posies.

And Miss Morning Glory (who is the belle of Tokio) shouldered a bench for the purpose of sustaining the coffin when they were tired.

The hill is precipitous.

The gentlemen stopped numberless times, before they stationed themselves on the top.

The grave was hollowed behind Mr. Poet's monument. They sank the coffin.

What a tremor of silence sharpened the air! I was shaking.

The poor papa read a chapter from the Bible. He described his loving son's life, in doleful honourableness.

"There are a thousand flowers in Spring,"—the poet spoke—"whose repute is not extensively spoken, like that of the rose or violet. Some of them are not given even a name. They spend their smile and odour into the breeze, and die without any repining. They are content, because they are true to God. So a poet's life should be. What is celebrity? Keats was told of his beautiful graveyard, and he said: 'I have already seemed to feel the flowers growing over me.' If this poet, whom we now bury, had been told of this hill, he might have said: 'I see already the butterflies beaming over my head.' Spring is coming. The poppies and buttercups shall dress the hill."

A church-bell chimed from the valley.

We left the buried to his solitude.

My uncle and I sat under an acacia tree, silent for some time.

"Look, Morning Glory!" he said, exhibiting a silver piece.

"Is there any story about that dollar?"

"The father of the dead paid me for carrying the coffin."

"Uncle, did you accept it?"

"Yes."

"Such a funny uncle!"

"Why not?"

"You have spoiled all your nobility for only one dollar."

I upturned my face, afterward, appealing in gleeful tone:

"O Uncle, you ought to give me half of it. Fifty cents! I carried the bench, you know."

15th—I arose at the first whistling of a meadow-lark.

Hearken to its hailing morning voice!

O simple bird!

Its so various moods are expressed only in its eternally changeless syllables. What a magical song!

How bungling seemed our human vocabularies!

I trod the garden in bare feet.

Naked feet, sir!

The delicious chilliness of the ground animated me rapturously. Do you believe me if I confess that I knelt and kissed it? I said that I would not mind burying my nude body for a few hours. Mother earth is so sweet.

I ran up the hill, humming an Oriental ditty.

The air was relishable, like an ice-cream on a summer midnight.

The beautiful sun was rising.

I clapped my palms thrice, reverently bowing.

Am I a sun-worshipper?

Yes!

I cleansed my feet in the water of the creek when I returned from the hill. I sat me on a rock, extending my bare feet in the sunlight. I thought that towel-wiping was too much of a modernism.

"Uncle! O Uncle!" I called.

"What is it, Miss Morning Glory?"

The poet jutted out from a bamboo bush by the wooden bridge over the creek.

"Such charming feet!" he said.

I instantly lowered my skirt, blushing.

He was carrying a spade and hoe. He said that he had been planting flowers about the grave of our friend, ever since four o'clock. "To make it beautiful is high poetry," he philosophised.

"What do you wish with Uncle, my child?" he continued.

"I want my shoes."

"Let me have the honour of fetching them for you!" he said in amiably dignified docility.

16th—The poet gave me five feet square, behind the Willow Cottage, for my potato garden.

I sticked a stick at each corner. I encircled it with my crape sash.

The note hanging on it read, "Graveyard of Morning Glory's Poem."

I hired uncle for ten cents, to clear off every weed.

I raked.

I set the seeds.

I got a suspicious coat and pants from a nook in the unrespectable barn. It was fortunate that the horse—who may also be a poet, he is so philosophically thin—didn't shout, "Hoa, clothes-thief!"

I put them on the limbs of an acacia tree.

I planted it on my graveyard to scare away wild intruders.

It is holy ground.

I wondered when the potatoes would grow.

17th—Squirrel!

What admirable eyes!

He projected his head from a hole by my window. He withdrew it a bit, and bent it to one side, as if he were solving a question or two.

Then his eyes stabbed my face.

"I'm no questionable character, Mr. Squirrel," I said.

He hid himself altogether.

I amassed some crusts of bread by his hole, and watched humbly for his honourable presence.

He did not peep out at all.

The bread was not a worthy invitation. I varied it with a fragment of ham.

Mr. Squirrel wasn't void-stomached.

I thought he needed something to read. I tore a poem from the wall. I left it by his respectable cavern.

Lo!

His head sprouted out to pull it in.

"Aha, even the squirrel is a poetry devotee, in this hill!" I said in humourous mood.

18th—

"Most Beloved:

"Mamma was flogged with a bamboo rod some hundred times when she was a girl, her exchanging of a word with a boy over the fence being deemed an obscenity. My papa spent his lonely days in a room with Confucius till one night a middleman left him with my mamma as with a dolly. I do believe they never wrote any love letter.

"What would they say, I wonder, if they knew that their daughter had taken to Love-Letter Writing as a profession in Amerikey?

"You shouldn't censure my penury in writing, knowing that I am a musume from such a source.

"Oscar, are your windows clean?

"Every window of my Willow Cottage was washed yesterday. Is there anything more happy to see (your beautiful eyes excepted) than a shiny window? I pressed my cheek to the window mirthfully, when Mr. Poet tried to pinch it from the outside. My dearest, if he had been my very Mr. Ellis!

"I made a discovery while I was trimming about the kitchen.

"Can you guess what it was?

"'Love-Letter Writer!'

"'Gift from Heaven!' I said, trusting it would help me in my composition.

"I lit a candle last night. I hid it behind the cover of such a huge bible which I had borrowed for the purpose. I was heedful of two old men who might disturb me, mistaking the light for a sign that something had happened. Poor Mrs. Heine almost cried, she was so pleased to think that I loved the Bible. Do I love it? Oho, ho, ho—

"Bakabakashi, how sad!

"The whole bunch of letters wasn't fit for my taste at all, at all.

"I'm sorry that I used up two candles that were all we had in this hill.

"So, my darling, my letter has to be woven from my truest heart.

"Good morning, my sweet lord! How are you? Have you breakfasted? Did you eat a beefsteak? I dislike a hearty morning eater. My ideal man shouldn't be given more than a cup of coffee and one trembling leaf of bacon.

"Mr. Poet kills a frog every morning. He says that his fancy springs like a pond singer when he tastes it. I should say that his idea bounds too far in his case.

"Do you eat frog?

"I beseech you not to incline toward it.

"What should I do if your thought ran off from me?

"Failure of my life! Love is the whole business of woman, you know.

"Have you any shirt to mend?

"I have been fixing the poet's.

"Pray, express it to me!

"Should you ask such a pleasure of any other girl, it would be a fatal mistake for you. Remember, Oscar, that the Japanese girl is a mightily jealous thing!

"My sweetheart, I dreamed a dream.

"You were a dragonfly, while I was a butterfly. It is needless to say that we loved. One spring day we floated down along the canyon from a mountain a thousand miles afar. Our path was suddenly barred by a dense bush. We couldn't attain to The Garden of Life without adventuring in it. So, then, you stole in from one place, I from another. Alas! We got parted forever.

"Isn't that a terrible indication?

"Do you know any spell to turn it good? I am awfully agitated by it.

"Oh, kiss!

"Kiss me, my dear!

"I have to ascertain your love in it.

"Your
MORNING GLORY"

19th—A little "chui chui" was building a nest under the roof, by my door.

Dear jovial toiler!

I must help him in some way.

I unravelled one of my stockings, hoping it might be servicable in bettering his home.

I stood me on a chair, raising up my arms with my gift.

The poor sparrow was scared. He cast a gray "honourableness" on my hand.

O naughty "chui chui!"

He winged away, twittering, "chui, chui, chui!"

20th—The squirrel by my window shows a great fancy for me. He honoured me three times already this morning. He bore a somewhat scholarly air. A retired professor, I reckon.

Is he regular with his diary?

Possibly he is idle with a pen, like any other professor.

Let me scribble for him to-day!

My one bottle of ink has some time to dry up yet.

I will name it "The Cave Journal." I will leave it to the Professor for a souvenir upon my sayonara to this hill.

A

Where are my spectacles?

B

Upon my soul, I believe that some mischief is raging. I can never trust even the poet abode. Who stole my two-cent stamp?

God bless you, my precious daughter at Sierra Nevada!

By and by I will erect my private telegraph between us.

C

The idea of an idiotic spider tying his net across my front gate!

How ever could he be so ambitious as even to incline to arrest me!

He may very likely be a detective. A railroad brigand is hiding in these Heights, I suppose.

The world is running worse every day.

How shocking!

It was a fundamental error of God, to create that adventuress Eve. The offspring of a crow can't be other than a crow.

Our squirrel history is not blotted by any criminal. I feel a bit conceited in speaking about it. How can I help it?

The trouble with God is that he was awfully vain to express his own ability by so many useless things.

Rifle, for instance.

My poor wife!

D

To-day is the anniversary of my beloved. She was shot by one two-legged barbarian.

I appealed to the police. American police are rotten through and through. The murderer bribed them, I fancy.

I found my wife, but she was only a skin.

How often did I tell her that she was risking too much in sporting around! But she didn't mind me, insisting that sight-seeing was a better education.

I carried her skin into my home.

I cleansed it, and altered its form a trifle, because it was a lady's. I am still keeping it for church-wear.

I feel dreadful, thinking of her.

E

A butterfly passed by my cavern, a hundred times.

Each time she threw me a vulgar laugh.

Her face was thickly powdered in yellow. Does she think herself charming? I should say that I would prefer a girl in tights from a saloon-stage to her indecency.

Such a flirt!

I suppose that she wanted me to marry her.

No!

Am I not old enough to avoid running into such foolishness?

F

Rainy day!

I sat in a memorial corner of my cave, with an unfinished novel of my wife's.

I do judge she had flashes of genius. She was so deep, like the sky. I never suspected that she could gracefully have beaten George Eliot, if she had only survived.

Poor girl!

One tenderly loved by God passes away young.

I have fallen into the habit of crying unmanfully nowadays.

I cannot help it, can I?

G

One thing I must furnish is a bathroom.

Cleanliness is the first rule of heaven, I am told.

I went to the lily pond to take a gracious bath.

O such water gamins! Dirty-handed frogs!

How could I dip me in the turbid water?

The frogs ought to go to a reformatory school. They have no culture, whatever.

H

Camera hunters are thick as fogs.

To-day I came near being a victim.

No, sir!

I can't permit my picture to be seen with those of cheap matinee idols. I must keep some dignity.

Americans are too commercial altogether. The pictures of our race are in demand, I imagine.

I

Beautiful moon, last night!

I filled my stomach with the divine water from a creek.

My face waved in the water. I flattered myself that I was a pretty handsome gentleman.

I sang an ancient Chinese song:

> "Come 'long to-morrow moon,
> Carrying a harp!"

J

Stop your empty noise, meadow-larks!

Silence is the first study of this hill and the last, don't you know?

I am absorbed in my grave work, "The Secret of the World."

K

My neighbouring Jap girl is rather attractive, isn't she?

I heard a few scratches of her native bubbling.

The pagan speech is not so bad as I thought.

L

If there is one thing I cannot endure, it is ignorance.

What is the state of your roses, old boy?

The poet Heine is utterly alien to rose culture. Shall I order "How to Raise Roses" from a London publisher?

M

I went up the hill to pray to God. The higher the nearer.

When I came back, my honourable vestibule was blocked, I found, by the dirt. The poet was ditching close by my residence.

I couldn't blame his conduct, however, because no one could see my home. I don't hang out a sign like a quack doctor.

It occurred to me that I would strike into his cottage, and snatch the best poems from his drawer, and sell them with my name.

"I must secure the international copyright," I said.

But I couldn't dare it, my impulse being thwarted.

I am no wicked reporter, don't you see?

I hid me in his historical iron pot all day.

N

Heine was posting around the following card:

No Shooting.

I venture to say that he is the only one civilised Two-Legged in the whole world.

O

Where is my napkin?

Chinese laundry isn't punctual in delivery.

P

I think I must learn how to swear for a pastime.

Q

My fellow brother Mr. —— was shot this morning.

The paper says that there is a possibility of war between Russia and Japan. A preacher prophesies the disappearance of the universe.

Everything is precarious in the extreme.

I will not poke around outside during the day. I will loaf in the poet's orchard under the breezy moonlight.

Poetical existence is just enough. I will withdraw me to the sanctuary of the Muses.

R

Heaven be with my soul! Amen!

S

Good-bye, my dear old world!

21st—A Chinaman passed with a weighty load of washing on his shoulder.

"Friend, stop a minute! Take a glass with me before you go!"

The poet rolled out with a claret bottle.

Did you ever see a Chinee in love? Did you ever see one smile?

Mr. Charley smiled a serene smile of the Flower Kingdom pattern.

"God bless the Empress Dowager!" Mr. Poet said. Both raised their wine.

"The load is too heavy for you. You are killing yourself. I can't bear to see it. My friend, obey me! Let me help you! Don't leave till I come back!"

The poet hurried for his questionable buggy and horse. He cracked his whip—he never whips the horse, but he carries it for fashion's sake, as he remarks—when Mr. Charley protested, "Me oll-righ, you savvy!"

The Chinaman was dumbfounded, for the poet was unknown to him.

Mr. Heine pushed him in.

When he leaped up, he noticed his horse in tender tone:

"Go on, baby!"

"What a goody-goody! His act never parts from poetry, however," I said.

I was simply dying for an opportunity to explode my good heart, when I invited one tramp to my Willow Cottage.

I fed him with one dozen eggs.

I emptied out all my change for him.

"Don't you feel cold, lying outdoors?" I said.

"Yes, Miss!"

"Don't you need an overcoat?"

"Yes, Miss!"

When Mr. Tramp left me with an overcoat in his hand, looking like a proud Mayor of Tokio, my uncle was coming from Mrs. Heine's.

"Uncle, you do want to be good to a poor man, don't you? You have made yourself a great philanthropist with your overcoat."

"What have you done?"

"I presented it to a tramp."

"Morning Glory!"

"Never mind, Uncle! I will buy a swell coat in New York. You have some more, haven't you?"

"It cost me forty yens at 'Hama. You really are a foolish girl, Asagao!"

(Asagao is my humble name in Japanese.)

Then I kissed his hand most pathetically—in fun for my part, of course.

22nd—My superstitious Mamma!

She mailed me an o mikuji from the holy box of the Akiwa god.

The number written on the slip was fifty-one. The divine will read as follows:

"Faith in the Well-God will result fortunately."

Mamma bade me make my prayer long (not mixing it with any laughter whatever).

I wondered whether there was any well around here.

I explored. I came across one (such a doubtful well) by an apple tree.

I hastened to my cottage to cut a paper flag.

The poet gave me one cup of claret for the Well-God.

I sat by the well.

What did I pray?

I pried into the well for the fin of a fish. Well without a funa fish isn't holy to a Jap mind.

23rd—Uncle left the Heights for Frisco.

I have encountered somewhere one picture, "Stolen Kiss," symbolising sweetness.

I dare say the sweetest thing in the world is to steal into a gentleman's room and overturn his things.

The gentleman smell is provocative.

My uncle?

I can only say that he is more desirable than an old woman. Old woman is sad as a dry persimmon.

I stole into his room.

God will overlook my petty crime—how lovely to be scratched by guilt!—in consideration of the fact that a Jap girl never profanes.

I turned his pillow. Pillow is a fascination for me ever since I have read of a poet who hid his diary under it.

Look at the book, "A Random Note!"

He was working to beat me with his journal, I derided.

I sat on his bed, opening it.

"How original!" I exclaimed.
Uncle, you are a cynic, aren't you?
Let me pick a few pieces from his pen!

"Unfortunately! Japanese are accustomed from babyhood to depend on another's back. The hereditary fashion of nursing the baby on the back has thoroughly taught them dependence. Independence is only a coat of arms to distinguish man from the beasts—that is all. I urge that Emerson's essays be adopted in the Nippon schools. His 'Self-reliance' should be the first of all.

"Most unhappily! I have observed the Japanese fad in America for years, and it has not yet reached its culmination. Each month the books on Japan are placed before the public. It is verily sad even to cut their edges. (The practical Americans prove themselves unpractical in leaving the leaves of books uncut.) I say that our Japan is entitled to regard for worthier things than geisha girls or a fashion in bowing. We should decline your love, Americans, if it is rooted merely in your fancy for our paper lanterns. I have frequently come to conclude that Americans are eminently the freakish nation. I feel not only occasionally that they lack the reasoning power. I do not assume the phenomena of the yellow journals as my proof.

"A year or two ago, one Japanese theatrical troup roamed. They are not catalogued at home as actors. They chose to skip on the stage, simply because a bit more money is in it than in the calling of 'lantern-carrying for politicians.' Any wild animal can skip. I am now confronted with the question whether American generosity is not without sense. They piled up their money for them. Even the first-class critics struggled to find out something from such poor art. I am bound to be thankful, however, for the Americans saved these poor players from bankruptcy in Japan. It reminds me of a story. Our Nippon government many years ago appointed a certain loafing sailor as an English instructor, giving him a monthly pay of three hundred dollars. Sailor with an anchor-tatoo on his hand! Three hundred dollars are no small coin in Japan. Our sailor professor said, I am told, that he had not heard of any Milton. Ignorance can easily be a philanthropist, if it can be anything.

"Japanese love Nature? They do. But how sad to glance at Japanese garden! It is painful to notice the dwarf trees. Japs never permit one thing to grow naturally. Country of deformity! America, most natural, most manly nation!"

24th—My uncle didn't come back yesterday. Mr. Poet condescended to the town.

I am alone.

I spent the entire forenoon with Grandma, peeling potatoes, strewing sweet pea seeds on the ground.

I ascended the hill with the root of a white rose—believing in the Nippon idea that blossoms for the dead should be white—and set it by the grave.

Then I stole into the canyon.

I amassed the dead leaves of redwood by the brook for a camp fire.

The smoke rose like a soul unto heaven.

I watched its beautiful confusion.

When I left, a snake obstructed my path, flashing its needle of a tongue.

Snake, one of my greatest foes! (The others being cheese and mathematics.)

I turned pale.

But I bravely faced it, hoping that it would speak a word or two, as one did to Eve. I placed my eyes on it, though in fear. Perhaps it wasn't as intelligent as the one in the garden of Eden. Maybe it thought it nothing but a waste of time to address a Jap poorly stored in English. It crept away.

I ran down the hill.

A storm of laughter struck me from within when I came to my Willow Cottage. I examined it from the window. Half a dozen young ladies were biting pie. (Pie! Rustic pastry I ever so hate!)

"Picnic!" I murmured.

My blood gushed up. I was on the verge of denouncing their irruption. The cottage belongs to any one, I said in my afterthought, as it does to me.

I slipped away.

I found myself in the plum orchard with a hoe.

I began to root the weeds. I waited silently for their departure.

25th—The spring hills were coquetting like a tea-house maiden, singing:

"The air is lovely like wine;
Come Lord! Come Lord!"

The curtain for the spring comedy has not yet risen.

Already the picnic band invades.

To-day I will make myself mistress of a hillside coffee-house.

The poet—the eternally sweet poet—hastened to borrow a tent from a neighbour.

He set it on the greenest spot of grass before my cottage. I must excuse his conceit, he entreated, in showing his skill by baking a cake for me.

"Accept my hundred arigatos!"

I bowed demonstratively.

I pasted a paper—such a bashful brown piece from a butcher's table—with the sign of

"BISHOPS' REST."

The poet tacked "Ten Cents for Coffee and Cake" on the fence by the tent.

The cups (what a shame that their arms were all off) were rinsed, when he showed me an imperial poundcake, declaring it his own manufacture.

At three o'clock I was fully prepared for an honourable guest.

The coffee on the oil-stove was surging, when two parties went by, not spending even one look at my sign.

"Times are awfully hard, I think. People have not luxury enough to spare even a dime," I murmured sadly.

I said that I would have no business, if I didn't make the next party my victim.

I appeared before the tent, when a few girls—who were born for laughing, but not for thinking—came close by.

"Will you rest and taste the cake that the poet made, ladies?" I said.

"That's nice," they said, rolling into the tent.

I served them with coffee and cake.

"Is this surely the poet's cake? It looks like baker's cake," one girl said.

"Mr. Poet assured me it was of his own making," I replied in cool reserve.

After they left, I scrutinised the cake. Oya! A little bakery mark was seen.

"Mighty liar!" I grumbled.

Abrupt clouds clouded the sun. The winds scolded bitterly. I decided there was no business remaining.

I called Mr. Heine and uncle into the Bishops' Rest.

"Your cake was fine, Mr. Poet."

"I know it, Miss Morning Glory. I'm a pretty good cook, you see. I cooked once in a Sierra camp for fifty miners. I was paid twenty dollars a week. Alas! It was the biggest money I ever earned."

"By the way, Mr. Heine, the bakery sent a bill for you."

I placed before him a slip that I had prepared for the purpose.

"Ha! Ha, ha, ha!"

His open laughter was as from a simple Faun.

I noticed, afterward, a black mass heaped in a ditch. The whole situation grew plain to me. He couldn't bake, but only burn, in the oven, and had despatched his neighbour for the cake.

Dear Poet!

26th—We pressed the poet to receive some money as just a sign of our gratitude.

Mr. Heine despised our thought.

Honourable gentleman!

I found a tin box. I put the money in—ask me not how much!

I dug a hole by the willow tree beside the lily pond, and buried the money box. I tumbled a stone over it to mark it.

"I'll write him about it from New York. See, Uncle! Isn't it unique?" I said.

Uncle wasn't enthusiastic in approving my idea. He couldn't check me, however, as the money was mine.

He said he would order an elegant vase from Tokio.

27th—I intended to keep a sweet fashion of old Japan in presenting a poem at my sayonara.

We will take leave to-morrow.

O gracious graceful poet abode!

My farewell poem in seventeen syllable form is as follows:

"Sayonara no
Ureiya nokore
Mizu no neni!"

"Remain, oh, remain,
My grief of sayonara,
There in water sound!"

28th—Mrs. Heine kissed me.

Dear old Grandma!

"Do you know what this is, Miss Morning Glory?" the poet said, plucking a leaf from a tree by his door.

"Fig-leaf! Isn't it?"

"Yes, my child! It is a fig-leaf. Do you know the fig tree? It is the shyest tree in the world. Classical tree indeed! It has no blossom, being so modest of display, but it has the fruits. Remember, my young lady, its teaching of 'Modesty! Modesty!'"

"Sayonara, Mr. Poet!"

"One minute, Uncle!" I said.

I ran into the Willow Cottage to get a cupful of water. I watered my friend Miss Poppy with love.

Bye-bye, little girl!

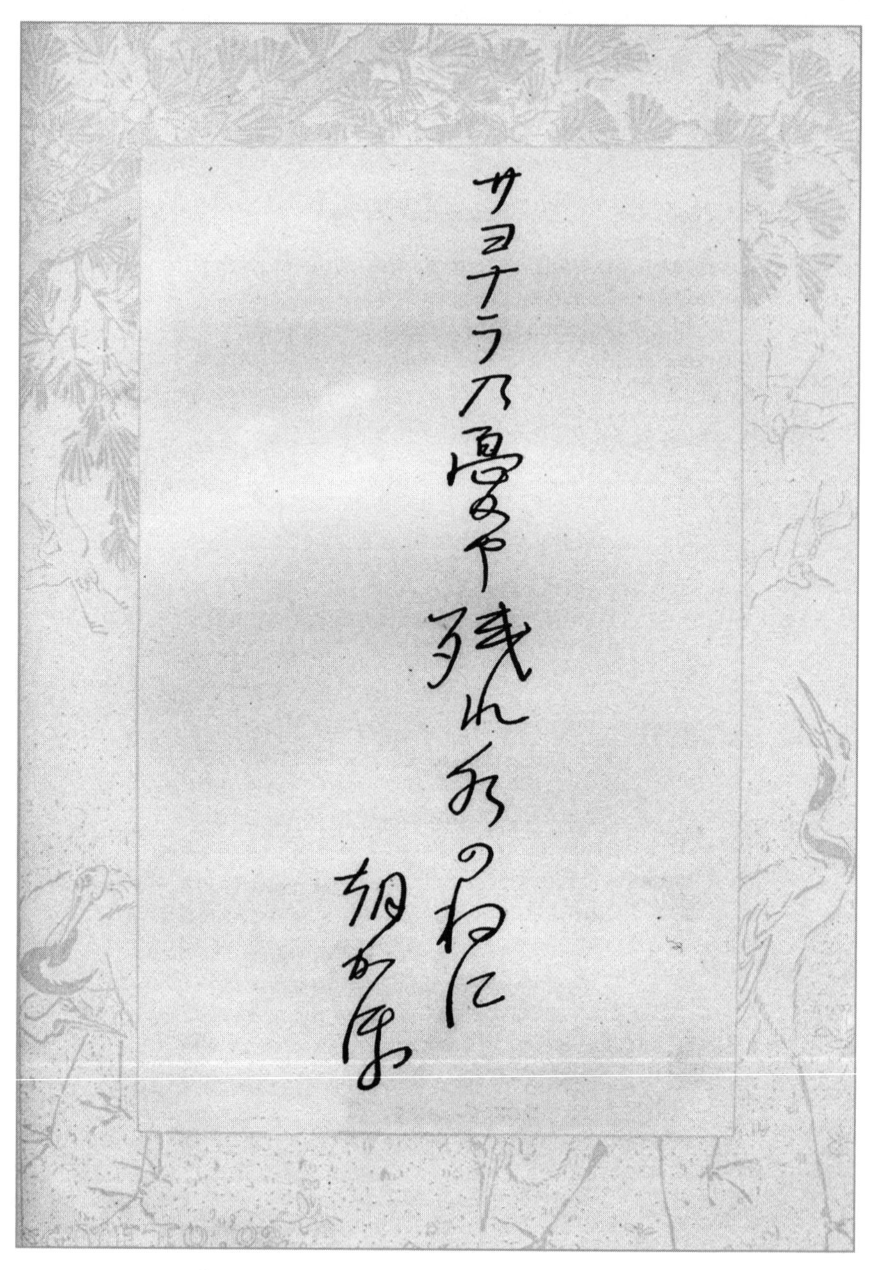

"My sayonara poem in Japanese autograph"

San Francisco, March 1st.

Civilisation again!

The first thing was to buy a cake of the best soap.

Because my hands had perfected their transformation into worthless leather while I dwelt on the hill.

What kind of soap did I use, do you suppose?

Laundry soap.

2nd—Delightful Ada!

We drove to the Cliff House, Ada to laugh at the stupid song of the seals, I to say my adieu.

Good-bye, Pacific Ocean!

We cried in hugging.

We shall not see each other for some time—maybe never again!

Ada!

O Ada San!

3rd—This afternoon!

Eastward, ho, ho!

Overland Train, March 4th

"Madame Butterfly" lay by me, appealing to be read.

"No, iya, I'll never open! I erred in buying you," I said.

I dislike that "Madame." It sounds indecent ever since the "gentleman" Loti spoiled it with his "Madame Chrysanthème."

The honourable author of "Madame Butterfly" is Mr. Wrong. (Do you know that Japanese have no boundary between L and R?) Undoubtedly, he is qualified to be a Wrong.

Authorship is nothing at all, nowadays, since authors are thick as Chinese laundries. Well, still, it can be honourable, if it is honourable.

Japanese fiction penned by the tojin!

It is a completely sad affair. I wonder why the author (God bless him) didn't fit himself for brooming the streets instead of scrawling.

The characters in his book—I am grateful I see no lady writer of Japanese novels yet—remind me of the "devils of mixture" swarming in Yokohama or Kobe, whose Jap mother was a professional "hell." It is lamentable to set the verdict on them that they have inherited the art of framing lies from their mamma.

Do I vex you, gentleman, when I say that your Japanese type could only be an unprincipled half-caste?

Your Nippon character eyed in blue, and hairy-skinned always. Isn't it absurd when it puts a 'Merican shoe on one foot and a wooden clog on the other?

And if you insist on registering it as a Jap, I shall merely laugh loudly.

One heroine I have read of placed a light summer haori over her heavily padded midwinter clothes.

Your Oriental novel, let me be courageous enough to say, is a farce at its best.

Oh, just wait, my sweet Americans! A genuine one will soon be offered to you by Morning Glory.

I stepped out to the platform, and threw out "Madame Butterfly."

Poor "Madame!"

I trust in the mountain lions of high Nevada to cherish her lovingly.

5th—

"Matsuba Sama, the following letter creeps 'under your honourable table.'

"How is yourself?

"I imagine that the breeze fills your bower with the odour of ume flowers. I am definite in saying that the Japanese ume is of different origin from the California plum tree, which has no expression in divine fragrance as I am told. I see your indolent face in the air, awaiting poetical inspiration on your bamboo piazza where the ume petals are beautifully blotched.

"There are several months yet till we shall quarrel face-to-face over the superiority of English or Oriental literature.

"Miss Pine Leaf, I—or rather we—have said farewell to Frisco.

"It was said that I never saw any battleship (excepting one shamefaced gunboat) in the bay of the Golden Gate. A bay without battleship is like a door without a lock.

"Can you fancy any Japanese city without soldiers?

"American soldier?

"I am sorry to say that I have met no soldier in my four months at the Pacific.

"I presume that the practical Meriken jins can't bear to see such a useless ornamentation. Yes! Soldiers are degenerating, in my opinion, to the rank of a fireplace on a hot summer day. How stimulating, however, was the sound of the fearless hoofs of a cavalier! When the sabres of a regiment flashed in the sunlight, I could never keep from fluttering my paper handkerchief.

"I shall not excite myself in such a joy in Amerikey.

"I made the acquaintance of one colonel at Mrs. Willis'. He is a jolly business man. Just think of a colonel plus merchant! Is it possible? He changes his white shirt every morning, and shines his shoes twice a day. I should say that he will carry a sheet and opera hat, and leave his gun behind, whenever he is summoned to a battle-field. Possibly he has hidden his colonelship in his trunk.

"I found afterward that every old gentleman is a colonel or judge.

"Everything in California is made for just a woman.

"California gentleman isn't privileged to raise one question against a lady. He is provided with all sorts of exclamations to please the woman. If he should ever miss one dinner with his wife, he would be divorced in court on the morrow.

"Uncle says that the Eastern gents are not so devoted to the lady.

"If it be true!

"Am I now entering the city of Man?

"How sad!

"Have you any experience of writing by the car-window?

"I feel a strange delight in scanning my romantically tremulous handwriting. A certain famous Jap penman takes wine before he begins, for the sake of putting his mind in a fine frenzy, as you know. The shaking of the car produces in me the same effect. Isn't this letter great enough to be honoured on your tokonama?

"Can you ever imagine how vast Amerikey is?

"Yesterday our car ran all day long, over the mountains and prairies, seeing only a few huts.

"O such a snowstorm in the evening!

"The train rushed like a maddened dragon. It was verily an astonishingly ghastly spectacle as any human thought could ever picture. I thrilled with a feeling of tragic ecstasy, which is the highest emotion.

"Can you recollect that you and I once stood under the darkest rains without an umbrella, and laughed hysterically?

"I love shocking emotion.

"Since I was touched by the continental air, I measure my lungs dilating two inches bigger. How sorry I shall be for you when I return! You are so tiny! I expect myself to be five inches higher within the next few months.

"Amerikey is the country where everything grows, don't you know?

"Even the stars look a deal larger than in Japan.

"Looking back at the Rocky Mountains,

"Yours,
"Asagao"

6th—The rocking of the train makes us babies in the cradle.

The car is a modern opium resort, where we sleep and sleep.

I shouldn't wonder if we all turned into nodding Rip Van Winkles.

To-day I had a sleeping contest with uncle.

I was defeated.

CHICAGO, 7th

Chicago water is a perfect horror.

Gomenyo! That's no way to begin, is it?

I never waver in saying that California girls borrow their fairness from their water.

There is no question in my mind why the Chicago women—certain hundreds I saw, if you please—are barren in their complexion.

"O Uncle, how many days have we to tarry here?" I asked, within an hour after we had set foot in this city.

I grieve over my contact with such a city. It is no place for a lady. (Is here any lady?) It is just the place for a man.

No show marked "Only for a Man" is respectable, I dare say.

Are Chicago men "gentlemen?"

They are not sensitive about their hats in the hotel elevator. The laundry work isn't superb, I judge, as not every one's shirt is snowy as a San Franciscan's. I cannot blame their black fingernails, as they live in smoke.

Even the Frisco smoke hindered my breath at my opening moment in Amerikey. I should have died, if it had been Chicago.

Bodily cleanliness is the first chapter in the whitening of the soul. How many mortals are there here with a clear soul?

"Chicago is Mr. Nobody without the smoke, like Japan without a fan. The prosperity of a modern city is measured by the bulk of its smoke, Morning Glory. But I don't approve of their using a cheap coal. Health has to be guarded," my uncle said.

A driver carried us from the station as if we were pigs.

Mind you, this is Chicago illustrious for its hams.

I barred my ears with my hands in the carriage. The thunderous noise menaced me so.

Do roses blossom well in the turbulent air?

I have no doubt that Chicago has no poet.

"Cook County fosters three thousand poets, one paper says, my young woman," Uncle said in laughter.

"Don't say so!"

As soon as I had established myself in the hotel, I inscribed—with the longest apologetical ojigi to Mr. Shelley—as follows:

"Hell is a city much like Chicago,
A populous and a smoky city."

8th—How sad I felt, not to be greeted by even one star from my hotel window last night!

"Uncle, please count how many stories in that building."

I was disgusted with the poor taste of the coffee. Such a first-class hotel! Coffee and maxim, I have said, should be of the very best. Commonplace words with the golden heading of Maxim would be as cheap as a negress with white powder. I would choose even a bread pudding rather than a suspicious cup of coffee.

Uncle failed to secure a box of cigarettes.

The most delicate shape for smoking is the slender stalk of a cigarette. The cigar ever so much impresses me as barbarous. Chicagoans might say it was the only manly smoke.

Truly!

Chicago is the City of Man (whatever that means).

I'm glad that the young gentlemen with genteel canes under their arms don't open any cigar stand conference here. Such an abomination in Frisco!

No drones, whatever.

My uncle was going out sight-seeing with me in a silk hat.

I objected to it.

Plug hat doesn't suit informal Chicago.

He changed his frock-coat for a sack-coat.

"Now, Uncle, you look more like a Chicago gentleman!" I said.

Yes, this is a plain sack-coat city.

He was fussing with a handkerchief. I said, laughing: "Never mind, Uncle! I am sure the men don't carry it here, since the women never carry a purse in their hand."

Isn't it awful that one (even a stranger) ought to know everything in Chicago? A slight question to the street people would be condemned as a nuisance.

Even the policeman shows no chivalry.

I was sorry that the colour of his suit was bitterly faded.

Isn't Chicago rich enough to furnish a new one?

I suppose many dogs must be hanging around here, because the policeman arms himself with a piece of wood for chasing them off.

I should like to know if there is any blacker house than the City Hall.

It will be a matter of a short time before the Chicago River turns to ink.

Then we went to observe the Lake of Michigan from Lincoln Park.

I scoffed at my absurdity in being ready with the first line for my poem on the lake. If you knew that "O minstrel of Heaven and Truth!" was the beginning, you would laugh surely. The lake wasn't a huge singer like the Pacific Ocean, at all.

"Uncle, please, count how many stories in that building!" I begged.

Chicago structures "crush my little liver" completely. Did I ever dream that I would eye such pillars of the sky in my life?

When I returned to my hotel, I declared that I would not open my trunk, because my everyday dress was good enough for Chicago.

I regret to say that the gentlemen are so homely.

9th—How dear is the green crispy paper money.

What a historical look!

It made me feel as if I were at home.

I hated ever so much the gold coin in California. Its threateningly mercantile aspect made me shudder as at a speculator of Kakigara Cho of Tokio.

If I like Chicago it must be on account of its soiled paper money.

I will exchange all my gold to it.

I went to one store for a short skirt like that Chicago woman wears.

It may be a change, though shortness in hair and dress is my aversion. It may be advantageous in showing one's shoes, though eternal exhibition isn't tasty.

It would be an accurate account of my reason for buying to say that I singularly wished to use up a few jumbles of money.

I dulled myself reading the advertising bills through my hotel window.

There's no block free from them.

'Vertisement!

Isn't it horrid?

I laughed, wondering why those enterprising Meriken jins don't employ the extensive backs of prizefighters in the ring.

Uncle and I went to see the Injuns dance.

How fantastically they sang!

There was a Japanese tea-house.

It is no "tea-house" at all. It was the saddest thing I ever saw.

I thought that Chicagoans were not fastidious with anything.

"Any old thing will do!" they might say jollily.

Open, hard-working Chicago!

Has she much education?

10th—My uncle wanted me to join him in visiting a stockyard to see the doomed pigs groaning, "Fu, fu, fu!"

I declined.

Uncle started off alone.

There was some time before I heard someone fisting on my door.

"A Japanese gentleman wishes to see your husband, madam," a hotel attendant addressed me.

"Good God! My husband?" I cried.

Satemo!

How could any porter be such an ignoramus as not to distinguish between Mrs. and Miss!

Possibly he esteemed me "modern" enough to marry an old man for money's sake.

Oya, he was Mr. Consul of Chicago.

"Walk in, sir! Uchino hito will return within an hour or so."

Then I explained about "my husband."

We both laughed.

There is nothing more pleasing when in an alien country than a chit-chat in our native "becha becha."

Japanese speech!

Such a beautifully indefinite, poetically untidy language!

I love it.

11th—It would be too much of a risk of one's life to stay in Chicago.

Good-bye!

Flowerless, birdless city, sayonara!

BUFFALO, 12th

Niagara Falls was a disappointment.

Uncle says I have still to learn how to be appreciative of things.

A red brick chimney by the Fall spoils the whole affair, I do think.

My uncle was cross, saying that he had eaten the toughest beef of his life.

He seized two Canadian dimes and a bogus half-dollar in an hour.

"Poor Uncle! Isn't this Buffalo town awful?" I said.

NEW YORK, 13th

Miss Morning Glory has stepped into Greater New York, at last.

Thirteenth of March, 1900.

To-day will be the special day of my family history.

My entrance was delightful to the full.

The train stole gracefully into the city at early morn. The sky was distinct like the lake of Biwa. The respectable face of the city accepted us charmingly.

I bounced my little body in my happy thought of another chapter of life.

I felt like Dante crawled out of darkest Hell, after the torture of the terrible show. (O Chicago!)

Our kind Japanese consul of New York was looking after our arrival with a carriage.

I saw a horse-car trotting.

It encouraged me to think that even an ignorant Jap might find her own living here, since such an old-fashioned thing exists perfectly.

I secretly fixed in my mind that I will adventure my independent life when the crisis demands.

Our carriage rolled up Fifth Avenue to Central Park.

How often had I imagined laying me in this celebrated ground!

"Pray, let me off to smell the smell of the New York breeze!" I exclaimed.

When I was stationed on the third floor of an edifice on Riverside Drive—what a brisk name in the world!—which was Mr. Consul's home, my bubbling fancies hastened down with the waters of the Hudson River under my window.

Hudson River?

It is my dear old acquaintance, introduced by the ever so pleasing Mr. Irving.

See its classical profundity before my face!

Where's "Sleepy Hollow," I wonder!

The spectacle of the river reminded me of the Sumida Gawa of Tokio, mirroring the clouds of affectionate cherry blossoms which border its bank. It would be a remarkable idea, I thought, to petition the Mayor of New York for the Japanese cherry-trees to parade on this side of the Hudson. When they are in flower, I will open a tea-house under them, of course. My attire as a mistress should be a little red crape apron to begin with. My head will be wound with a Japanese towel to endow my Oriental eyes with certain better results. I will raise my voice, calling, "Honourable rest! Honourable tea plucked by the choicest musumes!" What a novel!

Romance!

How can I live without it!

In that case I must entreat the removal of the characters on the other side, which are:

"Lots For Sale!"

Because I don't see any such unaristocratic sign by the Sumida Gawa.

14th—O snow, yukiya fure, fure!

The season of the city is still within the fence of winter. I was grateful to my fate that conveyed me here to overtake my loving snow.

I settled me by my window in absorption with the snow view of Hudson Gawa.

How busily the snowflakes fall!

Their cautiously silent hurry made me recollect the drama of the China-Japan war. How stealthily the soldiers marched at midnight! Can I ever forget how I tugged my shoji, crying "Victory, Dai Nippon!"

I raised the window, stretching out my arm. I collected the snow-petals in the hollow of my palm. I tasted them.

"Uncle, New York snow is as deliciously savoured as at home," I said.

Central Park must have been artistically attired.

"Oji San, let us go to the park for snow-viewing! I advise you to till a bit more poetry in yourself, Uncle," I announced.

I began to change my dress before his decision.

15th—We went to the famous Brooklyn Bridge.

Verily, New York gentlemen are interested with their papers in the car. Newspapers, O newspapers! There's no slip of a doubt that they would die without the sight of their newspapers. The unheroic part about them is that they forget nearly to offer their seats to a lady. Woman loves an absent-minded man once in a while, but never on the car, I do say.

I suppose every woman of this city has to be rich.

Must I equip a carriage?

I do not see why I could not win the first prize with my Louisiana ticket.

How I wish to fabric an every-inch-a-Japanese mansion on Fifth Avenue, and welcome a thousand tojins to hear my Jap song on Sunday!

"Is this bridge built for Americans or Europeans, Uncle? People crossing here use no English," I said.

"Liberty Statue!"

I will let the Beauty statue hail from the Bay of Yedo, when I am wealthy enough to afford it.

Doesn't Nippon signify beauty?

"How dear is that sign, 'Beware of Pickpockets!' It makes me just feel as if I were at Shinbashi station in Tokio, doesn't it you, Uncle?"

Humbly humble 'rikisha men!

If I were besieged by them imploring me to take a little honourable ride, the scene would be complete.

I miss such a merry car in Amerikey.

We walked down Broadway. We came to a graveyard.

Tombstones in the midst of commerce!

O romantic New York!

I wondered how Wall Street gentlemen would be struck glancing at them.

What a soft silence hovered!

The old Gothic Church was my own ideal.

"Uncle, let us fall in and rest!" I cried.

The morning service was proceeding.

Alas and alas!

Not one soul was there.

Is this a religious city?

The inside was compact of heavenly purple air. Mr. Bishop—whatever he may be—gestured like another being from a loftier realm. A beautiful boy (there's no greater fascination than a boy with a prayer-book) supported the service. Intangibleness of speech is itself a divine charm.

"Will you mind asking Mr. Bishop whether he wants a sweeping girl? I wish I were given just a chance to clean such a holy church, uncle."

Then I looked up to Mr. Secretary.

16th—It seems to me a recent style that New York ladies discard their babies to leave them in the hands of European immigrants (very likely they want them to learn an ungrammatical hodge-podge, as respectableness is old-fashioned) and accompany a dog with mighty affection.

O my dear "chin" that I left at home!

Shall I call it to Amerikey?

Little loyal thing, pathetic, clinging!

I am sure it would beat any other in a dog contest.

17th—I never saw such hungry eyes in my life as those of an organ-grinder, set upon the windows for a dropping penny.

To an artist they would hint of a prisoner's bloodshot eyes numbed by useless gazing toward the light of the world.

Poor Italians!

They don't know one thing but turning the handle.

The last two days they placed their organ—read their sign, "Garibaldi & Co."—under my apartment at the same hour for my bit money.

I thought one of them might be a grandson of the renowned Italian patriot. How interesting it would be to be told of his shipwreck in life!

Now three o'clock.

There's one more hour before their frolic music will gush.

I must wrap some money in paper for them.

God bless them—simple creatures who work hard!

18th—Mr. Consul—an old man who sips the grayness of celibacy—never strays out from his official duty. He calls society and novels two recent pieces of foolery.

The family of Uncle's intimate is off in Europe.

The possibility of a nice time for me is verily illegible. Tsumaranai!

Last night I sketched an adventure of enlisting in the band of domestics.

"Capital idea to examine a New York household!" I said, when I left my breakfast table.

I humbled myself to a newspaper office with the following shamefaced advertisement:

"Jap girl, nineteen, good-looking, longs for a place in family of the first rank."

I used every kind of oratory to bring my uncle to agree to my two weeks of freedom.

19th—Two letters were waiting me at the office.

One from No. 296 of a certain part.

296?

Unfortunately it sounds like "nikumu" in Japanese, meaning hatred.

And the other was from Fifth Avenue.

Parlour maid.

Twelve dollars for a month.

I shall accept it, since it is the proper quarter for seeing the high-toned New Yorker.

I feel already a servant feeling.

I am sorry that I didn't discipline myself before in dusting.

I will style me an honest worker for awhile. "Toiling for my daily bread," does ring an American sound, doesn't it?

"Domestic girl has no right, I think, to sit with Messrs. Consul and Secretary," I said, moving my dinner plate to the kitchen table.

Morning Glory, isn't it time you changed the book of your diary?

Really, sir!

Let me close now with a ceremonious bow!

My next book shall be entitled:

"THE DIARY OF A PARLOUR MAID."

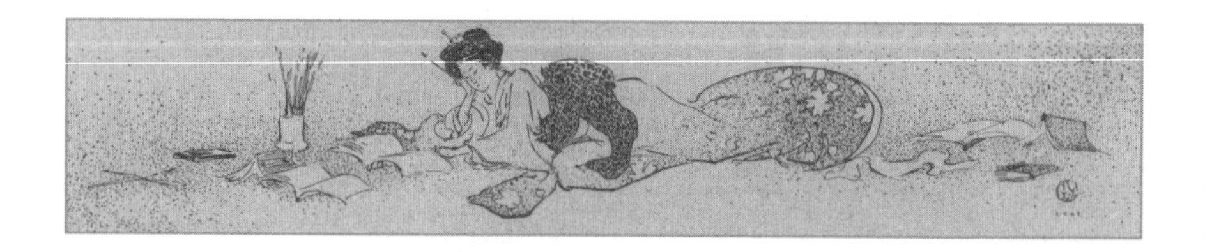

Afterword

IN THE EARLY SUMMER OF 1901, Noguchi left the "cozy and nice room" on Manhattan's prestigious Riverside Drive he had occupied rent free since November and moved to 41 East 19th Street, two blocks north of Union Square, a building he later described to Charles Warren Stoddard as "a Jap boarding[house], full of prank and noise."[1] He had finished the manuscript of his novel, and he apologized to Stoddard for his long silence, explaining he had been "writing some long piece" since February. "They are an American diary of certain Japanese girl. Think how charming they must be!" The manuscript had been accepted by *Frank Leslie's Popular Monthly Magazine,* and Noguchi was about to meet a Japanese artist the editor had arranged to do illustrations. "As for me," he complained, "I rather prefer some good one among American artists." He was planning to leave shortly for Bayonne, New Jersey, and "if the editor will pay a big money," he told Stoddard, "I will come to you to spend a few weeks."[2]

Ellery Sedgwick, the chief editor at *Leslie's,* had said his manuscript "was the best one he ever came across for many years."[3] The opinion should not be taken lightly, for Sedgwick, a twenty-nine-year-old Harvard graduate, was well on his way to becoming one of the most influential editors of his day (he eventually became president of the *Atlantic Monthly*). But the manuscript's favorable reception probably owed something to the magazine's glamorous owner, Mrs. Frank Leslie, an intimate friend, admirer, and—purportedly—lover of Noguchi's mentor, Joaquin Miller.[4] Though Miller's reputation rose and fell precipitously over the years, his literary productions had always received the most favorable treatment within the *Leslie's* organization, and

Mrs. Leslie had recently given public recitations of Miller's poetry.[5] Noguchi had already benefited from his connection to Mrs. Leslie's beloved poet: in 1897 a short article, "Joaquin Miller and Yone Naguchi [*sic*]," appeared in *Leslie's Illustrated Weekly* around the time Noguchi's first book of poems was published. The article had announced that "our virile poet of the Sierras" was devoting himself "to the cultivation of an exotic talent" whose work "shows unmistakable evidences of native genius." Noguchi presumably hoped to avail himself further of this special treatment by including in his manuscript a monthlong visit by Miss Morning Glory to the home of Heine, a poet easily recognizable as a stand-in for Miller.

Sedgwick's enthusiasm had its limits, however, and he informed Noguchi on 25 July that the novel was too long for serial publication (a curious claim, since the novel was short by contemporary standards). Serial publication, he explained to Noguchi, required "that a reader's interest from month to month must be stimulated by a definite plot, if he is to retain the previous installments in his memory," and the *Diary* was rather lacking in plot—although he was quick to assure Noguchi that the story did have "a springliness and originality which I find quite delightful and which will not be lost, I think, upon readers who have ideas of what literary merit means." Sedgwick thought it best to "select two or three passages . . . and publish them in two or three installments in the Magazine" with some compression, though the editing would be under Noguchi's supervision. The whole could then be published as a book in the spring, and Sedgwick promised, "Whatever I can do about introducing you to publishers or steering you to your goal, I will do gladly." This steering effort proved effective, for Noguchi ended up contracting with the respectable firm of Frederick A. Stokes, whose *Pocket Magazine* had recently merged with *Leslie's Monthly*. Stokes, a Brooklyn-born Yale graduate, had some interest in Japan; his firm sold English translations of several books by Pierre Loti and was about to bring out a U.S. edition of Clive Holland's 1895 novel, *My Japanese Wife*. A decade later, Stokes would make a respectable contribution to the literature on Japan with the U.S. edition of Ernest Fenollosa's *Epochs of Chinese and Japanese Art*.[6]

Noguchi was not unhappy with the arrangement and thought the artist, Genjirō Yeto, "pretty good, but not very great."[7] Yeto, born Genjirō Kataoka (1867–1924), had come to the United States in 1893, the same year Noguchi arrived. A native of Arita, a Kyūshū town famous for export pottery, he had enrolled in 1895 at the New York Art Students' League (later attended by Noguchi's son, Isamu Noguchi), working under the Japanese-influenced painters John Twachtman and Robert Blum, among others, and spending his summers with them in the Connecticut art colony of Cos Cob. As an illustrator of books related to Japan, he had risen to prominence with his design and illustrations for the Harper and Brothers edition of Onoto Watanna's

A Japanese Nightingale in 1901; along with Noguchi's book, he was illustrating Lafcadio Hearn's *Kottó* for Macmillan.[8]

Noguchi continued "dreaming of success" and warned his friends to keep his authorship a secret. "If you expose," he admonished Stoddard, "our friendship will be end. Isn't it awful? So, keep the secret!"[9] The first of two excerpts from the story appeared in *Frank Leslie's Popular Monthly* in November 1901, and Stoddard wrote to send his congratulations on 5 November. Noguchi assured him the congratulations were somewhat premature, as the book would not be out until March, and "Leslie's article is not satisfactory, because it has so many mis-spellings, and the editor condensed horribly." The magazine had left out "some charming part in the girl's living with Joaquin Miller . . . because the public might know who wrote it before the publication as a book." But Noguchi was pleased with the story's reception thus far: "Everybody who has read it praises it so much, although I don't think it as my best work. It is only a girl's diary. The girlish originality was the whole key, you know. It is not Yone Noguchi, but a Japanese girl you know." Noguchi was planning "a companion book if that diary will go well. I mean a 'Japanese girl in England.' Then I must go to England, and it is an easy thing to sail over there."[10] A few weeks later Noguchi had the contract from Stokes, which he sent to Stoddard to sign as witness. The contract stipulated that Noguchi was to get 10 percent of retail after the first thousand copies sold and 15 percent after five thousand. "Oh, Heaven knows when so many copies will be sold!" Noguchi wrote Stoddard.[11]

Toward the end of February 1902, Noguchi left Manhattan for Rochester, in upstate New York, where he stayed with an unidentified friend. Exhausted, he was depressed by an unpleasant meeting the previous week with Stokes, who wanted to delay publication of the *Diary* for the Christmas market. Noguchi was eagerly awaiting the promised April publication and thought it "really foolish to wait so long, without any definite idea how many copies should go when it were published in Christmas season." After the meeting he wrote to Stokes, who seemed to acquiesce but in fact did not change his plan. (The delay and the depressing tone of the meeting may have been related to turmoil in the *Leslie's* organization: Mrs. Frank Leslie had suffered a debilitating stroke in December, and the syndicate with which she had contracted to run her publications was in the process of ousting her from the organization.) Though Noguchi played down the seriousness of the meeting, writing his collaborator Léonie Gilmour that he thought "the book will go all the same when it made a fine starting," he tried to prepare for the worst, conceding in a postscript that he really didn't see "any bright prospect" for it. "I am not disappointed if it made a failure," he told her.[12]

Noguchi was in better spirits at the end of March, and the proofs finally arrived in April, after some delay. He planned to leave Rochester at the end of

April, perhaps for England, but ended up going to see Stoddard in Washington, returning to Rochester in May. He thought about returning to New York City, but "truly I am afraid to go back to New York in Summer season, which cruel impression I felt last year. Perhaps I will not return till Autumn that is to say September or October." Instead, he would remain in Rochester and start working on a sequel, which, he explained to Gilmour, "will be the group of letters written by a Jap girl (M[orning]. G[lory].) who adventures as a chamber maid in some New York rich family." "You will see how clever she could be," he promised. "I am writing the letter already in my mind, not on the paper yet. And I am trying how they will look."[13] He expected to start writing in June and was counting on Gilmour's help when she returned from her summer trip. By 11 September, the manuscripts for the sequel, *The American Letters of a Japanese Parlor-Maid*, were in Gilmour's hands, and Noguchi was relieved to hear her opinion that they were "all right."[14]

In early October 1902, the first copies of the *Diary* arrived from Stokes. Reviews began appearing in the second week of October, mainly the short notices typical of the holiday season, and for the most part they were favorable. Stokes gave a fair amount of publicity to the book, sending review copies to newspapers nationwide and employing an agency to collect reviews (more than sixty of which were eventually forwarded to Noguchi).[15] Noguchi remained in New York a few weeks after publication, then departed on his long-deferred transatlantic voyage in early November, arriving in London on 20 November. During his absence, Gilmour kept him informed of the fortunes of the *Diary*.

Miss Morning Glory's Fortunes

The popularity of "exotic" literature created special difficulties for reviewers. Misleading or false claims of authenticity and authorship were common, and reviewers were rarely in a position to make accurate assessments. Faced with this unprecedented work, they were even more at sea than usual.[16] Many readers had some acquaintance with the subject of Japan, for "everything Japanese seems now fashionable in literature," as a reviewer for the Des Moines *Register Leader* complained. But the barrage of information seemed often contradictory, and this was particularly the case with the ever-fascinating subject of the Japanese woman. Was she, like Loti's Madame Chrysanthème, a coquettish and deceitful mercenary; an amusing, domesticated curiosity like Mousmé in Clive Holland's *My Japanese Wife*; or an easily misled tragic victim as in John Luther Long's famous tale? Did she resemble the otherworldly wraiths of Lafcadio Hearn's supernatural stories, the diligent samurai daughters of

Alice Bacon's *Japanese Girls and Women*, or the melodramatic heroines of Onoto Watanna? Miss Morning Glory expressed her views on the matter clearly enough by accusing Loti of spoiling the word "Madame" and by throwing "Mr. Wrong's" book from a train platform. Curiously, Noguchi left Watanna out of the attack—Morning Glory noted simply, "I am glad I see no lady writer of Japanese novels yet" (119).[17]

Noguchi had first heard of Watanna (whose real name was Winnifred Eaton) in February 1899, when he received an inquiring letter from Chicago journalist Frank Putnam, Watanna's close friend and possibly her lover. "You say Onoto Watanna?" Noguchi wrote back. "Such is not Japanese name. Is she real Japanese lady?"[18] Watanna welcomed Noguchi when he passed through Chicago the following June. Noguchi told Stoddard to write him at Groveland Avenue, "where my dearest friend lives and I visit nearly every evening. She is a half caste woman with the name Onoto Watanna; her mother was Japanese, father being an English [*sic*]; she herself being very bright writes now and then very clever short stories for magazines. . . . She published one book from Rand McNally & Co. last year, I believe."[19] Her short story "A Half Caste" had been published in *Leslie's Monthly* in September 1899, and her first novel, *Miss Numè of Japan* (1899), had been favorably reviewed in the *New York Times*. Like Noguchi, Watanna was heading to New York in hopes of greater glory. She took a job writing for the *Brooklyn Eagle*, married, within weeks, a respectable if alcoholic fellow journalist, Bertrand Babcock, and by year's end had published her second novel, *A Japanese Nightingale*, to enthusiastic reviews and brisk sales that eventually reached two hundred thousand copies.[20]

Noguchi, quietly tending his furnace on Riverside Drive as he labored to complete his own relatively unacclaimed novel, observed Watanna's activities at a distance, perhaps through the intermediary of their shared illustrator, Genjirō Yeto. "I don't quarrel with her," he explained to Putnam. "But she is not the woman I admire you know. So I slipped away from her long time ago."[21] Reluctance to criticize a former friend was his explanation for declining to review the disastrous dramatic adaptation of Watanna's *A Japanese Nightingale* in 1903, and it probably explains her absence from the *Diary*.[22] But Morning Glory's oblique jab at the "unprincipled half-caste" type points to the simmering animosity that eventually emerged in a scathing article Noguchi published a few years after his return to Japan, "Onoto Watanna and Her Japanese Work." Remarkably, there is no indication he ever guessed the secret that her half-Japanese identity was a fabrication.[23]

Despite Watanna's odd absence from the novel's critique of the "Japanese fad in America," Noguchi's targets were clear enough. But if Noguchi hoped to expel the Japanese women of Long, Watanna, Loti, and company from the

American imagination, he was to be sadly disappointed, for readers clung tenaciously to their favorite character types. The *New York Evening Sun* reviewer, who mistook Genjirō Yeto as the author of the *Diary*, was among those whose expectations Miss Morning Glory disappointed:

> It is hard to believe that a real Japanese girl's conversation, when translated into English, is anything like that of Miss Morning Glory in "The American Diary of a Japanese Girl" by "Genjiro Yeto." We have always understood that women's Japanese—which, by the way, differs materially from the men's talk, both in words and form of sentences, was poetic, charming and anything but grotesque.
>
> "The Diary of a Japanese Girl," however, has a little too much of the consciously grotesque and of smart effect to convince one that it is genuinely Oriental. "Genjiro Yeto" may possibly be Japanese, but there is a fair showing of the twentieth century Occidental hand in the diary, although the writer of it clearly knows something of Tokio ways.

Most of the early reviews did accept the authenticity of the *Diary*. The *Buffalo Express* confidently declared it "an impossible feat for anyone with a drop of Western blood." This review may have been planted by someone connected with *Leslie's Monthly*, for it appeared there the following week, but other reviewers followed suit, implicitly or explicitly accepting the book as authored by a Japanese girl. The reviewer for *Town and Country* thought the book "evidently genuine." "It is edifying to see ourselves at times as others see us," said the *Boston Gazette*, a sentiment echoed by the *Albany Times-Union*.

After a month, however, doubts became apparent. The book "purports to be written by a Japanese girl," began the *Philadelphia Inquirer's* review on 16 November. The *Gloucester (Mass.) Times* also used the word "purports" the following day, as did the *Pittsburgh Dispatch* the next week. "One would like to believe in a tangible, actual Miss Morning Glory, she is such a flesh and blood little Japanese," wrote a wary but hopeful reviewer in the *New York Tribune*. Several reviews published on 22 November articulated the doubts more explicitly. Miss Morning Glory "expresses herself like a 'Jap,' and her observations are such as seem natural for one new to the concomitants of Occidental civilization," wrote the *Milwaukee Wisconsin* reviewer, "and yet there is a something 'between the lines' that seems to reveal the cunning work of one who is more American than Japanese." The *Pittsburgh Chronicle* reviewer declared the book "a highly fantastical diary of an imaginary Japanese girl" (though an amusing one) and predicted that "its greatest claim to favor will be as a curiosity of many sided modern authorship." The *Des Moines Register-Leader's* doubting reviewer injected a note of racism, observing snidely that the book "purports to be the experiences and impressions of a slant-eyed young miss from Japan." The same reviewer correctly surmised that Miss Morning Glory, "if born in the land of the fuzzy flowers, has at least lived long and much in this country." The *San Francisco Bulletin* reviewer, also "compelled to doubt the authenticity of Miss Morning Glory's journal," got still closer to the truth, suggesting that "her piquancies would be possible in a Japanese man, but they are hardly such as the best authorities indicate that the Japanese female is capable of." (The "best authorities" here meant Lafcadio Hearn, from whom the reviewer had gathered that "the girls of that populous island are not flirtatious in a very active fashion, and are taught to be practical and obedient rather than frivolous and venturesome.")

One of the more curious racially tinged critiques appeared in William Randolph Hearst's New York magazine, *Town and Country*:

> Although the little Japanese girl here published in very attractive form the diary of her visit to the States, she gives us really very little insight into the impressions made upon her by the extraordinary novelty which our customs must have been to her. This is probably because she is merely an unsophisticated little Japanese mousmi [*sic*], with a mind untrained to the analysis of emotion. These pages mainly contain the artless prattlings of an Oriental maiden interested more in her pretty self, her pretty clothes and pretty compliments, than in the vast differences between the East and West. There is a fulness, an ingenuousness in her confidences that is delightful, and as there is no plot and barely a suggestion of a love theme, the book is evidently genuine.

Aside from this ambivalent attack on the sophistication of the Japanese "mousmi" and the gratuitous "slant-eyed miss" slur of the *Des Moines* writer, there was little overt racism in some three dozen reviews. We may partly attribute this to the lack of organized racial antagonism toward the Japanese at this time. But considering the virulent animosity toward the Chinese, and Americans' poor understanding of the difference between the two countries, Noguchi deserves credit for his success in navigating the perilous waters of American racial discourse.

In total, about half the reviews were strongly or moderately favorable, and most of the remainder were ambivalent or noncommittal, with negative reviews accounting for only 10 or 15 percent of the total. There were, to be sure, a fair number of criticisms of Miss Morning Glory's general manner, but these attacks focused on factors other than race. To understand these criticisms, which were present also in some of the favorable reviews, one must look deeper into the question of the novel's generic affinities. Although, as we have noted, the novel was compared to other stories about Japanese women by writers like Loti, Holland, Long, Watanna, and Hearn, in fact *The American Diary of a Japanese Girl* bears little resemblance to these works in style, narrative, or the characteristics of its protagonist. What, then, were its antecedents?

One answer to this question is suggested by the name of a now largely forgotten author to whom at least three reviewers compared Miss Morning Glory. "And behold! Now we have a Japanese Mary MacLane," announced the *San Francisco Bulletin*. The *Chicago Advance* thought the book "might be a second edition of Mary MacLane, refined and tamed and stripped of her intensity." The *Chicago Record-Herald* observed: "It sounds like 'Mary McLane' [*sic*] in its absence of delicate reserve, and its patent belief that what the writer thinks is sure to be of interest." In fact, MacLane's sensational diary, *The Story of Mary MacLane*, which sold eighty thousand copies in its first four weeks, could not have influenced Noguchi's *Diary*, for it had only been published in April—months after the serialized *American Diary*. Nevertheless, reviewers were right to notice a resemblance between the scandalous twenty-one-year-old diarist from Butte, Montana, and her Japanese counterpart. Miss Morning Glory was mild compared to MacLane, who called herself "a genius, a thief, a liar—a general moral vagabond, a fool more or less, and a philosopher of the peripatetic school"—and wrote brazenly of devil worship and her passionate desire for a female teacher.[24] But both were outspoken, iconoclastic, mischievous, and vain, and deeper similarities in the style of the diaries point to common influences.

MacLane was the best known and most outrageous of the confessional diarists, but she was by no means the first. The vogue for confessional women's diaries, as Cathryn Halverson explains in her informative account of the MacLane phenomenon, began with *Le journal de Marie Bashkirtseff*, posthumously published in 1887 and appearing in English in 1889 as *The Journal of a Young Artist, 1860–1884*.[25] The popularity of these uninhibited confessions of an astonishingly self-absorbed young woman artist in pursuit of fame, love, and artistic glory, struggling simultaneously against bourgeois morals, the restricted role of women, and a fatal disease, encouraged many imitations—some authentic diaries and some fictional ones, though the distinction was often hard to make. These included Octave Mirbeau's *Le journal d'une femme de chambre* (1900), published in English as *A Chambermaid's Diary* (1900); *An Englishwoman's Love-Letters* (written by Laurence Housman, published anonymously in 1900 but subsequently acknowledged by its author); and Miles Franklin's *My Brilliant Career* (1901), which purported to be the diary of a rural Australian heroine, dubbed "the Bashkirtseff of the bush" by Havelock Ellis. Beyond question, the most dramatic American follower was MacLane, "the Butte Bashkirtseff," whom a critic for the *Literary World* described as "Marie Bashkirtseff raised to the 9th power of ignorance, indecency, and an illimitable absorption, with a dash of delirium tremens added."[26] It is difficult to know how many of these books Noguchi read, but he certainly read Bashkirtseff, as he was eager to read her newly published *Last Confessions* in July 1901 and told Gilmour afterward that, although he "expected much more," he "was not disappointed."[27] He later met Laurence Housman in London, and his letter to Gilmour about the meeting indicates they were both familiar with Housman's *An Englishwoman's Love-Letters*.[28] And he corresponded with MacLane, who initially disliked the copy of the *Diary* he sent her but later revised her opinion to call it "charming," adding, "You are clever, aren't you?"[29]

The confessional diaries were highly popular, but while their admirers praised their amusing, iconoclastic, and liberating qualities, critics broadly condemned them as frivolous, immoral, and disgusting. The debate over their value and popularity created the terms in which *The American Diary* was evaluated, as critics viewed Miss Morning Glory's mannerisms, her egoism and apparent lack of seriousness, and her snippy attacks on bourgeois culture, and then attempted to locate her place within the disreputable subgenre. The reviewer for the *Newark News* wrote, "'Miss Morning Glory's comments on this country would perhaps awaken mild interest were it not for the disgust they occasionally inspire." "The tone of the book is light to frivolity and the satire is light, even frothy," said the *Pittsburgh Dispatch*, which nevertheless conceded: "Still much of it goes home and many a thrust at national foibles will touch to the quick the supersensitive patriot by its truth." The *Chicago Record-Herald* was not so generous:

> The greatest part of the volume is flat and unprofitable, and we regret to say, when it rises beyond flatness, it takes the direction of coarseness. Miss Morning Glory's thoughts, expressed tete-a-tete, might seem highly piquant, but read in cold type they either bore or arouse repugnance. Pierre Loti and John Luther Long have given us portrayals of delicately feminine creatures whom, by the way, Miss Morning Glory ridicules. But candidly we prefer their fiction to her truth, if truth it be. She is funny sometimes and lively, but unmaidenly, in our sense of the word, and she betrays a curious familiarity with the alleys of life. Miss Morning Glory is too sophisticated for her role.

Like other confessional diaries, Noguchi's book was also criticized for its absence of plot. Long's *Madame Butterfly* owed much of its success to an effective tragic plot, and Onoto Watanna made heavy use of melodramatic plot devices to stimulate reader interest. Noguchi refused to follow their lead, telling Gilmour: "You know how I hate the plot in a story. Whenever I see any bungling invention in it I am disgusted."[30] He had earlier refused to include even a romantic interest, telling Blanche Partington: "I wish you will stop to plan to make the Diary as a story; because O'cho-san is a new comer to this country and naturally cannot have any romance."[31] Finally, he did allow Miss Morning Glory to develop a romantic interest in a young artist, Oscar Ellis. But as the reviewer for the *New York News and Mail* wrote: "Nothing serious happens, and she goes on her butterfly way serenely, gurgling over her own jokes and getting no end of satisfaction out of her own quick perceptions." The book was "decidedly light," but lightness was for many readers a positive attribute, and other reviews referred favorably to the diarist's "light touch."

In short, the reviews suggest that the book was received, as its creators presumably intended, as an exotic twist on a trendy if somewhat disreputable subgenre. Nevertheless, Stokes began to send disappointing news in December 1902, two months after publication. Sales, which started out well, were proving somewhat disappointing. Stokes informed Gilmour that some bookstores had begun returning their overstock, and that reorders were few. Stokes returned the manuscript for the sequel, *The American Letters of a Japanese Parlor-Maid*, although he politely suggested that if Noguchi did not succeed in making "advantageous arrangements" for its publication he would reconsider the matter in 1904.[32] Apparently *Leslie's Monthly* was also declining to serialize the sequel. Although the magazine still carried the name of Mrs. Frank Leslie, control was now in the hands of a syndicate, and the former owner, now calling herself the Baroness of Bazus, no longer wielded any editorial power.

Noguchi, receiving the bad news, wrote back despondently to Gilmour on 2 January 1903:

> Oh, Léonie! Such Stokes! D—!! What he means in the world! Can't help it though! He is a business man. I cannot blame him a bit. Simply it is my misfortune. Such a letter made me awful bad in feeling. I asked him a few times whether he was sure about publication of my second book. "Certainly", he said. Well, at that time he wasn't sure that the Diary may not go. So my venture was quite a failure. Isn't it really too bad? What do you advise me to do with the American Letters, I wonder? I think that I will try elsewhere. It may be wiser than to wait for some encouraging letter from Stokes. I know that he was trying best he could.[33]

Noguchi advised Gilmour to continue trying for serial publication of the *Letters*, suggesting the *Saturday Evening Post* or the *Smart Set*. "If the 'Smart-set' also [r]ejected it I think I will drop such an idea to publish in any paper," he wrote. The planned third volume of Miss Morning Glory's English adventures had gotten off to a slow start, as Noguchi found London "hard to penetrate in." "I think that it would be better to give up my hope to bring Miss Morning Glory here in London," he had told Gilmour soon after his arrival, explaining that "she cannot do much actually, you know." Noguchi turned his energy to his poetic project in England with fairly spectacular results—he was soon the talk of literary London—but Miss Morning Glory ended her fictional existence after a mere four days in London.[34]

The secret of Miss Morning Glory's identity remained more or less intact. No one seems to have paid much attention to Noguchi's friend Frank Putnam, an editor for *National Magazine*, who could not resist blurting out the truth in a note entitled "Is This Another of Noguchi's Pranks?" published in the December 1902 number, which "speculated" that Noguchi was the author and even included a portrait of Noguchi by Genjirō Yeto. Another writer friend, Zona Gale, also let the cat out of the bag in the summer of 1903, when she gave an exaggerated account of Noguchi's life to a reporter for the *New York Evening World*. The reporter "may ornament her story with some details that are not true," Gale warned Noguchi, "but you will not mind that if it helps on, I am sure." Noguchi's friends were amused at the resulting article's exaggerations: "To think that we should learn at the same time that you are Lord Marquis as well as Miss Morning-Glory!" wrote Thomas Walsh. "What a many sided life you must lead!"[35] Ellery Sedgwick, however, was furious at the journalist's exposure of the author, and he reprimanded Noguchi: "How often have I told you that you should be under my care to avoid such dangers from reporters and things."[36] Of course, Sedgwick was speaking on behalf of *Leslie's*, which might have suffered from readers' accusations of deception, for the revelations could hardly have endangered the reputation of either Noguchi or Miss Morning Glory, as Morning Glory's American prospects were all but finished.[37]

But Noguchi was not about to let Morning Glory's literary life end so prematurely. After his return to Japan in 1904, he arranged to have the Tokyo publisher Fuzanbō issue both *The American Diary of a Japanese Girl* and its sequel, *The American Letters of a Japanese Parlor-Maid*.[38] He also prepared a Japanese translation of *American Diary*, which was published by Tōadō shobō in 1905 as *Hōbun nihon shōjo no beikoku nikki* (The American Diary of a Japanese Girl in the Vernacular).[39] "A Japanese Girl's One Week in London" appeared in 1906 in *Eigo Seinen*, a prominent magazine for Japanese students of English language and literature. The Tokyo publications all clearly identified

Noguchi as the author and dispensed with any pretense of a "tangible, actual Miss Morning Glory." As in the Fuzanbō edition of Noguchi's 1903 poetry collection, *From the Eastern Sea*, the Fuzanbō *Diary* included a long appendix detailing the book's reception, framing it as an experiment in Japanese authorship in the English literary world. Where the former volume incorporated an appendix documenting the favorable reception of Noguchi's poetry by English "men of letters," the Fuzanbō *American Diary's* documentary appendix emphasized the success of Noguchi's impersonation, with a lengthy discussion devoted to Gelett Burgess's comical efforts to meet the purported author. A final "fifth edition" of the *Diary* appeared a few years later, after Noguchi had established an arrangement to sell his books under Elkin Mathews's imprint in London. Appearing under Noguchi's name, the novel thus belatedly achieved a small circulation in Britain.[40] But its authorship remained somewhat obscure in the United States, where the book has received little attention in the century following its publication.

Miss Morning Glory in Japan

"The Novel and Its Reception The impact of these works in Japan has also received little attention, for Japanese critics, like their U.S. counterparts, tend to regard Noguchi as an essentially foreign writer. This oversight is unfortunate, for there is ample evidence that internationally minded younger Japanese writers read and discussed Noguchi's work extensively after his return in 1904. Many of these writers read English fiction, and the Japanese translation of the *American Diary* (which went through several printings) made the work available even to those who did not. It is interesting to note certain resemblances between Noguchi's work and Sōseki Natsume's important first novel, *Wagahai wa neko de aru* (I Am a Cat [1905–6]), the satirical diary of a cat living in the house of a Japanese English professor, which may have been inspired by Morning Glory's squirrel-diary experiment. It is possible that Miss Morning Glory had some influence on the *shi-shōsetsu*, or "I-novel," an important genre of autobiographical fiction, usually offering little plot or characterization, that made its appearance around 1907. Noguchi was on friendly terms with a number of leading fiction writers of the period, including Tōson Shimazaki, Katai Tayama, and Hōmei Iwano, as well as the leading fiction theorist of the day, Shōyō Tsubouchi, who wrote a prefatory note for the *American Letters*.

Tsubouchi's note helps place Noguchi's work in Japanese literary history in another way, for Tsubouchi is regarded as one of the founders of the modern Japanese novel. Tsubouchi's *Shōsetsu Shinzui* (The Essence of the Novel [1886]) the first attempt to "transplant to Japan the concept of the modern novel in a well-delineated form,"[41] as Noguchi put it, was widely read and discussed at the time Noguchi attended college, as was the 1887 novel in which Tsubouchi put his method into practice. "His 'Shosei Katagi' was a sweeping triumph," Noguchi wrote. "It was an example of a realistic novel with little plot of dramatic incident but made up of graphic sketches which successfully carried out the Western idea of characterization. Its clever fellow and beautiful girl—'saishi' and 'kajin,' as we say in Japanese—won the perfect confidence of the young readers."[42] The *American Diary*, too, offered readers "a realistic novel with little plot of dramatic incident," and Noguchi clearly sought to create in Miss Morning Glory a heroine both clever and beautiful.

There is also a far older Japanese tradition to which the *American Diary* lays claim, for *nikki bungaku*, or diary literature, is one of the oldest Japanese literary genres. It is said to have its roots in government annals of the seventh century written in *kanbun*, a Japanese form of the Chinese language. The first diary considered to have literary value, Ki no Tsurayuki's *Tosa Diary* (written in 935), was, like Noguchi's book, written by a male author posing as a Japanese woman. "His dignity forced him to apologize by saying that he was a woman writer," Noguchi explains in an article, "Japanese Women in Literature."[43] Tsurayuki's imposture enabled him to discard *kanbun* for the more familiar Japanese, then thought to be an appropriate literary language only for women, who were not schooled in Chinese learning. Miss Morning Glory's closer spiritual ancestor, however, may be Sei Shōnagon, whose well-known *Pillow-Book*, written around the end of the tenth century, shares the whimsical quality of the *American Diary*. "It is the best example of a style of elegance, refinement, delicacy, and the perspicacity of sentiment, which afterward set the fashion called 'Following the Pen,'" Noguchi explained. "Her book is a thousand little sketches and observations of her court-life." "Following the pen," or *zuihitsu*, refers to a personal, impressionistic, spontaneous style of literary essay that also bears a close relationship to Noguchi's production.[44] These classical Japanese women's diaries, Tomi Suzuki has pointed out, had been "rediscovered" by Japanese writers in the 1880s and 1890s. In the prevailing atmosphere of cultural nationalism, the women's diaries, written in hiragana and thus thought to be less tainted by Chinese influences, were celebrated for their qualities of immediacy, elegance, and grace, ostensible Japanese qualities contrasted to the "heroic and grand" qualities attributed to Chinese literature.[45] The "New Woman Novel" in its Japanese, U.S., and English forms seems also to have influenced Noguchi. In his essay on modern Japanese literature, he writes of Nansui Sudō's *Ladies of a New Style* (*Shinsō no kajin* [1887]), which "inspired a revolution among Japanese ladyhood. The heroine was in the van of the progressive movement. She taught that labor was sacred.

She became a dairymaid. (How new it was if you consider that we didn't use milk in those days!) Her favorite reading was Spencer's 'Education.'"[46]

Miss Morning Glory Today

Whether the *American Diary* is a work best viewed from the perspective of Euro-American literature or from that of Japanese literature is a question that should inspire lively discussion. But today, a century after its first publication, *The American Diary of a Japanese Girl* is likely to be of interest to us primarily as a pioneering work in the new and increasingly important field of Asian American literature. It can justly claim to be the first Japanese American novel, if we take a broad view of Japanese American literature as the literature of Japanese America, as I have suggested elsewhere.[47] Those who prefer to define Japanese American literature exclusively as "the literature of Japanese Americans" may call it the first American novel by a writer of Japanese descent. Either way, it is a remarkable achievement. Literary historians may indeed be baffled by the enormous gap that separates the *American Diary* from the usually cited "first Japanese American novel," John Okada's *No-No Boy*, which did not appear until 1957. Considered within the field of Japanese American life writing, on the other hand, the book takes a less remarkable position. It follows a number of earlier Anglophone Japanese American works, notably Shiukichi Shigemi's *A Japanese Boy* (1890), Tel Sono's *The Japanese Reformer* (1891), and Joseph Heco's *Narrative of a Japanese* (1895), as well as a number of works in Japanese, including earlier travelogues by Joseph Heco and John Manjirō and the autobiography of Yukichi Fukuzawa. Placed in this company—to which we might add U.S.-educated Japanese essayists like Inazō Nitobe, whose *Bushidō* was first published in 1899—we find that Noguchi is not alone in being dismissed as an essentially foreign writer whose writings allegedly "did not express the concerns of Japanese Americans," for none of these works has received much more than a glance in the field of Asian American literature.[48] Yet Noguchi's *Diary* is undoubtedly a novel of Japanese America, although it may not seem, on the surface, to resemble the way early Japanese America is usually imagined today.

One might characterize these "Americanized Japanese" writers, as they are sometimes called, as the "unsettling" Japanese Americans—because they did not, in most cases, settle in America, and because their work may help unsettle some restrictive conceptions of Japanese America created by subsequent generations. It is not surprising that later generations of Japanese Americans, who passed through the usual generational conflicts experienced by immigrant communities under the intensified pressure of wartime nationalism, tended to view first-generation immigrants as deficiently American, obstacles to the

American attachments of their Nisei children. The Issei were indeed ambivalent, as Eiichirō Azuma writes in his informative study *Between Two Empires:* "Because they were always faced with the need to reconcile simultaneous national belongings as citizen-subjects of one state and yet resident-members (denizens) of another, the Issei refused to make a unilateral choice, electing instead to take an eclectic approach to the presumed contradiction between things Japanese and American."[49] For the Issei, this ambivalence represented not a deficiency of nationality, but an enabling doubleness. As internationally inclined Asian Americanists like Yunte Huang have begun to argue forcibly against "nativist trends in literary studies that seek to construct a history of American literature deprived of its transnational character," such views seem to be gaining momentum.[50] In today's globalizing world, multiple identities have again become opportunities, and nationalistic "settling" looks again like settling for less.

At the same time, historical hindsight may remind us, as we read, that things are not always what they seem. In light of the hard experiences of later Japanese American settlers, the perspective of Noguchi's Morning Glory novels may seem idealized, at times even delusory. As citizens of a country closed to the rapidly modernizing outside world for two and a half centuries, Meiji-era Japanese intellectuals were conscious of being perceived as members of a backward nation but believed Japan would be accorded its proper place in the hierarchy of nations as soon as it caught up with the West. This idealism is present in *American Diary* but is perhaps best illustrated by its sequel, *The American Letters of a Japanese Parlor-Maid*, in which Morning Glory undertakes the "adventure" of working as a servant girl. Eventually, her true identity is revealed by the arrival of her wealthy Yale-graduate uncle and the Japanese foreign minister. She then bids a sad farewell to her fellow servants and is welcomed as an equal by her employer, who, it turns out, is a friend of the foreign minister. The Japanese aspirations underlying this allegorical tale would begin to shatter a few years later, when the Japanese, after short-lived congratulations for defeating a powerful Western opponent in the Russo-Japanese War (1904–5), found themselves branded "the new Yellow Peril" and increasingly shunned rather than welcomed as equals. As Japanese idealism about international relations crumbled amid escalating anti-Japanese political agitation and violence, Japanese belatedly began to realize the incorrigibility of American racism and devised more aggressive strategies to achieve recognition.

The Japanese, of course, had chauvinisms of their own. Noguchi would have been deeply uncomfortable with the category "Asian American literature" in which his inclusion is now debated. Morning Glory does not, for example, acknowledge any special sense of connection to the Chinese characters who frequently appear in cameo roles in the *Diary;* on the contrary, she seems mainly interested in mocking the Americans who confuse the Chinese with the Japanese. The Japanese had recently defeated China in the Sino-Japanese War and did not wish to be placed in the same category as their widely reviled Chinese counterparts, let alone the Koreans, who were then being treated to the early stages of Japanese colonization.[51] Noguchi's famous teacher, Yukichi Fukuzawa (who had visited pre–Civil War America in his youth as a junior member of the "Errand Bearers" celebrated in Whitman's famous poem) is now also remembered for counseling Japanese on the need to "escape from Asia" and follow the ways of the powerful Western nations. There is, to be sure, a strong sensitivity to ethnicity in *American Diary* and some evident effort to treat all ethnic groups ambivalently, if not impartially. But one finds little sense of cultural commonality or the shared fate of ethnic exclusion that would later come to characterize Asian American identities. Nor was the Japanese immigrant community itself as cohesive as is sometimes believed, for the sense of national unity in Japan was of fairly recent development, and divisions between Japanese social classes and disparate regional groups remained strong. The cigar-shop proprietress O Fuji san is the nearest thing to a working-class Japanese immigrant that Miss Morning Glory encounters in the novel. Elsewhere in Noguchi's writings, where there is evidence of a wider range of contacts, there are strong indications of class consciousness, and the encounters usually have a practical, rather than a social, basis. For instance, Noguchi writes in a typical passage describing his California travels: "It was fortunate, perhaps, to find a Japanese keeping a bamboo store or laundry shop, or working on a farm, wherever I went along the coast, who welcomed me, as my name was very well known to him; I was often begged to stay, if possible, indefinitely. I was glad that I could wash my stockings, or shirts even, with hot water prepared by him; he would be pleased also if I served him by writing an English letter or interpreting a business transaction."[52]

All this is not to say that we cannot find parallels between Noguchi's novel and other works of the period by Asian Americans and writers from other immigrant groups. Indeed, intergroup rivalries are undoubtedly more prevalent in immigrant discourses of identity in this period than any sense of panethnic solidarity. Morning Glory's journey through the United States is a journey through the signs and discourses of racial difference, which she studies with great interest and learns to use in ways that enhance her self-valuation. She is fascinated that her white friend Ada "would rather mumble a nigger song than a chapter from the Bible," and she picks up on the key phrases in the "coon songs" made famous by white musicians in blackface in which blackness signifies anxieties about money and social class. In one song, the singer's girlfriend informs him: "If you ain't got no money, you needn't come round" (this tune, significantly, emanates from a bar called the Klondyke, evoking the failed dreams of would-be gold miners). In another, the supposedly black singer rejoices that his gal "is a high born lady," noting that "she's dark but not too shady." Like the Irish, who, as David Roediger has argued, discovered that "the pleasures of whiteness could function as a 'wage'" and that "status and privileges conferred by race could be used to make up for alienating and exploitative class relationships," the Japanese perceived both the tangible and symbolic goods claimed by whiteness and the enormous losses of these goods entailed by blackness.[53] The power of racial stereotypes in a culture where even the dictionary refuses to explain the meaning of "coons" is abundantly clear, and Morning Glory's plaintive "Tell me what it means?" signifies a somewhat hesitant willingness to latch onto these ready substitutes for knowledge in her engagement with ethnic cultures. Noguchi also demonstrates his acceptance of the U.S. ethnic system by offering a protagonist who not only is a "high born lady" with "de dough" (as the song puts it) but also demonstrates that she is above such things. Thus, while Noguchi carefully dissects American stereotypes of the Japanese (as his cross-cultural picaresque heroine explores her relation to, and possible place in, American society) he leaves intact, and even reaffirms, stereotypes of other groups: the "Chinee" pidgin-speaking laundryman, the famous Jewish noses, the poor Italian organ-grinder.

A useful paradigm of inclusion to apply to Noguchi as an "ethnic" writer is that proposed by the authors of the critical anthology *Tricksterism in Turn-of-the-Century American Literature* (1994). As the coeditor of that volume, Annette White-Parks, explains: "The modern trickster can be said to grow out of a political system that oppresses certain cultures" and "out of the exclusion and persecution of women and ethnic minority male writers in Canada and the United States, in particular." American tricksterism, White-Parks suggests, developed into unique cultural styles "from the earliest oral pieces forward, as a means of achieving voice and visibility in a context of oppression, even of overturning the established hegemony—and without those in power being the wiser."[54] Tricksterism is not a genre but a kind of energy prevalent in certain texts: we might speak of a "trickster spirit" and perhaps a "tradition of tricksterism." In retrospect, we may find this spirit and tradition prevalent (though by no means universal) among writers hailing from a variety of disempowered groups, including a number of early Asian American writers. We can consider *The American Diary of a Japanese Girl,* with its elaborate impostures, strategies, dissimulations, and provocations, a manifestation of this trickster spirit, a minor classic in the literature of the ethnic American trickster.

The trickster spirit is not, of course, restricted to ethnic American minority groups. Noguchi's trickster spirit was evidently born in his Japanese surroundings: his autobiographical writings include numerous references to his early propensity for pranks and theft, and his fondness for mythical shape-changing tricksters like the *tengu* and *kitsune*. But he developed tricksterism into an art in California, that great breeding ground for tricksters, where Native American tales of the trickster Coyote found new relevance in a carnivalesque culture of gold diggers and gamblers. Noguchi's training in the arts of literary tricksterism came largely from his two white male mentors, the "splendid poseur" Joaquin Miller and the "consummate wag" Gelett Burgess. Miller, a gold digger, horse thief, and lawyer who rose to fame in London's drawing rooms as the first Wild West performance poet, might have learned a trick or two from Coyote during his year among the native Wintu people of Mount Shasta. But Burgess, a literary jokester of no mean talent, graduated from that most serious of American academic institutions, the Massachusetts Institute of Technology.[55] The tradition of literary tricksterism among Asian American writers connects Noguchi to some of his closest peers: Onoto Watanna; Henry Kiyama, whose *Four Immigrants Manga* is a worthy comic successor to Noguchi's novel; and Maxine Hong Kingston, whose more recent *Tripmaster Monkey* celebrates California's powerful tradition of Chinese tricksterism.[56] "Given the pervasive ideas of Asian Americans as somehow never being able to be 'American' enough," Tina Chen has suggested, "the very nature of Asian American identity might be thought of as *one that requires one to impersonate fundamentally oneself*."[57] When we enlarge our view of literary tricksterism to include African American trickster writers like Frederick Douglass, Paul Laurence Dunbar, James Weldon Johnson, and Nella Larsen, as well as Native American writers like John Rollin Ridge and Emily Pauline Johnson, we begin to discern the outlines of a diverse ethnic trickster tradition emerging in the late nineteenth century and continuing until the present day.[58] Some of these trickster writers may be white writers who traffic with the other—writers like Miller, Stoddard, Whitman, MacLane, or, in a more contemporary view, Allen Ginsberg and Gary Snyder—but this does not distract from the sense that the trickster, always looking anxiously toward the border or beyond, belongs to a tradition of others.

Like many of these trickster writers, Noguchi was a master humorist. His playfully provocative humor is one of his distinctively American characteristics, for Noguchi was not entirely exaggerating when he complained, in a 1904 article, "Japanese Humor and Caricature," that "Japan has no literature of laughter and humour." The Japanese, he lamented, did not know how to laugh, they regarded laughter as degenerate, and Japanese humorists were content with clever wordplay. "You could never measure them with the scale which you use for Artemus Ward or Mark Twain," for they were "rarely philosophical, wholesome and sunny. They never laughed with their faces turned to the sky." Japan "was and is the country of tragedy and tears."[59] And yet Noguchi later said that he was not entirely satisfied with "the huge laughter of American humor" because he found it too dissociated from reality. "It is always fed by the unreality of the American optimism, and it has, naturally, no footing on life's inevitable realism," he complained. "I find it, in eight or nine cases out of ten, to be merely a joke or horselaugh not backed by life's tragedy or tears." "The true humor," he argued, "is but another phase of the real tear laughingly interpreted, and is, let me say, a twin sister or brother of the tear differently born by a twist of evolution."[60] The humor of the *American Diary* may have appeared "light to frivolity," but there is no doubt that it was "backed by life's tragedy or tears" and could have taken a darker course but for a "twist of evolution." Noguchi's first volume of poetry had been literally full of "tears," the word appearing twenty-six times among fifty poems ("laugh" appears only once, in the phrase "the mist-wreathed phantoms laugh me to scorn"). Noguchi's second volume, written scarcely a year later, mocks this melancholy tendency. "'Buy my tears that I sucked from the breast of Truth—tears, sister spirits of Heaven's smile!' sobs the Wind," begins one poem. "Thou pale Wind, tear-vender of the hideous night," Noguchi continues, "no one welcomes thee with thy unsold tears!"[61] In the *American Diary*, the evolution of tears into humor is complete, for there is scarcely a teardrop in view; and here, nothing escapes the vortex of Noguchi's satire, least of all himself or his heroine. But as he told Léonie Gilmour, it was "very hard work to keep Miss M.G. to be sweet, capricious, romantic all the time. Anytime my own self jumps in you know."[62]

These days, the queer is often attributed a transformative power not unlike that of the trickster: as a disturbing force that unsettles simple binary oppositions of sex and gender, and here, as well, the evidently bisexual Noguchi invites reconsideration. "We slept in the same bed, Charley and I," he tells us, describing his relationship with Stoddard in *The Story of Yone Noguchi*.[63] "Yone is most queer boy among all Nipponese," Noguchi's artist friend Kosen Takahashi once explained to Blanche Partington. "I woo to him as a boy do so for a girl. well! Yone is my lover forever."[64] There is plenty of evidence, too, of Noguchi's sympathy for gay writers: Stoddard and Whitman, of course, but also Oscar Wilde and Edward Carpenter. He had an avowed nostalgia for the Genroku era in Japanese history, when "narrow-minded theory and learning, conservative manner and customs, failed to satisfy people's mind; and they, as it appears, chose their own free ways, according to their taste and purpose."[65] Though he retained many of the prerogatives of the Meiji-era male and has been particularly criticized for his callous behavior toward his American "wife," Noguchi was also a tireless opponent of gender stereotyping. When Rabindranath Tagore was criticized in the Japanese press for being insufficiently masculine, Noguchi explained that "Sir Rabindranath's personality[,] somewhat feminine, like that of any other true prophet or poet, proves him to be a son of Nature whose feminine grace procreates itself."[66] In one of his later poems (unpublished in its English version), he writes, with evident pleasure, about the female Nō mask called by the masculine name Magojirō, explaining: "Contradiction is delightful / And often tantalizing indeed."[67] To read *The American Diary of a Japanese Girl* as a queer novel is first of all to attend to this delight in contradiction. Contradiction, which may involve "speaking against" as a form of opposition, is crucial to our concept of law, whether we mean the law of the courtroom, the social codes governing sexual behavior and gender roles, or the Lacanian "Law of the Father." "If I ever build my ideal city," Miss Morning Glory tells us, "two things shall not be tolerated. One is a lawyer's office and the other is a church" (83).

The relationship between this humorous, ethnically other, ambiguously gendered bisexual American trickster tradition and the serious, straight white male-dominated tradition of American literary naturalism that has long served to represent American fiction at the turn of the twentieth century is elucidated by Elizabeth Ammons's introduction to the aforementioned collection, *Tricksterism in Turn-of-the-Century American Literature*. In the "master narrative" of this genre, which pits the individual against society or "hierarchical authority," she explains, "resistance ends with the individual overpowered, brought into line, controlled by the superior authority of the state/system/group." Trickster, Ammons tells us, "offers a different plot" that embodies "a principle of human rebellion and resistance that exists both within a protagonist/antagonist framework *and* within a totally different context, one in which the disruly—the transgressive—is accepted as part of the community's life."[68]

As a vivid illustration of the antagonistic relationship between the naturalist and the trickster, we might place Noguchi's work beside a contemporaneous naturalist classic, Frank Norris's novel *The Octopus* (1901). At one point in this weighty exposition of the powerlessness of hard-working, idealistic California ranchers in their struggle against the inexorable expansion of the corrupt railroad monopolies (the first volume of a projected trilogy left incomplete by the author's early death), the narrator describes a protagonist's encounter with San Francisco's literary bohemia. Among the bohemians with their "veritable mania for declamation and fancy dress," the reader may easily recognize Joaquin Miller as "the bearded poet, perspiring in furs and boots of reindeer skin," who "declaimed verses of his own composition about the wild life of the Alaskan mining camps," and Noguchi as "the Japanese youth, in the silk robes of the Samurai two-sworded nobles," who "read from his own works" (for two of Noguchi's poems are quoted). Norris adds a Russian countess, an aesthete, a Christian Scientist, a university professor, a Cherokee, a toga-clad elocutionist, a "high caste Chinaman," an Armenian, and a mandolin player. As his narrator sums up:

> It was the Fake, the eternal, irrepressible Sham; glib, nimble, ubiquitous, tricked out in all the paraphernalia of imposture, an endless defile of charlatans that passed interminably before the gaze of the city, marshalled by "lady presidents," exploited by clubs of women, by literary societies, reading circles, and culture organisations. The attention the Fake received, the time devoted to it, the money which it absorbed, were incredible. It was all one that impostor after impostor was exposed; it was all one that the clubs, the circles, the societies were proved beyond doubt to have been swindled. The more the Philistine press of the city railed and guyed, the more the women rallied to the defence of their *protégé* of the hour.[69]

In this "irrepressible Sham, nimble, ubiquitous" (an early image of a now-familiar postmodern California), we find an American ethnic trickster culture emerging from the margins (or is it really the center?) aided by sympathetic women, despite strong opposition from better-pedigreed male members of the literary establishment like Benjamin Franklin Norris, whose literary task was serious, important, and authentically American.

Of course, not only the literary tricksters opposed naturalism. In Britain, Irish and Welsh writers like Oscar Wilde, William Butler Yeats, and Arthur Symons, who formed the center of the decadent and aesthetic movements, were strongly opposed to Émile Zola, Henrik Ibsen, and their crowd and sought alternative inspiration in French symbolism, Celtic legend, and non-Western cultural traditions. Though Oscar Wilde (Miller's friend and Mrs. Frank Leslie's former brother-in-law) was no longer a viable force on the London scene when Noguchi arrived there in 1902, Noguchi did befriend Yeats and Symons and played a leading role in importing their ideas to Japan, where the internationally minded literati soon divided along similar lines of naturalism versus symbolism. Noguchi was well aware of the decadent and aesthetic movements admired by Les Jeunes, as Gelett Burgess and his group called themselves. While Noguchi probably did not (contra Norris) give many California readings clad in kimono, he undoubtedly modeled his poetic persona on the fashionable aesthete, and many features of this aesthetic persona carry over to Miss Morning Glory. The New Woman phenomenon, often associated with the decadent movement, also had its direct and indirect influence on *American Diary,* as has been noted.[70] As a New Woman with aesthetic and decadent tendencies, Miss Morning Glory is not about to be dragged down into a morbid and depressing naturalism. True, she is momentarily dismayed by the "sky-invading dragon of smoke" whose impact Norris analyzes at such length. "Gentlemen, is this real Amerikey?" she exclaims, reaching in vain for her perfume. A realist like Norris would scoff at Miss Morning

Glory's desire to disguise the evil odor of American industrial reality with the perfume of aesthetic escapism. But her denial has much in common with other West Coast quests for alternative realities, built on similar doubts about the obduracy of contemporary social and political realities. Miss Morning Glory retreats to the hills to live "near to God" with a theatrical poet, where she can give free rein to her imagination and creativity. "Dream and reality," she says from this more congenial abode, "are not marked here by different badges. They waltz round" (92).

The aesthetic perspective that informs this work is also recognized as the foundation of English and American literary modernism, which leads us to a final important issue: the extent to which we may regard *The American Diary of a Japanese Girl* as a work of modernist fiction. As early as 1919, *Poetry Magazine*'s associate editor, Eunice Tietjens, argued that Noguchi's early verse "directly . . . forecast the modern movement," and the *American Diary*, too, has significant modernist elements.[71] Among these, one may cite the Wildean insistence on the superiority of art to life, the rejection of traditional narrative in favor of a style approaching stream of consciousness, the profusion of incorporated genres, and the experimentalism of narrative style. Additionally, one may point to the novel's fascination with style, perspective, mirroring, and representation; its extensive use of parody, pastiche, and quotation; and its self-reflexive interest in textuality. The novel's incorporated genres range from haiku (Noguchi was probably the first important American advocate of this form) to Morning Glory's shredded "Things Seen in the Street," a kind of textual collage reminiscent of the later experiments of William Burroughs or John Ashbery.[72] There is much more to say about the many ways in which the novel engages with cultural modernity, raising provocative questions at every turn. Though this remarkable text has been for many decades buried under the accumulated rubble of cultural amnesia or international misunderstanding, it is fair to say that its transformative power is far from exhausted.

Edward Marx

Notes to the Introduction

I would like to thank the Hearin Foundation for summer funding in 2003 that allowed me to write a preliminary exploration of key issues in Noguchi's *The American Diary of a Japanese Girl.* I am also grateful to Millsaps College for a Faculty Development Grant that funded travel to the Bancroft Library at the University of California, Berkeley in the summer of 2002.

1. Present-day readers may find the squirrel diary very strange, yet when Zona Gale, a friend of Noguchi's and later an author of popular stories and novels, read *The American Diary*, she commented in an undated letter to Noguchi, *CEL* no. 246, how much she liked that particular section of the narrative: "The diary of the squirrel—it is the most charming thing imaginable."

2. *Chicago Journal*, quoted in "Some Press Opinions on *The American Diary of a Japanese Girl*" (unpaginated appended material in the 1912 edition of *The American Diary of a Japanese Girl*). Edward Marx provides an analysis of additional press reviews in the Afterword in this volume.

3. Marx's essay "'A Different Mode of Speech': Yone Noguchi in Meiji America" provides an overview of Noguchi's life. Information about Noguchi's early life can also be found in Noguchi's own (somewhat untrustworthy) *The Story of Yone Noguchi.* Concerning the development of Keiō University, see Fukuzawa.

4. The information in this paragraph concerning Noguchi's life with Joaquin Miller comes from *SYN* 55–83 and from Marberry 231–33.

5. Other residents of the Hights at the time Noguchi lived there are not mentioned in *The American Diary.* In *SYN*, Noguchi noted the presence of "Miss Alice" (Alice Oliver), Joaquin's lover and the mother of three of his sons (one died in infancy). For more information on Oliver, see Marberry 208 and 234. A Japanese poet named Takeshi Kanno (who married an American artist named Gertrude Boyle) also apparently lived there during at least some of Noguchi's stay. See Marberry 232.

6. On the first Tuesday of August 1899, Noguchi begged Partington to "stop to plan to make the Diary as a story; because O'cho San is a new comer to this country and naturally cannot have any romance" (*CEL* no. 44). All subsequent quotations from Noguchi's letters will be reproduced as written, without changes to grammar or spelling.

7. Letter to Partington, 5 September 1899, *CEL* no. 46.

8. [September 1899] *CEL* no. 49.

9. Regarding the burning of the manuscript, see Yone Noguchi to Charles W. Stoddard, 23 July 1901, *CEL* no. 88. The quotation regarding his "English composition" comes from a letter to Gilmour dated 4 February 1901, *CEL* no. 62.

10. Duus 19.

11. Noguchi to Gilmour, n.d., *CEL* no. 75, and Noguchi to Gilmour, n.d., *CEL* no. 79.

12. See Larkin as well as the Afterword for a fuller description of Yeto's life and career.

13. For additional information on Japanese-themed novels, plays, poetry, folktale collections, and magazines at the turn of the century, consult Wordell.

14. See the Afterword for additional discussion of Noguchi and Eaton's interesting relationship after they met in Chicago in 1900. For more information on Eaton's career, consult Ling and Birchall. Several of Eaton's Japanese-themed novels, including *Miss Numè of Japan*, *A Japanese Nightingale*, and *The Heart of Hyacinth*, have been reprinted (with *A Japanese Nightingale* appearing alongside *Madame Butterfly* in a book subtitled "Two Orientalist Texts").

15. Yoshihara 97.

16. Letter from Funk and Wagnalls to Noguchi, n.d., *CEL* no. 66.

17. Regarding Noguchi's opening of the bazaar, see Noguchi to Gilmour, 5 July [1903], *CEL* no. 217. The pressure Noguchi experienced to trade upon his Japanese identity to ensure his own financial well-being is also apparent in a letter from Thomas Walsh to Noguchi, 9 March 1904, *CEL* no. 290, in which Walsh encouraged him to lecture on Japanese literature: "If you really want to make money at once, why do you not prepare a lecture on Japanese Poets and Poetry and get some fashionable people to introduce you to lecture in the afternoon in their parlors? I might introduce you to some ladies who could help you. This would be perfectly dignified work for an author and you might ask fifty dollars for a lecture." Noguchi did present such a lecture, "Modern Women Writers of Japan," at a benefit for the Barnard College Reading Room in April 1904; see Barnard College to Yone Noguchi, 23 April [1904], *CEL* no. 317. In 1913 he had a more extensive lecture tour in the United States and England.

18. See Downer for a very detailed discussion of Kawakami, Sadayakko, and their tour.

19. For a discussion of ethnic impersonations or masquerades more generally in twentieth-century American literature, consult Browder.

20. Doniger 102, 70.

21. According to Sōfu Takai's *Eishijin Yone Noguchi no eiko* [English poet Yone Noguchi's glory], cited by Marx and by Masayo Duus in her biography of Isamu Noguchi, Yone's father claimed samurai ancestry but ran a store selling such items as *geta* and umbrellas. See Marx, "'A Different Mode of Speech,'" 290, and Duus 11.

22. Chen xviii.

23. Glenn 22. According to Glenn 31, census data suggest that in 1900 there were fewer than a thousand resident Japanese women over the age of fifteen in the United States.

24. See Ichioka 51–90 and Ichihashi 65–69.

25. See Ichioka 7–28.

26. *Japan Weekly Mail*, March 1890, quoted in Ichioka 9.

27. Glenn 70–73.

28. Ichioka 24.

29. It is possible that the encounter with a rude American described in *SYN* never happened. As Marx has pointed out, the story of Noguchi's taking a room at the Cosmopolitan Hotel immediately upon arriving in San Francisco appears apocryphal given his limited resources and contacts at the time. However, Marx suggests in "'A Different Mode of Speech'" (294) that the scene is truthful as a "composite picture of the shock of arrival and the reality of California racism." Similarly, the point of my comparison here is to suggest why Morning Glory's actions may represent a response to racism that was unlikely for immigrants, who sometimes felt physically vulnerable in a new land.

30. Noguchi began an intimate relationship with Gilmour sometime in 1903, and in November of that year he sent her a letter, *CEL* no. 254, stating: "I declare that Leonie Gilmour is my lawful wife." Sometime in early 1904 Gilmour became pregnant with Noguchi's child and moved to California. Noguchi then became engaged to Armes (to whom he had been introduced by Stoddard in 1900). This engagement ended only in the spring of 1905, after Noguchi had already moved back to Japan and Armes had found out about Gilmour and the baby.

31. Okihiro 180.

32. *SYN* 8.

Notes to the Text

DEDICATION

1 **Haruko, Empress of Japan** (1850–1914), born Masako Ichijō, married Mutsuhito, the Emperor Meiji, in 1867, shortly before the upheavals of the Meiji Restoration transformed the imperial institution. In line with Japan's efforts at modernization, Empress Haruko made public appearances with the emperor, took an active role in promoting women's education, and engaged in charity work. As she had no children, she officially adopted Yoshihito, the future Emperor Taishō, one of fifteen children the emperor fathered among his five ladies-in-waiting.

BEFORE I SAILED

Note: The first number of each entry indicates the page on which the word or pharase appears.

3 (23 September) **Meriken Kenbutsu** (メリケン見物): American sightseeing trip. The transliteration "Meriken" was a slangy alternative to the more accepted *"beikoku no"* or *"Amerika no,"* and survives today only in such quaint instances as Kobe's Meriken Park.

3–5 (24 September) **"Nono Sama"** (のの様): a childish name for any sort of transcendent deity: the Buddha, the gods, the sun, the moon, etc. **Mitsuho No Kuni** (瑞穂の國): usually "*mizuho no kuni*," an archaic name for Japan meaning "land of abundant rice." **Konpira shrine:** The main branch of the Shintō shrine popularly known as Konpira-san (金比羅さん) but officially known as Kotohira-gū (金刀比羅宮) is located on the island of Shikoku, but there are smaller Konpira shrines throughout Japan, including several in Tokyo; Morning Glory is probably referring to the famous one located at Toranomon, about one mile north of Shiba Park. The enshrined deity is said to be a protector of seafarers. Miss Morning Glory's comment, **"I didn't exactly see how to address him, being ignorant what sort of god he was,"** points to complex questions about the historical transformations of the shrine and its syncretic deity, identified at various periods with either Shintō or Buddhist practices and beliefs, according to the prevailing religious and political climate. Since the Meiji Restoration of 1868, when the Japanese government forcibly separated Shintō and Buddhist practice, the shrine deity Konpira Daigongen had been identified with the Shintō deity Okuninushi no Kami. For a detailed history, see Thal. **Amerikey:** Morning Glory's word for America does not appear to be of Japanese origin.

4–6 (26 September) **4 yens:** In 1900 four yen was equivalent to two dollars. By way of comparison, a copy of the moderately expensive *American Diary of a Japanese Girl* sold for $1.60. **"Sara! sara! sara!"** (さらさらさら): rustling or murmuring sound. **The steamer "Belgic":** Noguchi used the name of the ship that had carried him across the Pacific in 1893, which he described in his autobiography as "an almost unimaginably small affair for a Pacific liner, being only three thousand tons" (*SYN* 25), though, in fact, the *Belgic* had a more respectable gross tonnage of 4,212 tons. Built in 1885 by Belfast shipbuilders Harland and Wolff for the White Star Line, she was already small by the early 1890s, when White Star Liners typically weighed in at six- to eight-thousand tons, and a mere toy compared to Harland and Wolff's most famous production, the 1912 *Titanic* (the company always used names ending with *-ic*) which, at 46,328 tons, could have comfortably held ten *Belgics*. The 420-foot *Belgic* and its sister ship the *Gaelic* were chartered by the Oriental & Occidental Steamship Company, joining the *Doric* (1881) and *Coptic* (1883) on the company's Pacific service connecting San Francisco and Hong Kong with a stopover at Yokohama. Noguchi's choice of the ship for Morning Glory's passage was careless, however, because in 1899, the *Belgic* was no longer on the Pacific service and indeed, no longer existed, having been returned to Britain to be refurbished and resold the previous year; at the time of Morning Glory's supposed passage, she was doing duty between New York and London for the Atlantic Transport Line under the name *Mohawk*. Morning Glory could have sailed on the *Gaelic*, which ran the Pacific route through 1904, or on the *Coptic* or *Doric* until 1906.

6–7 (29 September) **my book of Longfellow** refers to an edition of the works of the very popular nineteenth-century American poet, Henry Wadsworth Longfellow (1807–82). Longfellow's career began with *Voices of the Night* (1839), *Ballads and Other Poems* (1841), and *Poems on Slavery* (1842); in the late 1840s and 1850s, he published several long narrative poems, including the famous *Evangeline* and *Song of Hiawatha*, both of which were based on American themes, although their style was derived from classical models and German Romanticism. **A poet need not always to sing, I assure you, of tragic lamentation and of "far-beyond":** The editor of Longfellow's *Selected Poems*, Lawrence Buell, concurs with Morning Glory's point about "tragic lamentation," arguing that modern critics' "preference for the self-divided, alienated, or pessimistic sensibility as against a socially well-adjusted, optimistic temperament" is largely responsible for their failure to give Longfellow "a fair hearing" (vii–viii). Morning Glory's praise of Longfellow for not always singing of "far-beyond" is more difficult to explicate. Noguchi may have in mind the Romantic fascination with the sublime (see note to 1 February). Noguchi may also have in mind English metaphysical and devotional poetry where "far beyond" suggests an orientation toward heavenly matters accompanied by a sense of earthly detachment, as in Henry Vaughan's widely anthologized "Peace," a brief poetic rendering of Christian heaven that begins: "My soul, there is a country / Far beyond the stars." Longfellow's **"A Psalm of Life,"** which appeared in *Voices of the Night*, urged readers to be active and goal oriented, while **"The Village Blacksmith,"** published in *Ballads and Other Poems*, praised the blacksmith for doing essential work for the community. ***Evangeline*** (1847) presented a sentimental tale of lost love during the British removal of French Acadians from what is now Nova Scotia. ***The Song of Hiawatha*** (1855) was based on Native American legends (as retold by Henry Rowe Schoolcraft). Noguchi wrote that he first encountered "The Village Blacksmith" while a student at Keiō University. A number of Longfellow's poems had been translated into Japanese, including Tetsujirō Inoue's version of "A Psalm of Life," in the 1882 *Shintaishi-shō* (the first important Japanese collection of Western verse). **"Arcadie":** Longfellow's *Evangeline* was subtitled *A Tale of Acadie*. Noguchi has evidently misunderstood this as "Arcadie," the French spelling of Arcadia (see note to 1 February). In fact, Acadia was the name of the French colony in Nova Scotia that the British seized in 1710. **I confess the poet of my taste isn't he:** In fact, the poet of Noguchi's taste was Edgar Allan Poe, an avowed anti-Longfellowist. Had Noguchi acknowledged his fondness for Poe, he would have risked identification as the author of the *Diary* as a result of his well-known Poe plagiarism scandal of 1896.

7 (30 September) **The Jap "gentleman"—who desires the old barbarity—persists still in fancying that girls are trading wares:** The status of Japanese women had changed considerably under pressure from foreign critics but was still a topic of rancorous discussion among educationists and reformers—Alice Bacon's *Japanese Girls and Women* (1891) was the most widely read English book on the subject. Japanese Christian activists like Tel Sono and Naomi Tamura found strong Western support for their zealous reformist projects but were regarded as extremists by most Japanese. **When he shall come to understand what is Love!** links the question of women's status in marriage to related Japanese intellectual debates concerning the meaning of the Western concept of "romantic love," which was commonly thought mysterious or even incomprehensible. For an extensive discussion, see "The Introduction of 'Love' into Modern Japan," in Yokota-Murakami's *Don Juan East/West* (35–80).

7–8 (1 October) **Butterfly mode!:** The *chōchō-mage* (蝶々髷) was a girlish hairstyle somewhat popular during the latter half of the nineteenth century. It was unusual in that the sides were allowed to fall freely, creating an effect resembling butterfly wings, while the front was formed into bangs and the back into a topknot suggesting the butterfly's body. Lafcadio Hearn in his essay "Of Women's Hair" (*Glimpses* v: 19) refers to a *shin-jōchō* or "new butterfly style" being worn by young women in Matsue, but his description suggests a style rather different from the original *chōchō*. **Sayo shikaraba!** (左様然らば): In that case, then.

8–9 (2 October) **Irving's . . . "Sketch Book":** Washington Irving (1783–1859) was a founding figure in American literature. Born in New York, he began his public writing career with satirical essays published in *The Morning Chronicle* in 1802–3. He is best known for his eclectic collection of essays and short tales, *The Sketch Book of Geoffrey Crayon* (1819–20). Though the book mostly focused on England, which Irving had visited on several occasions, some of the stories had American settings (including "Rip Van Winkle" and "The Legend of Sleepy Hollow"). In *SYN*, Noguchi tells two different stories about his first encounter with the *Sketch Book*. In the first chapter, he recalls being thrilled by Irving's book while he was studying at Keiō University in Japan. In the second chapter, he says he first encountered the *Sketch Book* while working and studying at Manzanita Hall, a "sort of preparatory school for Stanford" in Palo Alto (38). In both accounts, he mentions that the book motivated in him a desire to go to England. See also notes to 28 October and 13 March. **musume** (娘): girl, daughter. **"Karan Coron"** is an onomatopoetic representation of the sound made by wooden clogs. The phrase had recently become popular because of its use in the 1892 play *Botan Tōrō* (see note to 17 November). **Makey Hey Rah:** apparently a Chinese pidgin phrase.

9–10 (3 October) **The "silver" knife (large and sharp enough to fight the Russians):** The Japanese did eventually go to war against Russia in 1904 over Russian expansion in

Manchuria and Korea. After Japan was forced to return the Liaodong Peninsula to China after the Sino-Japanese War by the Tripartite Intervention of Russia, Germany, and France, Russia formed an antimilitary alliance with China, obtained the lease of the Liaodong port of Lüshun (Port Arthur), and in 1898 began constructing a railway line from Lüshun to Vladivostok that would insure Russian dominance in Manchuria. **A celebrated American restaurant, the "Western Sea House":** the Seiyōken (精養軒), a famous and expensive Western-style restaurant in Ueno founded in 1877 as an offshoot of the deluxe Western-style hotel of the same name in Tsukiji, near Ginza. The Japanese-run Seiyōken was ostensibly French rather than American, and the characters used in spelling the name did not mean "Western Sea" (西洋)—the word associated with foreigners from the West (known as *seiyōjin*, "Western Sea people")—but "refinement" and "nurture," intended to suggest the cultural sophistication to be attained by dining there. A **shōji** (障子), is a sliding paper door. A **toow,** (i.e., *toō*, 渡欧) is a European trip and, by extension, a person who has traveled to Europe. It is not clear why Morning Glory uses the awkward *"Meriken toō"* rather than simply *tobei* (渡米), the equivalent word for an American trip. **The Nippon Mining Company** did not exist until 1929 and is therefore presumably fictional. **Cheese** and other dairy products were virtually unknown in pre–Meiji Japan, the phrase *"batā-kusai"* (stinking of butter) surviving as a term of disparagement until well into the twentieth century. **Shall I hang them on the door, so that the pest may not come near to our house?** refers to a custom described in Noguchi's essay on "Setsubun," a winter festival concerned with the expulsion of domestic demons. Although Setsubun is still widely observed, the custom according to which "every front door is decorated with the Hiiragi leaves [a kind of holly] and some sardines' heads" is no longer widely practiced. As Noguchi explained: "The Hiiragi leaves with thorns round their edges and these fish heads were supposed to have power to keep off the invasion of the evil spirits" (6).

10–12 (5 October) **chin koro** (小犬): a small dog or puppy. **koshi goromo** (腰衣): underclothing worn around the waist. **Bikkuri shita!** (吃驚した): [I] was surprised. **ijin** (異人): foreigner. A less polite spelling (夷人) meant "barbarian-devil." **Bartlett's English Conversation Book** does not appear to have been the title of an actual book. It is possible that Morning Glory actually refers here to *Bartlett's Familiar Quotations*, first published in 1855. **mottainai** (勿体ない): wasteful; sacrilegious. **the great book of Confucius:** Confucianism (in Japanese, *jukyō*), a system of practices based on writings attributed to K'ung Ch'iu, known in Japan as Kōshi (孔子), is thought to have arrived in Japan from Korea in the fifth century. From the sixth to the ninth centuries, Confucian texts were adopted as the basis of a state-sponsored education system, but with the rise of Buddhism, *jukyō* diminished in prominence until the Tokugawa era. The famous 1716 Confucian compendium for women, the *Onna Daigaku* (女大学) (Women's Great Learning), popular until the end of the Edo period, emphasized obedience as the paramount feminine virtue. Noguchi does not clarify whether this or the influential *Analects* or *Classic of Filial Piety* is the "great book" Morning Glory sat on, but it is no doubt an act of some symbolic significance.

13 (7 October) **My house sits on the hill commanding a view over Tokio and the Bay of Yedo:** Taking this comment in conjunction with others made by Morning Glory that suggest the proximity of her house to Konpira shrine (24 September) and her familiarity with Shiba Park (7 January), Morning Glory's home is likely to be in southeastern Tokyo, the part of the city Noguchi knew well from his student days at the nearby Keiō Gijuku.

ON THE OCEAN

13 (7 October) **Dai Nippon** (大日本): great Japan, the Japanese Empire. **Balboa . . . caught his first view from the peak in Darien:** In 1513, Spaniard Vasco Nuñez de Balboa became the first European to see the Pacific Ocean from the Americas when he and a party of Spaniards and Native Americans saw it from a mountaintop near the Spanish settlement of Darién in what is now Panama. Though Noguchi implies that it was Balboa who (mistakenly) referred to this body of water as "pacific," or calm, it was actually the later explorer Ferdinand Magellan who gave the ocean its name. Balboa simply called the ocean Mar del Sur (South Sea).

13 (12 October) **new minister to the City of Mexico:** Japan reopened relations with Mexico in 1873 after an interval of two and a half centuries and subsequently negotiated with Mexico in 1888 Japan's first "equal" treaty with a foreign power. In 1890, Mexico's first minister arrived in Yokohama, and two years later Yoshibumi Murota (室田義文 1847–1938) arrived in Mexico City to establish a Japanese consulate. In 1897, a group of thirty-five Japanese colonists arrived in Mexico to grow coffee in Chiapas in a colonization project of Japanese foreign minister Takeaki Enomoto, but the poorly organized plan was declared a failure in 1901. Murota was still consul at the beginning of the colonization project. **The Chinese question** in October 1899 would have meant the beginnings of the Boxer Rebellion, a cult-based antiforeign uprising that emerged in Shandong in March 1898 and led to widespread open violence against foreigners in June 1900. The Japanese army contributed the largest number of troops among the eight nations allied to suppress the rebellion.

14 (13 October) **I am a mountain-worshipper:** Beyond a mere fondness for hiking, the Japanese phrase *sangaku shinkō* (山岳信仰) refers to a broad set of religious beliefs, ranging from folk belief in mountains as the habitat of ancestral spirits to ritual climbing of Mount Fuji by adherents of the Fujiko sect (who regard the mountain as sacred) and the ascetic-shamanic *shugendō* practiced by *yamabushi* mountain priests.

15 (14 October) **hair . . . negligence . . . would be fined by the police in Japan:** Morning Glory is not entirely joking; Japan (particularly before the Meiji Restoration) was famed for its draconian sumptuary laws which, as Lafcadio Hearn noted, "probably exceeded in multitude and minuteness anything of which Western legal history yields record" (*Japan* 79). Such laws—aimed at promoting class stability by insuring that members of each class dressed and behaved appropriately to their station—did dictate appropriate hairstyles and hair ornaments for various classes.

15 (15 October) **We die any moment "with bubbling groan, without a grave, unknelled, uncoffined, and unknown"** is from Lord Byron's *Childe Harold's Pilgrimage,* canto 4 (1818). The phrase appears in stanza 179. **Hotoke Sama** (仏様): Buddha.

15–16 (16 October) **I will proudly land on the historical island of Lotos Eaters:** Noguchi refers to the Lotos Eaters of both Homer and Tennyson. In book 9 of *The Odyssey,* Odysseus and his mariners land on a coastline inhabited by people who eat lotus blossoms and who offer the plants to them. Those mariners who eat the plants forget about the beauties of their homeland and become unwilling to leave the place, but Odysseus forces them onboard the ship. In Tennyson's version, published in 1832, the encounter is described in much greater detail. **I began my "Lotos Eaters":** Noguchi did indeed attempt to write an imitation of Tennyson's "Lotos Eaters," sending it to Frank Putnam on 11 January 1901 with the note: "Here is my poem in which I took much pain, perhaps you will like it. Have you a copy of Tennyson's poem in your library? Have you ever read his 'Lotos Eaters'? That piece many a people admire! I have a different expression of the land of Lotos-eaters, so I wrote [it] down. This is a very risky work since I make a race with the great poet" (FPL, 9). The lines quoted by Morning Glory appear in a different arrangement in the evidently unfinished 107-line version of the poem retained by Putnam. **Then I feared that some impertinent poet might have said the same thing many a year before** is a comment that recalls the controversy in November 1896 over accusations by Jay William Hudson that Noguchi had plagiarized the poems of Edgar Allan Poe. Noguchi had then allegedly responded: "I am thankful to God for giving me the moment when I felt the same thing with Poe" (*SYN* 42).

16 (17 October) **Red, a symbol of my sanguine attachment,** refers to the theory of temperament based on humors that was still popular in the 1890s. "Storm, darkness, war, images of disease, poverty, and perishing afflict unremittingly the imaginations of melancholiacs," wrote William James in *The Principles of Psychology* (1890), while "those of sanguine temperament, when their spirits are high, find it impossible to give any permanence to evil forebodings or to gloomy thoughts" (577). A sanguine person, according to Kant's *Anthropology from a Pragmatic Point of View* (1798), "is carefree and full of hope; he attaches great importance to each thing for the moment, and the next moment may not give it another thought. He makes promises in all honesty, but fails to keep his word because he has not reflected deeply enough beforehand whether he will be able to keep it. He is good-natured enough to help others, but he is a bad debtor and always asks for extensions. He is a good companion, jocular and high-spirited, who is reluctant to take anything seriously (*Vive la bagatelle!*) and all men are his friends. He is, as a rule, not a bad fellow; but he is a sinner hard to convert, who regrets something very much indeed, but soon forgets this regret (which never becomes an affliction). Business wears him out, and yet he busies himself indefatigably with mere play; for play involves change and perseverance is not in his line" (153–54).

17 (18 October) **"The Lady of the Lake":** Sir Walter Scott's Arthurian romance in verse, published in 1810, is about two hundred pages in length. **Oji San** (伯父さん): uncle.

17 (Morning, 21 October) **Tsumaranai!** (つまらない): worthless, dull. **He is not blockish, I thought, since he permits himself to employ irony:** The use of verbal irony—the Japanese edition uses the word *fūshi* (諷刺), which means innuendo or sarcasm—is comparatively rare in Japan.

IN AMERIKEY

19–21 (Night, 21 October) **San Francisco** was Noguchi's primary home from December 1893 to May 1900. **Kitsune ni tsukamareta wa!** (狐に掴まれたわ) does mean "seized by a fox! as Morning Glory suggests, but Noguchi evidently meant to say *Kitsune ni tsumamareta wa* (狐に抓まれたわ): "pinched by a fox," the phrase usually used to mean "bewitched by a fox!," which he used in later editions. The fox, like the Coyote of Native American mythology, is a shape-changing trickster figure, believed to have spiritual power and the ability to bewitch people. **Darwin:** Noguchi implies here that the smells and looks of the wagon drivers provide evidence for Charles Darwin's theory of evolution, first promulgated in his *Origin of Species* (1859), which was popularly thought to imply that human beings were descended from monkeys. In his autobiography, Noguchi confessed to actually knowing very little about Darwinian theory: "I cannot forget how he [Watari] tired me with his Darwinism, which I little understand, even to-day" (*SYN* 32–33). The **Oriental wharf,** the usual docking place for the Asia-bound steamships of the Oriental & Occidental Steamship Company (see notes to 26 September) was located at the end of Townsend Street, seven blocks south of Market Street, between First and Second streets (the present site of AT&T Park, home of the San Francisco giants). **Tamageta wa!** (たまげたわ): Astonishing! *"Wa"* is an emphatic particle used primarily in women's speech. **We 40,000,000 Japs must raise our heads from wee bits of land. There's no room to stretch elbows. We have to stay like dwarf trees.** The Japanese population was in fact closer to 45 million and rising at a rate of 1.2 percent per year. The increasing congestion of Japanese urban centers was blamed for various social ills and used as an argument for foreign colonization and expansion into previously restricted regions of Japan such as Hokkaidō. The fondness for *bonsai* (盆栽, literally, "tray planting") is here used as a metaphor for Japanese strategies of adaptation; the point is repeated more strongly by Morning Glory's uncle (23 February). **The *Chronicle* building,** at 690 Market Street, was San Francisco's first steel-frame high-rise building, constructed by the Chicago architectural firm Burnham and Root in 1890. "I was amazed to see the 13- or 14-story Chronicle Building," Noguchi wrote, describing in a Japanese essay his 1893 arrival in the city. "I never thought there could be a building so high" ("*San Furanshisuko*" 43). Noguchi placed ads for his schoolboy services in the *Chronicle*, and in his journalistic days visited the offices of the *Chronicle* and nearby *Examiner* to take notes from the files kept for the use of advertising customers. The minister's comment in the *Diary* is anachronistic, however, since after 1898 the twelve-story *Call* building (also known as the Spreckels building) across the street at 703 Market and Third Street held rank as the city's tallest building at 315 feet, with the help of its baroque dome. **Yokohama park**, constructed in the early 1870s as Japan's second modern Western-style park, was originally called Higa kōen (彼我公園), meaning "theirs and ours park," a name intended to suggest its openness to both Westerners and Japanese. **Yokohama**, like Nagasaki and Kobe, was a "treaty port" where foreigners were free to live under conditions of extraterritoriality. Few foreigners lived in the "interior" of Japan until the system was abolished in 1899. **Emerson's essays**, namely, the *Essays, First Series* (1841) and *Essays, Second Series* (1844), were available in numerous editions by the end of the nineteenth century. The Yokohama beggar might be reading "Self-Reliance" (see entry for 23 February), in which Emerson comments that "the reliance on Property, including the reliance on governments which protect it, is the want of self-reliance" (201). **The Palace Hotel** was the fabled predecessor of the postearthquake hotel of the same name at Market and New Montgomery streets. Built in 1875 at a price tag of $5 million, the original hotel, with its skylit interior and bay windows, was famed for such ultramodern features as electric call buttons in every room and hydraulic elevators (known as "rising rooms"). Noguchi's familiarity with it derived in part from his association with William Doxey, the bookseller-publisher whose shop was among those that lined its Market Street. An innovative English-born bookseller who introduced the latest local and international trends in thematic window displays, Doxey was also the publisher of the little magazine *The Lark* (in which Noguchi's first poems appeared in 1896), and of Noguchi's second volume of poems, *The Voice of the Valley*, published in 1897. Doxey's business ventures had been overly optimistic, however, and Miss Morning Glory, arriving on 21 October 1899, could not have visited the shop, as the recently bankrupted proprietor's books and shop fixtures had been auctioned off during September and October. **"Irasshai mashi"** is a colloquial form of "irasshaimase" (いらっしゃいませ), a standard welcoming phrase.

21–22 (22 October) **seriage** (迫上げ) in the kabuki theater means the raising of actors or scenery onto the stage by means of trapdoors and crank-operated platforms. Properly speaking, the "vanishing" of a ghost by such means would be called *serisage* (迫下げ). **O Binzuru** (お賓頭盧) is the Japanese name for Pindola Bharadvaja, one of the historical Buddha's sixteen disciples or *arhats* (*rakan* in Japanese), whose statue may be found in some Buddhist temples. He is associated with healing and said to have possessed supernatural powers; thus, it is popularly believed that rubbing his bald head may cure or ward off disease. **The august "Son of Heaven"** refers to the Japanese emperor or *tennō* (天皇)—literally "heavenly emperor"—said to be descended from the sun goddess Amaterasu.

22–23 (23 October) **Kara** (唐) and **Tenjiku** (天竺) are archaic names for China and India, respectively. The use of the archaic names suggests distant medieval journeys that might require many years. **"The negroes are horrid":** Morning Glory's reaction to the novel sight of black people seems to have been common among Japanese. Joseph Heco, who was among the first group of Japanese to arrive in San Francisco in 1851, had also written of his shock upon seeing "a black object driving a goods-cart or dray." "Its black face and white teeth and huge red lips, which formed such a contrast with its soot-like face were fearful and dreadful. I thought it was not human, and fancied it must be more akin to *Oni* (a Devil) than anything else" (I:90). A few thousand African Americans lived in San Francisco in the 1890s, when Noguchi arrived from Japan. Though some enjoyed success, many faced discrimination and difficulties in finding work. Such discrimination is evident in the fact that the Palace Hotel fired all its black employees in the 1880s after being pressured to do so by white labor unions. **"Coon,"** a derogatory slang term for African Americans, was in very wide use during the latter half of the 1890s, when the most successful genre of popular music was the "coon song." The first such song is thought to have been "Zip Coon," a comical impersonation of a black dandy performed by George Washington Dixon in 1834. The proliferation of the genre was notable by the 1880s (with the appearance of Paul Allen's 1883 "New Coon in Town," among other examples), but its golden age was unquestionably the late nineties, when the publication of hundreds of "coon songs" provided the sheet music and emerging phonograph industries with many of the chart toppers of the day. Popular black performer Ernest Hogan is often blamed for lending black prestige to the genre with his 1896 "All Coons Look Alike to Me," but the commercial lure proved irresistible even to the most talented black acts like Bert Williams and George Walker (who took to advertising themselves as "Two Real Coons") and Bob Cole and Billy Johnson, whose off-Broadway musical *A Trip to Coontown* (1898) was the first musical entirely written, performed, produced, and financed by black Americans.

24 (24 October) **From every corner in this nine-story hotel—think of its eight hundred and fifty-one rooms!—you are met by the greeting of the spittoon.** In fact the Palace Hotel was seven stories (eight in some parts) and had only 755 rooms. Porcelain spittoons were amply distributed throughout its spacious hallways and public areas. **The toilet room:** Indoor plumbing, private baths, and flush toilets were rarities in hotels at the time of the Palace Hotel's construction in 1875 and still luxury features at the turn of the century. An 1887 description of the hotel noted proudly that "every parlor and guest chamber has its

own private toilet, ample clothes closet and fire grate," and the private toilet must have included a "water closet," a deluxe accessory available since the 1860s. In contrast, the Japanese continued, until well into the twentieth century, to place "night soil" in various household receptacles to be periodically collected and, in many cases, purchased as a valuable crop fertilizer. Such practices would no doubt have seemed **three centuries behind** from the perspective of the Palace Hotel's toilet room, but they were environmentally efficient and largely free of health risks associated with untreated sewage that still plagued American and European cities. Morning Glory's enthusiasm about being able to **take off** her **shoes** and **play acrobat** alludes to the Japanese practice of wearing special toilet shoes (*benjo geta*), and to the differences between floor-level Japanese toilets (*daibenki*) and their chairlike Western counterparts. **Iya, haya** (いやはや): Honestly!

24–25 (25 October) **kissing:** *Seppun* (接吻), literally "lip contact," was "regarded by the Japanese as an act reserved solely for the privacy of the bedroom, if not indeed as something of an occult art" (Anderson and Richie 176). It was only in 1946, under U.S. military occupation, that *Aru yo no seppun* (A Certain Night's Kiss) dared to offer "the first kiss scene in any Japanese film"; even then, despite the salacious title, the shocking act was obscured by an open umbrella. **The Japanese consul** is evidently based on Hirokichi Mutsu (陸奥広吉 1869–1942), son of the late foreign minister and former Japanese ambassador to the United States, Munemitsu Mutsu (1844–97). The younger Mutsu headed the consular office in San Francisco from 1898 to 1901. His (according to Morning Glory) **Meriken wife**, Gertrude Ethel Passingham (1867–1930), was not, in fact, American, but English; Kōkichi had met her on an earlier diplomatic stint at the Japanese embassy in London. After the couple retired to Kamakura, Gertrude, now calling herself the Countess Iso Mutsu, published a well-regarded guide to the city, *Kamakura: Fact and Legend* (1918).

25–26 (26 October) **shrine of Tennō Sama:** refers (as one may surmise from Noguchi's other writings) to Gozu Tennō, patron deity of Noguchi's hometown Tsushima shrine—"the Ox-Head Emperor," as Noguchi calls him elsewhere (*SYN* 215). Gozu Tennō apparently began his complicated divine career in India as Gavagriva, a tutelary protector of a Buddhist monastery said to have been established during the lifetime of the historical Buddha. As a protector against pestilence (associated with the Hindu demon-slaying Indra), Gozu Tennō reached Japan via Tibet and China, where he acquired associations with both Vajrayana Buddhism and Chinese Taoism. In the year 869, worship of Gozu Tennō proved efficacious against an epidemic in Kyoto, and thereafter the deity, identified by the Japanese as a form of the Shintō deity Susanoo no Mikoto, was enshrined at the Gion shrine and celebrated in the annual Gion festival, now one of Japan's oldest and most famous festivals.

26 (27 October) **red demon in Jigoku:** Depictions of hell or *jigoku* (地獄, literally "earth-prison") have been popular in certain Japanese Buddhist sects—most notably the Pure Land (Jōdo) sect with which Noguchi's family was closely associated. Buddhist Jigoku is customarily described as the lowest of the *rokudō rinne* (六道輪廻) or "six paths of *samsara*" into which one may be reborn, a conception largely derived from the "five realms" of Hindu transmigrational thought. Typical pictorial representations of jigoku depict Emma, ruler of the underworld, assigning new recruits to appropriate subhells, those of a fiery sort being watched over by red demons (*aka-oni*), while blue demons (*ao-oni*) evoke the fashion of icy realms.

26–29 (28 October) **hanao** (鼻緒): thong (strap) of geta (wooden clogs) or zori (sandals). **O Fuji San**: Mount Fuji, Japan's tallest mountain. Longfellow's **"Psalm of Life"** (see note to 29 September) begins: "Tell me not, in mournful numbers, / Life is but an empty dream!—." **Golf** did not exist in Japan until the first decade of the twentieth century, when the first courses were constructed in the former foreign ports of Kobe and Yokohama. A century later, Japan claimed the second-largest golfing population in the world, after the United States. **Their English was neither Macaulay's nor Irving's:** Morning Glory here reveals her unfamiliarity with the styles of spoken English used by the women, at the same time implying their unfavorable comparison to the literary models she has studied in Japan. Thomas Babington Macaulay (1800–1859) was a British writer (and Member of Parliament) famed for his essays on political and literary subjects, while Washington Irving (1783–1859) was best known for his lively stories of American and British life (see note to 2 October). Noguchi noted in *The Story of Yone Noguchi* his appreciation of Macaulay's prose style: "The first English book I read in a Tokyo School was Macaulay's *Life of Lord Clive*, the beautiful style of which excited my adventurous enthusiasm" (6).

29 (29 October) **tongue and ox-tail soup . . . tripe . . . pig's feet**: Although Emperor Temmu's late-seventh-century Buddhism-derived prohibitions against eating certain animals were no longer strictly observed by the time the meat-eating foreigners returned to Japan in the mid-1850s, meat eating continued to be considered an unusual barbarous custom until the new Meiji government began promoting it as a beneficial practice, the turning point being the emperor's own 1872 proclamation accepting meat eating in the imperial palace. Around the same time, the new government moved to eliminate the stigma attached to meat handling by redefining the outcaste *burakumin* group (which included butchers and leather workers) as *shin heimin* ("new commoners"). Although beef restaurants were popular among urban Japanese cognoscenti in the late 1800s, they continued to be criticized and parodied as a Western fad until well into the twentieth century. **"western sea eggplant":** Western and Japanese eggplant varieties are nearly all members of the *Solanum melongena* family, but the common Western variety (var. *esculentum*) is generally thought to have a stronger, more disagreeable flavor than has its milder Japanese cousin, the *nasu*. Like other members of the *Solanum* (Nightshade) genus, eggplant contains the toxin Solanine, which may account for its shady reputation in medieval Europe, where it was linked with various maladies, including madness and leprosy. **Harai tamae! Kiyome tamae!** (祓い給え清め給え): a purification invocation.

29–30 (30 October) **chrysanthemum . . . show at Dangozaka:** The annual *kikkaten* (菊花展) held at Dangozaka (団子坂) in northwestern Tokyo was an elaborate affair, as Noguchi described in "Chrysanthemum" (*TT* 88–91). *Kikkaten* were a popular Edo-period (1600–1868) entertainment built on an older autumn chrysanthemum festival tradition: the *kiku no sekku* (菊の節句), one of five traditional *sekku* or seasonal festivals dating back at least to the Heian period (794–1185). The festivals are actually of Chinese origin, as were indeed, the mums themselves, which are thought to have been imported for medicinal purposes in the fifth century. A **tokonoma** (床の間) is an alcove for decorative objects. **The violet, . . . favourite of dear John Keats:** Although the violet is by no means dominant among the many references to flowers in the poetry of John Keats (1795–1821), it does make a few notable appearances. In "Adonais: An Elegy on the Death of John Keats," Shelley writes: "His head was bound with pansies overblown, / And faded violets, white, and pied, and blue"—an image that probably derives from Keats's "Ode to a Nightingale," which mentions "fast-fading violets cover'd up in leaves." Noguchi presumably means to suggest that Keats, with his early death from tuberculosis, was himself a fast-fading violet. The flower and color were notoriously popular in the 1890s (one famous study of the period is entitled *The Mauve Decade*) but do not make an appearance in Noguchi's poetry until his third volume, which contains such purple passages as "the evening stars of violet song," "her eloquent violet eyes," and "along a violet road" (*FTES* 4, 7, 22). A melodramatic love poem, "The Violet," appears in Noguchi's 1905 collaboration with Joaquin Miller, *Japan of Sword and Love*, and is reprinted in *The Pilgrimage* (7–9).

30 (31 October) **Longfellow . . . has ceased to be an idol of American ladies:** Longfellow's reputation in the United States began declining soon after his death in 1882 and reached its nadir in the years just before World War I, but his poems continued to be heavily anthologized in collections intended for use in schools. By the 1930s Ludwig Lewisohn's question—"Who, except wretched schoolchildren, now reads Longfellow?"—was widely echoed in the criticism (quoted in Arvin 321).

30–31 (1 November) **Van Ness Avenue,** which extends from City Hall to Pacific Heights at the northern end, was lined with mansions and private clubs. Noguchi wrote in a Japanese essay that his first domestic employment was in a "huge and splendid house" at the corner of Van Ness and Sacramento Street ("*San Furanshisuko*" 43; see also note to 26 January). **"Two Cherry Blossom Musumes"**—which the Japanese edition (51) renders as *futari no sakura musume* (二人の櫻娘)—is probably Noguchi's invention. In kabuki, the *musume* (unmarried woman or daughter) was typically portrayed as pure, innocent, and faithful. **"The Geisha,"** an early musical comedy, was the most successful production of the team credited with originating the modern musical: producer George Edwardes, composer Sidney Jones, librettist Owen Hall, and lyricist Harry Greenbank. *The Geisha* debuted at London's Daly Theatre on Leicester Square 25 April 1896 and ran for 760 performances; the New York production, which opened September 1896 at Daly's New York theatre, turned in a less spectacular but still respectable 160 performances. The play was also popular in San Francisco, where it opened at the old Tivoli opera house on Eddy Street on 26 October 1897 and ran for 50 performances, closing on 5 December. The play is largely responsible for introducing the figure of the geisha in England and America. The profession of *geisha* (芸者), which means "art-person," became popular in the 1700s and was early on restricted to entertainment districts or *yūkaku*, which were also home to prostitutes, known as *yūjo* or *jorō*. Geisha were in fact prohibited by law from directly engaging in prostitution, although financial support by wealthy patrons led to a considerable gray area between the two professions. Noguchi probably did not write the interesting essay entitled "The Geisha Girl of Japan" that appeared under his name in 1905.

33 (3 November) **our Mikado's birthday**: The Japanese emperor, Mutsuhito, better known by the title of his reign (Meiji), was born on 3 November 1852. The emperor's birthday is customarily celebrated as a holiday, although, rather unusually, Meiji's birthday continued to be celebrated even after his death in 1912. The holiday was renamed "Culture Day" after World War II. **"The Age of Our Sovereign"** is a rough translation of "*Kimigayo*," the title and first line of the Japanese national anthem, a *Kokinshū* tanka poem set to music in 1876 and recomposed in 1880. **Banzai** (万才), which literally means "ten thousand years," is a Japanese equivalent of the English "hurrah."

33 (4 November) **Robert Stevenson,** who had died in Samoa in 1894, was claimed as a California writer by virtue of his brief residence in the state from 1879, around the time of his marriage to San Francisco resident Fanny Osbourne; Noguchi was friendly with Fanny's children, Lloyd and Isobel, and especially Isobel's bohemian artist husband, Joseph

Strong, who had also lived with the Stevenson family in Samoa. Noguchi's friend Charles Warren Stoddard is credited with inspiring Stevenson's lust for South Seas travel. In 1897 Noguchi's *Lark* associates Bruce Porter and Willis Polk erected the Stevenson monument in Chinatown's Portsmouth Square.

34 (5 November) **darkey:** Among the various derogatory terms for black people popular among whites in the late nineteenth century, darkey (or "darky") conveyed nuances of cheerful contentment, in contrast to the ambitious dandyism of the "coon" (see note to 23 October) and the angry obnoxiousness of the "bully." White musicians as well as black (obliged, of course, to cater to white tastes) made liberal use of "darky" and the related "Darktown"—alternatives, as it were, to "coon" and "Coontown." "Warm coons a prancin' / Swell coons a dancin' / Tough coons who'll want to fight" were promised in "Darktown Is Out Tonight," the opening number of Paul Laurence Dunbar and Will Marion Cook's groundbreaking first all-black Broadway musical, *Clorindy or The Origin of the Cakewalk* (1898). **Hei, hei, hei** (へいへいへい): Okay, okay.

34 (6 November) **"para para"** (ぱらぱら): in large drops; scattering; making a pattering sound. **O Yuki San!** (お雪さん): honorable Ms. Snow. **ashida** (足駄): high clogs.

34–35 (8 November) **We drove to the Golden Gate Park.** Although Golden Gate Park, constructed in the 1870s and extensively developed for the 1894 Midwinter Exhibition, could be easily reached by streetcar, carriages, which were allowed to range freely through the park's spacious meadows were de rigeur for sophisticated picnickers. **and then to the Cliff House:** Perched on the cliffs above Ocean Beach (situated at the western end of Golden Gate Park) was Adolph Sutro's resplendent Cliff House, an eight-story entertainment complex built in 1896 in the style of a French chateau, replacing a less elaborate structure built in 1863 and destroyed by fire in 1894. Golden Gate Park's **Japanese tea garden**, one of the more famous and influential early examples of Japanese architecture in the United States, grew out of a Japanese village constructed for the 1894 Midwinter Exposition. The exhibit had been organized by George Turner Marsh, who is said to have contributed the Japanese entrance gate from his Mill Valley summer home. After the city took over the buildings, Makoto Hagiwara, an affluent immigrant from Yamanashi, proposed developing the site into a permanent tea garden, to be managed by himself and his family, who would occupy a small private area in the garden complex. The tea garden proved popular amid the fashionable *Japonisme* of the 1890s, but in the wake of the first organized anti-Japanese protests in 1900, the city ousted Hagiwara, who built a competing "Japanese village" outside of the park. In 1907, the city reconsidered the matter, and Hagiwara was invited to lease the site as a concession for one dollar a year, an arrangement that continued under Hagiwara's descendants until their eventual eviction in 1942 under Executive Order 9006. **o'senbe** (お煎餅): a rice cracker or biscuit. **shamisen** (三味線): three-stringed musical instrument. **Tenu, tenu! Tenu, tsunn shann!**: sound of plucking a shamisen. **My Gal's a High-Born Lady**, properly "My Gal Is a High Born Lady" (1896), was a popular "coon song" by Barney Fagan, leader of a large minstrel troupe and a pioneer tap dancer. It was recorded by Len Spencer and occupied the top of the charts for four weeks from 20 March 1897. The singer celebrates his "swell colored affair" in the catchy refrain: "My gal is a high born lady / She's black but not too shady / Feathered like a peacock, just as gay, / She is not colored, she was born that way." (Both Fagan and Spencer were white.) The song also makes a brief appearance in D. H. Lawrence's *Women in Love* (1920).

36 (9 November) **third anniversary of my grandmother's death:** The *sankaiki* (三回忌) or "third-time memorial," observed two years after a person's death, is one of a series prescribed by Buddhist tradition. **ijins**: See note to 5 October.

36–37 (10 November) **women coursing like a 'rikisha of 'Hama**: Though a Japanese invention, the *jinrikisha* (人力車), literally "human-powered vehicle," was originally developed for use in foreign settlements like Yokohama, where in 1870 it officially entered into competition with the newly imported horse-drawn carriages, creating unpredictable traffic conditions as the large and relatively high-speed vehicles, piloted by drivers of various nationalities, faced down pedestrians under protection of extraterritoriality. Morning Glory's carping observations are presumably meant to suggest a similar danger on American streets posed by American women strolling in their unwieldy bustle skirts, exacerbated by a sense of carelessness reiterated in the ensuing snippets: **their children crying at home** and **left somewhere their womanliness.** The **'vertisements of 'The Girl from Paris'** would have been left over from the San Francisco segment of the national tour that followed Edward E. Rice's New York production. An American burlesque revision of George Dance and Ivan Caryll's London musical comedy, *The Gay Parisienne*, it had opened at New York's Herald Square Theatre in December 1896, remaining there through the summer of 1897. One admirer of the play was William Randolph Hearst, who fell in love with a sixteen-year-old "bicycle girl" in the chorus, Millicent Willson, eventually marrying her in 1903.

37 (11 November) **"gokigen ukagai"** (御機嫌伺い): paying of respects.

37–38 (12 November) **the high hill of California Street,** i.e., Nob Hill. The elite neighborhood was certainly quieter than chaotic Market Street, but Morning Glory's comment that she is **"grateful there is no car quaking along there"** overstates the case, since the California Street cable car line had been in operation since 1878. The line was built by Leland Stanford, whose mansion stood at the southwest corner of California and Powell, beside the palatial home of the late Mark Hopkins (occupied after 1893 by the San Francisco Art Institute). Across the street were the mansions of the remaining "big four" railroad magnates: Collis Huntington and Charles Crocker. **The Chinese colony is close at hand:** Dupont or Grant Street, the central street of Chinatown, is about four blocks from the top of Nob Hill. **"karako"** (唐子): Chinese girl, usually referring to a conventional style, as in "*karako-mage*," a Chinese hairstyle, and "*karako-ningyō*," a doll in Chinese costume.

38 (13 November) **The Oakland boat joggled on happily as from a fairy isle:** Until the opening of the San Francisco–Oakland Bay Bridge in 1936, the main mode of travel to the East Bay was the Oakland Ferry's frequent service from the Ferry Building at the eastern end of Market Street to the Oakland pier. On the half-hour passage the steamers passed the small Yerba Buena Island that now provides the bridge's center support. In Noguchi's time, the island was the site of a small lighthouse and had been planted with trees on California's first Arbor Day in 1886, one of Joaquin Miller's more successful environmental projects.

38–39 (14 November) **haori** (羽織): formal coat, often emblazoned with a family crest.

39–40 (16 November) **"charin charan"** (ちゃりんちゃらん): compound of "*charin*," a clinking sound, and "*charan-charan*," "jingle-jangle." **The Yokohama Shōkin Ginkō** (横浜正金銀行) was the San Francisco branch of the Yokohama Specie bank, located at 515 Montgomery Street. The bank, founded in 1880, was the brainchild of Keiō founder Yukichi Fukuzawa, who saw it as a solution to the drain on Japan's precious metal reserves that resulted from Japan's unequal foreign treaties.

40 (17 November) **the gallery of the photographer Taber**: prominent San Francisco photographer Isaiah West Taber (1830–1912). In 1896, Noguchi had his first publicity photograph taken at Taber's 121 Post Street studio. **"pera pera"** (ぺらぺら): thin, flimsy [clothes]. The Japanese *Diary* (59) substitutes the *nihon no fuku* (日本の服), which means simply "Japanese clothes." The likely reason is the increasingly common use of "*pera pera*" to mean "quickly," and by extension "speaking fluently in a foreign language." **actress in the part of "Geisha"**: See note to 1 November. In the San Francisco production, Florence Wolcott played the role of O Mimosa, the lead geisha. **Botan Tōrō** (牡丹灯籠): "One of the never-failing attractions of the Tōkyō stage is the performance, by the famous **Kikugorō** and his company, of the *Botan-Dōrō*, or 'Peony-Lantern,'" wrote Lafcadio Hearn in his retelling of the tale, "A Passional Karma," which appeared in his 1899 collection *In Ghostly Japan*. A well-known ghost story of Chinese origin, "The Peony Lantern" revolves around the ultimately doomed efforts to rescue a young man, Shinsaburō, from the lingering attentions of a young woman, O-Tsuyu, who dies of longing when Shinsaburō proves unable to fulfill their mutual meeting pact. The kabuki play, *Kaidan Botan Tōrō* (The Peony Lantern ghost story), was a recent adaptation, premiering at Ginza's *Kabukiza* in July 1892, with the great Kikugorō Onoe stealing the show in dual, ostensibly minor, roles as Tomozō (Shinsaburō's corrupt servant) and the ghost of O-Yone (O-Tsuyu's devoted maid). There is an *ukiyoe* triptych by the artist Kunichika Toyohara depicting Kikugorō in both guises that provides a clue to what Noguchi had in mind in comparing the pseudo-Japanese hairstyles of American actresses in *The Geisha* to Kikugorō's "ghost style." Instead of the profusion of unruly, strangely colored hair favored by denizens of the Japanese spirit world, Kikugorō's O-Yone (as Kunichika renders it) gives just a suggestion of ghostliness in the wispy lock escaping from her slightly misshapen bundle of hair, no doubt because the storyline requires Shinsaburō to believe that she and her mistress are still alive until fairly late in the play.

40–41 (18 November) **"My Gal's a High-Born Lady"**: See note to 8 November. **a matinée of one vaudeville**: At the turn of the century, San Francisco's premiere vaudeville theatre was the Orpheum, located at 117 O'Farrell Street between Stockton and Powell. The program, which featured a series of short acts or "turns," was regularly changed. A typical program in late October 1897 offered continuing performances by "diminutive comedians" Arthur and Jennie Dunn, society sketch artists Hayden and Hetherton, Miss Edna Collins ("the whistler"), and singer Ola Hayden, plus two novelties, "the best machine yet made for projecting continuous photographs" from American Biograph, and Mlle. Irma Orbasany of Paris, "who directs a troop of trained cockatoos." A month later, the Biograph Pictures machine was still running, but the continuing acts were Fordyce's musical puppets, comedy duo Stanley and Jackson, juggler O. K. Sato, European illusionist Servais Le Roy, Morris' Trained Ponies, and Harry Edson and his dog "Doc." Ticket prices ranged from ten cents (balcony) to fifty cents (open chairs and box seats), and matinees were offered on Wednesday, Saturday, and Sunday. As noted in the text, 18 November 1899 was a Saturday.

41–42 (19 November) **the insignificant works of local poets**: Noguchi is satirizing the pretensions of his own poetical circle, which included such luminaries as Joaquin Miller, Edwin Markham, Ina Coolbrith, and future mayor Edward Robson Taylor. **Tasukatta wa!** (助かったわ): Saved! **"O'hayō"** (お早う): Good morning (informal). **"Chon kina! Chon kina!" . . . a Japanese song, she said, which the geisha girls sung in "The Geisha":** (See also note for 1 November.) Morning Glory's objections to the song would likely be connected with its improper associations, as the song had origins in a geisha-quarter musical variant of *chon-kina* or *jan-ken* (the Japanese game usually known in the West as "rock, scissors, paper"). "The Chonkina, I was told before I went to Japan, was a dance similar to the game of 'strip poker,'" explained Harry Hervey in 1924 in *Where Strange Gods Call.* "It was done to the twanging of a samisen and the song 'Chonkina'; and at the word 'Hoi!' the music stopped and the dancers, who were making figures with their hands, held their posture." The loser "forfeited one garment" (48). In Japan, Hervey allegedly witnessed the game in Yoshiwara and was informed by a more knowledgeable Western interlocutor that "Chonkina, as it was originally conceived, was a game for children," and that "the forfeit in Chonkina was some article of clothing, but the last garment was never removed" (50). In the play, the song is sung by the character of Molly, an Englishwoman posing as a geisha, in hopes of winning back her geisha-infatuated fiancé. (Other "authentic geisha" characters participate in the chorus.) In spite of Morning Glory's logical inference that the play was **practising a plenteous injustice to Dai Nippon,** its treatment of Japan was comparatively respectful toward Japan, reserving most of its offensive ethnic humor for Chinese and French characters. In contrast to the fantastical "Japan" of Gilbert and Sullivan's *Mikado, The Geisha* presented a comical but not essentially inaccurate picture of the relations between geisha, foreign sailors, and visiting Western women in the waning days of the treaty-port era. There were, of course, many lapses in verisimilitude, beginning with the improbable plot characteristic of the genre.

42–43 (21 November) **if our speech lapped justly**: Morning Glory's use of "lap" here follows the usage of Victorian tailors and seamstresses, who used the term to describe a method of insuring proper fit by the use of layered folds. The comment seems to revisit her 28 October complaint that the speech of the American women was "neither Macaulay's nor Irving's." **the English of Carlyle . . . intangible:** The literary style of nineteenth-century British historian and essayist Thomas Carlyle (1795–1881) was the subject of much debate in the nineteenth century. "Much twaddling criticism has been spent on Carlyle's style," George Eliot commented in 1855. "Unquestionably there are some genuine minds, not at all given to twaddle, to whom his style in antipathetic, who find it as unendurable as an English lady finds peppermint. Against antipathies there is no arguing; they are misfortunes. But instinctive repulsion apart, surely there is no one who can read and relish Carlyle feeling that they could no more wish him to have written in another style than they could wish Gothic architecture not to be Gothic, or Raffaelle not to be Raffaellesque" (Seigel 409). Carlyle wore his Germanic influences on his sleeve, as it were, in *Sartor Resartus* (1833), which claimed to be a commentary on the life and thought of Diogenes Teufelsdröckh ("god-born devil-shit"), a tailor-philosopher supposed to have authored a work entitled "Clothes: Their Origin and Influence." **furoshiki** (風呂敷): a square cloth two feet or more in width. In the early Edo period, *furoshiki* served a double function: to wrap bundled items for the bath (*o-furo*) and then act as a spread (*shiki*) to cover the floor while dressing. Later, the *furoshiki* became an all-purpose carryall. **O' ba san** (叔母さん): "aunt," used to denote a middle-aged woman.

43–45 (23 November) **Tamageta!:** See note to Night, 21 October. **O Ada San:** the honorific "O" was often added to Japanese women's names in the nineteenth century. **"buku buku"** (ぶくぶく): bubbling.

45 (25 November) **The Chute** on Haight Street between Clay and Cole streets, one of the city's most popular recreational facilities, featured the famous waterslide developed by

amusement-park pioneer Paul Boynton (who built similar attractions in Chicago in 1894 and at Coney Island in 1895); it also featured roller coasters, a vaudeville theater, carnival booths, and a zoo. **Oji San** (伯父さん): uncle.

45–46 (26 November) **"kotsu kotsu"** (こつこつ): a tapping or drumming sound.

46 (27 November) The phrase **"nigger song"** was a vague and disparaging term for any of the various musical styles associated with, or depicting, black people. Here, Morning Glory is apparently referring to Ada's fondness for "coon songs" (see note to 23 October).

47 (29 November) **hired "crying women":** refers to women paid to perform the crying and wailing traditionally required of certain female relatives of the deceased during a Chinese funeral.

47 (30 November) **Formosa:** now Taiwan. **Chinee:** the disparaging term for a Chinese person was popularized by San Francisco writer Bret Harte's poem, "Plain Language from Truthful James" or "The Heathen Chinee" (1870).

48 (1 December) **Louisiana lottery ticket:** Chartered in 1868 and operating through 1893, the Louisiana State Lottery Company, the only legal lottery in the United States, issued lottery tickets nationwide and made huge profits. The company paid the state only $40,000 a year despite bringing in approximately 20 to 30 million dollars per year in ticket sales and paying out less than 50 percent of those earnings in cash prizes. The lottery tickets were delivered by special trains to local agents (note Morning Glory's sadness, on 12 November, leaving the Palace Hotel butlers who "talk gently as a lottery-seller"). Although in 1890 Congress had banned the sale of interstate lottery tickets, and in 1893 the company's charter had ended, the company continued to operate illegally out of Honduras until its U.S. printing press was shut down by the federal government in 1907.

48 (3 December) **Los Angeles:** Noguchi claimed in his autobiography that he traveled from San Francisco to Los Angeles on foot. In one chapter, he states that he read Shelley and Keats en route and then "engaged to work one week at a wooden-box factory" in order to replace his lost copy of Shelley (*SYN 20*), while in another chapter, he describes various comical adventures as he passes through farming communities on his way south, stopping in towns like Santa Cruz, Monterey, San Lucas, San Luis Obispo, and Santa Barbara and receiving assistance from other Japanese immigrants (49–54). "It was fortunate," he said, "to find a Japanese keeping a bamboo store, or a laundry shop, or working on a farm, wherever I went along the coast, who welcomed me" (51). A letter to Blanche Partington (*CEL* no. 37) indicates that Noguchi did undertake the journey in March 1899, although the extent was exaggerated since he was back in San Francisco by early April. In the letter, he states that he met Charles Lummis (the well-known editor and amateur ethnologist) and spent "about two weeks" in Los Angeles. After his return, he resumed work on the "O'Cho san writing" (the early version of the *Diary*) begun before his departure.

50 (5 December) **Meriken Jin:** modified form of *Amerikajin* (米人), an American.

50–51 (6 December) **"Anata donata?"** (貴方何方): Who are you? (humble). **"Gokigen ikaga?"** (御機嫌如何): How are you? **"Nihonjin desu"** (日本人です): I am a Japanese.

51–52 (7 December) **Kawaii koto!** (かわいい事): How cute! **Robert Burns:** Scottish poet especially known for his lively poems in Scottish dialect (lived 1759–96). **Bakabakashii wa!** (バカバカしいわ): Absurd; ridiculous. "*Wa*" here is emphatic. **If American babies were like Chinese girls! / I would pile up all my coins to buy one** alludes to the reputedly flourishing Chinese child-slave trade of San Francisco. A favorite topic of the San Francisco newspapers, Chinese slave girls were mainly bought to stock Chinatown bordellos, although girls of all ages were apparently available. According to one authority, the Chinese Exclusion Act had caused a rise in prices, so that "during the early eighteen-nineties they ranged from about $100 for a one-year-old girl to a maximum of $1,200 for a girl of fourteen [and] about 1897 girls of twelve to fifteen sometimes sold for as high as $2,500 each" (Asbury 181).

52–53 (8 December) **"hipp goo":** apparently Chinese pidgin. The Japanese translation gives the parenthetical gloss *jōtō* (上等), meaning "superior quality." Morning Glory's comments on the resemblance of the **inviting heaviness** of the dinner to **an honourable poem by Milton,** and the **Miltonic presence** of the Schuylers' house, brings a new referent—the English poet John Milton (1608–74)—into her ongoing discussion of literary and spoken English styles. Whereas her discussion of Carlyle's "intangible" style (see note to 21 November) employed analogies of clothing and gardening, her discussion of Milton's style involves comparisons with styles of food and architecture. In the nineteenth century, Milton was widely praised as the exemplar of the "grand style" in English poetry, but in the twentieth century, T. S. Eliot famously condemned Milton for writing English "like a dead language," declaring that "Milton's poetry could only be an influence for the worse, upon any poet whatever" (*Milton* 11, 14). Noguchi evidently found Milton's intentionally archaic style as **lenitive** (an archaic Latinate word meaning "soothing") as the Schuylers' candelabra. He had consciously emulated it in his second book, *The Voice of the Valley*, written, he said, "in the Yosemite Valley, where I took Milton's book of poems, whose organ melody did well match the valley's rhapsodic grandeur" (*SYN* 20). **"chabu chabu"** (ちゃぶちゃぶ): trickle.

53 (9 December) **barefooted Arabs:** By the 1880s, the term "street Arabs" or simply "Arabs" had become a popular epithet in Great Britain and America for poor children roaming urban centers.

53–54 (10 December) **"Nenneko, Nenneko, / Nennekoyo! / Oraga akanbo wa / Itsudekita? / Sangatsu sakurano / Sakutoki ni! / Doride okawoga / Sakurairo"** (寝んねこ、寝んねこ / 寝んねこよ。 / をらが赤坊は / いつ出来た。 / 三月桜の / 咲く時に。 / どうりでお顔が / 桜色。): lullaby, as translated in text.

54–55 (12 December) **Echo Mountain** above Altadena was a popular attraction from 1893, when developer Thaddeus S. C. Lowe completed construction of the Scenic Mount Lowe Railway, California's first electric mountain railway. Passengers rode the "white chariot" to the 3,192 foot summit, where they could enjoy two hotels, a zoo, an observatory, gardens, hiking trails, and, after 1895, a second railway to take them another 1,500 feet to a rustic Alpine Tavern.

54–55 (12 December) **Areda mono!** (あれだもの): There it is! **Nikki** (日記): diary. **Carlyle wrote his "French Revolution" twice:** Thomas Carlyle (see note to 21 November) sent the manuscript of his magisterial study of the French Revolution to John Stuart Mill, but it was inadvertently burnt as wastepaper by Mill's servant. After beginning the project anew, Carlyle completed the three-volume work in 1837.

55 (13 December) **the venerable bishop who threw out candlesticks to Jean Valjean in Hugo's book:** Morning Glory's encounter with the bishop reminds her of Bishop Myriel, a character in Victor Hugo's popular novel *Les Misérables* (1862) who helps Jean Valjean reject his former life of crime and dedicate himself to the betterment of humanity. Noguchi first read Hugo while working as a "schoolboy" in Palo Alto (*SYN* 14). **As Napoleon said when he saw Myriel:** Morning Glory's question to the bishop echoes the words used by the

French emperor Napoleon when he meets the old curate, Monsieur Myriel, in the opening pages of *Les Misérables*.

55–56 (14 December) **"Pachi pachi pachi!"** (ぱちぱちぱち): sound of fire. **Namu Tenshoko Daijingu!** (南無天照皇大神宮): Hail, shrine of the sun goddess! Shinto invocation to Tenshōkō-daijin, the Sun Goddess (Amaterasu). **Iyani natta!** (いやになった): It became annoying.

56–57 (15 December) **"bebe"** (べべ): baby kimono (archaic).

57–58 (16 December) **"nenne"** (寝んね): a baby; going to sleep. **hana kanzashi** (花簪): floral hairpin.

58 (17 December) **kibisho** (急須): a teapot.

58–59 (18 December) **Ureshiya!** (嬉しや): Happy! **"otenba"** (お転婆): a boisterous or wild girl. **Hotoke Sama** (仏様): Buddha.

59–60 (19 December) **"anego!"** (姉御): elder sister (humble), often used to refer to a woman older than the speaker. Morning Glory is referring to herself as Miss Olive's clumsy "elder sister."

64 (24 December) **'. . . full of whispers and of shadows, / Thou art what all the winds have uttered not, / What the still night suggesteth to the heart':** The lines are a somewhat condensed version of a passage in Stephen Phillips's *Marpessa* (London: John Lane, 1900), in which the mortal Idas endeavors to woo the beautiful Marpessa, who must choose between his mortal love and the divine affections of Apollo. **"Gomen kudasai!"** (御免下さい): Excuse me! (polite).

64 (25 December) **every Chinee—ten thousand Mongols in all—is named one Charley:** Estimates of the Chinese population in San Francisco in 1900 range from eleven to fourteen thousand. Noguchi, who despised being called "Charley" or "Frank," knew that Chinese people in America were not named "Charley" but instead were given that nickname by some non–Chinese Americans. See also note to 30 November.

65 (26 December) **"Rubaiyat of Omar Khayyam,"** properly the *Rubáiyát of Omar Khayyám*, freely translated by Edward FitzGerald from the verses attributed to the Persian astronomer and mathematician (1048–1123). Rising from total obscurity at the time of publication (1859) to cult admiration among the Pre-Raphaelites in the 1860s, the book found mass appeal in the decadent 1890s, when the poems were among the most widely read and quoted of the age. The book was, as Noguchi implies, highly popular among California writers who identified with its decadent pastoralism and resigned fatalism; Noguchi was, indeed, explicitly hailed by Porter Garnett of the *Lark* group as a new avatar of the "Oriental" Omar at the time of his first poetry publications in 1896. It should be noted, however, that the *Rubáiyát* was often parodied in the pages of *The Lark*, particularly by the satirical Burgess, who subsequently illustrated *The Rubaiyat of Omar Khayyam, jr.* (a 1902 volume allegedly "translated from the original Bornese into English verse" by humorist Wallace Irwin) and wrote his own *Rubaiyat of Omar Cayenne*, published by Frederick Stokes in 1904. **"I came like Water, and like Wind I go"**: from FitzGerald's *Rubáiyát*. The *Rubáiyát* appeared in four variant editions during FitzGerald's lifetime (1859, 1868, 1872, 1879) plus a slightly altered posthumous fifth edition (1889). Noguchi's quotations follow the wording of the third and later editions. The present poem appears as number 28 in the three later editions.

65–67 (27 December) **Japanese cult**: Noguchi evidently means the "cult" of Japanese flower arrangement broadly referred to as *ikebana* (生花), meaning "live flowers," or *kadō* (花道) "the way of flowers." The Japanese text gives *Nihon-ryō* (日本流) which might be translated more simply as "Japanese style." **My style is the Enshiu.** We have emended the original text's reading, enshin, presumably a misreading of Noguchi's manuscript. (The Japanese edition renders the line as 私の流は遠州流なのよ [*watashi no ryū wa enshū-ryū nano yo*]: "my style is the Enshū style!") Enshū Kobori (小堀遠州 1579–1647) was a prominent tea master, pottery connoisseur, garden designer, architect, calligrapher, and poet. His floral arrangement style was "the most elaborate and the most popular of the more modern styles," according to Josiah Conder, who "chiefly followed" it in *The Flowers of Japan and the Art of Floral Arrangement* (1891), explaining that "compared with some of the other styles, that of Enshiu is characterized by a greater degree of artificiality or artistic affectation, and this makes it specially adapted for the purposes of a thorough explanation of the principles of the art" (79). **Joss house** was a vague term for a Chinese shrine or temple, derived from the Portuguese "*deus.*" **simplicity of the illustrious Mr. Rikiu**: Sakai merchant Sen no Rikyū (千利休 1522–91) had a profound impact on the aesthetics of the Japanese tea ceremony (*chanoyu*) in his capacity as tea master under Japan's first shoguns. Rikyū's *wabi* aesthetic deployed austere rustic simplicity in order to promote a spiritual liberation from material concerns.

67–68 (28 December) **shamisen . . . hard implement to handle . . . unending blind practice**: The shamisen, which is played with a large plectrum, has no frets. **"Don't fancy me a geisha!"**: Shamisen playing was one of the traditional arts in which geisha (see note to 1 November) received extensive training. **an old hauta**: a genre of short shamisen songs originating in Japan's Edo period. **"Haori kakushite"** (羽織隠して) **which was Englished by someone,** namely, the English poet Edwin Arnold, in his 1891 book *Japonica* (60). Noguchi was evidently dissatisfied with Arnold's rhymed translation and later offered his own free-verse version in *The Pilgrimage* (131). **mado** (窓): window.

68–69 (29 December) **classical "flower path":** The entrance to the Japanese Kabuki stage via the *hanamichi* (花道), a narrow stage-level walkway at stage right, gives actors greater intimacy with the audience. **iyadawa!** (いやだわ): how annoying! **Japan theatre is a hurly-burly.** For Noguchi's early views on the Japanese theatre, see his articles "Theatres and Theatre-Going in Japan" and "The Evolution of the Japanese Stage." **O'cha wa yoroshi?** (お茶はよろし): How about some tea? (informal).

69 (30 December) **Sah!:** (さあ) Well!

70 (1 January) **Is to-day the opening of another century?** In a word, no: the new century began in 1901, not 1900. **"Shinnen omedetō"** (新年御目出度う): Happy New Year. **shimenawa** (七五三縄 or 注連縄): sacred shrine rope of twisted straw, hung with **gohei** (御幣), zigzag-shaped strips of paper. The shimenawa marks the presence of a god or the boundary of a sacred area. Usually found in shrines and other sacred spaces, shimenawa are placed on doors of houses during the new-year festival to invite the *toshigami*, god of the new year, who is believed to bring good luck. The shimenawa are accompanied by a **"gate pine tree"** or *kadomatsu* (門松), an assemblage of sprigs that serves as a temporary dwelling place or *yorishiro* (依代) for the toshigami. Offerings to the toshigami are usually placed on a small wooden stand called a **sambow** (三方). These include ricecakes, or *mochi* (餅), and a spiced sweet sake called **toso** (屠蘇).

70–71 (3 January) **"Fold your tents like the Arabs, / And silently steal away":** lines from Henry Wadsworth Longfellow's poem "The Day Is Done" (1845).

71 (6 January) **"O'tabaco bon"** (おタバコ盆): "The hair of little girls from seven to eight years old is in Matsue dressed usually after the style called O-tabako-bon, unless it be

simply 'banged,'" Lafcadio Hearn explained in his essay "Of Women's Hair." "In the O-tabako-bon ('honourable smoking-box' style) the hair is cut to the length of about four inches all round except above the forehead, where it is clipped a little shorter; and on the summit of the head it is allowed to grow longer and is gathered up into a peculiarly shaped knot, which justifies the curious name of the coiffure" (*Glimpses* 2:421).

71–73 (7 January) **Shiba park** (芝公園) in southern Tokyo is the site of Zōjōji, the vast family temple of the Tokugawa shoguns, as well as the Tokugawa family mausoleum (see *SYN* 207). Rebuilt after World War II, the park is now known for its views of Tokyo Tower rather than of the ornate mausoleums and vast pine grove that Noguchi passed by on his way to classes at Keiō (see *TT* 21–26, 130–33). **"Miss Honorable Moon, how old are you?"** and subsequent lines are the beginning of an actual Japanese song of that title, "*O-tsuki-san ikutsu*" (お月さん幾つ). **O Hana San** (お花さん): Honorable Miss Flower. **The first worry of a girl after thirteen would naturally be about her hair.** Lafcadio Hearn, in his essay "Of Women's Hair" (see notes to 14 October and 6 January), observed that girls in Matsue changed from simple *katsurashita* or *sokuhatsu* styles to the more complex *Omoe-dzuki* at the age of twelve, and to "the beautiful coiffure called jorōwage" two years later (*Glimpses* 2:421). With due allowances for regional differences and changes in fashion, Hearn's description reflects the common practice for Japanese girls to wear more elaborate hairstyles from puberty until marriage, when they would shift to a more conservative hairstyle (usually the *shimada*). **Utsukushii nah!** (美しいな): Beautiful!

73 (8 January) **Imperial Menagerie of Tokio**: Onshi Ueno Dōbutsuen (恩賜上野動物園) which may be translated as "The Imperial Gift Ueno Animal Park," opened as Japan's first zoo in 1882.

73–74 (9 January) **Cribbage . . . the Lambs:** The essayist and literary critic Charles Lamb (1775–1834) enjoyed evenings of cribbage and whist with friends. The game, invented by the seventeenth-century English poet Sir John Suckling, was considered a genteel pastime suitable for both male and female players, while **poker** (which Morning Glory gamely suggests to "Mrs. Consul" as an alternative to cribbage) was an unsavory game associated with gamblers.

74–75 (10 January) **Cigar-stands** were ubiquitous in San Francisco in 1899. The *Crocker-Langley Directory* listed some 250 retailers, with 47 on Market Street alone. The city was home to more than a hundred cigar manufacturers (a mere five companies produced the still unpopular cigarette) and about sixty importers or wholesalers. The cigar-stand business was largely Jewish; there are no Japanese or Chinese names listed in the *Directory*, although this undoubtedly reflects inclusion policies of the *Directory* rather than absence of businesses owned or managed by Japanese or Chinese. (The category of "Japanese and Chinese Goods," by way of illustration, absurdly lists only two Chinese businesses.) **Dupont Street,** now Grant Street, is one of San Francisco's oldest streets (originally Calle de la Fundación); it had been renamed for Captain Samuel F. Du Pont, whose ship played a role in the conquest of California in the Mexican-American War of 1846. The second renaming, in honor of President (and Mexican-American War veteran) Ulysses S. Grant, took place not after the 1906 earthquake, as is often claimed, but several decades earlier. The 1896 Rand, McNally *Atlas of the World* shows "Dupont Or Grant St.," reflecting resistance to the change that was especially strong among Chinese residents, who preferred the old name, easily rendered in Chinese as "Du Pon Gai." The street has always been the center of Chinatown, which has grown from a few blocks around Portsmouth

Square in the early Gold Rush years to its current size of about sixteen blocks, extending from the Dragon Gate at Grant and Bush streets to Broadway on the northern end. In the 1890s, when the so-called Chinese colony occupied a ten-block area extending southward only to Sacramento Street, Pine Street (the location of O Fuji San's cigar shop) was two blocks outside Chinatown; it is now the first street inside the gate. **O Fuji San** (お藤さん): honorable Ms. Wistaria. **teishu** (亭主): master or husband. **"Komaru nei!"** (困るね): "It's a difficult situation, isn't it?" **Doshite** (如何して): "Why? What for?" **"Hello ma baby, hello ma honey"** is from the song, "Hello Ma Baby," which sold over a million copies within a few months of its publication in January 1899. Written by vaudeville duo Joseph E. Howard and Ida Emerson, it was marketed as a "coon song," although it was in actuality a novelty song about crossed telephone wires. Recorded by Arthur Collins, it became the Philadelphia-born Irish "coon" crooner's fourth consecutive recording to hold the top of the recording charts since mid-February, and it occupied the position for four weeks, until 27 May, when Len Spencer's recording of the same song took over until 7 August. The song dramatizes the singer's efforts to maintain a fledgling telephone romance initiated with the fortuitous help of crossed wires:

> Hello! ma baby, Hello! Ma honey, Hello! ma ragtime gal.
> Send me a kiss by wire, baby my heart's on fire!
> If you refuse me, Honey, you'll lose me, then you'll be left alone;
> Oh baby, telephone and tell me I'm your own.

75–76 (11 January) **slot machine**: The modern slot machine, known as the Liberty Bell, was invented by a German-born San Francisco immigrant electrician named Charles Fey in 1887. Since gaming devices were not at the time protected by patent laws, Fey did not sell the machines but instead offered them without charge to saloons and cigar shops in exchange for fifty percent of the profits. San Francisco outlawed the machines in 1909 and the State of California followed suit two years later. **Lillian Russell cigars** were named after the singer-actress (1861–1922) who dominated the American stage at the turn of the century. An intimate of millionaire Diamond Jim Brady, she was said to smoke five hundred cigars a month.

76–77 (12 January) **"The Klondyke," my neighbouring saloon**: Noguchi's disapproval of the Alaskan Gold Rush of 1897 and the Spanish-American War, which caused similar chaos in the port the following year, was no doubt a factor in his naming of the two saloons mentioned in the text. In August 1897, Noguchi, whose idyllic life at the Hights was disrupted when Miller himself joined the Yukon stampede, published a broadside poem entitled "Noguchi's Song unto Brother Americans," advising readers to scorn the Klondike hysteria in favor of "the gold at the proud gate of San Francisco Bay, aye, the divine gold of the majestic sun!" Miller did not return from the Yukon until the following summer (see note to 12 February). **"If you ain't got no money, you needn't come round"** is a slight simplification of the second of Arthur Collins's four number-one hits of early 1899, properly entitled, "When You Ain't Got No More Money, Well, You Needn't Come Around." (The song had been composed by Alfred Baldwin Sloane to lyrics by Clarence S. Brewster for the Broadway hit *Kate Kip, Buyer*, which opened at New York's Bijou Theatre on 31 October 1898 and ran for 128 performances). In the song—a highly appropriate selection for a bar called the Klondyke (see preceding note)—the singer complains of his gambling losses and the unsympathetic attitude of his "on-'ry niggar gal [*sic*]," who tells him: "De only coon dat I can see is da one dat blows his dough on me. / So when you bring de stuff Mister Nigger I'se to be found / But when you ain't got no money, well you needn't come 'round." **Go yukkuri** (ごゆっくり): Please take your time. **Lord Nono Sama**: See note to 24 September. Here, "memorial day of Lord Nono Sama" would probably suggest the Buddha's birthday, also called the Hana Matsuri (Flower Festival). Since this holiday is celebrated in April, not January, the reference is evidently part of Morning Glory's playacting. **Oku San** (奥さん): wife, here used in the sense of the polite greeting, "madam."

77–79 (13 January) **noise in the Jap colony**: San Francisco's Japanese "colony" was a rather diffuse social entity in 1900, in contrast to the Chinese colony concentrated in Chinatown (see notes to 12 November and 10 January). The 2,500 or so Japanese, who were nearly all *Issei* (first-generation immigrants), not only inhabited diverse sections of the city but also were divided along demarcations of class, regional origin, and education. As they were overwhelmingly male, however, it is likely that the appearance of an attractive, unmarried Japanese female cigar-shop proprietor would have created a buzz in the community, and might even have been noted in one or more of the city's several Japanese newspapers. The **General Arthur cigar** was named after General Chester A. Arthur (1829–86), who became president of the United States after the assassination of James Garfield in 1881. The General Arthur cigar was probably the most popular cigar in turn-of-the-century San Francisco; it was certainly the most heavily advertised.

79 (14 January) **"Pon pili, yon, pon, pon!"**: unidentified. Possibly the drunkard has picked up the syllables, which are somewhat meaningful in Japanese, from a Japanese song.

79–80 (15 January) **Tomales**: Morning Glory means *tamales*, a steamed Mexican food made from seasoned meat wrapped in cornmeal. **barkeeper of "Remember the Maine"**: the mysterious explosion that sank the battleship Maine in Cuba's Havana Harbor in February 1898 heightened anti-Spanish sentiments (the full slogan was "Remember the Maine, to hell with Spain") and led to the Spanish-American War, another U.S. international affair (like the Klondike Gold Rush) that elicited Noguchi's disapproval. Under the title "*W*A*R*," the first number of the short-lived *Twilight* (published by Noguchi and illustrator Kōsen Takahashi in 1898) advised: "STOP THY BATTLING, O AMERICANS AND SPANIARDS! BUY THE TWILIGHT, THIS MAGAZINELET, AND READ IT UNDER THE SPRING SHADE OF TREE! WHAT HAPPY RESIGNATION! LAY THY WEAPONS ASIDE, O MY COMRADES!"

81–82 (18 January) **Matsuba** (松葉): Pine Leaf. Morning Glory's correspondence with Miss Pine Leaf forms the basis of *The American Letters of a Japanese Parlor-Maid*. **Hitofude mairase sōrō** (一筆参らせ候): "Allow me to call on you with a few careless lines," a traditional and rather archaic salutation. **"Satetoya!"** (さてとや): well, then! **tegami** (手紙): a letter. **western sea painting**: *Seiyōga* (西洋画) means Western-style painting, as opposed to *Nihonga*, traditional Japanese-style painting. **'Tragedy To Be a Woman'** is rendered in the Japanese edition (165) as 女に産れるって頗る悲劇よ [*onna ni umareru-tte sukoburu higeki yo*]: "to be born a woman is indeed an extreme tragedy." As the Japanese edition's rendering of **"seen on a fiction"** suggests, Noguchi means to say that the phrase could only be seen in a novel (*shōsetsu no naka ni*).

82–83 (19 January) **sat like a Turk** refers to the cross-legged sitting posture, an informal style for Japanese men that was usually considered improper for women. **Oni** (鬼): demon (see note to 23 October). **Erai** (偉い): formidable. **Gibbon's "History of Rome"**: Edward Gibbon published his massive and influential *History of the Decline and Fall of the Roman Empire* in six volumes between 1776 and 1788.

83 (20 January) **Ohayō!** (お早う): Good morning!

84 (21 January) **harakiri** (腹切り): literally, stomach cutting, the well-known Japanese form of ritual suicide, also known as *seppuku*. Known since the Heian period and institutionalized by the samurai, the practice was rare by the end of the nineteenth century. It is not strictly true that Noguchi's own **ancestor did a harakiri**, but there was a famous case of seppuku by a brother of one of Noguchi's ancestors, Masahide Hirate (平手政秀), who, as a tutor of the young Nobunaga Oda, committed suicide in 1553 in order to take responsibility for a transgression of the future warlord. The loss of honor caused the remainder of the family to relinquish their samurai status and become farmers, thus the name Noguchi (野口), which means "entrance to the field." **A hired Chinese 'crying woman'**: See note to 29 November.

85 (22 January) **John Burroughs or Mr. Stedman**: Naturalist and poet John Burroughs (1837–1921) published his view that Whitman was the greatest American poet in his 1867 *Notes on Walt Whitman as Poet and Person* (which his friend Whitman, who fully concurred, helped him write). Burroughs reiterated his veneration in his *Whitman: A Study*, an expanded assessment of the late poet published in 1896. Edmund Clarence Stedman (1833–1908) had published a more guarded endorsement of Whitman in an 1880 essay reprinted in *Poets of America* (1885). **eraiwa**: emphatic use of *erai* (see note to 19 January), comparable to "brilliant indeed," here used sarcastically. **Mr. Whitman's fat book** almost certainly refers to Walt Whitman's *Leaves of Grass*, first published in 1855. This collection of interrelated poems that display Whitman's characteristically lengthy lines and his favorite themes of democracy and transcendent selfhood grew ever larger in the eight subsequent editions published during Whitman's lifetime. It was Joaquin Miller who suggested that Noguchi try writing poetry in Whitman's free-verse style, although Miller did not himself engage in the practice, which remained so unpopular in the United States that Noguchi and Stephen Crane were virtually its only practitioners in the 1890s. In 1897 Noguchi had initiated a correspondence with Horace Traubel, "the afterglow of the good grey poet," as he called him, and was subsequently considered a member of the "Whitman brotherhood," later playing an important role in the introduction of Whitman studies in Japan.

85–86 (23 January) **Otto San:** It is clear from the context (and from the text of the Japanese edition) that "uncle" means *otō-san* (お父さん): father. *Otto san* usually means "husband" (夫さん), but the pronunciation here may be a colloquial variant. An **ennichi** (縁日) is a temple festival or fair. **The dictionary for Jap girls comprises no such word as 'No'**: much has been said about the Japanese belief in the impoliteness of negative responses, most famously in *The Japan That Can Say 'No'* (1989), an angry dialogue between the founder of Sony and the mayor of Tokyo that proposed an end to Japan's smiling affirmativeness, at least in the international arena. In Morning Glory's case, the issue extends beyond questions of politeness into Confucian ethics (see note to 5 October), since the "no" involves a parent-supported marriage proposal.

86–87 (25 January) **take** (竹): bamboo. **The Lincoln night school** was a program of the Lincoln School, a public institution dating back to the 1860s that occupied a four-story Spanish-style building on the east side of Fifth Street, between Market and Mission, across from the old mint. **"See the boy and the dog"** was the first half of lesson 2 in *The New National First Reader*, from the popular five-volume series by Charles Joseph Barnes, published in 1883. **I was on the dangerous verge of clapping Byron's poem into my "Ocean"**: Since Byron did not write any short lyric poems about the ocean, it is likely that

Morning Glory refers to one of several well-known sections of *Childe Harold's Pilgrimage* that describe the ocean, such as the passage from canto 4 that Morning Glory quotes in the entry for 15 October. The suggestion of plagiarism (see also notes to 16 October and 20 February) was probably intended as a humorous jab at Joaquin Miller, "the Byron of the Rockies," who was often accused of plagiarizing from his idol (Marberry 97).

87 (26 January) **Mission Street . . . the famous Jewish noses**: Noguchi's poor immigrant Jewish merchant family is another in the novel's series of ethnic stereotypes, joining the horrid, beautiful-voiced negroes, unsmiling pidgin-speaking "Chinee" laundrymen, and a hungry-eyed, uneducated Italian organ-grinder. The nearly twenty thousand Jews who comprised 6 percent of San Francisco's population at the turn of the century did not occupy any single neighborhood. Their prominence in the used-clothing trade that still flourishes in the relatively low-rent South of Market and Mission districts was the legacy of centuries of European persecution that prohibited Jews from owning land and practicing most professions. Many Jews—like dry-goods seller Levi Strauss (1829–1902), who had introduced an innovative style of riveted-waist overalls in the 1870s (restyled as the blue denim "501" in 1890)—found success in the city. Noguchi stated that his first domestic service was in the home of a wealthy Jewish family where he mooned over the beautiful daughter, who tutored him in English, while the mother scolded him for breaking eggs and the father left him feeling "something like a slave" with daily boot-cleaning requests (*SYN* 8–11). A Japanese article locates the house at Van Ness and Sacramento (see note to 1 November), giving rise to the supposition that the young lady may even have been an inspiration for the character of Ada. Noguchi's bohemian circle briefly included the artist Ernest Peixotto, whose father was the president of the city's leading synagogue, Temple Emanu-El. **pan, pan** (ぱんぱん): onomatopoetic representation of percussive sound. **Kowaya** (こわや): colloquial form of "kowai ya": Frightful!

88 (27 January) **"When Knighthood was in Flower,"** a historical romance set in Tudor England, was the national best-seller for fifteen months following its publication in 1898. The first novel by Indiana lawyer Charles Major (who published it under the pseudonym Edwin Caskoden but later acknowledged authorship), it remained on the best-seller list for several years and inspired several theatrical and film adaptations. **Loo Choo** is the Okinawan pronunciation of Ryūkyū (琉球), the Japanese pronunciation of the Chinese word for lapis lazuli, used as a name for the Okinawan islands before their annexation by Japan in 1879. It is not clear which island Morning Glory means by **an isle close by . . . name[d] "Come and See"**; some islands in the group do have inviting names, such as Kikaigashima (喜界島): "pleasure world island."

89–90 (29 January) **Tennyson? I wish his life had been more hard up**: Given what we know of Tennyson's somewhat troubled early home life and the melancholy that was brought on by his friend Arthur Hallam's death in 1833, it might seem strange that Morning Glory complains of Tennyson's having been too well off in life. Yet Tennyson appeared to many at the turn of the twentieth century to have led a charmed life: his poetry enjoyed great commercial success from the late 1840s onward; he possessed the title of poet laureate after 1850; he established a stable family life after marrying his longtime love, Emily Sellwood, in the same year; and he was granted a peerage (thus becoming Lord Tennyson) in 1884. **Lotos Eaters**: See note to 16 October. **'Paradise Lost'**: Morning Glory evidently intends to imitate John Milton's monumental epic poem, published in 1667 (see note to 8 December). **our Empress . . . is a poetess.** Empress Haruko (known posthumously as Empress Shōken) was a respected writer of *waka* (traditional thirty-one-syllable poems). Although not quite as prolific as her husband, who is said to have composed more than a hundred thousand poems in his lifetime, the empress turned in a respectable thirty thousand.

91–92 (1 February) **The Heights**: Joaquin Miller, the model for Morning Glory's poet, referred to his hillside abode in Oakland as "The Hights" (*sic*). **Fruitvale car**: A traveler using public transportation to travel from San Francisco to Joaquin Miller's Hights in 1899 rode the Oakland Ferry (see note to 13 November) to the Southern Pacific Railroad's Oakland "mole" (a railway terminal that extended some distance into the bay), rode the train several stops east to the Fruitvale Avenue station, took the Fruitvale Avenue streetcar north to its end in rustic Dimond, and climbed the moderately steep hillside for about thirty minutes. **The breeze . . . enticed my soul . . . into "Far-Beyond"**: Morning Glory's view of "Far-Beyond" here is more favorable than her view expressed on 29 September, vis-à-vis Longfellow, that "a poet need not always to sing . . . of tragic lamentation and of 'far-beyond.'" Here, the concept suggests the idea of the sublime, which is developed in the entry for 4 February. Noguchi uses "beyond" in several poems of this period (notably "Under the Moon" and "Beyond the Silence") to suggest sublimity or dream. **A Jap girl also is provided with some soul**: This is certainly the case according to Shintō thought: both men and women possess a *tama* or *tamashii* (魂), roughly equivalent to the Western conception of soul. Buddhist views on the question are more complicated; strictly speaking, neither women nor men have souls, for the Buddhist doctrine of *anatman*, or "no-soul," holds that the soul or self is an illusion. Japanese Mahayana Buddhism, however, developed a variety of strategies to accommodate the world of illusion, and therefore, to some extent, tolerates the notion of souls. Japanese Buddhist apologists of Noguchi's era were sensitive to the criticism that Buddhism was nihilistic; even Sōen Shaku, the Zen priest who led the Japanese delegation to the 1893 World's Parliament of Religions in Chicago, made efforts to present a "soul-friendly" view of Buddhism, explaining that "most people are exceedingly alarmed when they are told that the self or the soul, which they cherished so fondly is void in its nature, and will overwhelm us with a multitude of questions" (Snodgrass 220). A second problematic implied by Morning Glory's comment is that Buddhism often does distinguish between male and female souls: a "Jap girl" is thus provided with *some* soul but perhaps not quite the whole kit and caboodle. The Pure Land sect, noted for its liberal views on the gender question, holds that only men can enter the Pure Land of Amida Buddha; women are not ineligible but must be reborn first as men. **"Ah, take the Cash, and let the Credit go, / Nor heed the rumble of a distant Drum!"** is from the third or a later edition of FitzGerald's *Rubáiyát of Omar Khayyám*. (It appears in slightly different translations in the first and second editions). The full verse reads:

> Some for the Glories of This World; and some
> Sigh for the Prophet's Paradise to come;
> Ah, take the Cash, and let the Credit go,
> Nor heed the rumble of a distant Drum!

Mr. Heine: Before discarding his given names, Cincinnatus Hiner, in favor of Joaquin, Miller attempted to substitute "Heine" for "Hiner," claiming he had been named after the German poet Heinrich Heine. In fact, he was named for a Dr. Hiner, who delivered him (Marberry 3). **Arcadia** was a mountainous region in Greece celebrated in Greek and Roman poetry as a pastoral paradise. The name was later used for pastoral romances in the sixteenth century by Italian writer Jacopo Sannazzaro and English writer Philip Sidney.

92–93 (2 February) **one Japanese essay, "The Poetry of a Tea Kettle,"** rendered in the Japanese *Diary* (189) as *"tetsubin no utau shi"* (鉄瓶の歌ふ詩), is evidently rather obscure. **"Tomb of Unknown Singers":** Noguchi states that he "inscribed by Miller's order the words, 'To the Unknown' on a little stone" by the side of the tomb Miller built for himself on the Hights (*SYN* 70). The phrase may allude to the first tomb of unknown soldiers in Arlington National Cemetery, dedicated in 1866, in which "repose the bones of two thousand one hundred and eleven unknown soldiers gathered after the war from the fields of Bull Run, and the route to the Rappahannock."

93–94 (3 February) **Ara ma** (あらま): Oh, but—.

94 (4 February) **I felt as if I were hurrying to the "Sermon on the Mount":** The sermon, as related in Matthew 5–7, contains what many believe to be the central teachings of Christian discipleship, including the Lord's Prayer and the Beatitudes. Harr Wagner writes of Joaquin Miller: "if anyone wanted to talk religion, he told them to read the Ten Commandments and forget everything else except the Sermon on the Mount" (125). **Sublimity vibrated in her soul:** See note to 1 February on "soul." The Romantic preoccupation with the sublime—a heightened encounter with the infinite or transcendent in nature—still thrived among late-nineteenth-century California nature writers like John Muir and John Burroughs and landscape painters like William Keith. **You would hardly believe Morning Glory . . . because she was just a little Oriental:** dismissive views of Japanese aesthetics were not only widespread among Westerners in the late nineteenth century, but also promoted by knowledgeable Japanologists like Basil Hall Chamberlain and W. G. Aston. "Japanese literature," Aston stated in the opening pages of *A History of Japanese Literature,* "is the literature of a brave, courteous, light-hearted, pleasure-loving people, sentimental rather than passionate, witty and humorous, of nimble apprehension, but not profound; ingenious and inventive, but hardly capable of high intellectual achievement; of receptive minds endowed with a voracious appetite for knowledge; with a turn for neatness and elegance of expression, but seldom or never rising to sublimity" (4). Another of Noguchi's attempts to elevate Japanese claims to sublimity was his translation of Bashō's hokku: "Ah, how sublime— / The green leaves, the young leaves, / In the light of the sun!" (*TT* 11). **The Gate of the Pacific Ocean:** In his essay on Miller, Noguchi explained: "I raised my head and looked down through the western window of my little cottage attached to Miller's; where my eyesight reached far away was the gate of the Bay, and lo! there the golden sun was sinking heavily down through that gate, as if a mighty king or poet at his departure for 'Far Beyond.' When I was told afterward by Miller that this was the very place where John C. Freemont [*sic*], the path-finder, once pitched his tent and was inspired to give the name of Chrysopylae or Golden Gate, the place became thrice more romantic" (*SYN* 61). Frémont is supposed to have coined the name for the Pacific entrance to the strait in 1846. **"The groves were God's first temples"** is the first line of William Cullen Bryant's "A Forest Hymn," a poem offering praise to God for the beauty of nature and suggesting that humans could worship God in nature rather than in manmade constructions like temples and churches. It is natural that Noguchi would find the ideas expressed in the poem appealing, from the Shintōesque notion expressed in the quoted first line to later passages celebrating "holy men who hid themselves / Deep in the woody wilderness, and gave / Their lives to thought and prayer," a conception common to a number of Asian religions. Noguchi, too, found it "almost impossible," when he was living in the Oakland Hills, "not to heed the calling voice of trees, hills, waters, and skies in the far distance" (*SYN*

46). The poem **Thanatopsis** was written by Bryant when he was a teenager and published in the *North American Review* in 1817. Like "A Forest Hymn," this poem lauds nature and invites the reader to "Go forth, under the open sky, and list / To Nature's teachings."

95 (5 February) **a huge statue of the Muse bidding sayonara to the dying sun would be the fitting ornamentation for these Heights:** In his poem "Upon the Heights" Noguchi wrote, "My feeling was that I stood as one / Serenely poised for flight, as a muse / Of golden melody and lofty grace." **Her eyes flash in divine sarcasm:** see note on irony (21 October). The Japanese edition here gives *chōshō de . . . mikudashite* (嘲笑で . . . 見下して), "looking down in scornful laughter" (195). "Upon the Heights" continues: "Yea, I stood as one scorning the swords / And wanton menace of the cities" (*FTES* 31).

97 (6 February) **poppy, beloved harbinger:** The poppy was named the state flower of California in 1903. **Ara, ara** (あら、あら): well, well. **a villainous fox who masquerades in the shape of an old woman:** The story is difficult to identify. It is somewhat unusual because the shape-changing *kitsune* (see note to Night, 21 October) usually appears as a beautiful young woman or man. **Sparrow never forgets . . . to dance in its hundredth year** is a translation of the proverb, "*suzume hyaku-made odori wasurezu*" (雀百まで踊り忘れず).

98 (7 February) **Longfellow, Lowell—they all loved high seasoning as I:** Miller's comment about the seasoning preferences of American poets Henry Wadsworth Longfellow (1807–82) and James Russell Lowell (1819–91) is echoed in Noguchi's essay on Miller (*SYN* 74–75). **Perfume of Omar's Rose** suggests the famous ninth verse of FitzGerald's *Rubáiyát of Omar Khayyám,* which Morning Glory herself quotes in the entry for 14 February. Roses also appear in six other *Rubáiyát.*

99–100 (8 February) Heine's **red crape sash** reminds Morning Glory of an ostentatious Japanese kimono sash (*obi*). A **large Japanese tobacco bag** would complete the look. Though formerly worn by "men of the plebian classes," elaborate *tabako-ire* had become an obligatory fashion accessory after the government banned the wearing of swords in 1876. **The cap with gay ribbons was like one of Li Hung Chang's:** The appearance of the Chinese warlord, viceroy, and diplomat Li Hongzhang (1823–1901) was well known in America, Europe, and Japan from photographs and early motion pictures. Li negotiated the settlement of the Sino-Japanese War in 1895, toured Europe and America in 1896, and negotiated the end of the Boxer rebellion in 1901. He appeared in Chinese dress, and (literally as well as figuratively) wore many hats. **"Victor of Life and Song, / O Muse of golden grace!"** is a slight variation on the opening lines of Noguchi's "Upon the Heights" (seen note to 5 February), which begins: "And victor of life and silence, / I stood upon the Heights; triumphant, . . . Serenely poised for flight, as a muse / Of golden melody and lofty grace" (*FTES* 31). **Dante Gabriel Rossetti's "House of Life":** When his first wife, Elizabeth Siddal, committed suicide in 1862, Dante Gabriel Rossetti (1828–82) buried his manuscript of "The House of Life" in her grave. In 1869, he recovered the manuscript from her grave and added more sonnets; he published the entire sonnet sequence in 1870.

100 (9 February) **the first goddess, Izanagi, standing on the "Floating Bridge of Heaven," before the creation:** The story is told in the *Kojiki*, a collection of legends compiled by the beginning of the eighth century: "Hereupon all the Heavenly deities commanded the two deities His Augustness the Male-Who-Invites and Her Augustness the Female-Who-Invites [Izanagi and Izanami] ordering them to 'make, consolidate, and give birth to this drifting land.' . . . So the two deities, standing upon the Floating Bridge of Heaven pushed down the jeweled spear and stirred with it, whereupon, when they had

stirred the brine till it went curdle-curdle, and drew the spear up, the brine that dripped down from the end of the spear was piled up and became an island." From this island, called Onogoro ("spontaneously congealed"), the two deities produce the islands of Japan. Noguchi repeats the comparison in his essay on Miller (*SYN* 70–71). **"Not in Books"** is an abbreviation of Joaquin Miller's favored lecture title, "Lessons Not Found in Books," which "consisted mostly of his tribute to outdoor life and of the impassioned reading of his own poems" (Marberry 215). It was first given in the autumn of 1891 in San Diego. **"Sail on! Sail! Sail on! And on!"** was the refrain of Joaquin Miller's most famous poem, "Columbus" (1892). One of the most popular poems for school recitation, it was praised by Tennyson as "a masterpiece" and called "the best poem ever written by an American" by the *Athenaeum* (Marberry 225–26). The poem lionizes the Spanish explorer Christopher Columbus for daring to "sail on" to the New World despite naysayers in his entourage. **Pan, pan!** (ぱんぱん): onomatopoetic representation of percussive sound. The phrase often represents two handclaps in succession, which may denote a summons or rhythmical accompaniment.

100–101 (10 February) **I carried it down on my shoulder in Chinese laundry style:** According to magazine illustrations from the late nineteenth century, Chinese laundrymen carried laundry in large sacks or baskets either slung or carried over the shoulder. Fruit and vegetable peddlers, in contrast, carried their goods in baskets suspended from poles resting across the shoulder blades.

101 (11 February) **Sōdah** (そうだ): indeed.

102–103 (12 February) **gallon of whiskey . . . demijohn:** The rye or corn whiskey Miller toted to the Hights in a two-gallon wicker-covered jug was, according to fellow hard-drinking poet George Sterling, 110 proof and tasted "like swallowing an oil burner" (Marberry 193, 202). **Mr. Chōmei Kamo wrote his immortal "Ten-Foot Square Record":** In the early thirteenth-century *Hōjōki* (方丈記), Kamo no Chōmei, a retired priest of Kyoto's Kamo shrine (now Kamigamo and Shimogamo shrines), recorded his reflections on life in rustic seclusion, first in the vicinity of ōhara (a mountain village north of Kyoto) and then in a ten-foot-square hut he built on Hinoyama, a mountain south of Kyoto near Uji. **A fountain . . . melody of rain:** Harr Wagner recalled that Miller "had the water pipes and sprays so fixed that he could produce a perfect imitation of rain. He loved to gather his visitors around his chapel home and chant the song of the Rain Bear, and the rain would pour down on them although the sun was shining, and he would rush out with umbrellas to protect them from his magical rain" (129). **Klondyke costume:** Miller's lack of success in the Klondike mines did not prevent him from turning a healthy profit from his yearlong gold-digging adventure (see note to 12 January). The Hearst and Pulitzer newspaper syndicates entered into a bidding war for his exaggerated reportage of the journey, which netted him about six thousand dollars. Furthermore, "when he returned from the Klondike with the picturesque costume of fur coat with gold nugget buttons, he was offered a contract to appear in the East in the Keith vaudeville circuit" (Wagner 171). The tour, which began in December 1898, involved Miller recounting his impressions of the Klondike and reciting what he claimed was Chinook poetry, clad in the aforementioned parka, fur pants, and sealskin boots—and pulling a sled. Five performances a day of this routine proved less enjoyable than anticipated, and Miller canceled his contract after six weeks. **Namu Daijingu:** See note to 14 December. Here the shrine deity is unspecified.

103 (13 February) **yonaka** (夜中): midnight.

103–104 (14 February) **"willy-nilly blowing":** from quatrain number 29 in FitzGerald's *Rubáiyát of Omar Khayyám:*

> Into this Universe, and why not knowing,
> Nor whence, like Water willy-nilly flowing:
> And out of it, as Wind along the Waste,
> I know not whither, willy-nilly blowing.

"Each Morn a thousand Roses brings, you say; / Yes, but where leaves the Rose of Yesterday?": from poem 9 of Fitzgerald's *Rubáiyát of Omar Khayyám* (3rd ed.).

106–107 (18 February) **Bakabakashi** (バカバカしい): absurd; ridiculous.

108–112 (20 February) **[The Cave Journal . . . C] A railroad brigand is hiding in these Heights** may be a veiled allusion to the lingering scandal surrounding the arrest of Miller's estranged son Joseph McKay (whose real name was Harold Miller) for armed stagecoach robbery in 1891 (see Marberry 218). **[E] A girl in tights from a saloon-stage** represented the height of indecency in the view of many late-nineteenth-century moral reformers. Concert saloons, which became popular in the late 1850s, offered alcoholic beverages and variety entertainments, a volatile combination for immorality. As in the English music halls, the American concert saloons provided a notorious haven for prostitution, and the more enterprising saloons took charge of the business themselves in the form of so-called "pretty waiter girls." **[F] George Eliot,** the pseudonym of Mary Ann Evans (1819–80), a highly intellectual and highly prolific English novelist and critic. **[I]** The **ancient Chinese song** sung by the squirrel is difficult to identify. **[M] "I must secure the international copyright":** The first U.S. international copyright law, the Chace Act of 1891, provided a limited extension of copyright protection to authors who were not citizens of the United States, but only if (1) their works were published in the United States, (2) a copy was deposited with the copyright office prior to the publication, and (3) the author was a citizen of a country extending reciprocal protections to U.S. authors. Morning Glory's squirrel obviously could not have claimed copyright protection for Heine's unpublished works because squirrels, like other nonhuman animals, cannot own property under U.S. law and, indeed, have no rights at all in the strictly legal sense. Yet the squirrel's case is hardly silly, for it draws attention to a number of very real copyright issues directly impacting Noguchi's work. Perhaps the most important of these is the question of whether Noguchi, as a Japanese citizen, could have asserted any copyright to his own works published in the United States, including *The American Diary of a Japanese Girl* (which was in fact copyrighted by the Frank Leslie Publishing House in 1901 and the Frederick A. Stokes Company in 1902). Although in 1899 Japan had joined the Berne Convention (the international agreement providing automatic reciprocal copyright protection for members of signatory nations), the United States did not become a signatory to Berne until 1989 and was therefore not bound by any copyright convention with Japan until the first one, signed at Tokyo on November 10, 1905, went into effect on May 17, 1906. Until that time, from the point of view of U.S. copyright law, it is unlikely that Noguchi held any more valid claim to U.S. copyright protection than did the squirrel. This point may also illuminate Noguchi's rather casual attitude toward plagiarism, of which he was both instigator and victim on numerous occasions. Here, it is, after all, the squirrel who aims to benefit from the legal ambiguity, only to be held back by the shame of appearing as a "wicked reporter." **possibility of war between Russia and Japan:** See note to 3 October.

112–113 (21 February) **Flower Kingdom:** epithet for China. **The Empress Dowager** Tsu-Hsi (1835–1908) was the de facto ruler of China for most of the period from 1861 until her death in 1908. **"Me oll-righ, you savvy!":** "I'm alright, you understand!" in the pidgin English often associated with Chinese immigrants at the turn of the century. **'Hama:** Yokohama. **Asagao** (朝顔): Morning-glory (literally, morning-face). This is Morning Glory's first mention of her Japanese name.

113 (22 February) **o mikuji** (お神籤): a written oracle. **Akiwa god** or Akiba daimyōjin (秋葉大明神) is a minor Shintō deity worshipped in certain Shintō shrines throughout Japan. Noguchi's short story "The Wedding Bell" takes place at a "mountain temple of Akiwa Daimyojin" in Tado (多度), a village near Kuwana, which Noguchi may have visited in 1890 on his way to the port of Yokkaichi, when he left Nagoya for Tokyo. From this or a similar shrine, Morning Glory's mother has obtained an *o-mikuji*, probably by drawing lots. The *o-mikuji* advises devotion to the **Well-God**, or *idogami* (井戸神), one of a broad class of deities known as **suijin** (水神) or *mizu no kami* (水の神) that includes ordinary well protectors as well as their more exotic relatives like dragons and *kappa*. Suijin are protectors of water sources, but they also serve as the patron deities of fertility, motherhood, and easy childbirth. **Well without a funa fish isn't holy to a Jap mind**. As Lafcadio Hearn explains in *Out of the East* (1898): "The [well-]god has little servants to help him in his work. These are the small fishes the Japanese call funa. One or two funa are kept in every well, to clear the water of larvae. When a well is cleaned, great care is taken of the little fish" (112).

113–114 (23 February) **one picture, "Stolen Kiss," symbolising sweetness:** Noguchi probably has in mind one of several famous paintings by the French painter Jean-Honoré Fragonard (1732–1806). **"The hereditary fashion of nursing the baby on the back has thoroughly taught them dependence":** Ruth Benedict makes a similar point that "the spread-eagle strapping of the baby on the back in Japan . . . makes for passivity" (257–58). **"I urge that Emerson's essays be adopted in the Nippon schools. His 'Self-Reliance' should be the first of all"**: Emerson's "Self-Reliance," published in 1841, spoke of the need for people to trust their intuition and to refuse to conform to existing convention and ritual unless reason encouraged it. One early advocate of Emersonian ideas in Japan was Baron Naibu Kanda (who had heard Emerson speak at Amherst College in 1879); Emerson's work was first translated into Japanese in 1890, only a few years before Noguchi came to America. **"Japanese fad in America"**: Japanese influence on American culture following the "opening" of Japan in the 1860s was apparent in changing fashions in home furnishings, dramatic performances, the visual arts, and fiction. The phenomenon, now generally known as Japonisme, has been most extensively studied in the visual arts, where Japanese techniques, styles, and models were employed by many U.S. artists, most notably John McNeil Whistler and Mary Cassatt (see studies by Lambourne, Berger, and Cate for art, and by Lancaster for architecture). In the field of literature, interest in Japan fueled the publication of numerous travelogues, a few adaptations and translations of Japanese stories, a rather larger number of pseudo-Japanese tales, including the works of Long and Watanna (see notes to 4 March), and essays on various aspects of Japanese culture and history by Lafcadio Hearn and many others, including important early works by Anglophone Japanese writers such as Inazō Nitobe's *Bushidō* (1899) and Kakuzō Okakura's *Ideals of the East* (1903). See Miner for a useful if outdated survey. In the field of drama, Japanese-style plays were decidedly in vogue at the turn of the century, when revivals of British imports like *The*

Mikado and *The Geisha* (see note to 1 November) competed with homegrown productions like Belasco's *Madame Butterfly* and Klaw and Erlanger's *Japanese Nightingale,* as well as actual Japanese plays staged by the Kawakami troupe. For a discussion of the impact of Japanese material culture, see Yoshihara's chapter "Asia as Spectacle and Commodity" (15–44), and comments on Japanese furniture and kimono elsewhere in the present volume. **"A year or two ago, one Japanese theatrical troup roamed":** The uncle is probably not thinking here of the famous troupe of Otojirō and Sadayakko Kawakami, who were at that moment enjoying favorable reviews on the East Coast for their hybrid dramatic performances after a rocky start in San Francisco. (Had they arrived a few months earlier, he and Morning Glory might have met the Kawakamis in the elevator of the Palace Hotel, where the couple had resided until their local manager absconded with the troupe's earnings). Rather, the uncle would be alluding to one of the many troupes of acrobats and jugglers known as *karuwaza* (軽業, meaning "light entertainers") that frequently traveled abroad in the decades after the opening of Japan. Such troupes, appearing in theatres, international expositions, and traveling circuses, provided the first glimpses of Japanese performance for many foreigners, including Jules Verne (who included a memorable if somewhat garbled impression of one such troupe in *Around the World in Eighty Days* [1872]) and Lewis Carroll, who saw a *karuwaza* troupe perform in 1874. Constantin Stanislavsky (1863–1938), the pioneer of method acting, described in his autobiography how, in his youth, he and his family learned "all the Japanese customs" and "all the enchanting habits of the geishas" while hosting a Japanese acrobatic troupe in preparation for a Russian production of *The Mikado* (126–28). There is an extensive study in Japanese by Kurata. **"a certain loafing sailor as an English instructor":** In "How I Learned English," Noguchi recalled his surprise on discovering that his first foreign teacher in Nagoya was only "a common sort of sailor" (*SYN* 4). "In those days when we had little experience with foreigners," he explains, "a white skin and red hair were a sufficient passport for a Western teacher in any Japanese school" (5). **"It is painful to notice the dwarf trees":** The uncle's comments elaborate on those made by Morning Glory on 21 October.

114–115 (24 February) **Eve . . . Eden:** Chapter 3 of Genesis, the first book of the Jewish and Christian Bible, tells of Eve's temptation by the snake to eat the fruit of the tree of the knowledge of good and evil. The talking snake convinces Eve to eat the fruit by telling her that she and Adam will not die if they do so; rather, they will become like gods themselves.

115–116 (25 February) **a tea-house maiden, singing: "The air is lovely like wine; / Come, Lord! Come, Lord!":** Teahouse or *chaya* (茶屋) usually referred to a venue for geisha entertainment (see note to 1 November). Teahouses usually were quite distinct from the *kōshi-zashiki* (latticed rooms) in which prostitutes plied their trade, although in entertainment districts like Yoshiwara, "introducing tea-houses" known as *hikite-jaya* (引手茶屋) often assisted customers by arranging assignations. Ordinary *chaya* offered only entertainment and drink (and sometimes food). The song is evidently a translation of a ditty used to attract customers. **Mighty liar:** Joaquin Miller does not seem to have been much bothered by comments on his propensity for lying. On one occasion, when Harr Wagner informed him that "[Ambrose] Bierce has written a whole [newspaper] page to prove that you are a liar," Miller merely replied: "[W]hy take a whole page[?] I will admit I am a liar in three words" (Wagner 130). **"I cooked once in a Sierra camp for fifty miners. I was paid twenty dollars a week":** Miller twice worked as a cook in mining camps soon after he left his family's farm in Oregon at the age of seventeen. In the second of these jobs, he was paid fifty dollars a month (not twenty dollars a week) and cooked for only twenty-seven men rather than fifty (Marberry 23–24). **His open laughter was as from a simple Faun:** In the late nineteenth century, the classical figure of the faun (a half-animal, half-human quasi-divine Roman version of the Greek satyr) acquired new importance among artists and poets. Often taking the form of Pan, the lecherous shepherd-god of Arcadia (see note to 1 February) whose pipe-playing was said (by the unfortunate Midas at least) to rival the lyre of Apollo, the faun symbolized the irrepressible eroticism of creative energy, and, by extension, the argument for artistic and sexual freedom against the demand for regulation. In France, the faun was celebrated by Mallarmé and Debussy, and later by Matisse and Picasso; in Britain, by Swinburne and Yeats, among others; and among Noguchi's American poetical circle, by Bliss Carman and Richard Hovey in their popular *Songs from Vagabondia* (1894) and by Gelett Burgess and others in the pages of *The Lark*. Florence Lundborg's cover design for *The Lark*, number 17, which featured Noguchi's literary debut, portrays a pipe-playing Pan figure bearing a striking resemblance to Noguchi.

117 (27 February) **farewell poem in seventeen syllable form:** Noguchi's inclusion of this hokku (now usually called haiku) represented a modest step in his important effort to popularize the Japanese form. **Sayōnara no ureiya nokore mizu no neni** (サヨナラ乃憂や残れ水のねに) ("Grief of sayonara, remain in the sound of the water"): Morning Glory's "mizu no neni" recalls the *"mizu no oto"* of Bashō's famous poem (in Noguchi's translation): "The old pond! / A frog leapt into— / List, the water sound!" (*Spirit of Japanese Poetry* 45). Morning Glory's writing of "*sayōnara*" in *katakana* (usually employed for foreign loanwords) adds a creative touch.

117 (28 February) **fig tree:** In Genesis 3, Adam and Eve don fig leaves after eating the fruit of knowledge (see note to 24 February) leads them to discover that nakedness is a sin.

119 (2 March) **Cliff House . . . stupid song of the seals:** Seals still frolic on the Seal Rocks off Ocean Beach near the Cliff House (see note to 8 November).

119–120 (4 March) **"Madame Butterfly":** The novella by John Luther Long was published in the *Century Illustrated Magazine* in January 1898 and in book form a few months later. Long had never visited Japan himself but had heard stories about it from his sister, Sarah Jane Correll, the wife of a Methodist missionary. His story followed the life of Cho-Cho-San, or Miss Butterfly, the daughter of a samurai, from her marriage to an American, Benjamin Franklin Pinkerton, through her attempted suicide after she realizes he has permanently abandoned her and married a white American woman who now wishes to rear Butterfly and Pinkerton's young son. David Belasco adapted the story to the stage in 1900 but changed the ending: his Cho-Cho-San successfully commits suicide and her child (now a girl, not a boy) is taken away by Pinkerton and his American wife. Giacomo Puccini saw the play in London and was inspired to create his operatic adaptation, *Madama Butterfly* (1904). **Loti spoiled it with his "Madame Chrysanthème":** While living in Japan in the summer of 1885, Julien Marie Viaud, a lieutenant in the French navy, married a seventeen-year-old Japanese girl named Kane. Later he fictionalized this experience in the novel *Madame Chrysanthème* (published in 1887 under his pseudonym Pierre Loti). The first-person narrator of the novel registers a marriage with a young Japanese girl named Kiku (Chrysanthemum) and lives with her between his tours of duty in a French naval vessel. Eventually, he leaves Kiku when his ship is called to China, but neither he nor Kiku seems particularly sad at their parting. Two translations into English existed at the time Noguchi lived in the United States: Hettie E. Miller's translation for Donohue,

Henneberry and Company (published in 1892) and Laura Ensor's translation for Routledge (published in 1897). The story was also made into a four-act light opera that played in Paris in 1893 (see Van Rij 33). **tojin** (唐人): foreigner(s). **I am grateful I see no lady writer of Japanese novels yet:** Morning Glory overlooks Onoto Watanna's *Miss Numè of Japan*, published the previous year (see the Afterword for further discussion). **the "devils of mixture" swarming in Yokohama or Kobe, whose Jap mother was a professional "hell":** "*jigoku*" (hell) was a euphemism for an unlicensed prostitute. **Oriental novel:** See note for 23 February on the "Japanese fad in America."

120–121 (5 March) **letter creeps 'under your honourable table':** *onkika* (御机下 or 御几下) is a now rather quaint salutation conveying the sense of "your humble servant." **ume** (梅) is the Japanese plum tree, whose blossoms are widely admired as a harbinger of spring. It is a polite Japanese custom to begin a letter with a seasonal reference. **A certain famous Jap penman takes wine before he begins, for the sake of putting his mind in a fine frenzy:** The practice is probably too common to be identified with a single individual. The phrase "fine frenzy" is found in Shakespeare's *A Midsummer Night's Dream:*

> The poet's eye, in a fine frenzy rolling,
> Doth glance from heaven to earth, from earth to heaven;
> And as imagination bodies forth
> The forms of things unknown, the poet's pen
> Turns them to shapes, and gives to airy nothing
> A local habitation and a name. (5:1: 12–17)

121 (6 March) **The car is a modern opium resort, where we sleep and sleep:** Opium resorts, or "dens," existed in many large American cities in the late nineteenth century, though in some places, such as California, they were illegal by 1900. (A law passed in California in 1881 had made it illegal to own or operate an establishment where opium could be smoked and sold.) An opium establishment usually featured beds where customers could smoke opium and relax or sleep. **Rip Van Winkle** refers to the titular hero of Washington Irving's story "Rip Van Winkle" (1819), who falls asleep in his colonial American village only to wake up years later in the now-independent United States of America. Describing his Japanese homecoming in 1904, Noguchi wrote, "I was no other than Rip Van Winkle, only not so romantic as Joseph Jefferson's" (*SYN* 169), alluding to the impersonation of the character by actor Joseph Jefferson III (1829–1905) who created the role with playwright Dion Boucicault in 1865 and performed it to great acclaim for the last forty years of his life.

122 (7 March) **Chicago:** Noguchi spent several weeks in Chicago in May and June of 1900, en route to the East Coast. His impressions of the city, commissioned by the Chicago *Evening Post*, are reprinted in *SYN* (84–118). There, he also comments that **Chicago water is a perfect horror;** evidently, residents did not regard "a thick sediment of mud or sand at the bottom of the glass" as harmful (*SYN* 85). **Gomenyo!** (ご免よ): Sorry! (informal). **Cook County** is a large county in northeastern Illinois, founded in 1831, comprising the city of Chicago and numerous surrounding municipalities. **ojigi** (お辞儀): bow. **"Hell is a city much like Chicago, / A populous and a smoky city":** variation on the famous lines that begin part 3 of Percy Shelley's "*Peter Bell the Third*:"

> Hell is a city much like London—
> A populous and a smoky city;

There are all sorts of people undone,
And there is little or no fun done;
Small justice shown, and still less pity.

122–124 (8 March) **silk hat . . . Plug hat doesn't suit informal Chicago:** In the second half of the nineteenth century, the silk top hat supplanted the beaver-skin top hat as a staple in men's high-end fashion. "Plug hat" was another name for either a top hat or a bowler; clearly Morning Glory here uses the phrase to refer to a top hat. During his visit to Chicago, Noguchi noticed "only one or two gentlemen in silk hats" (*SYN* 110). **He changed his frock-coat for a sack-coat:** A frock-coat is a close-fitting knee-length men's suit coat, usually double-breasted, vented in the back, and with skirts that are the same length in front as in back. The more informal sack coat is a loose-fitting suit coat that comes down to the midthigh and usually has a small collar and four buttons. Noguchi believed that while Washington was "the city of the dress coat" and Boston "the city of the frock coat," Chicago was "the city of the sack coat" (*SYN* 98). **City Hall:** The City Hall Noguchi saw when he visited Chicago in 1900 had been built in 1885. Located at the intersection of Adams and LaSalle, the building was demolished in 1908 and replaced with a new structure. **Chicago River:** Today, the Chicago River winds its way through downtown Chicago and empties into the Des Plaines and Illinois river systems through three artificial channels that were built between 1900 and 1922. In 1900, the year of Noguchi's visit to the city, the flow of the river was permanently reversed in the first of these engineering projects. Instead of flowing into Lake Michigan, as it had done previously, the main branch of the river was diverted into the newly built Sanitary and Ship Canal so that the city's waste would not pollute the lake. **Lake of Michigan from Lincoln Park:** Lincoln Park, which Noguchi considered "beautiful" (*SYN* 92), is a large city-owned park located on the north side of Chicago, along the Lake Michigan waterfront. Part of the site originally functioned as a public cemetery, but the city decided to turn the land into a park in 1864. The Lincoln Park Zoo, one of the main attractions of the park today, was founded in 1868. **how many stories in that building:** Until the 1920s, Chicago's tallest building was the 302-foot Masonic Temple at the corner of Randolph and State Streets, built in 1892 by Burnham and Root, the same firm that designed San Francisco's *Chronicle* building (see note to Night, 21 October). "Chicago is the city of high buildings," Noguchi wrote in his Chicago articles. "[D]id I expect to see a twenty-story-high-building in my life, I who being a Japanese [was] used to living in a ridiculously small house, like a bird's home?" (*SYN* 89).

125 (9 March) **Kakigara Chō:** (蠣殻町) in Nihonbashi, site of the stock exchange. **jins:** anglicized plural of jin (人): person(s). **Uncle and I went to see the Injuns dance:** One of the most popular features of the 1893 World's Columbian Exhibition in Chicago's Jackson Park had been the Midway Plaisance, a sort of evolutionary theme park exhibiting the allegedly semi-civilized races of the world, which many visitors found more entertaining than the White City housing the exhibits of white "civilization." The Midway survived the closure of the exhibition to continue as an independent entertainment venue. **A Japanese tea-house** was included among the Japanese buildings at the World's Columbian Exposition, which accompanied an extremely expensive reconstruction of the beautiful, ancient Hōōden on a separate island, the construction having been funded by the Japanese government in a clever bid to remove the Japanese exhibits from the "uncivilized" Midway.

Morning Glory's negative comments are surprising, since the Hōōden, at least, was considered very impressive by most observers.

125–126 (10 March) **stockyard:** Meatpacking was Chicago's most important industry in the late nineteenth century, and foreign visitors often took tours of the city's stockyards. Noguchi commented: "The great dream of Chicago is to invent a machine that will kill 10,000 hogs a minute" (*SYN* 98–99). Since the meatpacking process required large numbers of human laborers, it is indeed possible that some magnates envisioned a day when the process could be mechanized so as to reduce costs. **Satemo!** (さても): Indeed; truly. **Uchino hito** (家の人): the man of the house (literally, the person of the house). **"becha becha"** (べちゃべちゃ): chattering; prattling.

126 (12 March) **Buffalo:** Noguchi spent part of the summer of 1900 in upstate New York, primarily in the town of Avon, near Rochester (see *CEL* no. 58). **Niagara Falls:** the famous falls (located about seventeen miles northwest of Buffalo, New York) on the Niagara River, which flows from Lake Erie to Lake Ontario between the state of New York and the Canadian province of Ontario. Niagara Reservation State Park, created in 1885, is the oldest of New York's state parks.

126–127 (13 March) **New York:** Noguchi himself arrived in New York in June of 1900. **the lake of Biwa:** Lake Biwa, in Shiga, was famed for its crystal-clear water. **I felt like Dante crawled out of darkest Hell, after the torture of the terrible show:** a reference to the *Divine Comedy*, the epic poem by Dante Alighieri (1265–1321) depicting the author's imagined visit to Hell, Purgatory, and Paradise in the company of the Roman poet Virgil. In Canto 34, the final canto of *The Inferno*, the first section of the *Divine Comedy*, Dante expresses relief at finally leaving hell after witnessing the tortures experienced by sinners condemned to eternal torment. **the third floor of an edifice on Riverside Drive . . . which was Mr. Consul's home:** Noguchi lived in a four-story mansion at 80 Riverside Drive, overlooking the **Hudson River**, for about six months beginning in November 1900. **the ever so pleasing Irving . . . "Sleepy Hollow":** Morning Glory considers the Hudson River a "dear old acquaintance" because she has read "The Legend of Sleepy Hollow" (1819), Irving's famous story of a headless horseman who terrorizes the Dutch settlement of Tarry Town (a "sequestered glen" on the Hudson River in what is now Westchester County) a decade after the Revolutionary War. **Sumida Gawa**, Tokyo's primary waterway, remained a popular site for cherry-blossom viewing and riverboat parties, despite heavy transportation use and industrialization.

127 (14 March) **yukiya fure, fure!** (雪や降れ降れ): snow! Fall, fall! **The China-Japan War** (usually called the Sino-Japanese War), which marked Japan's arrival as an imperialist power, took place during the fall and winter of 1894–95.

128 (15 March) **Brooklyn Bridge:** A monumental engineering feat, the Brooklyn Bridge was begun in 1869 and finally opened for use in 1883. Spanning the East River from Brooklyn to Manhattan, it was the first bridge to employ steel for cable wire. **Louisiana ticket:** See note to 1 December. **"People crossing here use no English":** From 1880 to 1900, more than nine million immigrants came to the United States, many of them entering the country through New York City. From the mid-1890s until the passing of the Immigration Act of 1924, the majority of these immigrants hailed from southern and eastern Europe. **Liberty Statue:** From the Brooklyn Bridge, Morning Glory sees the impressive Statue of Liberty, a gift from France that had been erected on Bedloe's Island (now Liberty Island) in Upper New York Bay and dedicated in 1886, just seven years before Noguchi

arrived in the United States. **The Bay of Yedo** (in Japanese, Edo-wan 江戸湾): Morning Glory uses the antiquated but evocative name of Edo, which meant "rivergate," as the site of her proposed statue of "Beauty," rather than "Tokyo" (東京), "eastern capital," the name used since the time of the Meiji Restoration in 1868. **Shinbashi station** (新橋駅): The first Japanese railway, built under British supervision, linked Yokohama with Shinagawa on the outskirts of Tokyo in 1872. In the same year, a line connecting Shinagawa with Shinbashi ("New Bridge," named after a bridge crossing what was then the Shiodome River) was completed as the first link of what eventually became the Tokaidō line. In the social and political turmoil of the 1870s, the flow of foreign barbarians, crowds, and the noise of steam locomotives made the station an attractive site for thieves, but such concerns would have seemed somewhat quaint in the relative stability of 1890s Tokyo. **Tombstones in the midst of commerce!:** The tombstones are in Trinity Churchyard, adjacent to Trinity Church (Episcopalian). Located at the intersection of Broadway and Wall Street (hence Morning Glory's reference to **"Wall Street gentlemen"**), Trinity Church was designed in Gothic Revival style by Richard Upjohn and built in the 1840s.

129 (16 March) **"chin":** See note to 5 October.

129 (17 March) **organ-grinder:** Noguchi's image of the organ-grinders coincides with the usually sympathetic portrayal of poor organ-grinders in poetry, novels, music, and newspaper and magazine articles of the time. One poem appearing in *Harper's New Monthly Magazine* in 1873, for example, laments the plight of the "worn-out brother" who waits patiently not only for the pennies that "fall rarely" but also for the death that alone can bring him rest from his labor. In keeping with her criticism of Chinese immigrants and black Americans, Morning Glory implies that Italian immigrants know nothing except for itinerant music-making. Yet she displays more sympathy for the Italians because she believes they are **"simple creatures who work hard!" Garibaldi:** Giuseppe Garibaldi (1807–82) gained a worldwide reputation in the 1850s and 1860s for his military successes during the unification of Italy. He believed strongly in the vision of a single unified Italian nation comprising the kingdoms, municipalities, and other political entities (such as the Papal States) that in the early nineteenth century either functioned independently or were under the control of foreign powers (especially Austria and France).

129 (18 March) **Tsumaranai!:** see note to morning, 21 October.

130 (19 March) **"nikumu"** (憎む): to hate. Because numerals have several pronunciations in Japanese, it is often possible to render numbers as mnemonically useful words. **"The Diary of a Parlour Maid":** The sequel to *The American Diary of a Japanese Girl, actually called The American Letters of a Japanese Parlor-Maid,* recounts Morning Glory's month-long domestic service adventure in epistolary form.

Notes to the Afterword

1. Noguchi to Stoddard, [6] August 1901, *CEL* no. 91.

2. Ibid., 23 July 1901, *CEL* no. 88.

3. Ibid., *CEL* no. 88.

4. See Marberry 139, 151–55.

5. Stern 172.

6. *Frank Leslie's Popular Monthly* to Noguchi, 25 July 1901, *CEL* no. 89.

7. Noguchi to Stoddard, 26 July 1901, *CEL* no. 90.

8. The following year Yeto was involved with a special edition of *Madame Butterfly* for the Century Company and also assisted with the second Long-Belasco theatrical production, *The Darling of the Gods*. Soon afterward, he returned to Japan, subsequently visiting the United States for exhibitions of his paintings and drawings. Though his renown began to fade a few years later, his work remains worthy of recognition, as art historian Susan Larkin has argued.

9. Noguchi to Stoddard, 26 July 1901, *CEL* no. 90.

10. Ibid., 5 November [1901], *CEL* no. 100.

11. Ibid., [November 1901], *CEL* no. 104. The Stokes contract is in the Noguchi collection at Keiō University.

12. Noguchi to Gilmour, 23 February 1902, *CEL* no. 116; Stern 175.

13. Noguchi to Gilmour, 23 May [1902], *CEL* no. 121.

14. Ibid., 11 September 1902, *CEL* no. 122.

15. The agency was Henry Romeike, 110 Fifth Avenue, "The First Established and Most Complete Newspaper Cutting Bureau in the World." Some sixty review clippings were discovered by Ikuko Atsumi and listed in her bibliography, "*Yone Noguchi Bunken* (2)," 89–90. The discussion here is based on sixteen surviving photocopies of the original clippings and an additional fifteen of the remaining reviews located in microfilm collections. All these reviews are listed in a separate section at the end of Works Cited in this volume.

16. For a further discussion of exoticism and the problem of authenticity, see Marx, *The Idea of a Colony*, 41–44.

17. Citations to *Diary* appear in the text as page numbers in parentheses.

18. FPL 1.

19. Noguchi to Stoddard, 19 June 1900, *CEL* no. 54.

20. Birchall 75.

21. Noguchi to Putnam, n.d., FPL 15.

22. "I thought that to say nothing was only the way to be kind to the play," he told Putnam (FPL 27).

23. Yuko Matsukawa provides an interesting critique of Noguchi's anti-Watanna stance in "Onoto Watanna's Japanese Collaborators and Commentators," 47–50.

24. MacLane 12.

25. Halverson 20–27.

26. Cited in Halverson 27.

27. Noguchi to Gilmour, n.d., *CEL* no. 86.

28. Noguchi's letter to Gilmour, 19 February 1903, *CEL* no. 167, alludes to their common knowledge of Housman's book: "I have met with Laurence Housman—the author of 'An English Woman's Love-letters', and talked with him upon many a things. He was most agreeable man in London. I have met also with some other fellows whose names were not known to you."

29. MacLane to Noguchi, [27] February 1904, *CEL* no. 287.

30. Noguchi to Gilmour, [July 1901], *CEL* no. 85.

31. Noguchi to Partington, 1 August 1899, *CEL* no. 44.

32. Noguchi to Gilmour, 2 January 1903, *CEL* no. 128; Stokes to Noguchi, 21 January 1903, *CEL* no. 148.

33. Noguchi to Gilmour, 2 January 1903, *CEL* no. 128.

34. See Noguchi, "A Japanese Girl's One Week in London."

35. Gale to Noguchi, [July–August1903], *CEL* no. 214; Walsh to Noguchi, 10 July 1903, *CEL* no. 220.

36. *Leslie's Monthly* to Noguchi, 6 July 1903, *CEL* no. 218.

37. Sedgwick did maintain friendly relations with Noguchi and accepted one subsequent article, "Admiration from Japan: An Oriental Critic on the Anglo-Saxon Girl."

38. The sequel, *The American Letters of a Japanese Parlor-Maid by Miss Morning Glory (Yone Noguchi)*, was published simultaneously in two versions: one in a Japanese-style binding with cover design and illustrations by Genjirō Yeto and the other an unillustrated hardback. The beginnings of the projected third volume, "A Japanese Girl's One Week in London," appeared in five issues of *Eigo Seinen* (The Rising Generation) in 1906.

39. There were evidently multiple printings of the Japanese edition. A copy in the possession of Seiji Itoh gives 10 July 1906 as the date of the third printing.

40. The stated fifth edition of the *Diary* (1912) disposed with the Yeto illustrations and incorporated a new illustration in the form of a *kuchi-e* (foldout insert) by Eihō Hirezaki (1881–1968), an established woodblock-print artist who specialized in this format. Reviews of the London edition appear in *Academy* 83 (28 December 1912): 829 and *Bookman* 43 (January 1913): 240.

41. Nakamura 32.

42. Noguchi, "The Evolution of Modern Japanese Literature," 261. Tsubouchi's *Types of Students* was published in 1887; the full title was *Ichidoku Santan Tōsei Shosei Katagi* (Read and Deplore: Modern Types of Students).

43. Noguchi, "Japanese Women in Literature," 91.

44. Ibid., 89. One may, however, question the extent of Noguchi's readings in these Japanese literary traditions, as his articles "Japanese Women and Literature" and "The

Evolution of Modern Japanese Literature" borrowed much of their material and even phrasing from British Japanologist W. G. Aston's *A History of Japanese Literature* (1899).

45. See Suzuki.

46. Noguchi, "The Evolution of Modern Japanese Literature," 261.

47. Marx, "'A Different Mode of Speech,'" 288.

48. Knippling and Nelson, 128. Heco, the only writer of the group to become a U.S. citizen, is discussed in Van Sant 21–48.

49. Azuma 6.

50. Huang 5–6.

51. After Japan wrested control of Korea from Russia in the Russo-Japanese war, Noguchi published a number of English articles on Korea that displayed the belligerent cultural chauvinism of Japanese colonial discourse. For an early example, see "A Japanese on Korea."

52. *SYN* 51–52.

53. Roediger 13.

54. Ammons and White-Parks 6.

55. Perhaps there was something lacking in Burgess's trickster education, however, for when Noguchi sent him a copy of the *American Diary* with an inviting inscription from the authoress on the flyleaf, he credulously took the bait. Noguchi confessed the truth only after receiving several ardent letters from Burgess, sent in care of Stokes, which he later published in the postscript to the Japanese editions of the novel.

56. On Watanna as trickster, see Yuko Matsukawa, "Cross-Dressing and Cross-Naming: Decoding Onoto Watanna" in Ammons and White-Parks 106–25.

57. Chen, xviii.

58. See Lewis Hyde's *Trickster Makes This World* for a discussion of Douglass as trickster.

59. Noguchi, "Japanese Humor and Caricature," 472.

60. Noguchi, "The Failure of American Optimism," 501, 503.

61. Noguchi, *Voice of the Valley*, 24.

62. Noguchi to Gilmour, n.d., *CEL* no. 107.

63. *SYN* 252.

64. Takahashi to Partington, 29 March 1899, *Partington Family Papers*, ca. 1892–1946, BANC Mss. 89/123 z, Bancroft Library, University of California, Berkeley.

65. Noguchi, "The Genroku Period," 6.

66. Noguchi, "A Few Words at Tagore's Departure," 5.

67. "Magojiro," typescript in *Yone Noguchi Papers, 1948–1967*, BANC Mss 89/123 z, Bancroft Library, University of California, Berkeley.

68. Ammons and White-Parks viii–ix.

69. Norris 825. Don B. Graham first identified Noguchi as Norris's Japanese poet. The Japanese poet's recitation is derived from Noguchi's poems "The Invisible Night" and "The Brave Upright Rains," both published in *The Lark* in July 1896 (they appear also in *Seen and Unseen*). Joaquin Miller earned more than six thousand dollars for his inaccurate reportage from the Klondike in 1898–99, and perhaps as much for his subsequent exaggerated recounting of his adventures on vaudeville and lecture stages. Blanche Partington eventually became a Christian Scientist.

70. As Sally Ledger points out, ambivalence toward the maternal role, questioning of gender norms, and emphasis on women's education and access to culture are notable characteristics of the New Woman, and all these are evident in Noguchi's novel; equally evident

are the less favorable "feminine characteristics" like vanity, often depicted in New Woman novels as impinging on women's higher aspirations (465–66).

71. Tietjens 96.

72. For Noguchi's early advocacy of the haiku form, see Noguchi, "A Proposal to American Poets."

Works Cited

Reviews of *The American Diary of a Japanese Girl* cited in the text appear in a separate list at the end of Works Cited.

Works frequently cited in the notes are identified by the following abbreviations:

CEL Yone Noguchi. *Collected English Letters*. Ed. Ikuko Atsumi. Tokyo: Yone Noguchi Society, 1975. Cited by letter number.

FPL Frank Putnam letters, catalogued as *Yoné Noguchi letters and ephemera, 1899–1921*, BANC MSS 82/130 z. Bancroft Library, University of California, Berkeley. Cited by folder number.

FTES Yone Noguchi. *From the Eastern Sea*. London: Unicorn, 1903.

SYN Yone Noguchi. *The Story of Yone Noguchi*. 1914. Philadelphia: G. W. Jacobs, 1915.

TT Yone Noguchi. *Through the Torii*. 1914. Boston: Four Seas, 1922.

Ammons, Elizabeth, and Annette White-Parks, eds. *Tricksterism in Turn-of-the-Century American Literature: A Multicultural Perspective*. Hanover, N.H.: University Press of New England, 1994.

Anderson, Joseph L., and Donald Richie. *Japanese Film: Art and Industry*. Princeton: Princeton University Press, 1983.

Arnold, Edwin. *Japonica*. New York: Charles Scribner's Sons, 1891.

Arvin, Newton. *Longfellow: His Life and Work*. Boston: Little, Brown, 1962.

Asbury, Herbert. *The Barbary Coast*. New York: Knopf, 1933.

Aston, W. G. *A History of Japanese Literature*. London: Heinemann, 1899.

Atsumi, Ikuko. "*Yone Noguchi Bunken* (2)." *Hikaku Bungaku* 15 (1972): 63–92.

Azuma, Eiichiro. *Between Two Empires: Race, History, and Transnationalism in Japanese America*. Oxford: Oxford University Press, 2005.

Bacon, Alice. *Japanese Girls and Women*. Boston: Houghton, 1891.

Belasco, David. *The Darling of the Gods*. In *Six Plays: Madame Butterfly, Du Barry, The Darling of the Gods, Adrea, The Girl of the Golden West, The Return of Peter Grimm*, 145–224. Boston: Little, Brown, 1928.

———. *Madame Butterfly*. In *Six Plays: Madame Butterfly, Du Barry, The Darling of the Gods, Adrea, The Girl of the Golden West, The Return of Peter Grimm*, 11–32. Boston: Little, Brown, 1928.

Benedict, Ruth. *The Chrysanthemum and the Sword: Patterns of Japanese Culture*. Boston: Houghton Mifflin, 1946.

Berger, Klaus. *Japonisme in Western Painting from Whistler to Matisse*. Translated by David Britt. Cambridge: Cambridge University Press, 1992.

Birchall, Diana. *Onoto Watanna: The Story of Winnifred Eaton*. Urbana: University of Illinois Press, 2001.

Browder, Laura. *Slippery Characters: Ethnic Impersonation and American Identities*. Chapel Hill: University of North Carolina Press, 2000.

Cate, Phillip Dennis, ed. *Perspectives on Japonisme: The Japanese Influence on America*. New Brunswick, N.J.: International Center for Japonisme, Rutgers University, 1989.

Chamberlain, Basil Hall. *A Translation of the "Ko-Ji-Ki," or "Records of Ancient Matters."* Yokohama: Lane, 1882.

Chen, Tina. *Double Agency: Acts of Impersonation in Asian American Literature and Culture*. Menlo Park: Stanford University Press, 2005.

Conder, Josiah. *The Flowers of Japan and the Art of Floral Arrangement*. 1891. Tokyo: Kodansha International, 2004.

Doniger, Wendy. "Self-Impersonation in World Literature." *Kenyon Review* 26, 2 (Spring 2004): 101–25.

Downer, Lesley. *Madame Sadayakko: The Geisha Who Bewitched the West*. New York: Penguin, 2003.

Duus, Masayo. *The Life of Isamu Noguchi: Journey without Borders*. Translated by Peter Duus. Princeton: Princeton University Press, 2004.

Eliot, T. S. *Milton: Two Studies*. London: Faber and Faber, 1968.

Emerson, Ralph Waldo. *Nature and Selected Essays*. Edited by Larzer Ziff. New York: Penguin, 2003.

Fagan, Barney. *My Gal Is a High Born Lady*. New York: Witmark, 1896.

Fukuzawa, Yukichi. *The Autobiography of Yukichi Fukuzawa*. Translated by Eiichi Kiyooka. New York: Columbia University Press, 1966.

The Geisha: A Story of a Tea House: A Japanese Musical Play. Libretto by Owen Hall, lyrics by Harry Greenbank, and music by Sidney Jones. London: Hopwood, 1896.

Glenn, Evelyn Nakano. *Issei, Nisei, War Bride: Three Generations of Japanese American Women in Domestic Service*. Philadelphia: Temple University Press, 1986.

Graham, D.B. "Studio Art in *The Octopus*." *American Literature* 44, 4 (January 1973): 657–66.

Halverson, Cathryn. *Maverick Autobiographies: Women Writers and the American West, 1900–1936*. Madison: University of Wisconsin Press, 2004.

Hearn, Lafcadio. *Glimpses of Unfamiliar Japan*. 2 vols. Boston: Houghton, 1894.

———. *In Ghostly Japan*. 1899. Boston: Houghton, 1922.

———. *Japan: An Attempt at Interpretation*. New York: Macmillan, 1904.

———. *Out of the East*. 1895. Leipzig: Bernhard Tauchnitz, 1910.

Heco, Joseph. *The Narrative of a Japanese*. 2 vols. Tokyo: Maruzen, 1895.

Hervey, Harry. *Where Strange Gods Call: Pages out of the East*. New York: Century, 1924.

Holland, Clive. *My Japanese Wife, A Japanese Idyll*. London: Herbert Jenkins, 1895.

Huang, Yunte. *Transpacific Displacement: Ethnography, Translation, and Intertextual Travel in Twentieth-Century American Literature*. Berkeley: University of California Press, 2002.

Hyde, Lewis. *Trickster Makes This World: Mischief, Myth, and Art*. New York: North Point, 1999.

Ichihashi, Yamato. *Japanese in the United States*. Stanford: Stanford University Press, 1932.

Ichioka, Yuji. *The Issei: The World of the First Generation Japanese Immigrants, 1885–1924*. New York: Free Press, 1988.

James, William. *The Principles of Psychology*. New York: Holt, 1890.

"Joaquin Miller and Yone Naguchi [*sic*]." *Leslie's Illustrated Weekly* 84 (3 June 1897): 361.

Kant, Immanuel. *Anthropology from a Pragmatic Point of View*. 1798. Translated by Mary J. Gregor. Berlin: Springer, 1974.

Knippling, Alpana Sharma, and Emmanuel S. Nelson. *New Immigrant Literatures in the United States: A Sourcebook to Our Multicultural Literary Heritage*. Westport, Conn.: Greenwood, 1996.

Kurata, Yoshihiro. *Kaigai kōen kotohajime* [The Beginning of Japanese Performance outside Japan]. Tokyo: Shoseki, 1994.

Lambourne, Lionel. *Japonisme: Cultural Crossings between Japan and the West*. New York: Phaidon, 2005.

Lancaster, Clay. *The Japanese Influence in America*. New York: Rawls, 1963.

Larkin, Susan. "Genjiro Yeto: Between Japan and Japanism." *Journal of the Historical Society of the Town of Greenwich* 5 (2000): 8–31.

Ledger, Sally. "The New Woman." In *The Cambridge Guide to Women's Writing in English*, edited by Lorna Sage, 465-67. Cambridge: Cambridge University Press, 1999.

Lee, Josephine, Imogene L. Lim, and Yuko Matsukawa, eds. *Re/collecting Early Asian America: Essays in Cultural History*. Philadelphia: Temple University Press, 2002.

Ling, Amy. "Winnifred Eaton: Ethnic Chameleon and Popular Success." *MELUS* 11 (Fall 1984): 4–15.

Long, John Luther. *Madame Butterfly*. 1898. Madame Butterfly *and* A Japanese Nightingale: *Two Orientalist Texts*. Edited by Maureen Honey and Jean Lee Cole, 26–79. New Brunswick, N.J.: Rutgers University Press, 2002.

———. *Miss Cherry Blossom of Tokyo*. Philadelphia: Lippincott, 1895.

Longfellow, Henry Wadsworth. *Selected Poems*. Edited by Lawrence Buell. New York: Penguin, 1988.

MacLane, Mary. *The Story of Mary MacLane*. 1902. Edited by Julia Watson. Helena, Mont.: Riverbend, 2002.

Marberry, M. M. *Splendid Poseur: Joaquin Miller—American Poet*. New York: Crowell, 1953.

Marx, Edward. "'A Different Mode of Speech': Yone Noguchi in Meiji America." In Lee, Lim, and Matsukawa, 288–306.

———. *The Idea of a Colony: Cross-Culturalism in Modern Poetry*. Toronto: University of Toronto Press, 2004.

Matsukawa, Yuko. "Onoto Watanna's Japanese Collaborators and Commentators." *Japanese Journal of American Studies* 16 (2005): 31–54.

Miller, Joaquin, and Yone Noguchi. *Japan of Sword and Love.* Tokyo: Kanao Bunyendo, 1905.

Miner, Earl. *The Japanese Tradition in British and American Literature.* Princeton: Princeton University Press, 1958.

Nakamura, Mitsuo. *Japanese Fiction in the Meiji Era.* Tokyo: Kokusai Bunka Shinkōkai, 1966.

Noguchi, Yone. "Admiration from Japan: An Oriental Critic on the Anglo Saxon Girl." *Frank Leslie's Popular Monthly* 57, 2 (December 1903): 187–90.

——— [Miss Morning Glory]. "The American Diary of a Japanese Girl." *Frank Leslie's Popular Monthly* 53, 1 (November 1901): 69–82; 53, 2 (December 1901): 192–202.

——— [Miss Morning Glory]. *The American Diary of a Japanese Girl.* Illustrated by benjiro yeto. New York: Frederick A. 1902.

———. *The American Diary of a Japanese Girl.* Tokyo: Fuzanbo, 1904. Illustrated by. Yeiho Hiresaki. Tokyo: Fuzanbo; London: Elkin Mathews, 1912.

———. *The American Letters of a Japanese Parlor-Maid by Miss Morning Glory (Yone Noguchi).* Tokyo: Fuzanbō, 1905.

———. "The Evolution of the Japanese Stage." *New England Magazine* 31 (October 1904): 144–47.

———. "The Evolution of Modern Japanese Literature." *Critic* 44 (March 1904): 260–63.

———. "The Failure of American Optimism." *Bookman* 48 (December 1918): 501–3.

———. "A Few Words at Tagore's Departure." Osaka *Mainichi Shinbun*, 1 September 1916, 5.

———. "The Geisha Girl of Japan." *Theatre Magazine* 5 (January 1905): 20–22.

———. "The Genroku Period." *Japan Times*, 30 December 1917, 6.

———. *Hōbun nihon shōjo no beikoku nikki* [American Diary of a Japanese Girl in the Vernacular]. Tokyo: Tōadō Shobō, 1905.

———. "A Japanese Girl's One Week in London." *Eigo Seinen* 14, 10/11 (1 January 1906): 165–66; 13 (1 February 1906): 197; 15 (21 February 1906): 232–33; 17 (11 March 1906): 261; 18 (21 March 1906): 277.

———. "Japanese Humor and Caricature." *Bookman* (N.Y.) 19 (July 1904): 472–75.

———. "A Japanese on Korea." *Los Angeles Times*, 24 September 1905: v: 19.

———. "Japanese Women in Literature." *Poet Lore* 15, 3 (July 1904): 88–91.

———. *Nijūkokusekisha no shi* (Poems of a Dual National). Tokyo: Genbunsha, 1921.

———. "Noguchi's Song unto Brother Americans." Oakland: Yone Noguchi, 1897.

———. "Onoto Watanna and Her Japanese Work." *Taiyō* 13, 8 (June 1907): 18–21; 10 (1 July 1907): 19–21.

———. *The Pilgrimage.* 2 vols. Kamakura: Valley Press, 1909.

———. "A Proposal to American Poets." *Reader* 3, 3 (February 1904): 248.

———. *"San Furanshisuko"* [San Francisco]. *Keiō Gijuku Gakuhō* 106 (15 July 1906): 42–48.

———. *Seen and Unseen: Or, Monologues of a Homeless Snail.* San Francisco: Gelett Burgess and Porter Garnett, 1897.

———. "Setsubun." *Japan Times*, 28 January 1917, 6.
———. *The Spirit of Japanese Poetry*. New York: Dutton, 1914.
———. "Theatres and Theatre-Going in Japan." *Theatre Magazine* 4 (July 1904): 167–70.
———. *The Voice of the Valley*. San Francisco: William Doxey, 1897.
Norris, Frank. *Novels and Essays*. Edited by Donald Pizer. New York: Library of America, 1986.
Okihiro, Gary Y. *The Columbia Guide to Asian American History*. New York: Columbia University Press, 2001.
Roediger, David. *The Wages of Whiteness: Race and the Making of the American Working Class*. London: Verso, 1991.
Seigel, J. P., ed. *Thomas Carlyle: The Critical Heritage*. London: Routledge, 1971.
Snodgrass, Judith. *Presenting Japanese Buddhism to the West: Orientalism, Occidentalism, and the Columbian Exposition*. Chapel Hill: University of North Carolina Press, 2003.
Sono, Tel. *Tel Sono: The Japanese Reformer*. New York: Hunt, 1891.
Stanislavsky, Constantin. *My Life in Art*. Boston: Little, Brown, 1924.
Stern, Madeleine B. *Purple Passage: The Life of Mrs. Frank Leslie*. Norman: University of Oklahoma Press, 1953.
Suzuki, Tomi. "Gender and Genre: Modern Literary Histories and Women's Diary Literature." In *Inventing the Classics: Modernity, National Identity, and Japanese Literature*, edited by Haruo Shirane and Tomi Suzuki, 71–95. Stanford: Stanford University Press, 2000.
Tamura, Naomi. *The Japanese Bride*. New York: Harper, 1893.
Thal, Sarah. *Rearranging the Landscape of the Gods: The Politics of a Pilgrimage Site in Japan, 1573–1912*. Chicago: University of Chicago Press, 2005.
T[ietjens], E[unice]. "Yone Noguchi." *Poetry* 15 (November 1919): 96–98.
Van Rij, Jan. *Madame Butterfly: Japonisme, Puccini, and the Search for the Real Cho-Cho-San*. Berkeley: Stone Bridge, 2001.
Van Sant, John E. *Pacific Pioneers: Japanese Journeys to America and Hawaii, 1850–80*. Urbana: University of Illinois Press, 2000.
Wagner, Harr. *Joaquin Miller, His Other Self*. San Francisco: Harr Wagner, 1929.
Watanna, Onoto [Winnifred Eaton]. *The Heart of Hyacinth*. 1903. Introduction by Samina Najmi. Seattle: University of Washington Press, 2000.
———. *A Japanese Nightingale*. 1901. Madame Butterfly *and* A Japanese Nightingale: *Two Orientalist Texts*. Edited by Maureen Honey and Jean Lee Cole, 81–171. New Brunswick, N.J.: Rutgers University Press, 2002.
———. *Miss Numè of Japan: A Japanese–American Romance*. 1899. Introduction by Eve Oishi. Baltimore: Johns Hopkins University Press, 1999.
Wordell, Charles B. *Japan's Image in America: Popular Writing about Japan*, 1800–1941. Kyoto: Yamaguchi, 1998.
Yokota-Murakami, Takayuki. *Don Juan East/West: On the Problematics of Comparative Literature*. Albany: State University of New York Press, 1998.
Yoshihara, Mari. *Embracing the East: White Women and American Orientalism*. Oxford: Oxford University Press, 2003.
Yu, Henry. *Thinking Orientals: Migration, Contact, and Exoticism in Modern America*. Oxford: Oxford University Press, 2001.

Reviews of

THE AMERICAN DIARY OF A JAPANESE GIRL

(Most of these reviews were collected by a publicity agent. Titles and page numbers are provided where they have been identified.)

Albany Times Union, 15 November 1902
Boston Gazette, 25 October 1902
Buffalo Express, 22 October 1902. "Japanese in Literature."
Chicago (?) Advance, 27 November 1902
Chicago Dial, 1 December 1902. "Holiday Publications."
Chicago Evening Post, 29 November 1902
Chicago Record Herald, 1 January 1903
Chicago Tribune, 12 December 1902. "Miss Morning Glory's Opinions."
Current Literature, April 1904
Des Moines Register Leader, 23 November 1902
Frank Leslie's Popular Monthly, November 1902. "Men, Women, and Books."
Gloucester (Mass.) Times, 17 November 1902
Indianapolis Journal, 27 November 1902
Milwaukee Wisconsin, 22 November 1902
National Magazine, December 1902. "Is This Another of Noguchi's Pranks?" 367–68.
Newark News, 1 November 1902
New Bedford (Mass.) Standard, 24 October 1902
New York Commercial Advertiser, 29 November 1902
New York Evening Sun, 17 October 1902
New York Journal, 18 November 1902
New York Mail and Express, 22 November, 17 December 1902
New York Times, 6 December 1902. "Holiday Books."
New York Times Book Review, 26 July 1902. "Books and Men," 12.
New York Tribune, 17 December 1902. "A Japanese Fantasia."
Philadelphia Inquirer, 16 November 1902
Pittsburgh Chronicle, 22 November 1902
Pittsburgh Dispatch, 23 November 1902
Pittsburgh Post, 3 November 1902
Rochester (N.Y.) Democrat Chronicle, 3 November 1902
Rochester (N.Y.) Herald, 15 November 1902
San Francisco Bulletin, 21 November 1902. "A Japanese Maiden."
Seattle Times, 23 November 1902
St. Paul Pioneer Press, 1 November 1902
*Town and Country (*New York*)*, 15 November 1902

Yone Noguchi served as Professor of English at Keio University in Tokyo and was a prolific writer of essays, criticism, and translations, in both English and Japanese until his death in 1947. He was the father of the noted Japanese American sculptor Isamu Noguchi.

Laura E. Franey is Associate Professor of English at Millsaps College in Jackson, Mississippi. She is the author of *Victorian Travel Writting and Imperial Violence: British Writting on Africa, 1855-1902.*

Edward Marx is Associate Professor of Euro-American Culture, in the Faculty of Law and Letters, Ehime University. He is the author of *The Idea of a Colony: Cross-Culturalism in Modern Poetry* and is currently writing a biography of Yone Noguchi.